ENGELS EXTENSION

E. G. Ross

It's the ultimate military threat. Diplomats and politicians consider it unthinkable. Yet out of the turmoil of Russia, a new and more virulent Soviet Union unexpectedly arises—with an arsenal of secret weapons immensely superior to nuclear bombs and precision missiles. The poorly prepared, but courageous American president has a chance to stop the new Soviets from imposing their old strategic obsession with world domination. Is there time? Or has America been fatally trapped by the Engels Extension?

Drawing on little-known technical and strategic trends, international defense writer and newsletter editor E. G. Ross thrusts you into a tomorrow where the unthinkable becomes creepily real.

ENGELS EXTENSION

E. G. Ross

P PREMIERE EDITIONS INTERNATIONAL, INC.
CORVALLIS, OREGON

Premiere Editions International, Inc.

2397 NW Kings Blvd. #311, Corvallis OR 97330
Telephone (541) 752-4239 ~ FAX (541) 752-4463
email: *publish@premiere-editions.com*
web site: *http://www.premiere-editions.com*

EDITORS:
    Irene L. Gresick, Theresa Rolow, Darlene Ryan, Beatrice Stauss

DESIGNER:
    Nancy K. Marshall

GRAPHIC DESIGNER:
    René L. Redelsperger

Printed in the United States of America by Cascade Printing Company
First Edition, August 1997
ISBN 0-9633818-6-5
Library of Congress Catalog Card Number 97-66755

DEDICATED TO

B.H. Liddell Hart, who directed us to the indirect, and to Sun Tzu, who told us to expect the unexpected.

TOM CLANCY HAS A COMPETITOR . . .

Want to bet your life that the Soviet Union is dead, and permanent peace is at hand? Tom Clancy has a competitor in defense expert E.G. Ross, whose chilling technothriller is an urgent warning to those who would cut defense for domestic political expediency.

— *Durk Pearson and Sandy Shaw, international best-selling author-scientists*

SO DON'T PLAN ON GETTING ANY SLEEP . . .

This book picks up speed like a runaway train roaring down a mountain. If you think the Cold War is over and all of those dismantled nuclear weapons have made the world safe, you better read this book. E.G. Ross blends a resurgent Russia with military technology found in today's laboratories to produce a thought-provoking picture of war in the near future. Don't plan on reading this book if you have to go to work the next day because you won't sleep until you finish it.

— *Harold Hough, award-winning author of Satellite Surveillance*

READING THIS TOO-REALISTIC NIGHTMARE!

E. G. Ross's mastery of strategic capabilities propels his novel's scary scenario into a too-realistic nightmare. A MUST read for anyone "bearish" on the Reds.

—*Karen Reedstrom, editor, Full Context*

ACKNOWLEDGEMENTS

My wife, Suzy Peterson, for her wise and precious encouragement; Clint Eastwood, for showing what heroes can be and proving that persistence wins; Durk Pearson and Sandy Shaw, for their enthusiasm and expertise on a range of scientific issues; Larry Martines and Mark Dickinson, for their loyalty and lucid conversations on terrorism, special forces, security systems, and strategic history; Bob Bennett and Mike Dunn, for their tips on military rocketry; the late Dr. Peter Beckmann, for his patience with my questions about the darker corners of relativity theory and quantum mechanics; various guys at Beale and March Air Force bases, for letting me burn my ears at an SR-71 launch and participate in a mock nuclear attack; certain folks at Redstone, for insights into Patriot missiles; people at Lawrence Livermore, for patience with questions about high-energy lasers; several individuals at The American Civil Defense Association and Doctors for Disaster Preparedness, for a long-term education on nuclear war effects; Bill Lioio, for his insights into private investigative work; Brad Stewart, for his knowledge of digital processing; Harold Hough, for his discussions of satellite imagery; Dr. Yale Jay Lubkin, for enlightenment on mini-RPVs, exotic propulsions, and other devices and developments; several anonymous "good guys" at Chapter 191 of the American Society for Industrial Security, for insights into security technology and procedures; Eric Wingren, for tactical input; Dan Griffing, for rescuing a chapter from the bowels of my cannibalistic computer; Raymie Stata for website attention; Jonna Wingren, for generosity early in the game; countless backstage military and scientific contacts made over the years through my monthly newsletter, *Understanding Defense*; Jim Kemper, for keeping me legally straight; Jerry and Eileen Boal, for action when it counted; Karen Reedstrom at *Full Context*, for recommendations; Irene Gresick and the fine people at Premiere Editions International, for seeing the value and staying the course.

All extrapolations, expoundings, and errors are mine; these folks did their best to keep me true-to-target.

E.G.R.— April 1997

TABLE OF CONTENTS

~ *PART I* ~

LIGHTNING

PROLOGUE

Two hundred yards below and to the fuelman's left — from out of the top of a moonlit cloud bank — a winged shadow silently emerged. "Beautiful," he whispered. Like a great predator from a forgotten age, the shadow rose towards him. The man frowned in concentration and began adjusting a joystick which controlled and opened an outside basket, the guide for the fuel transfer connection. Within fifty feet of him, the shadow sharpened to that of an American B-1E nuclear bomber. It was the fourth generation of the B-1 series first deployed in the late 1980s and, in a sense, it was a dinosaur, the dead-end upgrade of its line. It was rapidly being replaced by far fewer, but substantially stealthier and faster B-2Cs — and, perhaps, thought the man, by a rumored B-3. Scuttlebutt said the B-3 employed a radical new super-stealth technology and resembled a razor-edged dinner plate — a true flying saucer.

He shook his head and shuddered. From his Plexiglas vantage on the under-belly tails of KC-135 tanker planes, the fuelman had serviced more of the graceful B-1s than he could remember. But the rumored B-3s were too weird to comprehend and probably too far in his professional future to matter. And the B-2s looked like mantas, like they belonged in sluggish water, not in effortless air. He knew his feelings were irrationally motivated by old concepts of planes as "birds," but he didn't care.

He caressed the joystick and opened and extended the basket. From his cramped angle, it looked like the silhouette of a badminton shuttlecock bobbing on a heavy black string. The outside airflow itself kept the fuel basket fairly steady on the end of the fuel hose, but air vanes also offered the fuelman limited horizontal/vertical control.

The big bomber moved closer, its pilot working constantly to keep his bird steady behind the tanker. So bright was the moonlight that the fuelman and pilot nodded to each other across the interval of night sea air rushing by at over 300 mph. That refueling speed was still quite slow for the B-1E. Unlike the old B-1Bs, it was a very fast bird, equipped with carbon/carbon turbine engines, a titanium aluminide skin and other modifications which allowed it to top out in the high Mach 3s. That was nearly quadruple its subsonic ancestors, although not as fast as the latest heavily modified B-2s.

The bomber's fuel nozzle extended, seeking. The fuelman lowered the basket a trifle and then saw it receive the B-1E's blunt nozzle, confirming the connection on his video screen. The fuel automatically pumped at high speed from one of the tanker's compartments, where fuels for several types of planes were stored.

The bomber pilot's face was invisible, sheathed in a slick super-cockpit helmet, the inside of which provided him three-dimensional images of everything around his aircraft in detail far better than his bare eyes ever could. The fuelman saw the bomber pilot hold up a thumb. The fuelman did the same.

It was the last action either man ever took.

In a gigantic, roiling globe of flame, the tanker blew, consuming itself and the bomber. Parts of both jets tumbled through the clouds to the sea, trailing grave markers of black smoke, which were quickly dispersed by cool night winds.

A hundred miles east, circling 250 miles off the coast of Southern California, an AWACS radar plane saw the tanker/bomber blip disappear from its sensitive screens.

Three nights and four days of searching recovered only stray bits and pieces of either craft: several seat cushions, some fuselage insulation, two life-preservers, a glove, part of a flight suit pant leg. These were packaged, sealed and saved for analysis. The homing-signal equipped data and voice flight recorders were eventually recovered off the Pacific bottom from the southeastern end of the Murray Fracture Zone depths. But the recorders were of no help to Defense Department investigators. The cause was listed as "unknown."

The incident received terse mention in the major media and was, for a time, forgotten by nearly everyone but the crews' relatives and friends, those who quietly lived to carry both the scars and memories which their beloved dead could not.

CHAPTER 1

THE COLD

I t was 6:30 a.m., June 25th, over two months into the long Antarctic winter and six months before the start of summer and Christmas. Inside a snow-dusted galvanized steel hut of the Russian research station, Engels I, sat a young communications officer. He punched through a rarely permitted, brief radio satellite call. The call was to his wife, Tanya Yublenka, who worked for the New Soviet Arctic/Antarctic Research Institute's southern base in the Buenos Aires embassy. The connection was exceptionally clear — partly due to low solar activity and partly due to unseasonable mildness in the turbulent far southern weather.

"Good morning, Gregor!" she said enthusiastically. "How *are* you?"

"So far, I am well," he answered in his normally grave voice, but grinned to himself at Tanya's vivaciousness. Coupled with her beauty and intelligence, her ebullient manner was a trait that helped her find satisfactory work in the good-job-scarce system.

"So far?" she asked. "Gregor, is something wrong? You haven't let that inadvertently indiscreet tongue of yours lead you into trouble, have you?"

Gregor noted the way she phrased a legitimate question to acknowledge his well-known temper while implying to the eavesdroppping ears of the new KGB that he harbored no complaints against the State. They both knew it was untrue. After all, inside himself every Russian grumbled. Public vocalization varied with the political winds. The winds blew cold since the passing of the brief, false spring of post-Gorbachev times.

Now the old Russian fears of chaos raged. The forces of reform—sweeping, alienly individualist, frightening — had received the blame. The last chief reformer himself had turned furiously on his people, shifting sides to try to stay in power. But he had moved late. Soon the Black Beret sadists of Interior Minister Boris Pugo and the KGB thugs of Vladimir Kruychkov were gleefully stomping the buds of democracy and markets back into the muddy earth of the Baltics, Georgia, Turkmenistan, Moldavia, Russia, and even Eastern Europe.

Red Army generals had renewed their raucous rhetoric about the dangers of "the main enemy," America. Kremlin bosses hunkered behind their ancient walls and again glared suspiciously at the West. The Cold War had come back, more frigid than ever.

Gregor shivered. Just now he admired Tanya's protectiveness, a warm cloak handed to him across 2,400 miles.

"I'm maturing to the Soviet way, as you have no reason to doubt, Tanya."

"I love you, too, Gregor."

"Yes."

"Your word of affection is so detailed. It's good I'm a practiced translator. What bothers you?" she asked, sipping her morning tea; they were, after all, only one time zone apart.

"First, I miss you," he said almost gruffly.

"Oh!" Tanya teased. "An explosion of articulation!"

"And second," Gregor went on, used to her theatrics, "a bad cold is going around."

"Be glad you're not in Vostok," she warned, referring to the Soviets' farthest-inland Antarctic station at 78 degrees latitude.

Gregor felt hair rise on his arms. Vostok was a haunted part of Soviet Antarctic history.

Vostok base, established in 1957 by the second Soviet Antarctic expedition, was 800 miles from the nearest Soviet coastal base of Mirniy on the Shackleton Ice Shelf directly south of India. West of Vostok, one had to travel a thousand miles to Ross Shelf to reach the U.S. McMurdo base, itself 2,300 miles from New Zealand. Vostok was known to drop below minus 125 degrees Fahrenheit. In 1982, a fire destroyed the base's diesel electric power plant, including the two main generators and a backup pair. One man died and twenty others struggled for months to survive the cold, too embarrassed to request U.S. aid, which could've easily been flown in from McMurdo station. To talk of Vostok was to speak of cold so severe that inhaling the raw air caused the nose, lips, and gums to bleed. A tube of toothpaste left out for minutes could be used to pound nails, except the nails might shatter.

As an employee of the refurbished Soviet Arctic/Antarctic Research Institute, Tanya knew all this. She also knew that her husband's base, on the ice off the east coast of the Antarctic, was relatively balmy compared to Vostok.

"You are a witch, Tanya," he kidded, grinning. "I meant the mess in the moustache kind of cold,"

"Crude, Gregor."

"Is there a Russian male who is not?"

"I haven't had time to check them all. Are you ordering me to?" she teased.

The absurdity set him laughing.

For a moment, she closed her eyes, pressing the receiver fiercely against her ear, listening to the strong rolling sound. It made her think of a powerful, soaring bird where none should be.

"Well, you've survived colds before," she said.

"Yes. It's just that there are so many of us down here who have caught this damned bug. Half the scientists and clerks alike. Some are seriously suffering, vomiting and so on."

"Germs don't recognize class distinctions."

"Watch your tart tongue, Tanya. Someone might think you do not believe scientists are members of the proletariat."

"Then after discovering the truth, someone would only embarrass himself. Are you feeling terrible?" she asked, her voice becoming unexpectedly tender.

He felt a surge of loneliness and roughly wiped away a tear. He was glad no other men were in the room with him. It was one thing to feel longing for a woman in front of family or closer friends, but among comrades on duty, not so.

"Oh, it's not so awful," he answered. "But for some of the others—"

"Yes, yes. Quickly now, Gregor," she interrupted, not wanting to hear about more messes in moustaches, "we have only a few moments. Tell me how many times you've thought of me today and in what ways. If you consume less than five minutes, I shall have to assume you've grown tired of me and wish a divorce."

He laughed. She tried to catch every nuance.

At 8:00 a.m., the next day, the supply ship *Siege of Leningrad* cruised within a stationary pattern two-hundred miles to sea from Engels — prudently far from the denser packs of icebergs. Though two months old, the natural winter in that part of the continent had been moderated by a warm current fed in from the Falkland Islands in the South Atlantic. As a consequence, the Larsen Ice Shelf still sloughed enormous bergs. They were like floating scales shed from the back of a molting monster.

In his small, crowded room, the ship's communications officer — a stringy young man who looked perpetually undernourished but was perfectly healthy — made a call to Engels station.

To the officer's surprise, his call went unanswered. Reluctantly, he notified his captain. The captain merely ordered the officer to let him know when communications were reestablished, and promptly forgot about the subject. The elder man had more important things on his mind.

Two small, 3,600-ton American Perry-class guided-missile frigates, and possibly one of those infernally difficult to detect new Lehman-class cloaked attack submarines, had paced the *Leningrad* for three days and nights. He was occupied directing procedures for learning all he could about the nosy foreign vessels. The *Leningrad* was, of course, well outfitted by military intelligence, the GRU, and the KGB for such work. The ship was equipped with sophisticated synthetic aperture and laser radars, sonars, digital photographic imaging gear and a half dozen other categories of gadgets — even an encrypted Internet connection for fast file searches direct from Mother Russia's military vaults. The fact was, few Soviet supply ships carried only supplies. The shell of his vessel was off the same assembly as a PROMORYE-class intelligence ship. It was gutted to carry a good measure of both lethal and non-lethal items for military operations. Meanwhile, its mission was to make the frigates of imperialist interventionist oppression react so that the ship of peace-loving worker liberation could measure and catalogue the consequences.

From the responses, the KGB's Service I intelligence analysts might glean something slightly important, some significant bit of data to whet the appetites of the 13 Politburo bosses, for whom Service I prepared daily intelligence digests, just as it did in the old days. The Politburo again ran things. True, the old 1990s "parliament" existed — but only as an artifact to please Western image-worshippers.

"All necessary," the burly, red-haired captain muttered to himself, "and ninety-nine times out of a hundred, as boring as my dead sister's opinions on sex."

Around 4:00 p.m., he was suffering a bad headache and wishing only to return to his warm cabin, a half bottle of vodka, and a few hours of sleep, when he received another call from the skinny com officer, "the Rat," as the captain had mentally nicknamed him.

"What was it?" he snapped. "Weather?"

"Unknown, Comrade Captain. I've tried everything, but still nothing from Engels."

"Surely even the worst weather would not prevent contact in eight hours, officer," the captain growled.

"Perhaps their radio is out. I'm sure our signal is reaching them." The Rat did not believe this, but it was prudent to answer optimistically. In the new Soviet system, it was risky to assume realism was in one's best interest.

The older man rubbed a calloused, short-fingered hand over his red, bushy brows and aching eyes and ordered, "Well, have your night man try every hour."

"Yes, Comrade."

When six o'clock came, Engels still failed to respond. Grumpily, the captain noted the clear sky and ordered a sea chopper in to investigate.

In about ninety minutes, the pilot reported that he had landed next to Engels and that he and his three men would go inside. Within three minutes, barely able to control his voice, he addressed his commander from Engels' own radio.

"Get hold of yourself!" barked his superior. "What's the situation?"

"They are, uh, gone, sir. That is, dead. The lot."

"Frozen?" asked the commander, remembering Vostok.

"No, sir. It looks like their —"

There was a sudden retching sound.

"By the grave of Gorbachev, pilot, if you do not pull yourself together and give me clear answers, I'll have you digging pipeline trenches with your teeth!"

"Yes, sir," the pilot replied, mustering himself weakly, "They appear to have — well, *melted*."

"Idiot! Make sense!"

"Sir, their faces and much of the tissue on their limbs seems to have dissolved. Beyond that, I am not competent, sir. Perhaps a medical officer —"

The pilot's voice trailed off into dry heaves.

The commander desperately wanted a drink. Could it be? His mind twisted down a dark alley of thought, recalling rumors of the Soviets' chemical warfare against the Afghan peasants, southern Iranians, Pakistanis, Azerjis, Georgians, others — chemicals which produced an effect like — but, no, not like this. And not the Americans, *they* wouldn't. Not the human-decency conscious Americans. Besides, America was in retreat. Everyone knew that. Then who or what—?

Forcing his mind back to the problem at hand, he ordered the copter crew to remain where it was and to stay in radio contact.

Every Soviet ship of any size carried at least one representative of the KGB, the Committee for State Security, the rejuvenated Soviet Union's secret police. The *Leningrad*'s commander called his KGB man and exchanged a few words, informing him of his plan. He then ordered the com officer to contact Field Forces Directory, the scrambled, ultra-wideband, worldwide automated Soviet military tactical information service, generally used only in emergencies. He told the officer to confirm the location of the nearest Soviet ship equipped with a helicopter or suitable plane, perhaps a cold-capable VSTOL jet, which could land straight down on the rough icy terrain. After being given the proper codes, a nameless bureaucratic voice said that it was the guided missile VSTOL carrier, *Nineteen Seventeen*. It was 30 miles north, barely over the horizon.

The *Leningrad*'s captain wondered briefly what a 273-meter, 37,000-ton VSTOL carrier was doing so far south. He hadn't thought the Soviets had any "gunboat" programs in Antarctic waters. He shrugged and called the KIEV-class vessel by encoded satellite link and explained the situation to its captain.

The carrier captain was a younger man, a star graduate of the Soviet Naval War College, nephew-by-marriage of an admiral serving the Main Military Council, or *Glavnyy Voyennyy Sovyet*, the organ of "strategic leadership" during peacetime.

The *Seventeen* was the youthful captain's first important command. He saw crises as opportunities for advancement rather than as dangers to his comfort. He said the *Seventeen* would dispatch a jetcopter with a medical crew of four.

"Sir," warned the older captain, "there are Americans in the area. Two 130-meter frigates and —"

"I know, Comrade. You are relieved of the problem."

Seven minutes later, the copter settled next to Engels station. After two days, the investigators had found no acceptable answers, but all the *Leningrad*'s copter crew had acquired severe colds. In another twenty-four hours, the doctor's voice was leaden with fear.

"Captain, we have lost two men; the pilot from *Leningrad* and one of his companions. Sir, their tissues simply oozed off their bones as though —"

"Absolutely no one is to leave Engels until we know more," the captain snapped.

After a long pause, the doctor answered, "Yes, sir."

"If any of you tries to fly out in some insane violation of my orders — remember, we have jets with air-to-air missiles."

Thirty more hours passed before the captain ordered a suited, second medical team into the air. By that time, no one at Engels responded to radio calls — except for a single man who gurgled incoherently off and on for several minutes before falling silent.

A few hours later, an American Air Force EF-22 reconnaissance plane attempted a fly-by at Navy request. The jet was sternly warned off by four Soviet Su-40 interceptors sent up to give "protective cover" to Engels. The Soviets rebuffed all U.S. efforts to approach the station, except for overflights by two unreachable transatmospheric (TAV) long-range Mach-25 Blackwings sent down from Beale Air Force Base in California. But even Blackwings could not see through steel walls and gathered little useful information about the events at Engels.

Eventually, the Russians ceased radio communication with Engels and established a copter courier system, presumably under heavy decontamination procedures.

For four months, the Soviet station was a wasp's nest of secretive activity. Then, suddenly, everything quieted. When the Americans requested permission to visit on the pretext of a scientific courtesy call, permission was granted. The American delegation found an ordinary meteorologic and geographic establishment engaged in weather and ice sampling projects. When the U.S. team inquired about the earlier strange events, none of the Soviet scientists could or would tell them. They claimed that there was no record of anything unusual at Engels, ever.

CHAPTER 2

THE INTELLIGENCE

F rankly, Mr. President, I don't think they knew anything."

"Oh?" President Sam Washington asked.

The hefty chief executive looked tiredly at his slender, 37-year-old Central Intelligence Agency chief, William F. "Whiz" Brighton. Whiz was competent, but rather humorless and often a bit long-winded. He'd been talking for over thirty minutes and Washington was still trying to figure out why he felt the Oval Office should be so all-fired interested in a bunch of long dead Russians down in Penguin Paradise. Didn't a president have enough to worry about with the latest and, it seemed, never-ending problems of the U.S. economy? He shook his head. Sometimes it was almost too much. It would make a hell of an epitaph: Creamed by Heavy Thoughts. Some well-aged hippie would probably read his gravestone and nod knowingly.

"The Russians brought in all new people after cleaning up whatever happened at Engels," Brighton said. "One of my boys was planted in the visiting U.S. scientific team."

"So what was the Rooskies' story?" Washington asked, stifling a yawn. The effort made his jaw ache.

"They said Engels had an uneventful winter. Claimed the station's logs backed them up. Faked, of course."

Washington leaned back and pursed his lips. Whiz's brain knew only one way—the long way. Creative people were sometimes like that; Washington didn't know why. He thought maybe a diversion would help. He let his light brown eyes gaze around the room, settling on his personally commissioned oil painting, a portrait of the nation's first president. The painting showed a close-up of George Washington gazing across the icy Delaware, moments before boarding the boat to lead his men in their surprise holiday raid that had so influenced the history of the early Republic. General Washington's face looked determined, strong — but also more than a touch worried.

"Whiz, did old George have to deal with so much, well — just plain weirdness?"

Brighton frowned, annoyed at the seemingly irrelevant question. Dutifully, he shifted in his seat to get a better look at the artwork.

"I don't doubt he thought so from time to time," he offered lamely. "Er, I suppose it's a matter of context."

Washington laughed, feeling the lingering irritation slide away like soap bubbles rinsed from his face. Maybe he had Whiz in a new perspective.

"Spoken like a true intelligence man, Bill," he said. "Or a politician."

"No ambitions in that direction," Brighton stated with conviction, as though he'd actually said, "I have no intention of living in a slime vat."

"Didn't mean it literally."

Washington straightened in his chair, and hoping to get lucky and hurry Brighton to the point, said, "Scrape the bucket bottom for me."

"Yes, sir. First, the Russians were experimenting with some new biological weapons which got out of hand. Second, and more likely, they were experimenting with chemical weapons —and the same thing happened."

Washington lifted his eyebrows. "Weapons? Wait a minute. Didn't you send me a memo on this several weeks ago?"

Brighton nodded.

"But I don't recall mention of weapons. I thought it was just a bad new flu."

"Well, to be precise, sir, there was only talk of people catching colds. That's what the first Soviets in there assumed."

"But you lean toward chemicals?"

"Uh-huh. The time frame fits. There are exceptions, but bad viruses don't usually act that fast that terribly!"

"You talkin' nerve gasses, then, or what?"

"Perhaps, sir. Like some of the Soviets' in the Islamic Wars, or what the rebel Serbs cooked up in their European terror campaign back in '99. With modifications, certain industrial compounds could do it, too. Remember the Union Carbide disaster in India? Grisly. A thousand or more dead."

"Maybe one of the Rooskies bumped a beaker."

"Maybe, sir."

"Hmmm," Washington frowned, stroking his heavy red beard. "I was under the impression that chemicals hit a person even faster than happened at Engels."

"There are in-between time-frames. You're forgetting your woodlore, Mr. President," Brighton chided. "Didn't you ever hunt mushrooms as a kid in those Oregon forests?"

"Nope. Dad threatened our backsides if we did. You're suggesting toadstools?"

"Very good, sir. Some of them don't show symptoms for a day or more. Then you're suddenly thrashing around like you swallowed a cattle prod, vomiting, maybe bleeding from both ends, and you've had it. Read up on the Deadly Amanita sometime, sir."

Washington grinned wryly. "I'll be sure to get a book for my bedside."

Brighton smiled big and seemed to relax. The president wondered if Whiz got off on horror movies.

"The point is," the CIA chief sped on with a lighter tone, "if the Soviets were fiddling around with deadly compounds, Antarctica is as isolated a place as you could pick. But if the stuff was too new, and an accident hit, they maybe didn't know what was going on until way too late."

"Think they know now?"

"They *should* have isolated the source of the problem. But our chemical boys say these things can be tricky. That the Soviets were hush-hush for so long might mean they found the going tough. Despite modern, analytical techniques, there's still plenty that takes time to tame. And they're not as advanced as we."

"We hope," Washington said, nodding. "And we can hope it was chemicals, because I'd sure hate to see some godawful new bugs loose. Black Death all over again, or worse." He tried to control a shudder.

"With our new anti-viral genetic engineering, we could combat it, sir."

"How many would die in the meantime?"

"Oh, the Soviets aren't *that* stu —"

"Not intentionally. Accidentally."

"Huh? Oh, uh, well —." Brighton stroked his chin and studied the ceiling for a few moments.

The President of the United States felt ridiculously smug — like a father who'd just gotten the concept of venereal disease through to an over-sexed teenage son.

Brighton finally conceded, "I suppose, quite a few would die, sir, but they likely wouldn't be ours. Not most of them."

"I don't follow you."

"Epidemics start somewhere, sir. We'd see one coming out of Russia or one of its satellites. If it was a virus that they developed down there, we can be fairly sure they took it home and put it under guard. They'd shelve it with the hundreds of other viruses, viroids, bacteria and fungal agents they've come up with over the years. That includes Yuri Ovchinnikov's infamous cobra-venom viruses, of course."

"Jesus," Washington said, feeling hair rise on the back of his hands.

"Never heard of that one, sir?" Brighton said, smirking in a way that reminded Washington of a mischievous coroner who enjoyed shocking people by handing them hunks of brain or liver. "It was devised at the Institute of Molecular Biology near Novosibirsk in the mid-1980s. The virus invades like ordinary flu. In fact, it *is* flu, except for one difference. At a certain point, after a week or so, the virus begins producing and releasing cobra venom. It's like being bitten a hundred times all over your body — from the inside."

Brighton laughed, then cut it off as he noted Washington's gray face. "Well, uh, anyway, after U.S. intelligence got wind of it, there were a few stories in the U.S. press, mostly *The Wall Street Journal*. But they passed. Too outlandish and awful; nobody wanted to dwell on it. Still don't, I guess."

He glanced accusingly at the president. "Some of our boys think the Soviets actually tested the venom virus, probably on Cambodians near the Thai border."

Washington grimaced and pushed up out of his seat. He worked his thick shoulders, then walked to the wetbar's fridge. He rummaged around, retrieved and twisted open a Henry's beer.

"Want one, Whiz?" he asked.

"Er, I'm a Mormon."

"Forgot. Well, no offense, but it's been a long day." He paused to swallow half the brew, then walked back to his desk and sat down, the bottle dwarfed by his large hand. He pulled his thoughts together and said, "Horrible chemical weapons have been around for years, Bill. I don't see the urgency of this."

He glanced purposefully at his watch.

Brighton's lips compressed tightly for a second before he replied. "I doubt if that's the interpretation potential victims would —"

"Get your dander down," Washington said. "We really can't police the world. I thought you knew that coming into my administration."

"Sometimes the line between world policing and our own security is awfully gray, sir."

"I'm a *politician*," the president snapped. "Don't lecture me on grayness, son. I get enough of that from the loyal opposition!"

He took another swig of beer, glowering at the younger man. Unexpectedly, Brighton seemed to relax, smiling broadly. I'll be damned, the president thought, maybe the kid just needed to know a person had a human temper. Washington remembered a conceited football quarterback in high school. You had to cuss him out to make him warm up to you.

"Yes, sir," Brighton said, no longer reserved at all. "But frankly, the kind of Soviet secrecy and cover-up we saw down there makes me think they found something we shouldn't ignore. I think I'd like a beer after all."

Washington shrugged and retrieved the beer for Brighton. As he handed it to him, he looked at him sideways and said, "Revisionist, Whiz, or just slipping?"

Brighton wiped his mouth with the back of his hand and said, "Actually, sir, I've never decided. Mom was old Mormon; Dad was new. I sort of swing."

"Nothing like the sanctity of principles," Washington remarked.

"No sacred seagulls from Utah shit on my head."

Washington guffawed and discovered that he didn't want the discussion to end quite yet. Unfortunately, he had things to do.

"Bill, understand me. I'm no fan of this resurrected Soviet system. It's glorified brutality. On the other hand," he continued, "I'm not terribly afraid. Yeah, our Pentagon budgets have been sliding for years and years. Even so, we're still strong enough to make the Rooskies or anyone else think twice. And they've had no more first strike options since we got the SDI flying. Surprise missile attack was always our main back-burner catastrophic worry. That's behind us."

The CIA chief thought to himself that the Soviets had had their SDI far longer than the U.S. and that they had kept parts of it totally secret. No one truly knew what they had. If they put this Engels thing on missiles —

He blurted out, "Sir, it wouldn't hurt to devote a few billion more to rough-and-dirty countermeasures. Just in case. Buy some better chem/bio suits for the troops and start rejuvenating civil defense shelters to —"

Washington shook his head, rapidly annoyed. "I've got an economy flat on its face and a stubborn, trough-slurping Congress that just might, if I go easy on defense, give me some budget reductions and tax cuts to get this nation moving again. It's been a damned near five-year recession. If I can't turn things around, we won't have the industry to support what defense we have. So don't try to sell me on bug nets."

He paused, looking out the window into space, then muttered, "Besides, I have more political housecleaning to do."

"Oh?" Brighton cocked an eyebrow, looking back at Washington's big, whiskered face. "Who've you decided to get rid of this time?" His eyes sparkled.

Washington smiled. "The word is 'fire,' Bill. The Soviets 'get rid of' people. Jason Johnson."

Brighton whistled. Johnson was Secretary of State. If Washington was ousting him, then there could be no doubt he intended to continue a serious pink-slipping of the numerous holdovers from the previous administration of Cranston McCaully.

President Samuel Washington was now well into his second year in office. When he'd taken his oath, he had been tempted to immediately kick out McCaully's appointees. His advisors had been all for it. But Washington had decided to tackle other matters first. He'd worried that another jarring upset in the affairs of state following the sudden death of one president and the disgrace of a second was not what America needed for her peace of mind — especially not in the storm of a badly mangled economy, the worst in decades.

"When's it happening?"

"Tomorrow morning. Replacing him with Craig Goldstein."

"He's been around," Brighton said. "My boys could get along with a guy like that."

Washington inwardly chuckled at the "my boys" reference. Most of Brighton's employees looked older than him. Many were.

"Goldstein understands that a little more than American English is spoken on this turbulent ball of dirt. He'll be with me at Camp David tomorrow. I'm making the announcement from there. Want to drop over for dinner?"

"Yes, sir, that'd be great."

"Maybe Annette will rustle up some of her down-home Oregon version of Russian Stroganov. Seems like an appropriate dish. Goldstein might as well get used to the word 'Russian.' With the new arms-reduction summit coming up next fall, he'll undoubtedly be hearing it a lot."

"I think he's used to it already," Brighton said. "He knows a lot about the Russians, believe me. We've kicked around ideas a few times."

"Well, er, good," Washington said. He'd been unaware that the two men knew each other personally. He stood and stretched, groaning. His sit-down session with

Brighton had gone on way too long. He walked around his desk and shook good-bye.

"Let's put this Engels fiasco aside, Whiz. I've got a feeling it's just another piece of Soviet dirty laundry that's fallen off the line."

Brighton nodded uncertainly.

After the CIA chief left, Washington punched his intercom and asked the White House switchboard to call General Wharton "Buck" Reed. Reed was the head of the Joint Chiefs of Staff.

"Yes, sir?" asked the familiar rock-hard face, one that looked like a general's — or so Washington had thought since his classmate days with Reed at West Point.

"Can you drop over here in couple hours? I'd like to knock around this Engels station thing."

Reed took a moment before answering. "Engels? Let's see, I'm not sure what you—" he said, as though trying to recall.

"The Antarctic bit," Washington interjected.

Reed snapped his fingers. "Right!" Then frowned. "Something new come up?"

"Something's *always* up in this office — and it's usually a downer, especially economic. Nothing to grind your teeth about, though, Buck. Just want another perspective."

In truth, the Engels case worried Washington more than he'd let on to Brighton. Not much more, but a little. It was like a faint sound echoing through the hills late at night. Something far away. Yet something that shouldn't be there.

CHAPTER 3

THE CANDLE

Across the continent, as President Washington waited for General Reed, a modified 195,000-pound missile thundered off a railcar into the clear sky. Soaring up out of Vandenberg Air Force Base, the mobile Peacemaker missile was visible for miles up and down the California coast. Reclaimed out of the old defunct Peacekeeper program, designed to eventually replace the few aging Minuteman missiles in the U.S. nuclear deterrent, this one was programmed to head for a test range in the Pacific.

Seventy-one feet high, the four-stage, 15-warhead weapon had never been used in combat. Most people hoped it never would be. Equipped with penetrator "wedgy" warheads and sophisticated anti-missile/anti-laser jammer/deflectors (AMALJADs), the Peacemaker could hit and collapse even the most hardened Soviet command bunkers. Unknown to the U.S., Red Army generals had dubbed the missile, "The Coffin Maker."

Most of the missile's several dozen test-firings had gone well. But there was special interest in seeing that this one fired and flew smoothly because it was the first to gather detailed information on full-profile warhead deployment.

Twelve minutes into the mission, a young colonel of Air Force Systems Command Ballistic Missile Office (BMO) intently watched the flight on his video terminal. The mechanics of the flight were actually handled by the Command's Space and Missile Test Organization personnel (SMTO).

"Sure, they get to light the candle," he muttered to himself, glancing at the SMTO people, who were already smugly winking at each other over the apparent success. "Their" missile had entered descent. It was preparing to release its decoys and dummy warheads against an assortment of mock target points. "But I made the wax," he added.

His project group had, working with engineers from the four original private contractors — Thiokol, Aerojet, Hercules and Rocketdyne — put together radical engine modifications involving "grown" ceramic linings and higher-thrust fuel mixtures. Solid fuel went into the first three stages, while liquid lit the last for guidance flexibility. You could turn off the tap on a liquid; solid-fuellers had to burn out on their own. But the new compounds burned better and more safely, and flew faster, cutting several minutes off the missile's attack time and making it a more formidable retaliatory, and hence deterrent, weapon. So the theory went.

Because he was watching the controllers at precisely the wrong moment, the colonel's first clue to what had happened was when he heard one of the men to his left hiss, "What the — ?" His second clue was the sense that everyone in the room and its adjacent glass cubicles was sitting straighter.

Perplexed, the colonel, who had never witnessed a live launch, looked away from his small terminal to the big screen. It was a high-resolution real video and digital graphic combo. The dual-mode monitor hung high above the front of the room.

At the moment, it showed a blinking red circle, indicating that the "bus," or last stage of the rocket, was in some kind of trouble. The video, broken into several sections, reflecting feeds from satellite and airborne cameras, showed why. The bus had disintegrated. Its thousands of parts were falling lazily into the Pacific, like a flock of birds burned out of the sky.

One of the SMTO men glared at him and said, "Some wax you guys put in our candle."

The colonel shook his head, "It shouldn't have done that."

The SMTO man snorted. "Yeah, well, it looks like you forgot to tell the candle. It did it anyway."

CHAPTER 4

THE WAIT

Tanya Yublenka lit a cigarette. She had three left in her last pack. She sat on the edge of a cheap, cracked brown vinyl couch and kept her long legs tightly crossed to keep them warm. She could no longer afford pantyhose and the sputtering steam heater in the waiting room was not a gift to efficiency. She had been smoking and getting angrier for three hours.

The first hour she had spent filling out a request, five separate copies, three pages each. The paper did not self-copy, there was no carbon paper, and the office copier was for "official use only" — whatever that meant. Two computer terminals sat unused, cobwebs across their screens.

The second hour she had waited for a records clerk "to become available" to look at her request. It turned out that there were only two clerks. One was a fat, hostile elderly woman with a bowl haircut. She had spent the entire time talking in whispered tones on the telephone, snapping at anyone who tried to interrupt. The other was a blond young man upon whose shoulders the burden of service fell.

He was returning from a back room for the fourth time. Tanya knew that she mustn't lose her temper. She told herself that Gregor's life could depend on her keeping a level head. If she lost control, the clerk could conclude that she was a fanatic, perhaps even a dissident.

"I'm sorry," the clerk said. "It's no use. There is simply no record of a Gregor Yublenka. Perhaps he was working under a different name," he offered. His voice was surprisingly deep, almost as deep as Gregor's, but softer.

For what felt like the twentieth time, she patiently said, "He is my husband. That is the name he's always used."

The clerk shook his head. "Maybe he was carrying an assignment of which you were unaware, from before you knew him. Yublenka might itself be a pseudonym and—"

"It was not that kind of job," Tanya interrupted, gripping the counter edge. "He wasn't some character in a movie."

The clerk looked embarrassed. "I've done what I can."

She felt her pulse quicken in frustration. Calm, calm, calm, she recited to herself.

"Please," she said. "Will you try just once more? Perhaps there's a place you haven't searched?"

The clerk glanced at the fat woman and grimaced, then let his eyes scan the room. There were ten other people waiting, at least half of them sending resentful stares their way. He looked back at Tanya, taking in her symmetrical, delicate features, high cheekbones, pouty lips, thick dark hair, her slender, proud figure. "Maybe if we tried another tactic. You'll have to go into it with me after hours," he whispered.

Tanya froze. So that was how the game would be played. Bribery, the blood of the new Soviet socialism.

"Tonight," he said. "Meet me near the gazebo at the Inspiration Park. I'll take us — somewhere better."

Sure. A public servant sacrificing his time to help a poor comrade — who happens to be built better than a sack of cement.

"Yes," she answered woodenly, unable to make herself sound enthusiastic, even though she knew it would probably help.

"Good," he said softly. "About five o'clock, then."

"Of course," was all she said.

The park was the only one in the small city of Krevesk. It's name was a sarcasm. The planners had overlooked a large piece of ground right in the middle of their beautiful schematic drawings. No one knew what to do with it at first and it had been too late to change the rest of the plans. Then, in the midst of an alcohol-propelled squall of recriminations about exactly which planner was responsible for wasting a minor tract of socialism, someone noticed another oversight. The planners had neglected to design any parks. Well, why not make one mistake the solution to the other? Declare the overlooked lot a park. Inspiration. Inspiration Park.

An icy Ural breeze blew his hair into a ragged yellow halo. He was smiling. A smug devil, she thought. He would probably suggest dinner at his apartment, she mused. Plenty to drink and a little caviar on the side. But it won't be caviar he'll want to spread, she observed, shivering more than the cold demanded. He stopped in front of her.

"Don't be offended if I say you look lovely, like Lara in Dr. Zhivago. Not a bad movie. But not really Russian. Too colorful."

"I heard once that New Pravda called the movie 'degenerate.'"

His smile faded.

Good, Tanya, she told herself. You've closed off that avenue to him; all that's left is the one between your legs.

He stamped his feet against the chill, glanced around and his smile slowly came back.

"Oh, well," he said, taking her by the elbow and briskly leading the way out of the park.

He found a small café where the music was mostly Polish renditions of old American jazz.

He seated them in a booth in the back of the establishment, getting an indifferent glance from a scruffy waiter who slouched by the battered bar smoking a heavy cigarette and chatting with the bartender. Their table was covered with what looked like bleached gunny sacks. A thick candle on the table was a mound of wax and could no longer hold a flame.

"No problem," he said, grinning broadly. "Watch."

He took a two-inch nail from his coat pocket and pushed it straight down into the mound of wax and pulled it out. Then he took out a short length of string and, using the nail, worked the string into the hole. He scraped a tiny amount of wax onto his thumb and rubbed it into the exposed string and lit it with a paper match.

"See?" he beamed. "Instant atmosphere!"

Tanya gave him a grudging smile.

The wall was recycled broken brick. Tanya spotted a cockroach scurrying between one of the gaps.

He chuckled, "One of the cafe's more loyal patrons."

She was remembering little places like this that she and Gregor had found. She looked around at the cafe's single chandelier twenty feet away, only half of its twelve weak bulbs working; at the pea-green swinging door to the kitchen; at the two tables to her left, each with four chairs around it, three of the eight unmatching. Tawdriness had not mattered when Gregor was around. Not as much.

"You are stiff, Mrs. Yublenka," he said. "Tense."

Bitterly, she forced her eyes to look at him. How could anyone know what it was like to miss a man like Gregor? What could anyone know of an ache so big it felt like her chest would split when she lay awake at night?

"Not *Mrs.* Yublenka. Tanya. It will make everything easier."

"Madeis Plechl. Servant of the state."

They shook. His hands were large and strong. Like Gregor's, she thought, feeling disloyal to his memory.

"German?"

"My grandfather grew up in Berlin, but my father moved to Moscow and then later, here, to Krevesk. Or rather, he was moved, along with other scientists. I was born here. I am now a wall-faced Soviet; part of the World's Greatest Edifice."

"The Edifice," she repeated.

He nodded, leaning out to wave the waiter over to the booth with a ruble note. "And after we plaster enough socialist bricks, someday our ladder of oppression will fade away, though it is a process slower than human sight can discern — unless you pursue truth."

"Which is?"

"Not the truth as it was, of course, but the truth as it is officially defined each minute. Which includes defining away any contradictions with the past. Excuse me, *what* contradictions? Right now, the truth is Great Russian. Even we blond-haired, blue-eyed Teutonics don't measure up to their genetics. Just ask. They claim to go all the way back to the Great Caesar — through the Great Rurik, the ninth century Scandinavian prince who founded what would become the Russian state. Royalty all, our socialist leaders."

His words were caustic, but his voice danced; his eyes sparkled. He's a good actor, she thought.

"I am?" Madeis asked, cocking his head.

She realized she'd said it aloud. Now what, you potato-headed slut? Tears unexpectedly trickled down her cheek. She was miserable at this game.

But suddenly he was sitting next to her, on her side of the booth, with his right arm around her, saying urgently, "It's all right, Tanya. If he's alive, we'll find him." She nodded, sniffling.

"Now let me get us some tea; I was going to order wine, but it would only make your emotions worse."

She leaned quietly against him. For a reason she didn't understand, she was no longer calling herself a fool inside.

Breaking the pattern of the cafe's lethargic service, the tea arrived almost as soon as ordered.

"And to compound wonders," he said, touching the side of the pot, "it's hot. Is there a lesson here for our system?"

Gregor used to say things like that, Tanya thought. She took a deep breath, wiped her eyes with a sleeve, and asked, "Have you lived in Krevesk all your life?"

"Presuming one can call it living, almost."

"Your father is still a scientist?"

"Absolutely. A dedicated one, diligently working to advance the perfection of Soviet man through the profession of chemistry. They all are, you know."

"Dedicated?"

"I meant that here in Krevesk, they all work in fields related to chemistry. Well, ninety percent of them. But, sadly, I inherited neither my father's talents for science nor his interest. It's another reason why this German will never get far up the ladder. Not here," he added, "not here."

He shrugged and poured the tea. She took her mug, warming her hands.

"We lived here earlier, Gregor and I, before we were transferred," she said. "Then I went straight to Buenos Aires, he first to Molodezhnaya, the main Soviet Antarctic base, and then to Engels. But we had spent two years in Krevesk right out of university."

"One wonders, if the state is omniscient, why does it need education at all?"

"To solve problems," she murmered through the tea's steam.

"Have you heard how the state will really solve them?"

She shook her head, letting tea trickle down her throat.

"There's the natural way and the supernatural way. Under the natural way, the head of the Kremlin will make a deal with God to again permit the flourishing of the Orthodox Church. In turn, God will send down a troop of angel economists to straighten out all the state's production and distribution problems."

"And the supernatural way?" she asked.

"Why, the state will find the answers itself."

In spite of herself, she laughed, looking around guiltily.

He smiled, slid out of the booth, and moved back to his side.

"It's not that I dislike warming myself against a beautiful woman, Tanya, but I find conversation more compelling when I can look directly at you. Now, then, about your husband's disappearance. Where have you searched?"

"Where could I search, but in Krevesk?"

His face clouded. "You are out of work?"

She realized only then that she'd assumed all this time that he knew. It affected her estimate of his intentions.

"Yes, since two weeks after my last conversation with Gregor. Transferred. No explanation. They put me on a plane from Argentina to Moscow, then by bus down to Krevesk. I was told to wait here for another assignment. Someone else had been given my old job, though. I've waited for over four months."

"Where? How have you lived?"

"When we were moved to the Southern Hemisphere, we had both been told that our jobs there would last only six or seven months. Miraculously, our apartment was still free when I returned. I've lived on savings. Nearly gone."

"I take it you've explained your predicament to your superiors? Who are they?"

She rubbed her eyes with thumb and forefinger. "I don't know anymore. I used to work as a translator in the foreign technical library. My job was to assist the researchers who had an inadequate command of English. Boris, that was the man I worked for, the library director, Boris Karpov. He said he might be able to work something out if only —"

"Yes?"

"If I became his mistress. I refused."

Madeis snorted. "The bastard. I deal with him every once in awhile. He sends his personnel records over to us for duplication into our computer files. We note new additions, subtractions, changes in staff, record them, forward it all to Moscow by Internet. When the connections are working, anyway. Boris is a horny little Tartar pig; a pig born with a semi-scientific brain. My father knows him and feels as I do. Actually, Karpov's fairly careful with married women. Years ago, he poked some empty-headed young bride who told her husband. He ambushed Karpov with a vodka bottle. He leaves the married ones alone now."

He looked at her, scanning her face. "But four months is a long time. Was Karpov the only one you asked for work?

"Oh, no! I have asked at all laboratories, the warehouses, even cafeterias."

"New jobs go only to scientists and to those who have friends, either here or elsewhere. I take it you have none."

"I did. But clearly not the kind who count. There were two girlfriends, but now they act as though I have anthrax."

"Karpov's spite. Warned them to stay away from you."

"I don't think so. They acted that way toward me *before* Karpov made his mistress proposal."

Madeis stared at her for a moment and then pulled out a pack of cigarettes. He offered her one, an American Camel.

"I was the fastest and most accurate translator in the library," she said. "At least the fastest with English."

"It almost sounds as though you're being punished."

"For what?" she asked, exhaling smoke.

"For what? Let me tell you a true story about a Jew in a Nazi concentration camp. He was dying of thirst and reached out to break off an icicle to suck. An SS guard broke his hand with a rifle barrel and told him to never try it again. 'What for?' the Jew asked. 'What for?' the guard answered. 'In here, there is no "what for."' In the new Soviet world, Tanya, there is no 'what for.'"

She shivered. He put a hand over hers and said, "I'm cynical. There are always motives. Two possibilities strike me. One, you've been lost in the cracks. Two, it's Gregor, something he did which spread the guilt to you, making you a 'non-person.'"

"He did nothing."

"We should find out. Coincidentally, it will prevent you from starving."

"That isn't important! Gregor is all —"

"You are the one who sits before me and grows gaunt from lack of food. You can't help him if you're dead."

She slid from the booth and ran out of the cafe.

He caught up half a block away, grabbing her arm and swinging her around to face him.

"All right, Tanya! We'll do it your way. On one condition."

"What?" She almost spat the word.

"Make it two."

She tried to jerk free.

He held tight. "First, you come back to the cafe and have dinner. Second, you promise to tell me when you run out of money so I can loan you some."

"I won't take —"

"No, you won't. A *loan*. That's not taking."

Her face remained tense, but her eyes were studying his.

"Please?" he asked, his voice low. "Is it so much to ask, a request to help keep you alive?"

He lifted her face in both hands and lightly kissed her lips. Tears filled her eyes. In a moment, he led her over the icy pavement and back into the warmth of the cafe.

You're crazy, Tanya, she thought.

CHAPTER 5

THE GENERAL

Thee general looked at his president and frowned. "Do you know something
I don't?"

"You never did like it when I did." Washington saw Reed stiffen slightly. "Oh,
I'm not worried about something disastrous, Buck. You'd probably see the signs
before me anyway, right?"

"An old jungle point-man's sixth sense."

Washington merely nodded. He'd never been in combat, but Buck had —
long ago, a two-year tour in Vietnam.

"Theoretically, Buck, tell me. Do you think the Russians are capable of initiating something big against us?"

"Huh? So that's the spider in the can, eh? Well, years ago, there was a window
of vulnerability. Not just in *some* things, either. We'd let defense slide badly after
Vietnam and the Soviets were lookin' to carve up the planet. Coordinated their big
phased array radars with their ASAT interceptors while conducting mock first strikes
with various ICBMs — including modified SS-20s that they fooled us into thinking were only intermediate range missiles; even sent a few up on U.S.-bound polar
trajectories and then blew them up. Then they conducted a mock missile attack on
Pearl Harbor in '87; that shook a few grass skirts loose. They sandbagged their
major industries, practiced mass evacuations and triage, and built whole new underground command, control, communications and intelligence shelters which they
didn't finish until the Clinton years. Looked bad. But after Gorbachev, it all im-
ploded. What a waste of an empire."

"True, but over the centuries, that kind of thinking made them into a big country," Washington said. "As I recall, in the half a millennium after their founding,
the Russians averaged territorial additions about the size of my old home state of
Oregon once every six years. They are patient builders."

"Yes, sir, but the fact is the Soviets have seldom moved except when there
was no chance of significant opposition. As to chemical and germ warfare, they
don't have the odds. Unless, of course, they get crazy and want to sacrifice a hell
of a hunk of everything, which they don't."

"What about ballistic or cruise missile delivery?"

"Same as for nuclear. Deter 'em with our SDI. Not foolproof, but then nobody who knows warfare ever really thought it would be."

The president nodded, making notes on a yellow pad. "What else, Buck?"

"We've got a no-holes radar. Our automatic border and rebuilt DEW systems with Canada and protected phased-arrays pick up everything over 5000 feet while our backscatter radars, AWACS planes, look-down/shoot-downs, satellites and so forth, get everything underneath. Couldn't put a gnat through it."

"So until they invent missiles that can make like moles, there's no way to sneak by us." Washington said. "What about biological? That one shortens my socks."

"Any sufficiently underdeveloped nation entertaining the idea of germ warfare faces an insurmountable problem — the 'biological boomerang,' it's called. Once you turn the little motherbuggers loose, how the *hell* do you control 'em? There's no point to any plan of conquest if implementing an epidemic carries the penalty of suicide. Anyway, the Sovs would be unsure that a bug attack — even if they got around the delivery systems difficulties — couldn't be quickly stopped."

"By us, you mean?"

"Of course. We still lead the world in genetic diagnostic and engineering capacities. Their stuff's primitive. That's why the boomerang'd get 'em worse than us."

"Well, I think Brighton covered that, but —"

"Sam," Reed interjected, "you're still fairly fresh in this office. I've never had the opportunity to thoroughly brief you on overall strength. Let me put the horse in the barn. I'm so confident of our defenses that I'm damned near complacent."

"That so?" Washington said, startled. He'd always been an opponent of overconfidence.

Reed grinned. "Oh, I've got reasons. Even though the conservative whiz kids say we should spend more — beware the new Commies and all that — I'm so sure the Russians understand and respect our dominant position that I'm considering the next time they ask for disarmament talks, we ought to take them up on it."

"They're scheduled."

"I don't mean those arms control card games," Reed said, his face growing stern. "I'm talking *real* disarmament."

Washington looked at him blankly for a moment, then got up and cracked another beer to cover his astonishment. No Joint Chief's head had ever suggested true disarmament talks. Arms *limitation* talks, sure — because that was merely a euphemism for modernization, especially for the Russians who'd violated from the outset virtually every agreement they'd ever signed. Both major parties now grudgingly agreed on that point.

"You're serious."

"Completely," Reed replied, spreading his hands wide in a gesture of simple honesty, "and so are the other chiefs — well, everybody except Glenn Young of the Space Command. But those space boys' escalators are missing a few steps. Always worrying about the wild stuff."

The president ignored Reed's jab at Young. Their feud was becoming legendary. "I don't know, Buck," he said. "As my daddy used to say, 'If a nail doesn't seem to be stuck' in anything, why hit it?"

"Eh? Well, consider this: disarmament talks are now a logical alternative."

"To what?"

"To economic foolishness."

Washington raised both eyebrows. "Am I talking to the leader of my Joint Chiefs?"

"It's the same old 'military-industrial complex' drainhole. Dwight Eisenhower said it, a man who wore both our shoes."

"Yes, he did," the president said, thinking as he had several times lately how much easier it'd be to give a swift kick to the economy if some major weapons systems could be scratched, or at least put on a long hold. It was not a new trade-off. It had been used by presidents ever since World War II. In the middle of a recession, it was tempting; tempting as hell. Especially if he wanted a second term in office.

"As short-sighted as I thought President McCaully was," Reed said, "I thought he was right about one thing—economically, military spending is a giant cowpie."

Washington pursed his lips. "Except that if we aren't strong in this world, we've got no confidence in the country. No confidence means no long-term investing. No long-term investing means no economic growth."

"Well, we don't have any growth now, sir. But we do have a defense amply adequate for the little jobs we're likely to face any time soon."

Washington sighed, rose, stretched, looked out the window. "I'll give it some thought."

"It could help the country a lot."

"Probably so. I've no doubt. But back to this Engels thing. Brighton says his crew doesn't think much came of all that Soviet secrecy down there."

"Well, Sam," Reed said, leaning forward, "I don't know what wild ideas Whiz may have run by you, but Engels was nothing unusual. Secrecy is *normal* to them. Nothing to worry about."

"I recall some Soviet secrets that sure worried us," remarked Washington soberly. "How about Sputnik? There was the H-bomb they got years sooner than we thought, too. There was the satellite-killer laser they popped up on those southern peaks. And then there was —"

"Okay, okay, okay," said Reed, "granted, they've nipped us in the nibs on a few things. Even the worst authoritarian regime with a practically decimated economy can *occasionally* make breakthroughs by concentrating scientific energies in certain fields. But you can't base policy on such exceptions. Spend yourself into oblivion if you do."

"Bluntly, you think Engels is piss iceballs?"

"I'm unconvinced the Russians had a chemical warfare project going. First, they don't have to go to Antarctica to do that. Second, Naval and Air Force Intelligence — which got the first info and were down there longer than Brighton's CIA boys — say Engels is what it appeared to be before and after the incident: a scientific weather and geographical station. Nothing more."

"But the chemicals ....."

Reed waved it away. "We've had accidents similar here in the U.S. at any number of institutions. Maybe a couple of compounds were inadvertently mixed. Who knows?"

"What about similarities to the yellow and blue rains that the Soviets used in the Mideast and Southeast Asia? Didn't they produce such symptoms?"

The general made a scoffing sound. "Crap — pardon me, sir — but Whiz is blowing it out his ear if he said that. Sure, some of the symptoms were similar. But a lot of 'em *weren't.*"

Reed steepled his fingers, then said, "I know you like Whiz, Sam. And there's no question he's got a lot of processors upstairs. But, frankly, I'd like to see a more experienced man in the position."

"A man only?"

"One Jeanne Allison is enough in intelligence," Reed replied stiffly, referring to the National Security Agency head.

"Another time on that one," the president said, looking at his watch. He stood up. "Okay, Buck. Thanks for coming by. Your judgment is always valued. Take care and let's pow-wow the Joint Chiefs on this disarmament idea. I'd like to hear first-hand everybody's real reasoning."

Reed smiled broadly and said, "Great, Sam. Have a nice weekend, sir." He saluted, as he always did.

Washington stared after the door for several seconds. There was something missing in Buck today, he thought. Or something extra.

CHAPTER 6

THE RESIDENT

There were few people among the three thousand scientists in Krevesk who knew that Library Director Boris Karpov was an "Internal Resident," a local head of the KGB. One person who knew was Madeis Plechl — for the simple reason that he was Karpov's chief deputy.

What better choice of jobs for KGB overseers than to work in the technical library and in the personnel bureau? Other than restrooms and cafeterias, these two places were the most frequented public structures.

"How is the Politburo these days, Boris?" Plechl asked.

"I expect to be First Secretary any day," Karpov answered.

It was an old joke between them. Boris Karpov had the misfortune to possess the same name as a powerful, well-known Politburo member. It made it difficult for others to take Karpov as seriously as he was sure he deserved.

"Vodka?" Karpov asked, as Plechl sat down in the creaky old wood swivel chair in front of the KGB chief's maple desk.

"A little, maybe."

"That's what all Russians say," Karpov observed, grinning. "Maybe we'll make one of you yet!"

Both men chuckled, raised their glasses and downed the smooth drink in single gulps. Karpov refilled them and eased his squat bulk into his stuffed leather chair, larger and four inches taller than Plechl's.

"So," Karpov began, "our little tundra flower, Yublenka — how is she?"

"She *is* a flower, but broken-hearted. Lonely."

"You've gained her trust?"

"I will have by the end of the week. But she's wary."

"Wonderful! The ones who start out wary and end up falling into your arms are the best. After you start shooting her with your pleasure pistol, she'll tell you anything."

Plechl laughed dutifully, but inside he felt uneasy. He pushed the feeling down, like stuffing a sock into a mouth.

"Remember," Karpov said sternly, "the first priority is to find out what her husband might have told her about Engels."

"Pardon me, Boris, but I still fail to understand why we fear she knows anything worthwhile. After all, weren't they both monitored constantly —" Plechl said, instantly cutting off the words as he saw Karpov's face darken.

"*Because,*" Karpov answered, his voice four shades louder than a moment earlier, "we take no chances. It's bigger than you know; than *I* know."

"Yes, but I —"

"You what?"

"I forgot my position." But he did not lower his eyes, staring at Karpov impassively.

"You know, Madeis," Karpov continued, holding the gaze, "one day your tendency to flirt on the edge of insubordination and insolence is going to find you with a piece of ice where it counts." But Karpov knew he needed Plechl and did not know, but feared, that Plechl had acquired enough against him to run the ice both ways.

Mutually assured destruction, thought Madeis. Who says it's an outdated concept? He felt it might be the only thing that kept them all from throwing the country into a repeat of the post-Yeltsin days of anarchy.

Besides, despite his outbursts, Madeis thought Karpov was secretly fond of him. For what reason, he couldn't guess.

In a characteristic lightning mood shift, Karpov threw his hands wide and smiled. "But why are we quarreling? I forget what it's like to be young. A toast to young upstarts!"

They both drank.

"Listen, Madeis," said Karpov, smacking his wide, fleshy lips, "they tell me we have pretty much mopped up this Engels fiasco. Our little part of it, anyway. Only Yublenka is left. Once we are sure she knows nothing, we'll send her flying on the Arctic Aeroflot and that will be the end of it."

"If she knows nothing, why not put her back to work here? I understand she was highly competent," Madeis said, toying with his glass.

Karpov burped loudly and wiped spit off the corner of his mouth with an index finger. "Oh, I agree. But take my word for it, Madeis, I know her type. Keep her here, and she'll eventually make trouble for us —and trouble is a *much* bigger waste than talent."

"But how? She's nothing but a lovely derelict."

"Look," Karpov explained, becoming avuncular, "After you engage in your phony search for her husband, she will be sufficiently satisfied. So, normally, I'd agree. After all, I'm not a Stalinist. I don't like to mindlessly resort to heavy methods. But I know her type. Under stress of memory and time, her emotions will erupt like coldsore blisters. Before she ever got back to Krevesk, we warned off her friends. Do you know what that will do?"

Madeis shook his head.

"No one can stand such an isolated condition for long, especially not a woman. She was popular with the researchers, you know. Considering that she is a vertical begging to be a horizontal, someone will take pity on her. Then, in bed, she will blubber things she shouldn't, perhaps even things about Engels. She has no future."

"But surely —"

"Spare me your altruism!" Karpov chided. "It's called 'softening the victim.' Necessary. And you get to be the handsome, sympathetic savior."

"You're smarter than me, Boris," Plechl said, shaking his head.

"Stalin's ass," Karpov replied, burping again. "I *am* immensely more experienced, though. My mind's been in and out of these Yublenka bitches, it's had time to grow callouses. You'd better grow some, too."

CHAPTER 7

THE TRAIN

As the engine of the Southern Pacific freight train rounded a bend out of the Cascade Mountains, the engineer could see the white concrete of Blue Beaver Dam three-quarters of a mile ahead. Primarily a flood-control project to squelch the unpredictability of the Middle Santiam River, the structure held back 12 miles of water above the town of Honey House, population 4,000. The reservoir was swollen with heavy spring runoff, although this day was clear. The engineer saw a brave early water skier cutting the sun-polished reservoir surface into a rippled V a few hundred yards above the dam.

"Too soon for that kind of stuff," the engineer thought, as he throttled down to take his 80-car load across the dam.

The train carried its usual variety, mostly lumber, but also a carload of new pickup trucks, three filled propane tanks, four flatcars of steel piping, and two cars of dynamite and TNT for a couple of construction firms in the Willamette Valley.

As the train traversed the dam, the skier waved. The engineer smiled and waved back and then waved again, as a striking, bikini-clad redheaded woman guiding the tow boat grinned at him. The engineer, middle-aged and single, thought that if he had a woman like that to warm him up afterwards, he might have the energy for chilly spring water sports, too.

Exactly one minute after his engine crossed the dam, a shock wave slammed the engineer across his cab against a steel gage panel. Several minutes later, he struggled up from a blackout, realizing that the train was stopped. Computerized braking had cut in to slow, halt, and hold the train. He blinked. Most of the cars were still on the other side of the river. On the dam, at least ten or fifteen cars were hidden beneath a towering, black and gray mushroom cloud, the base of which seemed, strangely, to be rushing over the dam.

The hair on his neck stood up a moment before things came together consciously. The ten or fifteen cars weren't hidden. They were *gone* — along with the entire mid-section of the Blue Beaver Dam. As he watched, enormous cracked and broken chunks of the remaining concrete/earthen retainer tumbled into the water and were swept away like dirt clods. What had been a small, five-foot-deep, narrow river downstream became an overflowing, 60-foot-high thundering wall of debris-laden, muddy water. He saw a boxcar surface for a second, tumble end over end, then disappear beneath the torrent, like a toy sucked into a storm sewer.

Along the banks, as far as he could see, 150-foot Douglas Fir trees were falling like popsicle sticks as the water ripped away the earth beneath their roots and flung them into the torrent. Large sections of the three-lane highway which paralleled the south bank of the river were already missing. As he watched with his mouth open, a one-eighth-mile stretch of road slid sideways into the water, like a massive black snake slipping in for a swim.

Remembering the skier, he glanced upstream. At first, he didn't see him. Then he spotted the power boat run aground some two-hundred yards to one side. He saw the skier standing next to it. The engineer sighed and waved. The skier looked at him and shook his head. The redheaded young woman was standing at his side, crying; he had his arm around her.

Then the engineer remembered the town of Honey House a few miles downstream.

"God help 'em," he muttered, reaching for his radio. He thumbed to the emergency channel to call the state police.

"Yeah, yeah, we know the dam's gone," a harried voice said. "So's the whole town. And once the water hits the Willamette River, everything through Salem on down to Portland's gonna get hit real hard. Worst dam break ever."

"Dead?" the engineer asked. "How many?"

"Couple thousand so far. But give it a few hours," the officer said gloomily. "Look, I'm no public service announcer, so if you've got something important to say, how about saying it, or get off the horn!"

The engineer began to sweat, "I think I'm responsible."

"Look, this is no time for crackpot confession —"

"It was my dynamite," the engineer said numbly.

"Huh? What's that?"

"Dynamite. I was carrying two train cars full. And propane tanks. I can't imagine how, but something must've sparked 'em as we crossed the dam."

The officer was saying something to him, but he didn't hear it. He was looking down at the redhead. She had turned to the skier and was sobbing against his chest. The engineer thought that she might have friends or relatives — or children — in Honey House. With all his heart, he hoped not.

CHAPTER 8

THE SPACEMAN

K evin Jones couldn't keep from staring at the Rocky Mountains. Seeing them on *National Geographic* specials was one thing. The reality was something else. Gawking, he'd twice almost driven off I-25. He forced his eyes away from the snowy majesty of Pike's Peak. He glanced at the digital dash clock of his rented Avis Ford T-bird.

"Be in Colorado Springs before you know it, Kev," he muttered to himself, as he frequently did when alone. "Still can't figure it, though. An interview with the friggin' Spaceman!"

The Spaceman was the U.S. Intelligence community's slang for Glenn Young, member of the Joint Chiefs, head of the USSC, the United States Space Command, the newest independent branch of the service.

On the basis of his high I.Q. scores and accurate memory, Jones had been shunted into Naval Intelligence almost immediately after his stint at the academy. He'd spent the next four years in the Mideast, then Antarctica. The Mideast had been only mildly interesting—except for when Lebanon effectively became part of Israel without admitted U.S. approval. Kevin remembered talking to a Mossad friend in Tel Aviv about the turn in U.S. sentiments ....

"Your nation is different," Moshe Trevis said as they sipped beer and whiskey in a liberal Arab bar and watched a dancer fling green veils and gyrate a Hollywood-sized glass-jeweled navel. "Something's happened to America."

"What might that be, Moe?" Kevin asked, his voice full of innocence.

"To put it bluntly, your country doesn't try to polish everyone's boots anymore. Your excursion against Iraq served you well. It restored your confidence."

Moshe raised his whiskey glass and smiled with a sparkle that doubtless broke many young female hearts. "I think many of us here had begun to wonder if the U.S. had taken its last turn long ago. Don't forget the disaster when we tried to settle the Lebanese chaos in the early 1980s. Your leaders pressured us to withdraw. And then, of all the idiotic things, rescued the terrorists—which encouraged them for a decade."

"Hell, that was way before *your* time, Moe."

"Before your time, too, Mr. Foreign Policy Expert. We Israelis study history."

"Which means Americans don't?"

"Perhaps Israelis preserve a clearer vision of the principles that move it."

"Uh-huh," Kevin said, "and now if you folks could wake up and junk your socialism, you might be able to get along without billions of green principles from Uncle Sam."

"Deserved," Moshe said.

They touched glasses and the conversation drifted.

Kevin recalled that they'd gotten drunk and lured the belly dancer to bed. Kevin had extracted her jewel with his lips, which Moshe had assured him was acceptable, since it was obviously a "navel operation."

Kevin hit the brakes and swore, "Damned daydreamer!"

He'd seen the sign, "Highway 24 Exit, Peterson AFB/Shuttle Base," shoot past his window. He'd missed his cut-off. He screeched the car to a stop on the road's shoulder, threw his right arm back over the seat and slammed the T-bird into reverse, burning rubber for an eighth of a mile on the asphalt emergency lane. A single car with a family passed him as he stopped, the driver honking angrily and the kids sticking out their tongues.

"Backbone of America," he muttered, shifting into drive and speeding up the exit ramp.

"The general will see you now," the receptionist told Kevin Jones, no more than a minute after he'd arrived. He looked her over as he rose and put down a magazine he'd just picked up. She was a perky, small-boned woman with dark hair. Too pretty to be wearing Lieutenant's bars, he thought. He immediately berated himself. Everyone knew promotions in the Space Command came hard.

She caught him staring at her and smiled. "Through there," she said, pointing.

"What?" he asked, then shook his head. "Oh! Don't know what I was thinkin'."

"I have an excellent idea," she said.

"Uh, well, that is, uh—"

"Cleverly stated, sailor. He's waiting."

Kevin nodded and began to do what he thought constituted straightening his tie. He was in civilian attire. That's how he'd been asked to arrive.

She shook her head, shoved her chair back, got up, and walked to him. She reached up and adjusted his tie with a few, quick motions. Kevin felt massive next to her. He could smell a subtle, cinnamon perfume. She stepped back and looked him over. Unbelievably, he felt as though he had no clothes on.

"Hmmm," she mused, "not bad." She turned and walked back to her desk. Hell of a set of legs, he thought. She sat down, raised an eyebrow, and nodded toward a closed door.

"Right," Kevin said. He stepped into the Spaceman's office.

General Young was not tall, not nearly Kevin's six-five. He had a compact gymnastic build; strong jaw and cheekbones; wide-set eyes; close-cropped, dark brown hair beginning to gray at the temples.

"After the Mideast, you were off to Antarctica. It wasn't much better, was it?" Young asked.

"Penguins dress for dinner, sir, but there's just no place to take 'em."

"No, I don't suppose there is. Sit down, Mr. Jones."

"Pardon me, sir," Kevin asked as he sat, "But what's the 'mister' all about? I'm in the service ."

"Not if you want to work for me, you're not. You won't have to figure it out," Young said, "because I am going to explain it in a minute."

He punched up something on his computer screen, scrolled through a couple pages, then looked squarely at Kevin and asked, "Jones, why the hell have you stayed in the Navy so long?"

"Wanted somethin' with a li'l more whistle."

"You could've gone into the private market, Mr. Jones. Any corporation would've taken a man with your brains, memory and intelligence training."

"The, uh, *scope* is different, sir. I guess I like being involved in the bigger picture."

"You saying Microsoft or Exxon or IBM or Mitsubishi are small potatoes for you? You too big for them, Mr. Jones?"

Kevin thought the question sounded like a trap. How did he answer that one? He felt his stress level rise like a thermometer in a fire. Then, as it had since late childhood during times of pressure or crisis, the Slowdown kicked in.

"I've got it, too, boy," his father had admitted. "So'd your grandpa and his daddy. Best I can make out, that's where it first showed up. It'll help you out now'n then, when things get tough, when you need to do some quick thinkin'. Got a physical side to it, but that's a might more unpredictable. Both your older brothers is possessed by it, too. I 'spect it'll continue in your kids. By the way, they'll likely be boys. Ain't been but a couple gals born in the family since the trait got goin'. Don't know why or what's behind it. Maybe the Lord's tryin' something new."

Everything around him seemed to suddenly flow like molasses and take on a slightly red tint. Except for the color shift, it was like a video tape run at one-twentieth of normal speed. It was some sort of mental overdrive and it was in operation now. He considered the general's question, feeling like he had all the time in the world.

If he answered negatively, Kevin figured the Spaceman would take it as a contradiction to wanting "the bigger picture." If he answered positively, it would sound like Kevin had his nose in the air. One would sound dishonest, the other would sound arrogant.

He went over it forward and backwards two or three times. Well, screw it, Kev, he thought. You won't be worse off for tellin' the truth. Besides, Young doesn't seem to like a man who tolerates manure shoveled onto his desk.

These thoughts happened in under a quarter of a second. The slowdown dissipated. The redshift faded as he returned to real time.

"Both, sir," he said. "I think I deserve bigger 'n' better."

Young threw back his head and guffawed. "That's the best answer I could've asked for! Now, the reason for the civilian clothes. You won't be needing a uniform if you work for this eye."

"Eye" was slang for intelligence agency, of which there were, by one count, 32 in the U.S. government.

"Excuse me, sir. But I didn't think the Space Command had an independent eye."

"Well, it does. We just don't talk about it much. Like it that way."

"I thought the Air Force provided you with everything, sir."

"Hah! Don't they frackin' wish!" Glenn snorted. "They did, you know, until I took over a few years back. Space is a different breed, son. Fewer illusions. More reality orientation. We've got our own intel system now that doesn't rely on resentful rival branches. I think it's a good system, but we're going to make it better. You like that attitude, spaceguy?"

"Yes, sir," Kevin said. He remembered hearing that only Young was Space-*man*. Everyone else in his command were "spaceguys," including women.

"You know what we call our intelligence service, Mr. Jones?"

"No, sir."

"High-eye. Think that sounds silly?"

"No, sir. Always 'preciated poetry."

Young chuckled. Then, in a characteristic subject-shift, said, "High-eye doesn't buy what the other eyes in Unc's government are telling us about Engels. We think the Sovs were onto something down there. I want you to help find out what."

All the dull years in the Navy seemed about to fade away, like ground dropping beneath clouds. Kevin knew something about Engels, of course. He'd been on duty in the frigid waters aboard the *USS Weinberger*, a 58,000-tonner, one or two new IOWA-class battleships outfitted especially for cold missions.

"Engels," he said aloud. "It had to do with those Russian deaths. Lotsa fragmentary stuff."

"The real questions are unanswered. Brighton's crowd at CIA thinks it was a chemical accident. That's the consensus of the eyes. Whatever it was, it appears the Joint Chiefs — and I mean General Reed, mainly — have written the incident off."

Kevin fidgeted in his chair and frowned.

"Bother you?"

"Well, sir, in a way. A few of us down there had a feelin' it was hot. Couldn't prove it, though. But felt we mighta if we'd been given more time."

Young nodded. "That's the leak in the suit. High-eye's the only branch of the military that still has its nose sniffing at Engel's trail, cold though it may be. You see, Mr. Jones," he said, clasping his hands behind his head as he stretched back in his chair, "if you're going to work for me, you have to understand something. I don't approve of this new Sov system and don't trust it."

"Actually, sir, I can't say I met many guys who did."

"You'd think it'd be true in the higher ranks, too, wouldn't you?" Young said.

"You'd especially think it of General Wharton Reed. After all, he's made some convincing speeches to military graduating classes about the need to keep up our guard."

Kevin looked confused.

"Mouths aren't legs," Young said. "What a man talks and where he walks are two different things, son. For instance, if he believes his own principles, why would Reed *drop* the Engels investigation?"

"I don't know, sir."

"How's that keeping up our guard?"

"Uh, well —"

"Exactly, Mr. Jones."

Young went to a coffee maker at the side of the room and poured two cups, black, handing one to Kevin. "Probably no better'n Navy acid," he said.

He sat down again and said, "I've made a bet with myself that you're our kind of man. Once I decide, I believe in giving an individual relevant information right away. It includes understanding what sort of politics High-eye's up against."

"Yes, sir. I'm with you."

"Fine. Don't worry about the intraservice transfer. We'll take care of the tape. Carmen — that's Lieutenant Carmen Sevens, the lovely lady you met in the outer office—will have forms for you to sign when you leave today. You'll find that your official record will list you as a colonel, assigned to cryptography. And then we'll have you killed."

Kevin stopped his coffee halfway to his lips. "Sir?"

Young grinned. "Colonel Kevin Jones will have a Humvee accident. He will be burned beyond recognition. Never mind the details. It's a cheap and easy way to take care of things. Space Command will issue a regretful press statement on the accident through channels. We'll set you up under a new identity. Then we're going to grind you through a brush-up course. It'll be like none you ever saw or felt."

"Yes, sir."

"We don't recruit lightly. We have a couple of special reasons for our confidence in you, Mr. Jones. And you'll have an excellent partner to help and guide you. I'm sure you'll get along."

Young hit the intercom again and said, "Carmen, is the other guy here yet?"

"Yes, sir," came the crisp reply.

"Shove him through the airlock."

Kevin turned around in his chair as the door opened.

"Pull your jaw off the floor, Kev, or something that craps bird-doo is going to build a nest in your mouth," Moshe Trevis said, smirking from ear to ear.

CHAPTER 9

THE CONTRADICTION

Alone, Madeis Plechl felt like an idiot. He paced the bare floor of his living room—which was also the dining room and bedroom. A personnel bureau clerk, KGB or not, did not rate much floor space. Nor a carpet. Not in Krevesk.

Madeis lit a cigarette and sat on the edge of his narrow bed, elbows on knees, shaking his head.

"Now, chill out," he muttered, using an American phrase which was twenty years out of date, but fresh in the new Soviet Union. "Oh, certainly, Tanya Yublenka is charming. Perhaps one might even say she is infatuating. But, isn't that all it is, really? Really! You've had it happen before. Of course! Be rational about this. Think it through, step by step."

"What is Yublenka, in *fact*? When you strip her qualities down to their material components, to their scientific parts, eh? She's merely more flesh and blood with arms and legs and torso and head. True, she's an attractive girl, but no more beautiful than a million other women."

He got up, walked the room once, then resumed his former position.

"Yes, she's lonely," he said, almost in a whisper. Then, louder, self-reassuring, "But I read once that some scientist had a theory that loneliness causes human beings to secrete chemicals that induce sympathy from others. So, you see? It's probably a purely physical response, Madeis. And you *are* being an idiot."

"However," he said, standing, crossing his arms. "However, she appears to be intelligent. That is a factor. You have always been drawn to intelligence. And she is disarmingly honest—or, at least, direct. Honesty and directness—yes, they can be seductive in a woman."

"But, who are you kidding? Here you are, an agent of the Committee for State Security, deluding yourself about such virtues. You, who lie to people as a matter of course, as a professional act!"

He took a heavy drag on the cigarette.

"Still, in one's mind, if he is careful, there is always room to form independent opinions."

He smacked his forehead with the heel of his left hand, walked across to his small kitchen table, roughly stubbed out the cigarette in a small, cracked saucer. He lifted a bottle of vodka off the shelf above a small refrigerator and poured himself a glass. He paced the room and sipped, feeling a surge of professional pride at how he'd handled himself with Karpov.

But he hadn't told Karpov, "And when I kissed her, Boris, it was like all the grayness, the shoddiness of Krevesk, the icy, pot-holed streets, the bad service in the restaurant, your ugly face, the KGB—all of it evaporated."

He laughed. "Right, hypocrite! The machine is too big, too vast to notice her. Neither must you, Madeis Plechl."

He tapped and lit another cigarette, accurately flipping the match three feet into the saucer. "Is it sad?" he asked the bare floor. "Does it rip at your soul, Madeis? Well, scrape that sentimental slime off your shoes before it makes you slip and fall."

For a few seconds he stood, silently whirling the remains of his vodka in the bottom of the glass. Then he sighed, drained it, set down the glass, crushed his cigarette, and flopped on the cot. Tanya, he thought, Boris feels you are a dangerous woman because you perhaps know too much.

"But Boris has a crude antenna," he mused aloud. "The antenna was right about the danger, but wrong about the source. It's not what you might know about Engels that makes you dangerous. It's what you are to me."

Madeis awoke with an erection. He'd dreamt that Tanya was straddling him there on his bed. She was naked, her head flung back, eyes tightly closed, her mouth wet and open in a grimace of passion. He threw himself up into a sitting position, and took several deep breaths. "By the Tomb of Lenin, Madeis," he said, "you haven't had a dream like that since you were thirteen."

He took two gulps of vodka and splashed cold water onto his face and tried to think of something else. It didn't work. He continued to flash back on the irritating erotic memory.

"You need to get moving," he told the room. "Take your *mind* off her."

It was no more than a ten-minute walk to his father's apartment. Johan "Hans" Plechl himself answered the knock.

"Ah, it's one of Krevesk's best record-keepers!" he said, grabbing his son by the arm and leading him in out of the cold. "How about something to drink, Madeis?"

The younger man shook his head and made no move to take off his coat or gloves. He shifted uncertainly, foot to foot.

Hans Plechl frowned and said, "Madeis, I've seen that look a hundred times. You're in some kind of emotional corner. When you were small, it took a piece of candy to get you to come out and talk. What will it take tonight? I've already tried liquor."

"How about a walk?"

After they'd strolled two blocks, Madeis had still said nothing. His father instructed softly, "Come on, now. You'd better get it off your chest before your ribs break."

"It's a woman."

His father pursed his lips and nodded. "Ah, it would not take a psychological genius to deduce that something about her upsets you."

"You are a man with incredible insight."

"True. But so far, you haven't made me use it. Talk."

"I can't have her."

The older man wanted to grin, but stifled it. "Married?"

"Yes. Well, in a way."

"That certainly clears things up."

Madeis glanced at him. He saw a man four inches shorter than himself, but just as broad and growing a little paunchy. Hans Plechl had white hair and a thick, white moustache, startling against his ruddy complexion. He looked like he should be operating a beer hall in Bonn, not a scientific laboratory in the USSR.

"She's married. But her husband is missing, probably dead."

"Probably?"

"Well, he *is*, but she doesn't know it."

"How do *you* know?"

"I stumbled across it. Remember Gregor, the radio technician? You met him once or twice in the library. You told me about it. You were walking up the library steps one night, near closing."

"Ah, I wanted a transcript from that lovely Yublenka woman, and she introduced me to—"

He stopped in his tracks and stared at his son.

"Yes," said Madeis. "*Her* husband."

"Oh my. And so young."

"She's broken-hearted. That's the problem. Part of it."

Hans Plechl sighed, rubbed a hand over his stomach and resumed walking, his broad feet thudding softly on the snow-dusted, broken asphalt. "Well," he said, after a minute of silence. "Well, well, well. You said she doesn't know?"

"He's been missing for months. That's all she's been told."

"Hmmmm, hmmmm, hmmmm," the elder Plechl said, a sound that Madeis had heard all his life whenever his father's brain was working hard.

"Are you thinking, Father? Or warming up a Gregorian chant?"

"Hmmmmmmmmm."

"The problem is, I can't tell her that he's dead—nor that I think I'm in love with her."

"I can see why you might be. I was not immune from her physical charms, either. I don't believe she was aware. All the more attractive. Madeis, what is the point of not telling her? It's somewhat cruel."

"It is ..." Madeis began, searching for words. "It's out of my hands."

"I don't understand."

"The KGB is involved."

"KGB?" Hans Plechl asked, stopping and blinking. "But how? She's just a translator. Did she see something? What?"

"They think her *husband* knew something, maybe told her."

The elder man looked at his son. He looked at him for several, long seconds. Then his face began to darken and he involuntarily took two steps backwards as he said, "Madeis, Madeis, you're not with *them!*"

Madeis looked down. He felt himself flush.

"My own son? An agent of that despicable—"

"You must not tell anyone or it's your head as well as mine. Those are the new rules."

Hans Plechl looked smaller, as though he'd shrunk several pounds inside his clothes. He whispered, "Why?"

"Why? To live. The same as you."

"The same as me? As *me!*" hissed Hans Plechl, straightening proudly. "I'm a respectable scientist—"

"A respectable one?" Madeis asked softly, dangerously. "In this nation? In this city? Don't tell me you've forgotten the Yellow Rain project, on which you worked. Which this oh-so-noble nation used against innocents in Asia!"

Hans Plechl's face had gone from ruddy to white. He glared at his son, who glared back. For a minute they stood like that, two stiffed-legged, riled dogs.

Finally, the father lowered his eyes and nodded. "Yes," he said quietly. "Who am I, indeed, to throw stones?"

Madeis felt an almost overwhelming shame for them both, and an urgent desire to embrace his father. The two urges seemed irreconcilable. His father saved him from the dilemma by turning and starting back toward his apartment. Madeis walked with him, stomach acid surging into the back of his throat.

After a few minutes, Hans Plechl said, "So then, this woman may be a danger to the state. This woman you love."

"No, but they think so. It's enough."

"And you? You think not?"

"No. A hunch. I'm supposed to make her fall in love with *me*. That way, the KGB thinks I may be able to find out what she knows about—well, about a project her husband worked on."

"And that's what you think, too, isn't it?"

"That she'll talk to me? If she knows. Is there any other way?"

"Callous."

"If I had only the KGB's feelings to consider, yes."

The father nodded, said, "hmmm," several times, then stopped. He squinted his eyes as he lifted his face against the falling snow, heavier now. "You know, Madeis, your mother once said something similar. It was the day she found out what some of my work was about. I'd tried to hide it but, after a few years, she suspected. So I told her."

Madeis stared at him. "I didn't know."

Hans spread his hands wide. "There was never a reason to tell you. I was more like you then, more reticent with my feelings. I finally squeezed out the truth. I expected her to leave, to spit on me in utter disgust. But son, I underestimated her. She took me in her arms and said, 'Hans, we're trapped. So be kind to yourself, and take me to bed.'"

"Did you?"

"Take her to bed?"

" Yes. First we made love. Then we made plans. To escape."

"*What!*"

"What else could we do? The nature of our lives was in the open. I'd forced the issue for us, for our happiness, even though I didn't intend to."

Hans kicked at a small mound of snow and dirt. "Because I was prominent then in the secret tricothocene and other chemical warfare projects, and would be closely watched, we decided that she would set things up. I don't know the details of her plans. I never did. In those days, we still lived in Moscow. You were not quite three. She said she had made the contacts, done the proper things, whatever they were. She had only one step to take before we could make our move."

Madeis put his hand over his father's shoulder and gave it a quick squeeze. His throat was tight.

"Well," the elder Plechel said, expelling a long breath, "your mother had worked out something with a relative in the south near Iran. The idea was that we would meet there and make our move across the border."

"How? That border's always been heavily guarded by the KGB."

"No, no, not always. There was a town years ago, Pekstan, I think it was called, which actually straddled it. Perhaps it's there again. It carried trade and was profitable for the Turkmen SSR to keep the business flowing. We were on good terms with Iran back then, at least better than later, after the Jihad crowd got control. It was far from impossible to gain permission to cross, especially for residents of Pekstan itself."

"And for relatives of residents?"

"Right. Many relatives resemble each other. A switched set of clothing, a changed set of papers, and your mother would have been someone else. So she said."

Johan walked on quietly.

"So she said?" Madeis asked. "What happened?"

"I don't know. She had already twice visited Pekstan. Her idea was to smooth potential suspicions by becoming a regular visitor. That was probably wise. Later, I wondered if it simply meant the border guards got to know her face better." Johan kicked an empty vodka bottle out of the way; it made a tinkling noise as it skittered across the empty street.

"And? *And?*" Madeis prodded.

"Travel for many Russians on Aeroflot was free then. Did you know the state used to grant passage to farmers in Georgia to fly their potatoes all the way to Moscow to sell in the peasant markets? The dirt-caked farmers would actually sit in the airliners with sacks of vegetables and fruit on their laps and on the floor between their legs. A funny picture; such a sadly Soviet contrast—the modern and the feudal, side by side. I recall once that a farmer could—"

"What about Mother?"

"Oh, sorry," Hans Plechl again stroked his moustache. "Well, I'd been at work. She'd left you in Moscow with a neighbor. She was supposed to be back in two days. You see, for the plan to work, for both of us, she was to return and then fly back to Pekstan a month later. At that time, I was also going to be there for a scientific gathering. Researchers from Russia were going to meet others from New Delhi and a couple of the Soviet satellites in Southeast Asia. It was a typical scientific idea-exchange among comradely countries. Of course, after the Khomeini revolution, the Soviet side of Pekstan was closed to Iran. That's an understatement. It was physically moved. Pekstan was turned into a military base and the original inhabitants were forcefully relocated, many on the Northern Express, to die working on pipelines in cold to which they were completely unresistant."

"The Khomeini matter was later, Father."

"Ah, yes. The mind wanders. It's been so long."

He kicked a cloud of snow, then said, "But I was supposed to meet her there, in Pekstan, before it was moved. We were all to get across to Iran and to the safety of the Americans. They were still in Iran and in good graces. Oh, I see; it had to have been before Khomeini. Yes, the days of Shah Reza Pahlavi, the so-called blood-thirsty Reza. Of course, the Jihaders later made him look like a puppy at a nipple."

"Was she caught?" Madeis asked, ignoring the history lesson.

Hans Plechl shook his head and shrugged. "I like to think that she decided to leave me."

"Betrayed you!"

"God, no! Perhaps her plan went awry and she had to choose freedom for herself or no freedom for any of us. If that was the choice, I'm glad she made it. Every night I tell myself she's living in America somewhere, somewhere warm. Maybe golden California. It's where she always wanted to live."

"I think I could feel the same," Madeis said, surprising himself. The thought had arisen and come out in words, unbidden.

But his father merely nodded and said, almost to himself, "My son. Mr. KGB."

They walked the rest of the way to Hans Plechl's apartment in silence, each lost in his own thoughts and memories—and plans.

Back in the warmth, both seated themselves in overstuffed, well-worn red velvet armchairs that Madeis remembered from his teenage years. They sipped dark German beer. The beer was a minor, defiant gesture by Johan against the Soviet preference for clearer, harder spirits.

"You're sure it's not—" Johan began, indicating the room with a sweep of his hand.

"No, not bugged. These are not the old days when one couldn't know."

"It was that little black calculator I saw you waving about."

"Yes. It's a sweeper."

The father squinted at his son, seeing not just the man, but the infant, the child, the teenager. You're turning into a soft old fart, he said to himself.

"I know all the tales of men and women who've become KGB and betrayed their families. After all, there's a monument in Moscow, erected in 1939. It honors a 12-year-old boy who turned in his father to Stalin's dogs. It went through my head, you know, asking myself, what could Madeis get from me, the scientist with sensitive information?"

"I got what I needed from you long ago. Values, principles. Not Soviet ones; ones for living."

Hans shifted his weight in his chair. "You should be proud of me. I think I'm showing considerable resiliency for a brittle-boned old man, no?"

Madeis raised his beer in a toast, a wide grin now erasing all traces of his former worry and turmoil. "To resiliency! May it keep us hard to our graves!"

Johan picked up the raunchy exchange. "May I be buried with a knothole in the top of my coffin!"

"And not for breathing!"

"Never! Only for the satisfaction of long-legged female cemetery strollers who will know what joys await them just beneath the surface—as long as they wear clothespins on their noses!"

"Do you think we're becoming, as the Americans say, 'gross'?"

"Absolutely!"

For a couple of minutes, both men basked in the warmth of their friendly obscenities, like lizards in the sun.

"When have they ever really tried to rape Mother Russia?" Madeis asked his father out of the blue. "That's what KGB doctrine says America and the West want to do."

"She cries rape whenever she doesn't get her way. One of the older forms of extortion. And yet," said the elder Plechl, "I doubt most of your KGB comrades see it as you do."

"They know. But they are too good at 'double-tracking.' They think one way on official business, another in private. The two are parallel; they never meet. We all do it. For survival. Public sacrifice of the mind in exchange for its private peace."

"Nicely turned. Maybe you should've been a writer. What do you do in the KGB? Or do you prefer to double-track away from the subject?"

Madeis swallowed beer and swished it over his teeth. "Mostly I do dull things, like—" He stopped.

"What?" Johan demanded.

"If ever, for any reason, Father, the Committee should find out that I talked to you about this—"

"Oh, forget that, Madeis. What can they do to an old man who holds as many state secrets in his head as I do?"

"Look what they did to Sakharov."

"Yes, well, talk anyway. Grant your father the respect to worry about his own future."

Madeis nodded slowly, pre-measuring his words. "Well, much of what I do is ordinary detective work. Boring. Mostly clerical, going through records and keeping things straight for Karpov; looking for information that might implicate; a lot of useless file-building on people who'll never do anything wrong."

"Nevertheless," his father interjected, "the state's appetite is insatiable. I understand; it was the same under the SS in old Germany. You said you're working for a man named Karpov? Not the *library* director? He's KGB?"

Madeis nodded and Johan expelled a huge, insulting guffaw. "My God, Madeis, that man is a dolt! If he's anybody important in the KGB, the Americans could probably steal the Committee's underwear in broad daylight!"

"Karpov is head of the Krevesk residency, Father."

"But I know Karpov. The man runs a library like a pig butcher would perform surgery."

"Doubtless."

"Eh?"

"Think. The library directorship; so what? Do you suppose the KGB cares if he does a wonderful job? Everyone complains about his work, focuses on him as a librarian. He's fooled *you*. You never suspected he was KGB, let alone the local Resident. Many probably feel that way. It makes them all putty to Karpov. They didn't put him in Krevesk because he's got a wandering eye for women. If anybody can keep the Engels project quiet—"

The words faded as Madeis regretted them.

"I'm virtually the senior scientist in Krevesk," Johan said, winking. "I already know something of the Engels Extension. It's not much different than many other vaccination projects now going on."

Madeis cocked his head.

"Karpov's obviously been feeding you some other story," his father said. "The Engels Extension is simply one of, oh, about a dozen. That kind of thing's been underway for years. It's going to counteract a piece of bad publicity the Soviet Union's suffered for decades. We have one of the highest rates of recurrence of some of the so-called 'conquered' diseases—measles, mumps, even smallpox. It's better than making Yellow Rain, no?"

"But you're a chemist. What does that have to—"

"Come, Madeis. Chemistry is modern medicine. Even the geneticists depend on us."

"What? The Soviet Union is going to surpass Bulgaria in disease control?" Madeis asked.

Johan chortled and replied, "Well, if that's what's meant by extending Engels, then it's at least a good step. Friedrich Engels once made an impassioned plea for an end to disease—about the time he was helping Karl Marx work out the philosophy that became communism."

Walking home, Madeis thought about what Karpov had told him about the Engels project—for it was not, in any fashion, consistent with what his father had told him. Karpov had spoken of it when he'd ordered Madeis onto what he called "the poker job," the job of gaining Tanya Yublenka's confidence ...

"You'll need to understand why this Yublenka task is important." Karpov said.

"If you think it's best," Madeis answered deferentially, out of habit rather than fundamental respect.

"It is, or so I'm told—Engels."

Madeis's face remained unconcerned as he asked, "Engels? I don't grasp your drift, Comrade."

Karpov's eyes darted back and forth in short jerks. "No. Well," he said, followed by what Madeis interpreted as relief, "sit down, my boy. There isn't so much to tell, but there's no reason not to let a chair squeeze some blood out of your butt while I explain, eh?" Karpov barked a sharp laugh at his words.

Madeis had never seen Karpov so nervous.

"It's like this," Karpov said, resting his swarthy elbows and forearms on his desk, hands clasped together, fingers squirming tensely. "The woman's husband, Gregor, was involved in a thing down in Antarctica. Some kind of research base. He heard things he wasn't supposed to, got caught and one of our agents took care of him."

A small smile, like a rat scurrying across the edge of a dark room, flickered over Karpov's face. "Yes, he and some others, drinking friends; all gone now."

"The problem?"

Karpov whacked his hand loudly on his desk. "Oh, shape up, Madeis," he said. "He may have talked to his wife about it."

"But she was stationed in Buenos Aires. How would they talk privately? They only did so by radio, no? Wouldn't it have been taped?"

"Hell," Karpov said. "You'll make it to a position like mine only on the day when alcohol flows from faucets. What should I expect from the incompetents the Committee sends to help me these days? Gregor Yublenka was a communications officer. Doesn't that tell you something?"

"Yes. With his technical expertise he might have been able to ensure that parts of his conversations with his wife would not be recorded—although I've no idea why. At least it seems possible. So what was the specific nature of the Engels project, Boris?"

Karpov shifted uncomfortably.

"You've no need to know," he said. "My department. However, I can tell you that it is important to the future security of the Soviet state."

"So is potato production," Madeis said.

Karpov looked at him sideways, pursed his lips, then laughed. "For all your shortcomings, my boy, including that unfortunate German background, you have a passable sense of humor. Nastily Russian. Did I tell you the one about the ladies in the Parachute Corps?"

"No."

"Even if there were women, there would never be *ladies*."

"Why is that?" Madeis asked dutifully.

"Because their first jump would not be by air, but by officers!"

Madeis smiled. "Is that all I should know about Engels, Boris?"

"Yes, yes. Go on now, boy get out so I can get work done."

He winked and opened a bottom desk drawer. Madeis heard a bottle slosh.

A swirling gust drove a fresh flurry of night snow across the bridge where he stood looking into Krevesk's "river," actually a polluted creek nicknamed The Urinal. He glanced at his watch. It was nearly two. As he bent into the wind and headed back to his own apartment, two questions alternated in his mind, first one flashing up, then the other, like competing warning lights. Why the discrepancy between his father's account of Engels and Karpov's? And what was going on?

Boris surely would be aware of Johan Plechl's mild version of Engels, that it was merely a small part of a vast state health plan for improved vaccinations. It would be common knowledge among the scientists. Yet Boris had acted as though he suspected something very different. Could both men be right? If so, why was his father so unconcerned and Boris so terribly nervous? How could they even be dealing with the same project?

"Think, man!" he growled to himself, as the wind picked up, howling among the low gray buildings of Krevesk.

CHAPTER 10

THE OFFER

I don't know about you but I'm starving," Annette Washington mumbled against her husband's bare chest. "In fact, I'm so hungry—"

"Ouch!" he said, as she nipped his skin. "Want me to turn into one of those husbands never seen by their wives at night?"

"Devil," she said, pecking him on the lips. She swung a bare leg out in a graceful arc and sat on the edge of the bed. As she ran her hands through her short brown hair, he shifted his weight and massaged her naked back with one hand.

"More," she said throatily.

"Hmmm, I don't think so. You have a tendency to pitch face down onto the rug. Besides, I want you alert. I need impressions."

"Oh, phooey!" She stood and stretched languidly. Then, as she strolled toward the bath, she deliberately threw her hips into a burlesque grind, giving him a sultry look over her shoulder. When he heard the shower start, he hurried after, cutting her off as she was about to step into the hot, steamy spray. "Me first, if M'Lady doesn't mind. You'll take longer; more efficient this way."

She placed her hands on her hips and glared in false outrage. He smiled as he got in. After a thirty-second rinsing, he stepped out and began to towel down as she took over the stall.

"So, what'd you think of Craig Goldstein?" he asked.

"Well, I sure like him better than Jason Johnson. Let me alone for a few minutes. Go to the kitchen. You can get the frying pan—no, never mind. Make coffee. You'll pull out all the wrong stuff in the wrong way."

"If you weren't so whimsical about what you wanted to eat after your romps in the hay with me—"

"Nummy, nummy," she said, sticking her head around the shower curtain and licking her lips.

"Keep it up, wench, and you shall be attacked where you stand."

"Promises, promises. I know your recovery time. I'm as safe as if I wore a chastity belt."

"Merely a clever impression I have been cultivating over the years, awaiting one of your unguarded moments."

"Uh-huh."

He took her wet face in his large hands, kissed her tenderly, and said, "You were wonderful, Net. See you in five."

"Make it ten. You've delayed my progress, you bully."

He laughed and pulled on a comfortable terry robe, then wandered into their private kitchen. They spent many weekends at the Maryland retreat of Camp David. It often reminded them of Oregon. In fifteen minutes, she joined him, damp hair held up by a hastily turbaned towel. She readjusted it and began taking out a frying pan, eggs, butter, jam and bread for toast.

"What happened to the bacon?" he asked.

"Too fattening. I think Goldstein is an honest man. That's point one. Point two, I think he's fairly in line with your angle on foreign policy. However—"

"Oh-oh."

She cracked two eggs, answering, "However, I wish I felt the same about Bill Brighton."

"I thought we were talking about Goldstein."

"My thoughts are wily and complex. Be patient and you'll eventually discern the connection."

The president grinned. He liked her assertiveness and was fascinated by the twists of her thinking. *Much different than mine,* he thought. *We're a good team,* he told himself, as he had many times over the years.

"Brighton is smart," she said, gesturing into the air with the egg turner, "but he's too almighty sure of himself. Still, I like him in a different way. I enjoy the boundless exploring he's willing to do mentally."

"Me, too. How'd you read Bill and Craig's argument?"

"About that Engels thingamajig? Well," she said, flipping the eggs, "Goldstein seemed cautious. He didn't want to rush into a decision about either the biological or the chemical explanation. Bill was rash."

"Because?"

"Oh, something Craig said based on his time in Israel. He picked up a distrustful outlook on anything to do with the Russians. Makes sense, if you consider history." Annette Washington had a masters in history.

"Of course," he said diplomatically, "hardly *anyone* trusts the Russians anymore. Not really."

"I was referring to Goldstein's remark about—oh, how did he put it?—Yes: 'Sooner or later, we get sparklers from the Sovs.' You picked up on it, too. I was watching your face."

"Spy."

"Compliment accepted. The first rule of spying is to be observant."

He frowned for a moment and then said, "You're right about Goldy—"

"Cute nickname, by the way. Is that what you call him in private? Will he let me?"

"You're a brave lady; try it and see."

"I'll wait 'til I'm invited."

"If you'd followed that policy, you'd never have snared me."

"But I'm not after Craig and I have you. These new Soviets are very old Russian, Sam," she said, suddenly serious again. "Like the Mob, they're so wary of each other that they project their fears outward. They even do it when they're trying to be cool. That's why they bluster."

She pushed the eggs around, then asked, "So what's your prognosis?"

The president shook his head.

"Just this. For all the pooh-poohing, the damned thing won't die." He chuckled nervously, flicking a glance at his wife.

She caught the look and frowned. "Speaking of the Joint Chiefs," she said, pulling toast out as it popped. She buttered-and-jammed it, then carefully sliced each piece into four squares, placing them on a plate with the eggs. She carried the ensemble over to the kitchen bar next to her husband, started to sit, then swore, "Oops, no forks."

"The Joint Chiefs?"

"What have you heard from Spaceman?"

"Not much. I've been meaning to invite him out here soon for an evening with us."

"That'd be nice. I like him. I haven't seen him since a few weeks after your inauguration. Glenn plays it close. So does Buck, but self-destructively. Nobody thinks Glenn is repressed."

The president rose and poured a half cup of coffee. "Well, it's not a groundhog's world anymore. In the long run, Glenn's got the appropriations lead and Buck's going to have to live with it."

"Man does not live by planet alone."

He sipped the fresh coffee. "But Buck will come around to the importance of space. He just takes awhile. It's his nature to buck trends. That's how he got his nickname back in school."

"The Soviets sure aren't slackening," Annette observed. "That string of solar/microwave power satellites is amazing. I read that they're selling electricity worldwide already. Ahead of schedule."

"Hell of an ingenious hard-currency goldmine. Not much works well over there, but that project sure seems to."

She poked at her food. "Sam, be careful with Buck. Sally says he's fuming inside these days, a boiler on overload."

Sally Reed was Buck's wife. She and Annette Washington had been friends for twenty years.

"Sal's sharp," he said cautiously, "when she's sober. When she's off the wire. But frankly, she seems goofed up every time we see her anymore. Has to affect her judgment."

"And his, too, Sam. There's anger and resentment in him. It's directed at both her wire addition and, in embarrassment and frustration, at others—especially Glenn."

"Maybe so. But 'til Glenn complains, I'm going to assume he can deal with Buck's moods. Glenn's tough, too. And right now, he's busy swatting the bugs in his new eye. Intelligence groups aren't easy to gear up. He doesn't want to be caught short in space. Lot of precedent for such caution."

She nodded and looked off, recalling history. "The French commanders and their knights learned the hard way against Henry V's long-bow archers. They could have saved 40,000 lives if their eyes had been opened wider."

"Of course, there's no reason why Buck can't be giving Glenn at least a civil amount of cooperation." He smoothed his beard contemplatively. "Maybe I'd better lean on Buck over a couple of brandies."

"So," Annette said, talking around a bite of toast and changing the subject, "how do you suppose the glorious American middle class is going to take your firing of Jason Johnson?"

"Fine, I'm sure. It's the economy they're worried about. My advisors, Congress, damned near everyone's yammering for more domestic spending 'stimulation.' But a tax cut is what we really need. John Kennedy and Ronald Reagan both proved that."

"Sooner or later, the domestic spending lobby is going to attack defense," Annette said. She wiped her mouth with a paper towel. "Even your tax cut idea will, because the loyal opposition will demand a 'compensating' spending cut. That way they can claim to be both for lowering the tax burden and budgetary responsibility. In the seventies, and again in the nineties, they paid for that claim out of defense."

He nodded. "Or by more borrowing."

"One thing that especially bothers me in this context," she said, sounding a little academic, "is that maybe the country's gotten too complacent about defense. Defense budgets move a lot more history than most people know."

"Buck says that it's *because* we're so strong that we can afford to cut. In fact, he and the other chiefs have prepared a disarmament proposal to present to the Russians."

Annette Washington stared at her husband for a full five seconds. "Disarmament? Doesn't that idea bother you?"

"Yes and no," he answered, pulling out a pack of cigarettes from his robe. He tapped out the last of the three smokes he allowed himself each day. "From *one* angle I don't see the point in negotiating anything with the sons of bitches. But from another angle, maybe Buck's got a point. The Russians ought to be able to learn civilized ways eventually."

"Yes, but—"

"They've stayed out of big trouble for awhile. I've been rethinking things, Net. They've opened their economy a bit. Not like in the Yeltsin days, true. But maybe it *is* a sign that they want democracy."

"Sam, this doesn't sound like you."

"Democracies tend to be less aggressive. You're the one always reminding me of that."

"The Soviets may not have done any major neighbor-stomping lately, but damn it, Sam—"

"It's been *years*, Net. Years."

"A few years is nothing to them. And they have had some important strategic successes." She began ticking them off on her fingers: "They got their Baluchistani warm water port five years back. Before that, they turned Burma into a puppet. And in between, the—"

"I know, I know, Mrs. History," he said, wiping his hand over suddenly weary eyes. He recalled that Buck had conveniently failed to mention the "BBs," as the Baluchistani and Burmese incidents were often called. "I don't know. I just don't know. But it's likely going to prove to be a moot point."

She looked confused. "I'm *not* following you, Sam."

"Well, I haven't mentioned it, but the behind-the-scenes arms control talks are going nowhere. The Sovs are dragging their feet on anything substantive. However, maybe a bold proposal like Buck's could get 'em off the dime. If so, given our economic mess, of course I'd be forced to listen."

"I don't like that 'of course' business."

"Think of the economic relief that serious defense cuts could bring."

"But what's serious for the Soviets? How can one ever know? They're so damned sneaky! We got nothing but hot air last time. They got Burma and Baluchistan."

Damn it, she thought, he's *way* off track! Or is the economy worse than he's letting on? What's he not telling me?

She started to say something, but Sam Washington cut her off with a gesture. "Net, we could argue this subject 'til doomsday. What's the point? I thought it over all day. The bottom line is that the Sovs will probably not go for a serious disarmament offer. I'll promise you this: if they offer to disarm, I'll give up smoking for good."

"Well, that's confirmation you *never* intend to quit," she remarked, a crooked smile accompanying her words.

He held up the last inch of his burning cigarette, looked at it, grinned. "Does this mean you'll be lobbying the Russians now?"

She sighed, shook her head, shoved her empty plate aside. "At three cigarettes a day, dear, I'm not terribly concerned anyway. Well, this night owl breakfast has made me sleepy. Let's head back to bed."

Fifteen minutes later, Sam and Annette Washington had drifted off. The phone rang and the president groggily grabbed the bedside extension. He listened, frowning, not quite able to understand what he was being told. For a moment, he wondered if he was dreaming some twisted version of his earlier discussion with his wife.

"Yes, okay. Fine," he said quietly. "No. She's asleep, I'll take it in the other room."

He replaced the receiver, sat up, and glanced at his wife to find her looking at him. "What?" she asked.

"I'm not sure," he replied, strapping on a robe and fishing out a cigarette. "Secretary Romanoff. On the hotline." He lit the cigarette. She seldom smoked, but now she motioned for his pack. He handed her a cigarette, lit it from his own, placed a hand on her cheek, and left the room.

It was half an hour before he returned. She was sitting up in bed, watching television, tuned to CNN International.

"Well," she said, "I guess you were on the phone too long for it to have been an attack warning."

He smiled and sat on the edge of the bed, elbows resting on knees, clasping his hands together.

"What is it, Sam?"

"I don't get it," he said. He reached into his pocket, pulled out the pack of cigarettes, and tossed them into the bedside wastebasket.

She noted the gesture and looked at him blankly.

"Romanoff has decided to dismantle all of their nuclear forces," he said. "Not just their ICBMs and SLBMs, but their intermediate range missiles, bombers, cruise missiles, artillery—the works. ICBMs first."

Too stunned to think of anything else, she asked, "You believe him?"

"Actually, he said he didn't think I would. He said he didn't expect to be believed. But he said we'd soon see proof. He offered on-demand site inspection. We can fly to the sites in our own planes. He said he wanted to tell me first because in a few hours he's going to make a worldwide announcement."

"The Russians have always had a flare for drama," she said drily.

"He's going to call for an international agency to oversee the destruction of the weapons as they are dismantled. Sounds like he wants to pick up where everything stopped in the late 90s—and then some."

"So he says."

"Yes."

"What does he want in return?"

"Nothing."

"Sam, if the Russians extend their hand, they want you to put something in their palm."

"'Til now, apparently. He says they've decided to disarm whether or not we ultimately do."

"It doesn't make sense. What's their motive?"

"Well, get this. He said defense spending is wrecking their economy. It's either disarmament or depression."

"That's what Gorbachev said, too," the First Lady scoffed. "He opted for depression. Romanoff rings about as true as a plastic church bell."

"He didn't ask me to believe him, Net. He said to wait and see. And he, well, he sounded genuinely happy."

"Hrmph! Well, I'm permanently awake. I'm going to make some coffee," she said.

She swung out of bed, stopped, reached into the wastebasket, and retrieved his cigarettes. "Don't chuck these yet, okay? I have a funny feeling that you're going to need them."

He hesitated, then put them back in his pocket.

She watched his face. The room was warm, but she felt a cold shiver run down her back. She didn't know why.

She took a heavy velour robe out of the closet, put it on and started to say, "Well, I expect you've got a few phone calls to—" But he already had the phone to his ear. She was no longer in his world.

Drawing the robe more tightly, she left the room, quietly closing the door to the President of the United States.

CHAPTER 11

THE CONFERENCE

Presenident Sam Washington walked briskly into the room. It was three in the morning. After a brief shower and a couple of squirts of vasopressin stimulant, he felt almost as though he'd had a reasonably decent night's sleep.

"Thank you all for coming in on such short notice," he said. "Please sit down." He remained standing at the head of the table.

"Ladies and gentlemen," he began. "I have unusual news for you, perhaps momentous."

"Five hours from now, at nine our time, President Alexandrovitch Romanoff is going to make a planet wide announcement that his nation is beginning unilateral nuclear disarmament."

People shifted in their seats, as though bracing themselves against an unexpected gust. Washington allowed a few seconds for the reaction to crest, then held up a hand.

"Mr. Romanoff seemed friendly and sincere. He told me that he will not be informing any of the world's media until an hour before his talk. That gives us four hours to prepare."

Quickly and efficiently, Washington recounted his conversation with the head of the new Soviet Union.

"Before I take questions," he said, "I will remind you all that we have a new Secretary of State with us. I hope I can count on you to give your respect to Craig Goldstein. Craig, I believe yours was one of the hands I saw raised."

Goldstein stood quickly, a slightly built man with curly, but receding dark hair. He wore a neatly trimmed goatee which had already turned white.

"Thank you for your vote of confidence, Mr. President," he said in a surprisingly clear, deep voice. "I'll do my best to live up to the office. I would like to begin with a question generally considered more military in flavor. What does Mr. Romanoff hope to gain *strategically* from this move?"

"General," said Washington, nodding to Buck Reed, "this sounds like your field. What about it?"

"Thank you, sir. Damn good question, Secretary Goldstein," he said, nodding at him. "I think most of the Joint Chiefs asked themselves the same thing right off the bat. Except for General Young, of course, whom I notice is not here."

The dig was so deliberate that Washington said curtly, "He hasn't ducked out, Buck. He's taking a TAV flight from the Rockies."

"I'm sure we'll let General Young copy our notes when he finally arrives—" Reed started to say.

A voice cut gently across the room from the door. "That's gracious of you, General Reed," said Glenn Young. "I'm sure notes from you would be scrupulously accurate."

Reed's face reddened for a second. He covered it with a crisp. "Good morning, General."

As Young seated himself, Washington said, "Glad to see you again, Glenn." He brought him up to date, then asked, "Buck was about to offer us his insight into Craig's question on strategy. Buck, continue, please."

"Thank you, sir," said Reed. He cleared his throat and rubbed the side of his nose with an index finger. "I think there's not a person at this table who'd play poker with a Sov wearing long sleeves—myself included. If we hadn't learned that long ago, we wouldn't have the tremendous military lead over them that we do."

Except for Young, most of the others at the table nodded. Washington confessed privately that he liked their confidence. He enjoyed being around optimists.

"We *do* have such a lead," Reed said, leaning forward to visually underscore his words. "Yes, defense budgets are down, but efficiency's up. We're in good shape, maybe the best ever. Everyone here is aware that I have a degree in economics. From what Romanoff seems to be doing, I think that the Soviets are offering us a hell of an opportunity. I say let's take advantage of it and get our own economy moving again!"

A half-dozen people applauded as Reed sat down. One person whooped and another whistled. The sounds died abruptly as the president raised a hand. That, he thought, sounded staged. Buck was not above some staging, but it bothered Washington. How had he managed it on such short order?

"Ladies and gentlemen," Washington said, "as Buck's former roommate, I know he's a hell of an orator. But we're here to calmly and rationally discuss a *serious* issue. Bill," he said, looking at CIA Chief Brighton, "you're always a man with ideas."

Brighton stood slowly. "Actually, Mr. President, I'd prefer to listen awhile. I'll say this, though: The CIA will be putting its best on the line to keep track of whether the Soviets do what they say."

"Goes for the military eyes, too, Mr. President," Buck Reed interjected.

"*All* of them," Glenn Young added, defending his own fledgling intelligence agency. Reed gave a soft snort.

"And us, too," said Jeanne Allison, head of the National Security Agency.

She stared directly at Reed, as if daring him to snort at *her* agency's intelligence value. The president wondered whether Allison and Young got along; it seemed they should.

"Fine," Washington said, but if I needed such assurances, none of you would have the jobs you have. General Young, what do you say to Romanoff's move?"

Young rose and surveyed the gathering. Most members of the cabinet were there, several key Senate and House members, including Speaker Baker Sunderleaf, Vice President Kurt Leininger, two members of the President's personal staff, and, of course, the military and intelligence VIPs.

"Mr. President, if this were a free spaceship they were offering me, I'd be asking myself how soon after liftoff would the engines explode."

Nearly all of the two-dozen conferees looked down, shifting uncomfortably at the undiplomatic directness of the statement and at the intensity of Young's feelings. Other than the president, only Allison, Goldstein, Sunderleaf, and Leininger met Young's eyes. Brighton was studying the ceiling, as he often did when thinking hard.

"What kind of evidence do you have for such Soviet-bashing?" Reed demanded.

"None," Young answered. "Except the swing of a thousand years of virtually uninterrupted Russian empire-building. And I think you've let a passion of yours cloud your judgment, General Reed. I refer to your dedication to the free market."

"That's a *vice?*" Asked Reed, his voice coated with sarcasm and disbelief.

"Not in itself, no. But just because the Russians have had to—and I stress the word—because they have *had* to free up some of their minor markets again recently, adding a few incentives and concessions to private property and so forth, it doesn't mean they've become trustworthy. Empirically and logically, it's a grave error."

"*May* I respond, Mr. President?" Reed asked, his tone demanding it.

"Air it out."

Reed stood and pointed at Young. "Yes, General, you're correct. I do believe the Russians are *more* trustworthy—and I stress the word. That doesn't mean I've gone jelly-brains. I know damn well that we have to be careful. But I say that this olive branch they're handing us has the fine, sweet smell of democratic capitalism to it. I say they want to enter the fold of free nations!"

"Glenn?" Washington asked.

"You're educated in economics, General Reed. Well, a degree of mine was in philosophy. One of the principles of good epistemology, of sound thinking, is this: you don't consider something a possibility when there is strong evidence to the contrary. Otherwise, the word loses all meaning: *anything* can then be considered possible."

"Excuse me if I say that's a funny statement coming from a man who flies rockets. Seems to me there used to be all kinds of 'evidence' to the effect that man would never fly in outer space."

Several people snickered.

"Sure, people said that, General," Young answered, unruffled. "But, they said it either because they didn't understand the evidence available, or because they wanted something else to be true, even if it wasn't."

Reed turned red, but stopped in mid-sentence as he saw Washington raise his hand.

"Gentlemen," he said, "the table has received the essence of your respective, respected views. Let's move on. Jeanne, how about some thoughts from the NSA?" Jeanne Allison nodded and rose. A small, but sturdy, early-middle-aged woman observed the president; she had a nice face and wasn't badly built if you didn't mind a certain chunkiness around the hips and breasts. He mused that his wife would love to hear him analyzing his National Security Agency head by such chauvinistic standards.

Allison brushed at a lock of her loose-cut, red-brown hair and took a deep breath. "I think," she began, her voice carrying a slight tone of exasperation, "that General Young's cautions are close to my own. General Reed is too optimistic about the Russians' intentions."

"God damn it, Jeanne—" Reed tried to interrupt. With a cold glance, Allison cut him off. "I would go farther. I would say that the Joint Chiefs—with the exception of General Young—are bordering on idiocy with their assessments of the Russian situation."

At least a half-dozen outraged voices shouted simultaneously. Three of the generals were out of their chairs. It took Washington thirty seconds to calm everybody down.

"We are at this moment taking steps to decide issues bearing on the future of this *nation,*" he said. "I had assumed you all knew that. Let's conduct ourselves as though we remember."

"Now then," he said into the silence, his voice as hard as scorched leather, "Speaker Sunderleaf, I believe you've had ample practice at addressing rowdies in the House."

In sharp contrast to the president, Baker Sunderleaf was not a large man. In fact, the adjective "diminutive" frequently graced descriptions of the South Carolina native. When he pushed his chair back and stood to speak, he barely topped five feet. He had a normal-sized head, but on his small body his cranium seemed extraordinarily large.

"Well now," he said with a drawl, "I suspect that the scufflin' defined the issues 'bout as well as a 'gator crunches ducks. Which is pretty good."

Several people winced at the graphic analogy.

"Oh, I know. Some o' you'll say we've barely got started here in pre-dawn's early dark. And so we have. But consider, if you will, the followin': Isn't trust o' the Rooskies what all this is goin' to boil down to once the heat's put to the pot? Isn't that what's goin' to turn us to one side or t'other? Isn't that what's tellin' Buck, there, to say, 'Why sure, Mr. President, the Rooskies've held out their hand far enough for me to shake it without losin' my arm if I'm careful'? And isn't it what's tellin' the lady from the radar room and the general from Pike's Peak to say, 'Hell, now Mr. President, you better be careful o' them ol' Sov boys, 'cause they've been known to snatch more'n a few of our chickens when we weren't watchin'!'

"Now, we all know we gotta look inside ourselves an' figure out on which side o' that fence we really want t' be. 'Course, as a life-long politician, for the moment I'm goin' to uphold my Congressional colleagues' reputation and sit *on* that fence."

Almost everyone chuckled. Sunderleaf was popular.

He glanced at his watch and continued, "However, Ladies and Gentlemen, all you who know me know I'm not and never have been a man who can't make up his mind. We've got us only three-and-a-half hours before whatever's goin' to hit the fan does. What we decide to do here'll determine whether or not we let ourselves get splattered with the wrong stuff or the right stuff."

He sat down.

The president said nothing at the speaker's last choice of words, but wondered if the "right stuff" reference was meant as a hint that Sunderleaf had already sided with "Spaceman" Young's views.

"All right, thanks Bake," he said. "My own sense of matters is that the speaker is right on target. I'm going to prescribe a fifteen-minute coffee break now, but while you're at it, think about the straw vote —the one I'm going to take after the break in order to find out what you think of a rough draft statement I worked out right before this meeting. Nobody's heard it yet, not even my wife," he said, smiling wryly.

Sunderleaf hurried in, balancing a cup of coffee and a pastry. "'Scuse me, Mr. President," he said, "but sometimes members of the older generation like me get slowed down by leg traffic."

"More than anything, it looks like you got slowed down by a detour to the pastry table," the president remarked.

Washington let his face grow serious. He wished that he had the advice of Defense Secretary Grieve McDouglas. But McDouglas was still in a coma in the hospital after a traffic accident months earlier. Washington didn't think much of McDouglas's assistant, inherited from the previous administration. The president had therefore continued to rely on Reed's advice on military matters. After all, there had been times when defense secretaries hadn't even existed. The nation would get by for a while without one.

He scanned the table, quickly meeting everyone's eyes. It was an old impromptu speaker's trick designed to make each person feel the responsibility of individual attention. He picked up a sheet of paper in one hand and said, "Here's what I intend to say in my announcement following Mr. Romanoff's address in"— he checked his watch — "about three hours."

He softly cleared his throat and began to read.

"Good morning, citizens of the United States and of the world.

"Naturally, the United States welcomes President Romanoff's astonishing decision. As any honest person must admit, the United States of America has never wished anything but peace in the world. But not, I must add, peace at any price."

"Further, any reasonable person must admit the Soviet Union's past record has been expansionist. I hope this unilateral move by the Soviets indicates that the USSR is giving up that record and reaching out to establish a new one: a record of peaceful trade and nonaggression towards other nations and, equally important, a new record of greater liberty for its own citizens. Too often has the Soviet Union opened up, only to fall back again into a closed society.

"As President Romanoff told me on the phone early this morning, he realizes that we will not be convinced of this first step until we are able to verify it. 'Trust, but verify.' We've heard that for years. Using all the resources of our nation's intelligence services, that is what we intend to do.

"I again thank Mr. Romanoff and his government for what we all hope will be a sincere step toward a better, brighter future. Not merely for our two nations, but for mankind."

Buck Reed immediately dove in. "Let me congratulate you, sir, on well-chosen words. However, since you—"

"Hold on, Buck," Washington said. "I want that straw vote. Will everyone who agrees with the thrust raise his or her hand?"

There were no unraised hands.

"Good. I'll take that to mean we've got a working start. Now, Buck, what's on your mind?"

"I have only two objections. Is it necessary to include either the reference to the Soviets' unseemly record or the prod that they improve the conditions of their own people?"

"My reasoning is that if they are serious, it's not going to make any difference."

"But, if—"

"Buck, I want them to know that I know who I'm dealing with. That was the gentlest way I could think to put it without losing the point in a lot of soft-sell euphemisms."

"Well, I don't know, sir. They're offering us something that has got to be damned hard for them. They've had to swallow a bucket of pride to do it."

Washington sat down and leaned forward, hands clasped in front of him. "Let me answer you with some questions of my own, Buck. What about the millions of people the Soviets have harassed, tortured, and killed over these decades? What about what *they*'ve had to swallow? In the name of their memory and regard for the way they've been mistreated, isn't it right that we indicate that we're not forgetting them?"

"But if you scare off the Soviets, those people will perhaps never have the freedoms you want for them!" Reed said hotly.

"Buck, I'm sticking by my guns. The Sovs respect strength. We want their respect if we're going to make this work and help get the defense drain off our economy's back."

"But, damn it, sir—!"

"Buck, my remarks stand. I meant it."

"Yes, sir," General Reed said. There was pure acid in his compliance. Washington vowed to have that talk with him, pronto. He could not have his Joint Chiefs' head twisted by personal problems. Especially not now.

"I believe," Craig Goldstein said, "that we are perhaps hitting what we've already knocked down. There's a rule that comes to mind about not making things more complicated than necessary. It strikes me that we are where we want to be. For once, let us sit back and wait for the Sovs to carry out what they promise. Too often we jump in to embrace them and then find they've picked our pockets."

"You bet!" Glenn Young said heartily, followed by Jeanne Allison's flat but emphatic, "Exactly."

"Thank you," said Washington. "The meeting's over. Time for us all to get some breakfast, to find a chair to watch Romanoff's speech—and for others to leave."

"Oh, by the way," he said, "the press will be getting an hour's notice of Romanoff's talk. They'll be all over you wanting statements and comments beforehand. Say nothing. I mean it. I'll brief my press secretary and he'll tell the media hounds to stop sniffing and simply watch and listen to my announcement following Romanoff's. They won't like it, of course, but they never like anything that doesn't instantly go their way. Issuing 'no comments' always makes the media feel something mysterious and momentous is going on. It'll make 'em holler loud enough to ensure everybody in the country tunes in."

"One other thing," he added. "Buck, I want you and the Chiefs to cap any objections you may have to my next words. In case, just on the off-chance, however remote, that this is an elaborate diversion by the Russians, I'm ordering our forces onto a raised state of readiness."

Everyone exchanged puzzled glances. Except for Glenn Young, the Joint Chiefs looked put out. Buck Reed started to open his mouth, then snapped it shut.

"That's it, then," Washington said. "Stay close; at least in the area, in case I need you over the next few hours. Anyone who wishes to stay here at Camp David is welcome. By the way, I'm sorry you all had to come way out here. But I work better on some things in a country atmosphere. The staff will see that you're properly accommodated. This does not apply to the military and security people, of course. I expect they'll want to be in various command posts." The Joint Chiefs looked at each other. The president's "expectation" was clearly an order.

CHAPTER 12

THE UFO

Tom Corman held the speedometer at a steady 85. He was 20 miles over Oregon's speed limit. But at three a.m., it was seldom enforced on the rural sections of the interstates. I-5 was practically deserted—unlike, he remembered, the same freeway 500 miles south near San Francisco, where he used to live. Two years ago, he'd moved his small, specialized chemical firm from the Bay Area to Beaverton, Oregon. The taxes were a bit lower, the incentives a bit higher, the traffic a lot lighter for himself and his employees. It had been a good move.

He punched his radio from a country-western channel to a rock station. Rock would help him stay awake for the two hours it'd take to finish the drive home after a long, grueling trade show in Oakland. He was tired, but satisfied. His firm had shown several new products, primarily plastics and propulsion mixes. He'd picked up important contracts, not to mention three significant orders, one from the Defense Department for what he suspected was a hush-hush anti-missile upgrade project.

"... in the sky this spooky morning," a female disc jockey with a low, scratchy voice was saying. "So, if *you* see anything, Darlin's—funny lights, weird noises, what*ever*!—give me a call here at KZOX UFO line or just tap into our Internet Web page, and we'll add *you* to the ZOX's Alien Witness List—AWL, for AWL *right*! So far I've got 46 *big* calls and 26 Webbie hits since two-bad-doo! I've got the feeling , night-lighters, that this is only the beginning! *I* don't know who's sending what to our part of the planet tonight, saucer-seers, but ain't it *weeeeeeird*!"

She rolled into a crazy, horror-show laugh, pulling up a driving drum-and-bass beat. It was the instrumental opening to a song by the heavy-metal group, Thrust-Busters.

Corman chuckled. He didn't believe in UFOs. Or, rather, he did—precisely. UFOs were *un*identified objects that flew, or appeared to. That didn't make them flying saucers; just unidentified. Usually never identified because they were, in fact, ordinary things, like copters, jets coming in for landings, even candle-and-balloon pranks—magnificently magnified by human imagination, fueled by superstitious media and blown into cult crazes. Or into one fun evening for an otherwise bored all-night announcer.

Corman noticed a sign which said, "Steep Grade With Curves, Next Six Miles—Slow to 55." He grudgingly adjusted the cruise control down to 75. He'd had his little Acura through 35 mph curves at this speed and didn't worry.

There was absolutely no warning when it struck.

One moment he was okay, the next moment his right hand and leg were severed. With stop-motion clarity, he watched his hand hang for a moment on the steering wheel, then drop to the floor with a thud to join his lower leg and foot. He noted that there was nothing gory about any of it. There was little blood, although he smelled burnt flesh. He also caught the odors of charred vinyl and metal. He glanced up and saw a nearly perfectly round hole in the roof of his car. There was another hole the same size through the floorboard. He could feel and hear night air rushing through both openings.

He flipped the cruise control off with his left hand. In order to get his left foot at the brakes, he had to kick his detached, lower right leg out of the way.

He pulled the car to a stop and looked at the stumps of his limbs. His leg was oozing blood; not spurting, as he'd have expected from severed arteries. Several years earlier, Corman had been in the Burma Battle. Injuries shocked, but did not stop him. Clinically, he noted that his wrist and leg stumps appeared to have been almost completely cauterized, the leg less effectively. He felt no pain. He reached into a tissue box and pulled out a handful, slapping it against the leg stump.

He reached for his cel phone and called state police. He told them only that he'd suffered a severe injury, was bleeding, couldn't drive. He was afraid to describe his precise condition. He was afraid they'd think he was a crackpot and ignore him.

Within ten minutes, a patrol car slowed rapidly in the opposite lanes, crossed the wide grass strip separating them, and pulled up behind Corman.

The patrolman hurried up to Corman's window and started to ask, "You're not the guy who—?"

Then he looked inside and saw the disconnected leg and hand and said, "Jesus to Sunday."

"I keep a big beer cooler in the trunk." Corman said, calmly. "It still has ice in it, although probably somewhat melted. I'd appreciate it if you'd toss the beer and carefully put the severed limbs in the cooler. It might help save them."

He had to repeat it. The policeman numbly took Corman's keys and did as asked. Corman handed the cop his own arm and leg through the window and then watched the patrolman settle the limbs in the crushed, wet ice.

"This is frackin' weird," the cop said stupidly.

Corman nodded, "Ain't it?"

The cop was as pale as a bleached newspaper, but was functioning efficiently. He put the cooler in the back seat of the patrol car, then helped Corman hop over and settle into the passenger seat.

The cop opened a first aid kit and taped a compress tightly over the leg stump. The arm was still not bleeding, but he did the same for it, just in case. He belted Corman in and took off at almost 90 mph through the six miles of curves, then upped his speed to 140, heading for Eugene's biggest hospital, which he notified on the way. The most shocking thing to the policeman was that Tom Corman remained awake and cogent, explaining the sequence of events. He finally lost consciousness when he was anesthetized in the operating room. The last thing he remembered was spotting his beer cooler on a metal table ten feet away from him. A doctor was holding up the neatly severed hand and shaking his head.

~ *PART II* ~

THUNDER

CHAPTER 13

THE MISSION

K evin Jones twisted and turned on the workout bench, stretching muscles and joints, feeling for damage. Once, in his early twenties, he'd been an enthusiastic weightlifter, but had learned the lesson of foolishly forcing progress. A painful stretch tear of his pectoral ligaments had given him a bout of costochondritis that resulted in a three-month layoff from most of his training. Worse, it had knocked him out of the karate competition his senior year in college.

Space Command—or SpaCom, as it was more commonly called—had given him the most thorough physical he'd ever undergone. Kevin rose to his feet. He felt wobbly a moment, then walked over to pick up the now-tattered printout, which he'd brought with him to the gym every day. His eye caught the phrase, "follow precisely in order to bring physiology up to standards."

"How?" he chuckled. "They've already *killed* me."

He was thinking of more than the five days of rigorous workouts. He was also remembering his phony car accident, the one which SpaCom had engineered. His name now graced a tombstone and numerous bureaucratic "dead" files.

"Any close relatives with heart conditions or the like whom news of your death could push over?" Young had asked.

"Not exactly, sir," Kevin had answered. "Folks are dead. Don't like my brothers. But I've got a nephew I kinda take a hankerin' to. Avery's his name; seven now, I believe. He thinks there's goin' to be some sort of interplanetary FBI someday and he wants to join. You ask me, he spends too much time breathin' Internet ether."

"Don't be so sure. If some of Tommy Mac's FTL ideas work out, who knows?" General Young said, almost to himself.

"Beg pardon, sir?"

"FTL"—faster-than-light."

"Huh?"

"Mr. Jones, for all the Einsteinian brew, it's never been *proven* that light is an absolute limit, you know."

"But my physics instructors all—"

"Dated. Old Pete Beckmann shoved that fact into the physicists' faces in the late eighties before he croaked. Then Tommy bit into it, wouldn't let go. Claims to've dragged it into a whole new orbit. We were together in school. I got him first, though General Reed made a grab. Jeanne Allison and I have been able to keep him at bay. If he had his way, Tommy's stuff would be permanently stuck in some sealed basement under a national security label. If there's anything to it, I want

Tommy's peers to be able to run it through open review."

Kevin had had only the vaguest notion what he was talking about. Young had gone on as though it made no difference: "Guys like Reed don't grasp that you can't straight-jacket the Tommy MacGregors of the world. If you try, their brains go on strike."

"Uh, you don't think this FTL thing is actually possible?"

"Don't know. Sorry. Not your nesting tree, I know. Now, about your nephew— Avery, you said? I'll see to it he won't worry about you. For now, it's better you don't know how I do that."

Kevin focused back on the present, forcing himself to plod once more through the printout sheet's nutritional specs.

"Extra doses," he read aloud. "Niacin; ascorbyl palmitate/calcium ascorbate; BHA, BHT—to lower serum cholesterol; 200 mg selenium selenite; L-argnine to optimize tissue repair and accelerate muscular development; 25,000 IU beta-carotene re: lung-damage repair, smoking; 85 mg aspirin daily."

Christ, he thought, I don't smoke more'n six weeds a day. He gave the sheet a final, quick scan to make sure it was locked in memory, then crumpled and tossed it away.

He was sitting and panting after another set of pumping when Moshe Trevis strode in.

"Got any belly dancers handy, Moe?" he asked.

"You'll never forget that, will you? Wait until you marry a jealous wife, as I did. I live in terror that I'll talk about it in my sleep."

"Aw, poor pokey. I'm all broke up," Kevin said, wiping sweat off his face and head with a gym towel.

"You look it. Will you live?"

"Hey, bud, I been bustin' buns faster'n a baker with a sledgehammer. So what's new?"

"The Russians are disarming."

Kevin snorted. "Yeah, and newlyweds hate sex."

"Seriously. Romanoff made a worldwide announcement. Washington came on afterwards for our side. Beneath the diplomatic daisies, he said we'd believe it when we see it."

"This the real poop?

Trevis shrugged. "The question is, are they serious about what they want *us* to believe?"

"Hmph," Kevin said. "If a grizzly gets friendly, check to see if it's already killed you. That's what my old man used to say. Hey, if the Sovs disarm, there ain't goin' t' be any need for my sniffin' at Engels' cold tailpipe, is there?"

"The Spaceman will keep his hounds working, believe me."

"That so? Quite a guy, ain't he?"

"Up there with the best, Kev. Never doubt it."

"Well, the sooner somebody tells me when I can get started, the better."

"Just keep up this rejuvenation therapy," Trevis advised.

"Any more rejuvenation, an' they can hammer up a pine box!" Kevin said, slapping the workout bench.

"For the next two weeks, mornings will be concerned with mission details. Our portion of Engels is underway," Trevis said, grinning. "Feel better yet?" Kevin threw his soggy towel at his friend. "Moe, you're not only a guilt-ridden womanizer, you're a goddamned sandbagger!"

At six the next morning, Kevin entered the cafeteria, hunger scraping at his stomach lining. He said, "Hi," to Moe, already in line.

Trevis nodded. "Don't overdo it. I want to leave in ten minutes so we can be early for our talk with the Chief."

"The Spaceman—?"

"No. His right-hand man, Walkingfar. Don't laugh. He is genuine American Indian. A Blackfoot from South Dakota, I believe. But everyone calls him Chief.

Colonel "Chief" Joseph Walkingfar was one of the few men whose physical presence had ever made Kevin Jones feel small. He estimated that the man would not look noticeably shorter than most NBA centers.

"How, paleface," Walkingfar said, looking sternly at Jones. "Little warrior sneak to Engels in quiet moccasins, come back to teepee, tell big red man what him see."

Kevin had no idea how to respond.

"Hi, Mr. Jones," the big man said after a few seconds of stone-faced silence. "Call me Chief, if you don't mind. I'm a rocket-bucked, former NSA civilian."

"Okay, Chief, sir."

"Don't pay attention to his pow-wow act," Trevis said drily. "I've probably been in more teepees than he has."

"Well, white, black, brown, red—if you go back far enough, we were all head-bashers," Walkingfar said. "What we are here to discuss is *modern* head-bashers, the new Soviets. Specifically, their project, the Engels Extension. That's their name for it. Let's start the movies."

A LANDSAT-5 map of Antarctica came up on the giant high-resolution screen. The picture was mostly white with several shades of brown and near-black, with some blues and greens offshore. Someone had circled the Engels base in red.

"In the twelve minutes while you were waiting for me to show up to talk to you, you had time to read the intelligence briefings left on your chairs. Did you?" Walkingfar asked.

Both men nodded.

"Good little braves. That means you now know almost as much as I do. Of course, what you don't know, Mr. Jones, is how to go about getting more. That's my specialty, and, of course, Mr. Trevis's. Together over the next two weeks, we're going to try to build you up to our levels of expertise. We won't succeed. It's impossible to bring a recruit along that fast. But, then, maybe we won't have to. Now," he said, bringing a new slide to the screen.

"Recognize?" he asked.

Jones frowned a moment. "Well, damn, Chief! That's a copy of my comprehensive exams for Naval eye."

"Right. Know why I'm showing it to you?"

"Because I finished it before anyone else that day?"

Walkingfar rolled his eyes. "No, Mr. Jones, no. You finished it faster than anyone *ever* did. Forty minutes faster, to be precise. Surely they told you it was an all-time record, one that stands to this day?"

"Well, uh, no, Chief. Nobody did."

"How did you manage, Mr. Jones?"

"Uh—you want t'know how I did it?"

"Bring the man a squaw for his bed tonight, Mr. Trevis."

"Reservation conscription or volunteer?" Moe asked.

"Either, I'm sure he'd never know the difference in his present state of fog."

Kevin was mulling it over. But should he tell them about the Slowdown? His dad had warned him to play it close to the vest, for good reason. Hell, they'd probably assume he was making it up. There was no way to demonstrate the effect on demand, either physical or mental. If his claim sounded screwballish, he might be chucked back into the salt-tub service. No one wanted a goofball underfoot. On the other hand, if he *could* convince them somehow, it would certainly seal his new career here.

He chose to explain.

After a ten-second silence, Walkingfar said, "Mr. Jones, that's about as believable as a singing turd."

"Yes, Chief. But it's true. I just don't know how to prove it to you on the spot."

Walkingfar stroked his chin, eyes narrowed. "On the other hand, they tell me I had a great grandfather who could dodge a spear or an arrow. Didn't matter whether it was shot at him from two feet or two hundred yards. I doubt it was true. But despite being in countless battles, he never lost blood and died at the age of 118. There's no way to tell about him. With you, though, maybe I can."

"I doubt it, Chief. It's so fly-buzzin' erratic. Seems to happen on its own, mainly under unexpected stress."

"That so?"

Walkingfar turned slightly away—then lunged at Jones with what must have been ...

... an eight-inch blade, Kevin noted, watching the knife begin to descend in one-twentieth motion toward his own chest. The idiot wanted to stick him! Kevin got out of his seat, side-stepped the knife and its wielder and watched the big Indian slowly stab the chair seat. Meanwhile, Trevis moved molasses-like toward

Walkingfar, apparently in a belated attempt to intercede. Kevin was shocked that the Chief had proven faster than his friend, whose martial reflexes Kevin had always respected. Kevin grabbed the huge wrist that held the knife. He chopped the hand, plucked the weapon, and stepped back ...
In a flash, everything sped up to normal. In real time, he watched Walkingfar crash into the chair and Trevis land on his back, groping for the already empty knife-arm.

"You boys lookin' for something?" Kevin asked from four feet away, holding the knife.

Walkingfar and Trevis whirled to stare.

"Great Blanched Daddy," the Chief said, "I send you prayers of forgiveness. You did not lie."

A few minutes later over fresh coffee, Kevin asked, "Uh, Chief, would you have really stabbed me if I hadn't moved?"

"Bruised you." Walkingfar pulled out his knife and plunged it into his own chest up to the hilt. He didn't flinch and there was no blood. "Collapsible circus blade. Magic tricks are a hobby. Figured in advance you had pretty amazing reflexes. Wanted a test option, though I didn't expect anything on this scale."

"Figured in advance, sir?"

"Hunch—based, among other things, on some incidents High Eye discovered from your high school and college days. For instance, it seems you and a date were once jumped by six guys outside an off-campus bar. You two were untouched, but the guys somehow ended up in pretty bad shape. The emergency room doctors couldn't make sense of their story."

"They wanted my wallet and her panties, sir. I couldn't agree to either."

"Apparently not," Walkingfar said, a hint of a grin cracking his impassive face.

Kevin asked nervously, "Chief, I don't want the Slowdown to become a liability. It will, you know, if word gets out."

Walkingfar slapped the fake knife against his palm, considered a moment, then said abruptly to Trevis, "We won't keep the secret from the Spaceman. But that's it. No farther."

"You expectin' me to see some hard stuff, Chief?"

"More than ninety percent of field work is non-physical, low-profile. That's how secret agents stay secret. But this is a crash project. You might have to bash a few fleshy brute obstacles. I hope not. I hope we've planned things well enough. But personally, you've got a permanent invitation to accompany me into dark alleys," he said, getting up and tapping the giant screen's keyboard control behind the podium.

Photographs of several people came up.

"Mr. Jones, here we have a half-dozen defectors from the new Soviet Union. All are reliable sources. Memorize. We've chosen these six because of the contacts High Eye has in Sovietville, one of these will probably stand the best chance of helping us find out more about Engels itself. The Ruskies had too much time to sweep the dirty snow away."

"Chief, is this all we really know?"

"No, Mr. Jones, it's not. One of Brighton's men got inside. Unfortunately, he found nothing more. He was undercover with the U.S. scientific team. We confirmed it because we had our man there, too, unknown to the CIA or the other eyes. Ours was a *real* scientist. The Spaceman himself recruited him years back. To make a long story somewhat shorter, he wasn't as timid as the CIA's boy. Our man's majors included chemistry and genetics with a minor in gab. He can get close to practically anyone. The American team visited for three days. The Ruskies couldn't resist trying to pump a scientist with our guy's background. They set him up with a looker-hooker KGB gal, ostensibly a scientist herself. While she was pumping him, *he* was pumping her. Some details classified, for reasons you may or may not eventually be told. Long of it is that he came away with a list.

"The list is of six research cities inside the USSR where chem and bio warfare work's going on at a rather intense rate. Four of those cities we already knew about from other sources. Two we didn't. Each of the faces I've shown you is of someone who's been inside those areas at one time, or who knows somebody well who was or is still there or has access.

"Now, Mr. Jones, lest you get your hopes up to where they suffer oxygen deprivation and dim your perceptions of the magnitude of the task, I have to tell you something else. We have no way of knowing if any of these six places—or the half-dozen we've chosen to match—is *really* related to Engels. For instance, it's possible that the KGB lady was smarter than we thought. She may've fed us a pound of rotten salmon eggs, not fresh caviar."

"Roe, roe, roe your boat," Trevis sang softly.

"Sounds like a shot in the dark, Chief."

"With a hunch for a gunsight. But we've got others working around the clock digging for angles. They may get lucky. In the meantime, we've run all of the six Sov towns through a computer. Our best brains have decided that one city has a high priority. It's a place from which we stand a reasonable chance of finding out where home base is and what it's about."

"You're sayin' you're gonna *send* me there? Hell, Chief, I don't even speak Roosky!"

"Well, I'm afraid there's no way we could get you ready for *that*, Mr. Jones. With your country drawl, that would be quite a challenge. But you won't have to speak Russian. We're sending you to a Mideastern city. Hence, our resident expert on the area," he said, nodding at Moe.

Trevis smiled.

"Hooh, boy," Kevin said. "Here come the belly dancers."

CHAPTER 14

THE COURIER

Hernando Valdez Garstona was growing nervous. He brushed at his trim, black-and-gray goatee and wondered if he should leave the pleasant out door cafe. He'd been sitting there for twenty minutes in downtown Mexico City.

"Ah, now," he told himself in a low voice, bringing calm to his veins, "take a deep breath, Hernando, and follow through your decision. It's always dangerous, but these days, routine. Now is far from the time to panic. If something *is* wrong, it's time for courage—and opportunity; the ordinary is frequently the less lucrative."

He thought that his uneasiness might merely be the lingering distaste of his stroll through a corner of one of the *pepenadores'* slums. He made himself look at them now and then, the garbage-sifters who worked ten-hour days for less than a total of two dollars. He looked in order to remind himself how far one could fall in this land. He did not really care about the *pepenadores*. There was nothing to be done about them. But he did care greatly about never falling to their level. And, of course, he did business with their *caciques*, their neighborhood bosses. Their $50,000 daily income led them to taste many material pleasures. Valdez could help the *caciques* obtain a few of those pleasures, either directly or through his network of connections.

He breathed in the *tierra templada* summer air. It smelled of auto exhaust and soot. He remembered he'd heard someone say that the city had started out centuries ago as a tiny retreat. It had been a refuge, actually, in the middle of what had been a large lake. Or so the legends said. You'd never know it now. If Mexico had been smart, this could've been the inland Venice of the New World.

"Now look at it," he grumbled. "It's a polluted pig sty—except, of course, for those areas with connections to the ruling party."

But that was old news, ancient, the oldest political news in the "free" world. There was nothing like yesterday's news to bore the restless soul.

Certainly nothing to worry over at this moment, he thought.

Smoothing his pale blue silk tie, he glanced into the plate glass window of the Contadora restaurant several yards away. He had not made himself wealthy by sloppiness—in either appearance or planning.

True, many clients failed to meet his standards of dress. Naturally, he felt contempt for them. On the other hand, he thought it gave him the upper hand. He believed that the Spanish—and that's how he thought of himself, not as a Mexican, even though he'd been born in Tijuana—understood the world of appearances.

They should have been followers of Immanuel Kant, he observed sarcastically.

He looked at his watch and felt the nervous churn of acid in his stomach. He sipped a little wine. The doctors said wine was bad for the stomach. But they said it was also good for the heart. Life was a trade-off. His client was late. That's all it was.

"No, be honest," he spoke softly into his wine glass. "Stay in touch with the phenomenal world. Something's different this time and, after all, it cannot be that you have never dealt with a Russian."

He snorted and raised his head in a disdainful, unconscious gesture. Russians! With their scruffy mix of false confidence and inferiority. Not so different from some of the *caciques*.

Still, these new Russians generally paid him well, if one recognized their nature and didn't grant them undeserved personal status. He wished it could have been an American instead. They paid well, too—far better, actually. True, they were also pushy and sometimes boorish. But, Mother Mary—at least the Americans generally kept honest self-interest at heart! One was not likely to have to listen to litanies about inevitable historical tides and the Second Proletarian Dictatorship just around the new Soviet corner.

Valdez had dealt with the Russians off and on for decades. He'd helped them raise cash for Central American operations through drug sales to his own connections in the U.S. The Russians did not like to take chances on such matters.

His operations had never suffered a major loss to the various American anti-drug forces operating along the border and, indeed, throughout the Latin nations. He worked through layers of intermediaries to protect himself. Nor did he advertise his success with the flamboyant, defiant lifestyles of the big drug lords. Together with a natural aptitude for tactics, these precautions allowed him to do a steady trade in his preferred commodities: cocaine's newer variations and substitutes, usually highly concentrated.

Always before, that's what the Russians had hired him for, to move their "see-see," their cocaine concentrates. They obtained them through their latest Cuban/Colombian network. He brought them into the U.S. for the Soviets whenever a particularly large delivery was at stake. Valdez laughed at newspaper reports alleging a dying drug trade in America due to the invention of the pleasure wire. To the contrary, the wire heightened the effects of drugs. He suspected the Drug Enforcement Administration had planted such stories to cover .

He frowned at his watch.

"There is another thing which makes you nervous, Hernando," he said in a whisper. "The Russians are not generally late. They are slobs, but timely."

He smiled at his reflection, then grew serious. In the glass, he saw a stocky figure with an enormous pot belly approaching. The man was waddling across the street, edgily dodging the melee of noisy traffic. He was dressed in a ridiculously loud red and white striped sport shirt.

"Pig," Valdez muttered, sipping more wine and raising a mask of regal indifference. It intimidated the Russians and usually got him a higher price. He *knew* it worked with Filatov because he'd dealt with him five times.

Nikolai Filatov puffed up to the table, wiping sweat with a large, stained red handkerchief.

The Russian grinned and said, "Valdez! *Buenos—*"

"Please," Valdez said, shaking his head sorrowfully. "As usual, your Spanish sounds atrocious. English. It's important that I be able to understand you in business."

"Very well," Filatov answered huffily, slumping with a thud into a white wicker chair. "My God, it's hot here this year. I long to return to Moscow."

"I read in the paper it was ninety-five in Moscow yesterday," Valdez offered nastily. "We have things to iron out and my time is short."

The Russian scowled. He'd never been able to soften Valdez. Filatov had been picked by the KGB for this sort of thing because of his supposed gregariousness. With Valdez, it was like trying to get a post to pucker.

"To business, then," he said. "We want something special."

"Oh?" Valdez glanced disinterestedly at the traffic. He watched a policeman accept a ten-thousand peso note from a motorist whom he'd stopped for a nonexistent violation.

"It will mean twice your million-dollar fee and percentage of the gross."

"So you say," Valdez said and sipped wine.

Filatov glared, then snatched his handkerchief and furiously dabbed his dripping face.

"I thought this was supposed to be a temperate climate. How do you keep from sweating in this heat?" he asked.

"I have better genes."

"Spare me your Moorish insults."

"How you interpret my innocent comment is doubtless the unfortunate fault of your having been born Russian. Naturally, I don't blame you *personally*."

Filatov dabbed his fleshy neck and plowed on. "This work we don't need for several months, so you may—"

Valdez rose and straightened his tie. "I'm a busy man. Perhaps you should call me when you are really ready."

"No, wait!" Filatov hissed. "All right, perhaps we can pay more. Greedy Spic," he said under his breath.

Ignoring the slur, Valdez thought: Well, well, well! He gives in so easily. This *must* be important.

Valdez's sense of adventure was fired, but he didn't let it show. He sat down with an irritated expression and looked at his watch. "Five minutes, Filatov," he said, thinking that it was much easier for a wealthy man to make money.

"We don't want you to deal with see-see this time."

"I don't do marijuana or heroin or any of the bulkier contraband. I've no need of juvenile dangers."

"No, no! A simple package. A small one. Well, several, but your people could carry them as one."

"Of what?"

Filatov shrugged.

"I don't deal in unknowns," Valdez snapped. "You know that."

"Yes, I told them. But they insist."

"Then they insist for nothing. Good-bye, Filatov. Call me when your *caciques* decide to be reasonable."

Valdez was several steps from the table before the Russian caught his arm. Valdez glared imperiously at the stubby fingers gripping him.

Filatov snaked his hand away. "Sorry," he said. "But I plead, Valdez. Reconsider. I *cannot* fail!"

They have his balls in a desk drawer on this one, Valdez thought. Fascinating.

"Best come back to the table and let me buy you a glass of wine," Valdez said. "Better still, vodka. After I name my price, you will need it."

CHAPTER 15

THE MISTRESS

At 10:30 the next morning, Valdez opened his eyes to darkness. For a fraction of a moment, he was afraid. Since witnessing a childhood friend blinded by a Zapatista car bomb, he had an irrational fear of losing his sight. Then, feeling extremely foolish, he realized that he was nose-down in his mistress's cleavage. He raised away from Maria. She was naked on her side, the sheet kicked down past her knees. Her black hair—after ten years finally carrying a bit of gray—fell in soft waves, framing high cheekbones. He ran his hand slowly down her body. She rolled over and opened her eyes, looked startled for a moment, then smiled and pulled him urgently forward.

"So now, in honesty," she asked smugly a few minutes later, "do you ever miss your wife?"

"She was a candle, but you are a beacon."

She sat cross-legged, the sheet carelessly across her knees. The ends of her dark hair were wet with sweat.

"You have taken another job," she said without preamble.

"What?" Well, yes," he said. The woman was uncannily perceptive. "I'll be one of the couriers this time."

"I can tell by the way you make love," she said.

"Adventure keeps a man young."

"You are only fifty. I have gray hairs at thirty-eight. What divides young from old in this modern age?"

"I know, I know," he said, snapping the cellophane on a pack of cigarettes. He laughed. "Maria, how did a drug smuggler acquire a psychologist for a mistress?"

"Because the psychologist knows that he is far more than a drug smuggler."

"If only U.S. Customs had your enlightened attitude."

"They haven't caught you."

"No, but while a rancher may not know which coyote steals his sheep, the coyote knows he will be shot if he is spotted."

"That's the Mayan in you."

"Spanish," he said, exhaling a stream of smoke.

"Light me one," she said.

"Bad for your skin."

"You're the one who worries about age!"

He sighed and complied. She drew on her cigarette, then blew smoke toward the ceiling, making a red "O" with her lips."

"It is the Russians you work for again?" she asked.

He nodded, then rose and paced around the spacious bedroom.

She admired his lean frame, dressed in a black and red-trimmed velvet robe. You are a hero by disposition, Hernando, she said to herself, and don't know it. But perhaps it is the nature of heroes not to know.

"It's a special mission," he explained. "I negotiated three million dollars for the job."

She raised her eyebrows. "That is an enormous sum for one job—even for you."

"No cocaine this time. Filatov says it will be several small packages. I suspect electronic equipment of some kind, but I will X-ray it."

"Is that wise?"

"Necessary. I will not chance taking something dangerous, such as—oh, who knows? Perhaps powdered plutonium for some crazy American neo-leftist or rightist terrorist. Drugs are one thing. People have a choice about whether or not to use them."

"My little smuggler the moralist."

"The illegal and unethical often differ, Maria."

"And I admire you for making the distinction—although it took me years to fully believe it."

She stubbed out her smoke, half-done, and set the ashtray on the nightstand. It amused him that she wasted cigarettes that way. It was a touch of luxury that added to her sensuality.

She asked, "It must be sophisticated contraband. Doesn't that in itself raise a moral concern?"

He barked out a short laugh. "That's like asking if it's immoral to provide a spear to be thrown at a tank."

"You feel no sense of vengeance against Americans — even though they are your enemies?"

He looked at her in astonishment. "How can you say that? I don't judge them by their drug-hunters. The Americans have the blood of achievers. They are unique."

"But you always talk of *Spain* with such admiration."

"Ah," he interjected with a wave of his hand, "I speak of Spain's face, its preservation of certain manners, dress, civilities—not of its soul, not of its spirit. Maria, such an American *I* would make; a perfect marriage of face and soul!"

"Then why not become one? Both of us."

"Preposterous," he said, dismissing the suggestion with a toss of his head.

"Your *attitude* is preposterous!" she shot back hotly. "You've already set up legitimate businesses in America under another name. America would welcome you."

"Dramatics. I would actually be out of place in the North. Impractical."

She took a deep breath and shook her head at his stubbornness. He was pacing again, impatiently, like a cornered *el tigre*.

"What are you afraid of, Hernando? Of challenge? Certainly, you'd have to leave your drug business behind. Oh! Oh, I see. You think you'll miss the rush to your crotch from the adventure. You are afraid it will dampen your manhood!" His face turned red.

"Hernando, Hernando," she said quietly. "Do you believe American businessmen and entrepreneurs are bored and impotent? Do you think *physical* risk is the only heater of blood?"

Hernando spread his hands and said, "No. Well, maybe. Hell, I don't know." He grinned in spite of himself. "I shall give it some deep thought, Mistress Psychology."

She blew him a kiss and winked. Just to show he could, he resisted a few moments.

He awoke to the sound of a television set. He yawned, stretched and got out of bed. He padded naked into the next room. Maria was curled on a couch, his robe around her.

Shhh. Listen," she said, pointing to the TV.

"Yes, your Majesty."

She made a brief face at him and patted the sofa beside her.

"... following which, President Washington made his own statement, expressing gratitude, but certainly gratitude dosed with more than a drop of caution," the announcer said. "Let's go now to our live camera at Camp David for an analysis from CNN correspondent Sandy Crestow. Sandy."

The scene fast-faded to a head shot of the reporter, a blonde woman in her thirties whose heavily lined face suggested that she spent too much time in the sun.

"Well, word of a possible summit meeting—yes, that had been rumored in the wake of reports still unconfirmed that the Joint Chiefs had prepared a proposal to the president for a U.S.-initiated major arms reduction. But no one, to a man, or woman," she added with a fake grin, "suspected this ..."

"What is she talking about?" Valdez asked, shifting restlessly. He was not the patient news junkie that Maria was.

She shook her head, turning up the volume with the remote.

"... and speculation is widespread that the president would welcome true disarmament as a budget-cutting aid in order to help the faltering economy and ..."

Maria hit the "off" button on the TV's remote. "I've heard enough," she said, then filled him in on what he'd missed.

"The Russians would never do such a thing," he pronounced. "I know them. It would be self-emasculation!"

"Like giving up drug smuggling?" she said dangerously.

He cursed. Sometimes her prodding was too much. He shot to his feet and stomped out of the room with as much dignity as a nude and disheveled man could muster.

CHAPTER 16

THE CAMP

I t's quite a place, sir," General Young said, motioning one arm in an encompassing gesture at the grounds of Camp David. He had never been there. "Glad I changed my mind about your invitation. My man Walkingfar threatened to shoot me if I didn't. Said I needed to get to know you."

"Smart man. I doubt there'll be trouble, but if there is, I'm sure he can handle things 'til you fly back."

"No doubt, sir. He says I have a tendency to over manage."

"Don't we all? General, did you know the White House once had grizzly bears on the premises."

"Beg your pardon, sir?"

Washington chuckled. "I'm not kidding. Thomas Jefferson kept 'em as pets. Got 'em from Merriweather Lewis, who brought 'em back from his 4,000-mile expedition out west. That was—oh, it would have been in the early 1800s, because Jefferson moved into the White House in 1801. I entertain the theory that Jefferson's success as a president may have been directly related to the number of senators and representatives to whom he personally showed his grizzlies—close up."

Young laughed. "Maybe so."

"Anyway, you're right," Washington continued, "the Camp is quite a place. Except for the higher humidity, this time of year it reminds me a great deal of the Willamette Valley of Oregon. Bigger evergreens out west, though. Not as many ash. Used to do a lot of hiking in that country when I was a kid."

He bent to pick up a stone, idly examining it as he and Young strolled on through the warm afternoon sunshine. Several wrens chased a crow overhead, dive-bombing the larger bird as it wildly pumped its wings to escape. A nearby cicada, oblivious to the overhead drama, droned raspily. Far away, in some hidden wet spot, several frogs croaked at irregular intervals. Off to the west, a couple of ominous thunderheads had begun to build.

"See any mean weather systems below as you flew in earlier today?" Washington asked, pointing to the clouds.

"Wasn't looking for them, sir. Wasn't piloting. Catching up on a batch of paperwork. But from the looks of the horizon, it appears something's going to bust water tonight."

"What'll it take to bust the problem between you and Buck, Glenn?" Washington said, shifting from small talk. "Looks to me like it's getting a tad out of hand."

Young pursed his lips, then shook his head in a mixture of revulsion and puzzlement. "Well, sir, you know by now that I'm the odd man out among the Chiefs. I think it boils down to how we view the Russians, just as Sunderleaf said."

"Is this causing serious problems for SpaCom?"

"I'm trying to end run them, sir."

"I understand that. It's the bane of any new service branch. But there's no reason for the other Chiefs not to cooperate. Especially Buck. He and I have been through a lot together, General. It beats my buns to see him act this way toward you. It's no excuse, but you should know that his wife's on the wire."

"Uh-oh."

"Most people can handle it, like alcohol. Not others. She was a bright and delightful woman once. It's got to *grind* deep on Buck."

Washington hurled the stone he'd been carrying. It hit a tree with a hard *thwack*. A blackbird squawked in outrage.

Young thought that a man might pay dearly to be on the president's wrong side. Washington clapped Young on the back and said, "Hey, I'm about ready for some lunch! What say we head back and corner the cook for cold roast beef sandwiches and a couple of beers?"

"Sounds good, sir."

Over the meal, Washington said, "On this Sov disarmament thing, Glenn, I don't personally expect much to happen for a few days. Even on the off-chance that they were planning some kind of ruse with disarmament as a cover, I imagine they'd go through at least a few weeks of trying to lull us into a false sense of security."

"That's how I'd figure it, too," Young said.

The two wandered into small talk about politics as they finished lunch, then Washington patted his stomach and said, "Now, *that's* what I call roast beef."

Young took a sip of his beer and nodded in agreement. He glanced around and asked, "Sir, has this place been scanned lately?"

"Huh? You mean for bugs? Sure. Right before you got here. Always. What's on your mind?"

"Remember the Engels thing, sir?"

Washington frowned. Not *that* again, he thought. "Yeah," he said cautiously, "I got a couple of briefings on it from both Whiz and Buck two days ago."

"Well, sir, I've started a small independent operation—just in case. I've pulled in a Mossad man on loan and a buddy of his from Naval Intelligence to follow some leads that both Jeanne Allison and Walkingfar have dug up."

Washington readjusted his position in his chair, moved a rivulet of beer foam off his glass with one finger, and said, "You sound as though you think Engels is more than a little warm. The other eyes don't go along with that."

"Alison does, sir. I haven't told you this—didn't see the need—after all, the word is 'warm,' not 'hot.' But I may as well mention it now that I've got this chance in private. Rather not have Reed and friends know just yet. I had a guy of my own on the scientific investigation of Engels."

"I see," Washington said neutrally.

"He got close to one of the female Ruskies," Young said, "and came away with a list of half a dozen Soviet cities possibly connected to the whole weird deal. I've run it by Jeanne and she feels the same, that this list is worth pursuing with some moderate active measures."

"Uh-huh," Washington said, finding for the dozenth time that week that his mind had wandered to the latest dismal poll numbers on his handling of the economy. In that looming context, this Engels business did not exactly inspire him. "Do what you think is best, Glenn. I can't deal with tenuous issues until they move up out of the lower forty. Understand me on that?"

"I believe so, sir."

"Good. Let's move on."

They discussed budget matters for twenty minutes, then the president rose, ending the meeting.

"Well, General, have a good flight," he said. "One of these days I'm going to get the guts to ride one of those transatmospheric vehicles—isn't that what TAV stands for? What do they do, Mach 24?"

"The older ones. The latest do Mach 30. *Grasshoppers* we call 'em, sir. The bugs with the giant jump. Nothing anywhere can touch 'em. Not even close."

CHAPTER 17

THE TAV

The Transatmospheric Vehicle, or TAV, was an old idea. The earliest the public had heard much about it was in the middle of the Reagan adminis tration with his endorsement of an "Orient Express" passenger version. A TAV vehicle flew high enough and fast enough to skim, like a stone, across the top of the atmosphere. It could descend and land as an ordinary plane. A TAV flew up to 30 times the speed of sound, several times faster than the old Blackbird SR-71s which had once been the fastest aircraft in the world. While it had been conceived in the 1940s, the TAV concept hadn't been proven with secret prototypes until the 1980s. As with many good ideas, man's imagination had run ahead of his technology, leading it onwards.

From the co-pilot's seat, General Young looked out the window at the curve of the earth. He was in one of SpaCom's smaller TAVs, not like the business-jet-size vehicle in which he'd been ferried out to Washington. Whenever possible, he sat in a front seat. He was now in mid-flight in the short hop from D.C. to Colorado Springs. This part of the journey was his favorite. They were high enough to be above most of the atmosphere. The sky had long ago lost its blue, turning purple/black. The stars were brilliant and untwinkling, mockingly far away. Young thought of Tomisito MacGregor's equations and what they might make possible.

"I may visit you pricks, yet!" he muttered at the twinkling suns so many trillions of miles away. The pilot, only twenty-five, glanced at him curiously.

"Sir?" he asked.

"Big wishes, that's all."

"Yes, sir," the younger man said, looking at the stars. "Me, too."

There was nothing for the pilot to do for several minutes. This portion of the flight was "coasting." A heads-up display—a detailed computer projection which overlaid the actual world outside—showed a simulated three-dimensional version of what was beneath the cloud cover miles below. A bright blue line indicated the location of the horizon. When SpaCom's base came into view, it would be projected first as a green dot, then, as they neared, would expand to a graphic of the airfield, major buildings, and so on. Almost as good as the real thing.

The pilot kept an eye on the display as Young chatted with him. He had a family—two young boys. He liked to race cars and read philosophy in his spare time. He wanted to be one of the first settlers on Moon Base—something planned for completion within the next ten years. Yes, his family would go, too. And after that—given his expected experience and the longer life he anticipated due to the moon's lower gravity—he wanted to move on to Mars.

Young had deliberately built SpaCom around this kind of man. He called them his "hooks in tomorrow."

A synthetic voice came on, announcing that the plane's autopilot was starting to take them into the atmosphere. But right on top of that, a diagnostic graphic began flashing red, showing a problem.

At first, Young could hardly believe it. The graphic indicated something incredible: the final foot of the plane's needle nose was completely gone. Nothing more, just the tip of the needle. It was enough.

The pilot gunned the rocket engines, sending the TAV up.

"Orbit's our only chance now, sir."

"Of course," Young said, stunned and bewildered.

Any attempt to descend through the atmosphere would burn up the plane. Without the needle streamlining, the plane would literally melt—and probably tear apart—starting from the nose back. In orbit, though, another TAV could rescue them. TAVs did not normally go into orbit, but most could in an emergency.

"What the frack happened?" Young asked.

"Whatever it was, it was back seat to lightning," the pilot said. "I didn't even see it. Something snipped us off clean as a guillotine, sir. Lucky it wasn't a few seconds later."

As the craft settled into a shallow orbit, Young said, "What occurred shouldn't be possible."

"No, sir," the pilot responded, his face at least two shades paler than normal. "It sure shouldn't."

CHAPTER 18

THE NOTE

Poor James Hoban, thought Annette Washington, he'd never recognize the place.

Nodding to the two tall Marine guards standing on either side of the elevator doors, she placed her thumb on the Print-a-Lock reader. At the electronic beep acknowledging her identity, the doors opened, and she stepped into the elevator. As the doors swished closed, she looked with her left eye into the retina-scanning laser above the floor selector buttons. She heard the expected beep and pushed the button marked "Sub-level 20."

The elevator surged downwards. When was it Hoban had designed the White House? She remembered that the first version was finished October 12th, 1792, exactly three hundred years after the "official" discovery of the New World by Columbus. She shook her head, unable to recall if she'd ever read anything as to precisely when the Irish-American Hoban had completed his design. She remembered that it was based on a late 18th century English country-house, contemporary for the time. His concept won out over several competitors, including one from Thomas Jefferson. Hoban won $500 in addition to the contract to build the White House.

The oldest portions of the new nation's official presidential residency were the big entrance hall, the large ceremonial room on the east, and the state dining room on the west. The structure was not known as the White House until 1809. The name derived from the white Virginia limestone used in part of its construction. The British—bless their devilish little hearts—burned the building in August of 1814. Hoban rebuilt it by the fall of 1817, adding east and west terraces overlooking the south lawn. The semicircular south portico was added in 1824—again by Hoban—and the north portico later, during the Jackson administration. Adams (the second one) and Van Buren fenced the grounds. The first piped water was in by 1832, open sewers shortly thereafter, gas lighting in 1848, the first telephone in 1880, and electricity in 1892.

Not bad, Annette, she thought to herself proudly.

The elevator hissed to a smooth stop and she placed her thumb on another scanner lens. The computer bleeped and opened the doors for her. She stepped out into a small "lock" room, about ten feet square. On the opposite side of the room was another set of sliding doors. All the doors were heavy steel. She sighed. This time she placed her index finger into proper position, got a sanction of her existence, and waited for the doors to open. She found herself in yet another room. This one was a little larger than the previous. She was met by two more guards—these with short shotguns at ready.

"Please step to the retina scanner, Ma'am," one of them said in a clipped Vermont accent.

She moved forward a pace and turned to the apparatus built into the wall, adjusting the eyepiece over her right eye this time. She waited for the laser to read and compare her retinal pattern with those in its memory—and then, as a final precaution, match the data to records of the exact proportions of her facial features. When the computer gave its okay, the guards stood aside. Both simultaneously placed their full hands on scanning plates set on opposite sides of the wide doors.

She imagined that the elaborate procedure was a small price to pay for the security it offered. After the attempt on the life of President Reagan, way back in his first term, the Secret Service had engaged in a slow, systematic upgrading of procedures. The work had culminated in the secret construction of new deep underground quarters for the president and his family. The quarters were designed for more than anti-terrorist, anti-assassination purposes. They were also designed to give the First Family as good a chance as could be given to survive a direct nuclear attack on Washington. Sam had even told her the designers had figured a way for the structure to survive the infamous "gopher" bombs which had come into U.S. and Russian strategic inventories in the 1990s. The gophers, such as the BLU-113 made by Northrop Grumman, were penetrator warheads. They burrowed far into the ground before exploding, causing a shelter-collapsing pressure wave. Annette Washington shuddered.

She had never been told exactly how deep the twentieth level was. In fact, the elevator was keyed to a random number generator which varied the time of descent or ascent among any and all floors, making insurgency of any kind difficult to plan. For safety's sake, First Families increasingly lived full-time in this underground "Black House."

She strode into their bedroom and called, "Sam?"

There was no answer. She shrugged and picked up a telephone, dialing the butler, also a member of the Secret Service.

"Yes?" answered the relaxed tones of Ernest Rogers.

"Hi, Ernie," Annette said, "Do you know where Sam is? I'm downstairs."

"He's up in Oval, talking with General Reed, I believe. He left a message. Don't expect him for dinner tonight, ma'am."

After she hung up, she pulled out a Post It™ notepad and scribbled a short message which she stuck to the bathroom mirror. It was their personal message clearinghouse.

Twenty levels up, President Sam Washington poured two brandies and handed one of them to General Reed.

"Buck," he said seriously, "I'm concerned about the way you've been cooking in your collar lately. When a man of your background and brains starts having trouble controlling his temper, something's on his mind. Is it your wife?"

The general's answer was defensive, "I know the rumors, Sam, but Sally's not *on* the wire."

For a few seconds, the president couldn't find a response. It didn't fit what he'd heard. "Send her to a clinic or something?" he asked.

"No. Didn't need that clinic babble. I just let her know that her addiction was tearing the hell out of us. She struggled for a week or two, threw stuff around, screamed, lost her appetite, slept too much—then she was off. We have our lives back, Sam," he said, giving an unconvincing grin. "But now you're *really* wondering what kind of burr's under my saddle, eh?"

"Buck, it's other people, too. People you need to have a smooth relationship with for the good of the country. For instance, Glenn Young."

Reed fidgeted in his chair.

"He claims you and the other Joint Chiefs in particular are shorting him on intelligence."

"Well, yes, sir. We've held back on him some. Young's intelligence service is poorly seasoned and we're consequently afraid of leaks, among other things."

"Like what?"

"We're leery that his High Eye group is going to compromise our agents. If we're right, Young's responsible for the death of at least one."

"Jesus, Buck. That's a serious charge. I assume you have proof?"

Reed's face became indignant. He almost snarled, "Well, don't assume it, Sam! You can't always *get* it in the intelligence business. Sometimes you have to go by instinct!"

"Don't use that tone with me, General!" Washington snapped.

Reed sighed, nodded, brought himself under control, and said, "Sorry, sir. Didn't sleep well last night is all."

"What else concerns you about Glenn, Buck?"

"Oh, he's a clever bellyacher. He knows the bugs aren't working out of his command, so he's scapegoating his problems to us. Be leery of him, Sam. He's mighty big trouble."

"I see," Washington said, thinking his old friend found a lot of people "mighty big trouble" lately.

Washington decided he wasn't getting anywhere. He glanced at his watch, stood, and said, "Well, thanks, Buck. I'll be wary. You just try to recover some of that chill under fire you've been so famous for, okay?"

Reed gave a passing imitation of a humble shake of his head, "Got it, sir. You know, Sam, maybe an old dog like me needs to be scolded once in awhile, eh?"

Reed left for the next ten minutes, Washington sat at his desk, mentally replaying the conversation. He didn't know why, but he felt like he'd found a spot of mold on what he'd assumed was good bread. Well, he thought, on to other matters.

He dialed his private NSA number for Jeanne Allison.

"Yes?" came her crisp voice.

"Up to anything?"

"Oh, the usual, Mr. President. Putting bugs in Romanoff's toilet and preparing poisoned pomade for a nice dictator in Latin America."

Washington smirked.

"Can you run over to Oval for awhile? I want to kick around an idea or two."

"No problem. You know I love to kick things, especially starving puppies and kittens with broken legs."

As they conferred, Annette Washington took a hot bath. After twenty minutes, feeling restless, she got out, dried off, and left the bathroom, intending to read in bed. Meanwhile, steam had taken its toll on the adhesive of the note she'd left on the mirror. The note slipped, hung for a few seconds by one corner, then fluttered down and lodged out of sight behind a large conch shell on the corner of the sink counter.

CHAPTER 19

THE DECISION

Hernando Valdez stretched out his hand to touch the dolphins. He was shocked at the warm, unfishy feel of the mammals. He had been to Planet Ocean six times, he recalled, but had never bothered to experience this. The dolphins squeaked and squealed, jostling each other roughly, competing for his attention.

He looked at his watch, petted the playful cetaceans in the raised pool for another several minutes, then regretfully turned away. He was finished with business today and wanted to get back to Maria.

Is that another sign of your weakness? he asked himself. Even five years ago, he could have been gone for weeks without feeling a gnawing need inside for the woman. This—he'd finally acknowledged, fully, helplessly—was the woman he'd met who fully challenged him.

He smiled, shifting focus. It had been an excellent trip. For two reasons he'd also come to San Diego. For Maria, he'd come to find them a place to build. They both liked the climate, especially near the coast, where the hot Santa Ana winds didn't reach as strongly. They wanted a romantic setting—preferably a granite and glass house on a bluff above the sea. It took Valdez two days to find such a location. If the architect was right, it would mean they would have plenty of time to wrap up their affairs in Mexico before leaving. She could end her psychiatric practice and perhaps establish a new one in San Diego.

For himself, he'd also come to work on setting up the Russians' special job. Originally, his idea had been to carry at least a part of the package himself. He'd decided against it. He shook his head. Never before had Maria been such a powerful consideration toward precaution. But the job could still follow his usual pattern. He needed an intermediary who would not know that he was carrying anything. He needed to find someone who looked and acted totally innocent—because he would be. He had found such a person. In fact, four.

The previous evening, he'd been sitting in Benihana's restaurant and overheard some women seated at the table behind him. They'd been talking about a vacation to Mexico planned for three months away. He'd turned to look at them and was pleasantly shocked to see that they were nuns. They were not the new type whom one could not properly distinguish from other women in public. Rather, they were from a sect of the older Benedictines. They wore white habits and full-length dreary black dresses. Apparently, he'd thought, an occasional night out was no longer considered a violation of the vows of poverty.

He'd introduced himself as a visitor from Mexico. They were delighted to question the handsome, distinguished, middle-aged man. He'd cringed at the term. They'd wanted to know about their intended destination, Mexico City. None of them had ever been there. Well, how did the good sisters plan to travel? By rented car? Fine, but of course in Mexico, Catholic nuns—dressed in the wonderful old fashioned style—could expect courtesy from the authorities. Yes, their travels would likely be quite safe and they would not be harassed, as long as they stayed on the main roads. Did they plan to travel continuously ...

In short order he'd gotten much more information, including their day of departure, and the date on which they planned to cross back into the States. He would make sure that he kept track of them. On their last night, before crossing back to the U.S., he would arrange—from mercenaries experienced in such matters—for their car to have installed in its body, securely hidden from casual observation by border guards, several small packages. After they returned to San Diego, Valdez would have one of his men—hired by telephone—be the next person to rent the car from the agency. From that point, delivery of the package to the Russians' destination would be a minor problem.

As he drove out of Planet Ocean's parking lot and headed for the airport to fly back to Mexico city, Valdez considered that he'd have to quickly inform Filatov of the date he intended to move the contraband. The nuns' trip was only two weeks earlier than the tentative "go" date which the Russians wanted. Valdez had made it clear to the sweating Filatov that assurance of safe delivery required some flexibility in scheduling.

It is a new life ahead of you, Hernando, he thought. Who would have imagined that you would actually be talked into emigrating to America permanently? Who, but a delicious and wise woman such as Maria? Perhaps, he mused, certain kinds of female pushiness were not so bad.

CHAPTER 20

THE BASEMENT

A h," Boris Karpov grunted, looking up. "No, don't take off your coat. Give me mine. We're going for another walk. Don't look so irritated. Afraid your most precious body part will freeze and crack off?" He jabbed Plechl in the ribs.

Madeis had seldom been to the police station. For the most part, Karpov did not want either of them there on the grounds that it would hurt their covers.

"Have you heard the news?" he asked. "We're disarming our country."

Madeis halted in his tracks.

Karpov laughed uproariously at the expression on the younger man's face. When Karpov regained control, he said, "Oh, quite true. It's already begun. It's just our nuclear missiles we're getting rid of for now."

"*Just* our nuclear missiles."

"First step. The Politburo has its reasons. We'll even be letting Americans in to watch the process, like we did on a much smaller scale with the old INF and START treaties."

"Getting rid of our best weapons, though. It sounds —"

"Crazy? Yes, *if* you think like an American." Karpov chuckled to himself as they reached the police station.

He pounded up the icy steps and through the door. Nodding curtly at the desk sergeant, he led Madeis down a maze of narrow halls and steps, finally halting against a steel-plated door hung on heavy hinges. A guard grunted and fished out a grimy key. They entered a small room and Karpov strode across to another unlocked door and opened it. As he did, Madeis noted the door's uncommon thickness.

"Soundproofing?" he asked.

"Obviously," Karpov answered and stepped through.

"So, Rastov, how's the patient?" Karpov asked a tall, emaciated man in a stained white coat.

"We had another round two hours ago," came the reply in a raspy voice like dry, crackling leaves. He led them to a cell.

On a filthy, bare, narrow cot, lay a naked woman, face down. She had long blond hair, now tangled with sweat and what looked like blood, but could have been anything.

"Okay, Rastov, turn her over."

Madeis was forced to turn away and retch into a corner. In a few seconds, he wiped his mouth with his handkerchief and turned back to face the men. They seemed amused.

Karpov slapped him on his back and said encouragingly, "Don't worry, Madeis, it's like that for some of us the first time, eh Rastov?"

"I've *never* minded," Rastov stated quietly.

"Bring her around."

Rastov injected something into the woman's arm. Madeis found that he could— barely—look at the woman without losing his stomach. Mostly, he analyzed, it's her nose. Or what's left of it. He decided from her bone structure that he could at least say she'd probably not been ugly. He made himself examine the rest of the damage to her, clinically, as though he were a doctor. Other than the signs of torture, the woman had full breasts and strong legs, although a little chubby near the upper thighs. She was not tanned at all, very white. Hardly unusual in this climate.

The woman moaned, opened her eyes, saw Rastov, then tried to curl into a ball against the wall.

Rastov breathed harder.

"Take her out and strap her in," snapped Karpov.

Almost lovingly, Rastov carried her out into the larger room and laid her on a long table. In a moment, she was spread-eagled on her back, held tight by canvas bands. Despite the harsh glare from the overhead lamp, her eyes were opened wide.

"What are you going . . .?" She stopped, saying no more, but her eyes pleaded desperately for a merciful answer.

"Oh, well, that depends on you," Karpov replied indifferently. "Actually, I do not normally answer questions from ugly ladies, you know."

"U - ug - ugly?" she stammered.

"Well, take a look for yourself," Karpov said softly, reaching to a nearby table and swinging a small mirror to her face.

The woman looked at her reflection for two horrified seconds, then screamed and began jerking wildly against the bands.

"Stop!" shouted Karpov. "All of what you saw can be fixed."

Madeis observed a sickening look of hope come into the woman's eyes.

"Oh, yes, yes," Kapov said encouragingly. "Our doctors can do wonderful things. And they will. If I tell them to." The woman began to cry. "Now, now," said Karpov, reaching into a pocket to get a clean white handkerchief. He began to lightly dab away her tears, which came away mixed with old blood. "Let's not cry. You don't want me to give you back to the tall man over there, do you?"

She turned her head where Karpov pointed to Rastov and then, recognizing him, whispered, "No!"

"And I won't," Karpov assured her. "As long as you tell me one little thing. You were stationed in Antarctica, weren't you? At Engels?"

"Ye—yes," the woman answered, her voice quite hoarse. "But they told me never to tell, except to my own resident controller. I am KGB, too!"

"But as you can see by your treatment, we need to make an exception. Now, when you were there, an American team of scientists came to visit. And you remember one particular one, with whom you had a little—er—official fun, eh?" She nodded. "A scientist. I had to."

"Mother Russia congratulates your patriotic vagina. But in the course of that duty, isn't it true that you talked perhaps a little too much?"

Fear shot into the woman's eyes.

"Yes, you *know* we know," Karpov said.

The woman shook her head, but even Madeis sensed she was lying.

"Oh, dear," said Karpov, sternly pursing his lips. "It appears you are not going to cooperate after all."

He reached down toward the woman's nose. Madeis closed his eyes. The woman screamed.

Karpov whispered something and soon the woman quieted down. Madeis opened his eyes.

Kapov said, "You see, it's this way. Your boyfriend in Antarctica—not the American scientist, the Russian one that you didn't think anyone knew you were having an affair with—he told us that you confessed to him that you *did* tell the American something you shouldn't have. Yes, yes—he betrayed you, of course. Why else would you be here? But he said you wouldn't tell him anything specific. That's what I want; the *specifics*, you stinking sow! If you tell us, we'll fix up your ugly face. But if you don't, well, unfortunately, the tall man over there badly wants to try something else on you."

As if on cue, Rastov fired a blowtorch; its hot hissing filled the quiet room.

"Cities," the woman blurted. "The American got a list of six cities. But I didn't tell them to him, I swear! I think he stole them while I was asleep." Each word sounded to Madeis like it scraped her throat raw.

Karpov considered for a moment, raising his eyebrows. "What cities? And what were you doing with such a list? A paper list was it?"

"It was—it was from my KGB controller. I was also sleeping with him—and watching him. On orders. The KGB did not trust him. I took the list from him to copy it. I had done that with other papers he had in his room. I was just doing my job!"

"Apparently not so well, if you let an American get hold of the list, too."

"But I don't know that he did! He might've gotten it from the resident himself, who could have lost the list!"

"Never mind," Karpov said harshly. "The important thing is that you tell me the names of those cities, and anything else printed with them.

"I—I can't."

Karpov started to reach for her nose again, but the woman cut him off with, "No! It's true. You see, I had just stolen it myself. I had barely glanced at it. I only remember one name—that's all, just one."

"And that was?"

"Krevesk."

Karpov took a step back.

"Scopolamine," Karpov yelled. "Inject her *now*. I have to know what else might be in that retarded brain of hers."

As Rastov administered the old "truth" drug, Karpov drew Madeis aside and winked. "Quite an education in one night, no? But you're doing okay, for a novice. Why don't you take a break?"

He gave Madeis a fatherly shove toward the door and turned back to the woman on the table.

My God, thought Madeis as he hurried out. My God, my God, my God! What kind of mission could ever justify such sickness?

CHAPTER 21

THE TEST

As he headed for the station's front door, the desk sergeant hardly glanced at him. A dutiful man, Madeis thought. Bury your nose in your secure little job and who gives a damn what might be going on beneath your feet? Double-track your life away. Don't think, don't see, don't object.

He stepped through the doors and walked a few paces down the front steps and to one side, into the shadows. The wind had died down slightly and the temperature seemed a touch less cold. He lit a cigarette and inhaled deeply.

He asked himself what he had learned from the experience—what of importance? First, of course, it appeared that the woman had made a terrible error leaving the list where the American could get hold of it. But could it be a frame-up? He wondered who would have had a motive to frame the unfortunate woman. Who would the top candidate have been? Probably her KGB resident sleeping partner. He may have sensed that she was spying on him. If so, he'd probably made sure more than his own superior in Buenos Aires knew about the woman's activities. He probably hadn't trusted his own boss at that point and, therefore, hadn't wanted to bring others in to widen his possible alibis. However, if—

Madeis sighed. He felt small, like a child thrown into a soccer game with boys several years older.

"Mr. KGB Einstein," he muttered, "so confident with Tanya, you were, spouting off your brainy insights about the corruption of the Soviet state."

Concepts that he'd glimpsed in the abstract about terror had fallen away, crumbling like old face putty. He ordered himself to remember the woman for the rest of his life, because *that* was the face of true corruption.

Abruptly he felt awash in guilt. The premises of a lifetime, countless propaganda "truths" from his earliest schooldays, reached up to slap him, and berate him for his unpatriotic ideas, to refasten the leash which had come unclasped and was slipping from his neck. To his surprise, Madeis thought that the leash had not merely become unfastened; it had broken. Then guilt hit him harder, almost physically collapsing him, drawing power from the depths of the horror he'd witnessed minutes earlier. He leaned against the station wall, eyes closed. The fear slowly passed and he was left with a piercing loneliness.

The icy wind picked up, chasing an empty paper milk carton down the street, making a hollow echo like a horse galloping far away. He blinked into the wind, deliberately letting it bite and rip at his skin. In a few seconds, he shuddered and tossed away his cigarette, turning to go back inside.

Karpov pounded out past Madeis.

"Move your German ass, Plechl!"

Karpov's heavy breathing came out in little steamy puffs.

"What's happened to the woman?"

"She'll be fertilizing potato fields by tomorrow."

"I meant, did she tell you what you wanted to know?"

"That's more of a good KGB attitude. Keep it in mind in the future—and don't let a few bruises and trickles of blood distract you. This nation is doomed to live in dungeons. Yes, she told me what I wanted to know, and a lot more. Damn, it's cold! Let's go back to my office. I need vodka."

Karpov did not even take off his coat as they entered. He went to his desk, fished a ring of keys out of his pocket, unlocked and roughly jerked open the bottom drawer where he kept his better liquor. As he reached into the drawer he slipped the key ring back into his coat.

"Hah!" Karpov said, holding up a still-sealed bottle, "Hood River vodka! American—but who cares? Made in their Northwest, the part that was ours once, until we foolishly sold it to them. Never underestimate the imperialist bastards," Karpov said, downing a glass in a gulp and immediately refilling it.

The glimmerings of a daring idea flashed into Madeis' mind.

"It's warm in here, Boris. May I take your coat and hang it with mine?"

"Huh? Oh, yes," Karpov said, shrugging out of his heavy garment and absently handing it to Madeis.

Keeping his back between Karpov and the coat tree, he deftly reached in and pulled out the keys, gripping them firmly to avoid clinking them together. Just as deftly, he slipped them into his own coat. His heart raced as though he'd sprinted up four flights of stairs. Carefully, he hung the two coats on the rack, making a show of smoothing them with his hands. When Madeis turned around, Karpov was sitting, not looking toward his subordinate, but wearing a fierce frown.

Madeis felt suddenly like a cat stuck out on the end of a fragile branch, unable to back up, committed to a dangerous leap.

"Engels," Karpov muttered darkly. "The bitch may have cost us Engels. Oh. That's right. You don't know much." He pursed his lips, considering something. "Well, perhaps you should." He lit a cigarette and smiled. "You did, after all, handle yourself well in the basement, Madeis."

"I felt I did poorly."

Karpov studied the younger man for a second. His next words caught Madeis totally off guard. "Did you know your mother was a defector?"

"I knew she left Russia when I was young."

"Yes—three, wasn't it?"

"I'm not sure. Father never told me."

"He wouldn't. Already had a black mark by just being German. You know he was lucky to have held his position after that."

"I don't comprehend his work."

"You have some right to be proud of him, despite the sauerkraut in his veins."

"What has this to do with today?"

Karpov leaned back in his chair. For a few moments he sat motionless, his glass cupped in both pudgy hands.

"The one thing wrong with you, Madeis, is probably attributable to your being young. You don't question things enough. You are intelligent, but damn it, boy," Karpov shouted, slapping the desk, "do you think I'll be around forever to pave your roads? Has it never occurred to you that you should not have advanced even as far as you have? It's me. *My* connection!"

Madeis shook his head, unable to follow.

"I'm dealing with a moron," Karpov said, chuckling, filling and draining another glass. "Look at what's against you, boy! First, your father is a German not particularly overjoyed with his Russian citizenship. He's not all that careful with his opinions, you know.

"Second, you have no relatives with any significant connections. You don't even have friends like that. In other words, you have no one to vouch for your standing to the Party.

"Third, as I just mentioned, your mother defected. Now, add it up, Madeis. Sinking in?" Karpov asked harshly. "Better late up the river than to miss the mouth."

"But I didn't even know you when I was recruited."

Karpov rolled his eyes. "Do you think most new recruits know their new bosses beforehand? Oh, certainly, some do—the ones who have friendly relatives highly placed to begin with."

Karpov leaned back, wiped his face with one fleshy hand, then said, "Over twenty years ago, I was on duty in a small southern border town. The town was called Pekstan. Next to Iran."

Madeis felt himself stiffen, but Karpov was speaking into his glass.

"It was my first full resident assignment, and a relatively important one. The Americans were friends with the Shah then, of course, and Iran was a threat to us. Because Pekstan straddled the border, it was an ideal place for picking up information. I oversaw its collection and forwarded it to Moscow. Why me? Boris Ivanovich Karpov, Minister of Trade, member of the Politburo, is *my* father, Madeis."

"My God."

Karpov laughed. "No, not my God. But certainly my patron. As I am yours. Anyway, in Pekstan I met a lovely lady on vacation from Moscow. As I plowed my car through a street, there was suddenly a huge ox loaded with baggage in my way. It panicked and jumped, and there, in the direct path of my car, was this woman, frozen as I bore down on her. I hit the brakes, but it was too late. I bumped her and she flew up onto the hood. For a second, I could only think that she did not look like she belonged in Pekstan.

"I recovered my wits and jumped out of the car. I gave her a handkerchief to stop her bleeding nose and helped her into the car. Both her legs were badly bruised and she could hardly walk. It wasn't until she was settled in the seat that I realized I'd been talking to her and she had answered me in Russian. When I got her home to my apartment in the Soviet sector, I treated her as best I could. She was surely in shock, for she offered not the slightest resistence when I undressed her, examined her legs, applied ice to them, and then, after a few minutes, placed her in a cool bath. Despite her swollen face and limbs, it took no effort to see that this woman was a beauty. I was enthralled with her—and I couldn't explain it. I felt extreme tenderness toward her. Protective. Me, the Tartar ass."

Karpov's voice had grown almost soft, slurring slightly from the vodka. "I had given the woman my own, comfortable bed, and sat up all night in a chair, watching her. I could have taken her a dozen times, if I'd wanted—but the thought of doing so repelled me."

Madeis was amazed that such things could come out of a man he'd considered no more than a crude, clever brute. He hoped Karpov didn't get drunk too fast. He wanted to hear the end of the story.

"It doesn't matter, though," Karpov said, his voice quiet and far away, "it makes no difference what one calls it in retrospect—including me. The fact was, she had inexplicably, in a mere moment of time, changed my world. Was I in love? I didn't even question it. It just *was*, like sunshine when you don't expect it."

He sighed heavily, rubbing the bridge of his nose.

"Well, she finally awoke, before dawn. 'It's all right,' I said, 'you've been in an accident; you're safe.'

"That's all I said then. I didn't tell her my name, either. It seemed entirely irrelevant at the moment. I got her some of the bottled water I kept in the apartment and helped her to drink it. She needed help, because it turned out she'd severely sprained her wrists in the accident.

"Soon we were talking. It was as though—and I know this sounds like cinematic idiocy—as though we'd known each other for years. That evening, I had dinner brought to the room. Afterwards, we sipped wine—and still we talked; about her family, about mine, about her work and about mine.

"I didn't realize what it meant until days later, but she didn't flinch or show the slightest sign of fright when I told her I was KGB. She asked me about what I did. I violated every principle of secrecy, telling her whatever—"

Karpov straightened himself and his focus came back to the present. "Well, now you *do* have dirt on me, don't you? A lot of it." He slumped back. "Doesn't matter, doesn't matter," he mumbled, his voice getting heavy and thick, but still understandable. "Pour me another, Madeis."

Madeis did so as Karpov went on.

"Sometime early in the next morning we were making love. Don't remember how that happened now. I had to be careful not to hurt her, but it was wonderful. Magnificent—and so . . . so *close*. Know how that is, boy?"

Madeis shook his head—but he thought of Tanya, even though he'd not made love to her.

"Well, 's all right, perhaps someday."

"What happened to her, Boris?"

"Got to me, she did," Karpov said, his voice fast becoming unintelligible. "Got to me, an' knew it. Knew it. Used what I tol' her about KGB methods and border security to—to get—to—"

"To get what?" Madeis prompted.

"Out," Karpov whispered. Madeis had to strain to hear him. "To defect. Your damned mother left me. Mud-dog bitch whore. But she'd told me about you. And after I got—got through being furious with her, well, I felt an obligation. I could remember her through you, see? Stupid, eh? I know, I know. I knew then. Yet I did. And all this time, since you were three, you know, I kept an eye on you, watched, watched out for you, Madeis, made sure that you didn't fall into, uh, that blithering whuh—"

Karpov's words degenerated into nonsense. His head drooped forward onto his chest as the alcohol claimed his brain. He began snoring.

Madeis sat perfectly still for several minutes. He listened to the crackling of the electric heater, the tinkling of wind-driven snow on the glass, the creaking of the building as it settled ever so slightly. He slowly got up and retrieved Karpov's keys from his coat. Then he pushed him, chair and all, out of the way and began rapidly opening locked drawers.

After finding nothing noteworthy, he started on the filing cabinets. It took no more than ten minutes to discover what he was after. As he scanned the folder's contents, he sucked in his breath. He felt the hair on his neck slowly bristle.

"And I thought I'd seen horror in the basement," he hissed.

Quickly he carried the folder down the hall to the locked copying room. One of Boris's keys opened the door and another turned the lock of the machine itself. After he finished copying the folder's contents, making two of each page, he set the machine's counter back to the reading he'd noted before turning it on. Boris had shown him the trick.

Within five minutes, he was back in Karpov's office. Karpov was snoring louder.

Madeis replaced the folder and carefully re-locked the drawers. He pushed Karpov back to the desk, went to the coat rack, dropped the key ring into Karpov's coat pocket, put on his own coat, and hurried out into the frigid early morning air.

CHAPTER 22

THE IRRETRIEVABLE

He seems different tonight, Tanya speculated
She watched Madeis restlessly pace her living room, a cigarette dangling from his long fingers, lamplight highlighting his blond hair and high cheekbones. She felt an unexpected chill of goose bumps along the insides of her legs. Well, she thought, there's something left after all.

"What?" she asked, noticing that he was looking at her.

"I was about to use the same word."

"You are odd this evening," she said. She often talked that way to him the past few weeks. It was direct, comfortable conversation; pleasant and sometimes close, though she'd not let matters progress beyond a kiss or two.

"I *feel* odd," Madeis said.

"Your face has a look I saw on a high-wire artist once—simultaneously thrilled and frightened."

Hell, thought Madeis, if I took her to the Institute of Paranormal Research in Moscow she could pass for a telepathist. He suddenly yelped and shook his head. His cigarette had burned down to his fingers.

"The dangers of preoccupation," she said; then, seriously, "Madeis, I'm sorry that I feel I can't — I mean, I know you would like to. To, well, more than kiss."

"I'm a realist, and not a satyr like Karpov."

"But consider how little I give you!"

He went to her where she sat on the couch. He dropped to one knee and held her hands in his.

"Tanya, I'll wait. For now it's enough that you are my warmth in a city of emotional ice."

He pressed his lips against the back of her hand for several seconds, then looked up at her.

She kissed him lightly on the lips. "And the other side of what you're feeling tonight, Madeis? The side that is frightened."

He pulled away, stood, and yanked out another cigarette.

"Talk," she urged. "Let me have the pleasure of doing something in return for what you are doing to find Gregor."

He wondered what she would think if she found out that he already knew what had happened to Gregor.

He had resumed pacing, but stopped as a thought, a wild, improbable thought, struck him. *Could* he tell her? Could he somehow make her see past the KGB skin that he'd chosen to wear? Was there some resource of persuasion inside him that could give her a faculty of sight to which the monster's skin would be transparent?

"Where are you, Madeis Plechl?" she asked.

He shrugged, aware that her apartment had long ago been wired for sound. "I need some fresh air. Let's go for a walk."

As soon as they stepped out into the chilly night, he realized that he could not admit it. It was simply a fantasy. He'd have to do something else. He was on his own. The effort to involve Tanya could destroy any chances of his doing what he must. There was no longer doubt. No human being—not even a Russian, not even KGB—could let happen what was about to happen. Not if it meant anything at all to *be* human, to atone for the terrors he'd seen in the basement, and for those he'd never seen.

He made himself pretend that he was working out of a bad mood. Soon, he was telling jokes and Tanya was laughing—something she had never done so freely, so easily with him.

It was a good walk, and when they returned to the apartment they shared a bottle of wine. It was a reasonably decent Chablis from the Ukraine, provided by Karpov at Madeis' request a few days earlier for just such an occasion. Despite all they'd said to each other about understanding her state of mind, about her lingering, deep feelings for Gregor, he was soon watching her undress in front of him. He marveled at her nakedness; at her round, high breasts; at her small waist; at her strong, slender legs and the auburn thatch between them; at her pleading face streaked with tears.

"Tanya," he said, "this won't help."

He picked up her slip and held it out, like a knight presenting a garland.

She dropped her eyes, shook her head, and took it.

He lit a cigarette as she dressed. When she finished, she came to him. He held her as she pressed her face against his chest.

"Thank you," she said, her voice muffled.

"As the Americans say, 'no problem.'"

She laughed, a small laugh, filtered through sobs.

He felt his throat tighten, aching from what he wished to tell her.

Now, he thought, matters *are* irretrievable.

CHAPTER 23

THE TAIL

N othing," Jeanne Allison said to the president's face on the screen in front of her.

Washington sighed. "You've been at it what? A month? You're *sure*, Jeanne?"

"Nix beyond what I told you a couple weeks ago. We confirmed that his wife's kicked the damn wire. Between you and me, I would've liked to have found something more. I don't think he's stable. But I'm no psychologist."

Washington shook his head. "Anything new, let me know."

As he clicked off the video phone function on his computer, his press assistant, Tom Rosco, poked his head into the open doorway.

"I slipped right by your secretary, sir. Am I violating any national security laws?"

"Probably. If I really believed that's what you did."

"Naw, you're right. Nobody gets by Ella," Rosco said, referring to Ella Paxson, whom Washington had brought with him through twenty years of political ladder-climbing. "But she said you might have a moment."

"She's a mind reader."

Rosco handed Washington a torn piece of copy from one of the major news services. "Give this tip a gander."

Washington read:

(WASHINGTON, D.C.)—BY UPI NET CORRESPONDENT, ERNEST POMP . . .

THE PENTAGON OFFICE OF GENERAL WHARTON "BUCK" REED, CHAIRMAN OF THE JOINT CHIEFS OF STAFF, ANNOUNCED FIFTEEN MINUTES AGO THAT HE WILL HOLD A NEWS CONFERENCE AT THREE P.M., EASTERN TIME TODAY.

A SPOKESMAN FOR THE GENERAL REFUSED TO ELABORATE ON THE SUBJECT REED INTENDS TO COVER, BUT TOLD UPI THAT IT WOULD BE "OF MAJOR FOREIGN POLICY PROPORTIONS."

Washington flipped the wire copy into his desk-side wastebasket. "What the hell is Reed doing? He can't go making foreign policy on his own!"

As the president reached to click the computer's phone key, Rosco looked at his watch and said, "Uh, sir, it's almost three now."

"Well, flip on the friggin' TV, then."

"Yes, sir." Rosco liked to see the president upset; it usually meant action. The office's five-by-eight foot screen came on in the middle of a sentence by CBS's Washington correspondent, James Shorelake.

". . . it *has* been nearly two months since Mr. Romanoff made his magnanimous offer to divest his sad nation of the awful temptations of nuclear weapons, a goal, I might point out, which administrations in the West have feared to fully grasp. While President Washington has so far suffered few of the usual slings and arrows of press—"

"You've just received notice that your honeymoon is over," Rosco said.

"I suppose I ought to be grateful," Washington replied. "After all, the notice has come from one of the media gods himself. Anything to drink, Tom?"

"Splash of whiskey. Sit tight. I'll get it."

". . . it has come to the attention of certain people in the press and others elsewhere, that President Washington has waited long and entertained an unnecessarily outdated suspicion of the Russians. After all, the Soviets *have* set aside their childish ways, and now, apparently, are also setting aside childish playthings—"

"He means nuclear weapons?" Rosco asked incredulously. "I've never exactly thought of 'em as toys."

"Wouldn't mind beating bombs into plowshares if Romanoff is serious. We'll know soon enough. Our spy-eyes are the best in the business."

"But are they good enough? Remember how back in the '80s the Saudis hid those mid-range Chinese missiles from our eyes for damned near two years?"

"Technology's more sophisticated now," Washington muttered, turning his attention back to the TV as Reed strode to the podium.

"He looks nervous," offered Rosco.

"He's got reason. Tom, get on the phone to his Pentagon lackey and tell him I want Reed on the line as soon as he gets through."

"Right."

Washington turned full-bore back to the television.

"Good evening, my fellow Americans," Reed began, and then cleared his throat. "I'll keep it honey sweet and hokum short. For a number of months, I and the other Joint chiefs of Staff have been preparing a move toward not just nuclear disarmament, but toward limits on *all* forms of armament—while simultaneously opening America to nothing less than full, free trade with the new Soviet Union."

Cameras shifted for better angles, lights were adjusted, microphones held higher, and reporters began shouting questions.

Playing the moment for its full impact, Reed waited and then held up his hand with a smile.

"Please, ladies and gentlemen!"

"Pentagon says it'll pass along your orders," Rosco said to the president, punching off his pocket cellular phone. Washington nodded.

I wish to emphasize," Reed said, "that the president has been fully aware of the JCS plan for sometime."

Washington growled, "What! That's a crock!"

Almost as though he could read his mind, Reed said, "While my good friend the president and I disagree on some of the finer points, we'll work it out one way or another. But, hey, disagreements are normal in this clumsy system we call a democracy."

The press laughed, nodding tolerantly, as though to say, "Ah, yes, it's the best those goofy, unimaginative, uncultured American people can do, the slobs."

Reed beamed at the media. "Ladies and Gentlemen, I hope that Mr. Romanoff will respond to this initiative in the humble spirit in which it is intended. Now, let's hear your questions."

Reed pointed to a brown-haired, tall reporter below the podium.

"Bill Braxon of NBC, General. Am I to understand that this discussion you're proposing with the Russians was something you'd been planning *prior* to Mr. Romanoff's disarmament move? And if so, can you tell us why the American public shouldn't be suspicious of such a claim?"

Reed smiled and shifted his weight into a more comfortable posture, "Yes, we kicked this idea around quite a spell before Mr. Romanoff did his thing. And any of the other Joint Chiefs will verify it."

Reed ignored the second part of Braxon's question and said, "Right there; no, sorry, not you—the pretty one behind you." Reed pointed to a statuesque blonde in a bright blue dress.

"Thank you, sir. Judy Roughfir, of ABC. General, as you know, the White House has been reluctant—some of my colleagues would actually say stingy—in offering specifics on verification. Any comment?"

"Well, Judy, I don't want to tread on the president's prerogatives. However, I can tell you that major intelligence services throughout this country have found no reason to believe that the Russians are doing anything wrong."

"Is it true that General Young has doubts?" Roughfir pressed.

"Oh, well. We have *some*," Reed said, smiling ruefully.

Roughfir was not so easily put off. "Are you saying that General Young's doubts are not serious?" she probed.

Reed sighed. "Well, let's just say that a general who is unwilling to extend his hand to an old enemy who wants to lay down his arms *is* violating one of the most sacrosanct of strategic principles: the best way to win is to convince your enemy that he shouldn't fight. I like to think that our years of 'peace through strength' have brought the Soviets to that point. Now we need to jump on it."

The reporters liked the answer.

"I've never seen anybody turn that school of sharks into goldfish before," Rosco remarked.

"You might say he's achieved a form of disarmament," Washington said under his breath, smelling political blood in the water. What the hell was Reed really playing at?

". . . so you're saying," a young reporter from the *Washington Times* was asking Reed, "that in fact the Russians are putting the past behind them? Are you saying the Russians haven't had the opportunity to do this before? What stopped them, sir?"

Several reporters turned hostile glances at the *Times* man.

"As I see it," Reed said generously, winking at the reporter, "the Soviets are showing considerable courage in recent steps—some taken even before their disarmament gesture. For instance, take their notable lack of belligerent tendencies against their neighbors recently; their introduction of not enough, but many American consumer products; their—"

"Excuse me," the reporter boldly inserted, "but wouldn't you consider maintenance of oppressive totalitarian regimes in the so-called Soviet Republics and satellite countries to be evidence of continued belligerence?"

Reed covered well, assuming a patronizing smile and shaking his head. "Well, that's not really fair. For one thing, many of the East European rulers have shown themselves more resistant to change than the Soviets themselves. They've elected several neo-Communist governments, yet continue to hold grudges at being brought back into the traditional Russian fold of nations rather than being wholesale admitted into NATO—which, I add, was always a hasty hope on their part. We can thank God that President Clinton back then had the sense to squash wholesale NATO expansion with his brilliant backdoor deal with the Russians."

"That's hardly the only—"

"As you *should* know," Reed rolled on, stabbing a finger at the *Times* reporter, "even our nation had to have time to solve its bigger problems. For instance, I'll remind you that it took America hundreds of years to free her slaves. In many ways that was a worse mark on our history than any besmirchments in the Russian experience."

Nobody looked at the reporter from the *Times* who appeared shocked and disgusted.

"Hell," Reed said to the room at large, "let's give the new Soviets a chance. Let's give peace a chance!"

A few reporters broke into applause; unprofessional behavior, but increasingly common in recent years.

"Who's the stud?" the President asked Rosco, motioning to the *Times* reporter.

"He's new."

"If he were less rigid in his views, we could use someone like that on our staff."

"Someone like that may not be for sale."

Washington shrugged. "Well, as I said, he's a bit rigid."

But as he said it, he wondered if he'd have thought the same way a few months earlier. He thought it was odd how, with the weight of the economy's sickness bearing on his shoulders, he found his views . . . well, evolving. Disarmament talk, back in January, would've seemed impossibly silly. Oh, sure, principles were important, but as Reagan used to say, "You can't let the perfect become the enemy of the good."

He lit a cigarette and watched Reed continue.

"Precisely when will this proposal be officially presented to the Russians, General?" the ever-aggressive Don Samuelson demanded.

"Precisely when the president himself says, Don. I'm quite sure you could suggest a date. I understand he listens intently to your every word."

"General Reed," CNN's Harry MacBride, one of the more respected "white-haired" reporters asked, "could you confirm or deny the talk that you plan to run against the president, a member of your own party, in the next election?"

The question blind-sided everyone.

So that's the blood I smelled, Washington thought, smiling grimly. Well, well, well.

"MacBride must be fishing," Rosco said skeptically.

"Never known him to troll, Tom."

Reed smiled benevolently and responded without answering: "Harry, I think I'll have to sidestep you on that one for now. Next question."

But of course the reporters were accepting no diversions. One after another, for a dozen questions in a row, they tried to get Reed to give something specific in answer to MacBride's bombshell. Reed kept smiling mysteriously, almost imperiously, and evaded direct answers—while skillfully giving the impression that he certainly could have said more if he'd wished.

After ten minutes of exchanges with the media, in whose eyes Reed had risen fifty percentage points, he waved, winked, and left the podium. The main event concluded, 150 reporters simultaneously snapped on their portable computer phones and began faxing, talking, or vid-feeding stories to their bureaus.

"JOINT CHIEFS CHAIR ANNOUNCES ARMS-TALKS PROPOSAL, HINTS AT PRESIDENTIAL RUN!" screamed the front-page headline of the *New York Times*.

"REED OLIVE-BRANCHES SOVIETS, WINGS FOR WHITE HOUSE!" belted the *Washington Post*.

"GENERAL REED SHOCKS PARTY WITH SHOT AT PRESIDENT: AP-PEASEMENT MOVE TOWARD RUSSIANS!" the *Washington Times* offered in outrage.

"PENTAGON TOP DOG HOWLS FOR COMMANDER-IN-CHIEF POST! WAGS TAIL AT RUSSIAN DISARMAMENT" barked *Rolling Stone*.

"JCS HEAD TAKES EARLY AIM AT PRESIDENCY; TRIES TO BROADEN ARMS-REDUCTION; REED NOTES ECONOMIC AWAKENING OF MOS-COW; WHITE HOUSE HAS NO COMMENT ON EARLY IN-PARTY CHAL-

LENGE," *The Wall Street Journal* said in its sedate and lengthy headline style. "GHOST OF ELVIS TELLS PENTAGON HEAD HE CAN BEAT WASHINGTON! UFO RECONNAISSANCE CONVINCED REED RUSSIANS REALLY DISARMING!" the *Enquirer-Star* announced in two-inch high red headlines in supermarket stands across the country.

"Well, it might as *well* have been Elvis and flying saucers," the First Lady said to her husband in disgust. "What did he say to you on the phone afterwards?"

"Ella couldn't even get his call through for fifteen minutes. Said the switchboard had never been so badly jammed. And that was my *private* line. I didn't know so many people even had access to the frackin' thing."

"He didn't try to use one of the military direct circuits?"

"No. He had some cock-and-bull story about how the lines were only for emergencies. Hell, he's right. I guess what's an emergency in politics to the likes of me, isn't to the Chairman of the Joint Chiefs."

Annette Washington scoffed and sat back in the cream-colored, deep-cushioned couch. She picked up and sipped a cola. "Sam, what did he *say?*"

"Eh? Oh, he apologized for going public with the disarmament idea, but claimed the press was already onto it and he didn't feel it served any purpose keeping it to himself any longer. Actually, when I think back, he handled it pretty well. Still galls me, but not as much."

"Fire the son of a bitch, Sam," his wife said intensely. "I sure would."

"Cool down, Net. I'm not ready to say Buck's bad for Defense. He told me I most likely would have approved his total arms talk idea eventually. And I probably would have. But now I've got to think of the political ramifications of firing the man. After all, he's a challenger. To fire him would look like I couldn't take the heat. Like I was playing dirty."

"Well, I'll have to honestly admit that I didn't think he had the political smarts to do it like he did. How's that for female intuition?"

Washington threw her a salute. "Well, dear, male intuition didn't fare any better."

"Still, there's something about all this that bothers me," she said, pushing her drink aside and crossing her arms as she looked at him. "What are you going to do about it?"

"Same as I've always done when challenged. When the time comes, I'll beat his pants off!"

"He'll be tough."

"He went light on me with the media, Net."

"It's mainly the D.C. media he hooked. The rest of the press may not bite so deep," she said, rising from the couch. She stretched, then suddenly stripped her dress off over her head and tossed it in his lap.

"Mr. President, I'm going to take a shower and I think I'm going to need some executive help."

Afterwards, as they dried off, she wanted to know, "Sam, how come you never asked me about that note concerning Sally? You didn't even mention it."

"What note?"

"The one I left right there on the mirror. You're not going to beat the pants off *any* challenger if you let your memory—" she started to chide, then stopped. "Damn! Look at this," she said, reaching behind the conch shell. With two fingers she delicately pulled the note out. It was wrinkled and moisture-stained, but readable. She handed it to Washington. "It's the funniest thing about Sally. I guess you know she's off the wire."

"Right. Buck said it was willpower."

"Willpower?" the First Lady snorted. "Yeah, sure, if it's the kind that comes in a capsule."

"You mean she's switched from the wire to drugs?"

"Uh-huh. She seemed so inexplicably light and happy again, when I visited her the other day. On a hunch, I asked her what she was taking and she said, almost shyly, 'Just a little magic pill that Buck gets me.'"

"He probably got a line on something new from one of the Pentagon medical staff."

"I don't know, Sam. Don't drug bottles usually have labels? I mean, aren't they legally required to list the actual drug?"

"I think so."

"When I used her bathroom, I snooped in her medicine cabinet. Naughty, I know; invasion of privacy and all that. But Sally's my friend, Sam. I found a bottle in there that had these little blue and green capsules—which is how she'd described them. Said Buck had told her to keep 'em quiet. Well, I took one."

"What!"

"I don't mean swallowed one. I slipped it into my purse. Sam, that bottle didn't have ingredients listed on it. In fact, there wasn't even a pharmacy label. Just a typed piece of paper curled up inside which instructed her to take two a day on an empty stomach, once in the morning and once at night."

"Peculiar. Wonder where Buck's getting them."

"*That*, pin-brain," Annette Washington said with good-natured sarcasm, thumping him on the chest with her index finger, "is precisely why I stole one of them. I thought maybe you could find somebody to analyze the ingredients."

"Maybe I can get Jeanne Allison to look into it. Her agency's not just electronic anymore. She's got a whole crew of chemists locked up in her basement."

"Good," she said, smiling and tossing her towel into a corner. She sauntered nude out the bathroom door. "Now I'm going to bed and if you know what's good for me, you'll come, too."

"The woman's appetite is shameless."

"Just the way you like it."

CHAPTER 24

THE LIFEBOAT

Ｈouse Speaker Baker Sunderleaf poured himself a small, neat whiskey from the Octagon side bar. He took it back to his place at the large, eight-sided table and looked around. Most of the Cabinet and other top Congressional and agency chiefs were there—one of several meeting rooms in the Black House.

This was the fourth such meeting of the month. Sunderleaf was getting tired of them. The subject was again the economy and what to do about its anemic condition.

The story was far from pretty. Unemployment had hit 13% that spring and was up another point now in mid-summer. Consumer prices were rising at an 18% annualized clip. Industrial production had plunged by 16% in the last half year alone, a drop unprecedented since the Great Depression. Europe was sinking, stridently demanding that America "get its house in order for the good of the West."

The administration had been in power a year-and-a-half and the economy had acted no more resilient than an old dishrag. In Sunderleaf's view, the president's advisors had acted about as innovative as a 'possum in headlights.'

"It's the damned plant-closing notification bill, I tell you, the Treasury Secretary argued. "That was the trip-wire. This whole mess got started right before we took over eighteen months ago. Who the hell can help lose money when they've got to keep employees they don't need for a whole friggin' *year*? It's a friggin' shame!"

"He's a reg'lar friggin' orator, ain't he?" Sunderleaf whispered to Jeanne Allison.

"Don't forget that coercive disability insurance," the Human Services Secretary said. "It started out innocently enough. Only a few billion a year, paid by the recipients themselves, no less. Now it's $100 billion a year and sucking us dry."

"Which is it? Sucked dry or soaked?" Sunderleaf drawled to the room at large. "Or was it a dry boondoggle that got soaked and became a weighty issue?"

Several people chuckled darkly.

"It's the deficit," the Federal Reserve Board chairman said in a deep drone. "One cannot discount the cumulative macroeconomic disequilibria. Decades of negative fiscal budgeting have resulted in a compounded set of consequences wherein bond and note distortions have risen to the forefront of rational expectations, as evidenced by high-interest weekly treasury auctions." He nodded to the treasury secretary to his right. "This concerted compendium of phenomenal data has, by a confluence of factors, shifted pre-tax, non-seasonally adjusted capital outlays overseas, verifiable by econometric expert-system database models and statistics—medianed-out, of course, for extraneous fluctuations over the past 1.6 fiscal years. This incipiently punctuated pattern has reappeared at the time when foreign investors are entertaining understandably computed doubts about U.S. productive viability via possibly disaffirmative demand inter-border-wise."

"Huh?" someone asked.

"Foreigners don't want to keep their money in our lousy economy and that's making it tougher for the treasury to raise money to pay its bills," Vice President Leininger said drily.

"Oh."

The Fed chairman nodded solemnly.

"Well, I think it's the tax burden," the Senate Finance Committee head said. "We've jostled tax rates for the middle class from a low of 28% back in the late 1980s up to 45% now—80% for so-called high-incomers, which include half the middle class anymore. What the hell did we expect? A boom?"

"*Well*," Sunderleaf said loudly, instantly getting the floor, "Out of all this extended discussion, two facts are as plain as a bullfrog on a lily pad. Lowerin' taxes is the only proven way to jostle an economy back on track. Worked like gangbusters after World War II for Erhard in Germany. Worked for Kennedy. Worked for Reagan, too. Doesn't take long, either. Just the prospect of doin' it shucks up confidence and pumps the blood 'round faster.

"The second fact is that it's politically impossible to trim almost any major program in order t' get the wiggle room to do the tax cuttin'. Used to be that only Social Security was sacred. Even tried a little tweakin' of that after Clinton. But it just slowed things, didn't reverse 'em. Now they're all growin' to where they're too big with too many dependents. Might as well try to steal a panther's teeth."

Sunderleaf sipped his bourbon, smacked his lips, adjusted his vest, and smiled at the gathering.

"Every Congressman on the Hill—Hell, everybody *here*! —got himself either elected or appointed by bein' beholden to one sacred cow or 'nother. Now there's a herd of 'em. You spook one and you start a stampede. And we know what administration'll get trampled and whose faces'll be smashed down in the cowpies."

Around the Octagon, people fidgeted nervously. The obvious bottom line was finally named.

"Let me put it another way," Sunderleaf continued. "We're in a lifeboat. It's overloaded and somebody has to jump. Who? Well, now, I'd say it'd better be someone who won't cause too much fuss. But to do any good, it's gotta be somebody a bit on the heavy side and strong enough to swim on his own for awhile. Then, maybe if we get the boat bailed out enough, we can let him crawl back in."

"Right," someone said. "It doesn't necessarily mean a sacrifice."

"Exactly," another voice added. "For the common good, we're just asking for temporary cooperation."

"Sure," someone else chimed in, "only long enough to put things right. Otherwise we'll all drown."

"After all, it's in the public *interest*," a final voice intoned, as though performing a benediction.

It was decision time.

One by one, heads turned toward the president.

The room was as silent as a cold desert night. He looked slowly from person to person.

"Bake is correct," the president said. "And I note that he said, 'it's politically impossible to trim *almost* any major program.' That means we have an option."

He looked at General Wharton "Buck" Reed.

Reed smiled.

CHAPTER 25

THE REACTION

P RESIDENT CLAIMS 'NEW DIRECTION,'" yelled the *New York Times*. "CHIEF EXEC EMBRACES REED'S DISARMAMENT PLAN," the *Washington Post* proclaimed. "HIGH TIME FOR LOW TIMES!" squawked *Newsweek*. "ONE MILLION SERVICEMEN TO BE RETIRED, CUTTING ARMED FORCES BY OVER TWO-THIRDS," noted *Businessweek*. "SCORES OF KILL.SYS TO BE SACRIFICED ON NEO.ECON ALTAR," *Net Times* asserted. "PREZ AXES WEAPONS CULT!" squealed *The Nation*. "WASHINGTON AND JCS AGREE ON BIG MILITARY CUT-BACK," declared *The Wall Street Journal*. "FEW DISSENT ON PLAN TO CUT DEFENSE & TAXES TO REVITALIZE ECONOMY. PRESIDENT TELLS NATION, 'I CAN DO BUSINESS WITH ROMANOFF.' EUROPE HOPES OF U.S. BUSINESS REVIVAL."

"WEAPONS PARING FOR ECON'S SPARING!" *Ebony* quipped.

"POLITICAL FOES, WASHINGTON AND REED, SEE EYE-TO-EYE," noted *The Los Angeles Times*, "BUT WHO'S CAREER IS HELPED MORE?"

"WASHINGTON BRAVELY, IF BELATEDLY, AGREES TO PRESIDENT ROMANOFF'S DISARMAMENT INITIATIVE," *Pravda* pronounced.

"U.S. TOP DOG BUGGERS BRASS'S BUDGET," sneered *Daily Inquiry of London*.

"CUTBACK! U.S. MILITARY TO SPORT G-STRINGS?" asked *The Tower of Paris,* sarcastically.

"MAJOR AEROSPACE PRODUCTION LINES TO WIND DOWN," *Aviation Week* announced. "ARMY, SPACOM TO ABSORB 'SUBSTANTIAL' SHARE OF DEFENSE CUTS."

"REED SAYS ARMY'LL BE ABLE TO 'LIVE WITH IT'," *Armed Forces Journal* reported. "THREE ARMY GENERALS, ONE DEFENSE UNDERSEC RESIGN IN PROTEST, BUT MOST TAKE 'WAIT AND SEE' POSTURE."

"SPACOM'S YOUNG DECLARES, 'IT'S A DISASTER'," reported *MilSci Aerospace*. "SAYS U.S. ENTERING 'ERA OF GREAT VULNERABILITY.' REED REJECTS CLAIM AS 'ALARMIST NONSENSE'."

CHAPTER 26

THE REDEFINITION

"If misery *really* loved company," Kevin Jones said, looking around the seedy bar, "this joint would be boomin'."

Moshe Trevis smiled grimly. The ancient air conditioning always worked in the summer and the drinks were cheap. As far as they knew, no one else from SpaCom ever came here. They could talk freely. The subject today was SpaCom's unexpected decision to shut down the Engels investigation.

"So, Moe, what iced Young's jets?"

"He'd still like to pry the Engels lid open, but the budget's gone. He doesn't even have the money now for missile defense upgrades."

"Serious situation."

"Yeah. The Sovs have new systems planned, Kev. Gotta counter 'em. Fortunately, we may have breathing room. Their launch fleet's totally occupied hoisting their MIPS network."

"MIPS?"

"Microwave power-satellites. The birds convert solar radiation to microwaves, beam it to earth, reconvert it to electricity. The system serves not only the new USSR, but their surrogates, including those in this hemisphere, like Sendero Peru and New Cuba. It's a cash cow, like their oil once was. Got about 800 of the units up, but only about a quarter functioning so far."

Kevin leaned forward, winked, and asked, "I'm hearin' rumors, Moe. Somethin' about the Spaceman almost buyin' the farm a while back. What gives? Don't give me any of this classified bullcrap. You know I'm a good boy."

"This stays here when we leave, okay?"

"Cross my heart, hope to die; stick kablooie in my fly."

"Spaceman's TAV may've been screwed with. Lost it's nose as it was about to descend into full atmosphere."

Kevin stopped his glass halfway to his mouth.

"Lost its—? What? As in *sabotaged*?"

Moshe shrugged. "That's the operational theory. It's weird. Not much was inferred from the brief space walk by Young himself before the rescue. Wasn't anything conclusive gleaned from rough pics taken by the rescue TAV's co-pilot. They left the bad TAV in orbit, intending to patch and retrieve it later. But about an hour after Young was back dirtside, the damaged TAV blew. It was just coming into good ground-eye view by then. Definitely not hit by a rocket, smart rock, or a beam. Maybe a fuel explosion, or an onboard bomb."

"But the nose—"

"Yeah, the creepy part. It's got all the engineers looking over their shoulders. Walkingfar says they're so scared their pocket-protectors are popping out."

"You got a theory, Moe?"

"Kev, it wasn't anything visible. Yet *no* known laser or particle weapon would leave that kind of result. I used one of SpaCom's artificial agent Internet searchers—the best—to check the scientific literature. Even if it was a deep black project, there'd at least be hints of it in the open sources."

Kevin looked at the wet spot left by his glass. His eyes brightened. "How 'bout a ringed-shaped charge? A strip of special plastique or magnesium or powdered titanium? Maybe planted durin' maintenance, say, 'round the nose, but inside the skin?"

Trevis waved away the suggestion. "Been considered. It would've been too time-consuming and the result too ragged. The available ground-eyes didn't have a good angle on it in real-time, so they videoed the cut only by a fairly gross grained, synthetic aperture radar. It was cloudy over TAV's flight path at that point, so no good motion optics caught the nose job in action. Had we followed old Piotrowski's advice back in the late eighties and put up a high-orbit, continuous-function, all-spectrum sensor network, we might have seen it happen. A budget-victim of another age."

"Comin' home to roost."

"Perhaps. My intuition tells me this was a test. By someone unknown, using something no one's heard of. Kev, the cut was so *clean*. It was like God himself had used a straight razor on it."

Kevin gulped his drink. "Oops!" he said in a low voice, nodding toward the door. "How'd *Walkingfar* end up in here?"

Trevis replied, "He is. That's what matters."

"Can you white girls still walk?" Walkingfar asked as he stopped before their table, eyeing the whiskey.

"Chief, if I've ever heard the call of wild duty, this is it," Kevin drawled.

"Bingo, Bonzo. Let's move, ladies. I'm driving. My car's outside. Leave yours. And perk up. Seems Engels didn't die after all."

After a moment, the Chief added, "If you girls grin any wider than that, I'm gonna have to get a sex-change operation to be appreciative."

On the way back to High Eye, he briefed them.

"A Mexican citizen who travels regularly to this country—we'll call him Valdez—has contacted us, concerned about an unusual business deal he'd made with a Russian named Filatov. Filatov is a known Soviet drug-supplier."

"Why come to us and not the FBI?"

"You're way ahead of me, Mr. Trevis. Seems Valdez is a bigger fan of America than of the FBI. In his business, I can understand it. He plans to move here and live off drug bucks. Seeing how SpaCom is so all-American that it turns your balls black-and-blue—our official colors—he comes to us. Walks right in the front door at the Springs. Demands to see Seen-yor Spaceman himself. We're rewarding him by ignoring how he came by his wealth. That was the requested price, and a small one, because it wasn't drugs that Filatov gave him. It was a virus, ladies."

Trevis and Kevin exchanged looks.

"And no ordinary bug," Walkingfar continued. "As we'll show you, it knocks off our labs' guinea pigs exactly like it did those Rooskie icemen down at Engels."

"So where do we come in?" Kevin eventually asked back at High Eye. He, Moshe, and the Chief had left the lab and a first-hand viewing of the grisly effects of the virus.

"Sobering?" Walkingfar asked, watching the scowling expressions of his two charges. "Oddly, you two come in exactly where you were jerked out. Filatov let slip to Valdez that the bug—which Filatov apparently didn't know was one, although he knew it was *something* dangerous—had come through to Mexico by way of northern Iran. Filatov was to pick up another there in a couple weeks from now. So we want you guys to find out where in the great Soviet Mommyland this crawly originated."

"I don't get it," Kevin said, trying to shake the alcohol fuzz from his brain. "If you intercepted the shipment here, wouldn't the Sovs' operation already be blown?"

Walkingfar rolled his eyes heavenward. "Forgive him, Great Bleached Dad, for he knows not what he mutters. Mr. Jones, we only *delayed* the Soviet shipment. We borrowed enough of the virus to culture it. We irradiated the rest to kill it. We repacked the now-dead virus and had Valdez complete the delivery. It's harmless now, but they won't know that. Got it?"

"Who's they?" Kevin asked. "I mean, I know they're Russians, but—"

"Spetsnaz," Trevis spat.

"Right. Combination commandos and undercover agents—"

"Trained for assassination, sabotage, mass killings," Kevin interrupted. "I'm not completely under the table, guys."

"Good for you, tub-boy. Tell him Moe', jus' to make sho'."

"Spetsnaz members are often long-time citizens of a target nation. They are frequently immigrant-plants, indistinguishable from the regular immigration population. For instance, to this day, the Spetsnaz have agents in every NATO nation. The agents' job in case of war is, among other things, to kill American and other top-grade fighter pilots in their homes, before they can reach their planes. No pilots, no air defenses. But the Spetsnaz go after anything they are told. The program's cruised straight through from the old Sovs through the Russian Republic right into the new Sovs' days."

"Persistent pests," Kevin said.

"Indeed. In this case," Walkingfar went on, "their job would be to disperse the virus at key times and locations. We've neutralized the only shipment so far. At least we're pretty sure it's the only one. We have classified reasons for thinking so. Anyway, now we need a preemptive strike to stop the bug where it's made and stored so no more of it reaches us or anyone else the Sovs decide they don't like to see healthy. Your job will end when and if you pinpoint the strike target. Uncle Sam's flying spirits will take it from there."

"Jesus Crisco!" Kevin exclaimed after a few heartbeats to absorb what he'd heard. "You're going to strike *inside* the frackin' USSR? What happened to stavin' off World War III?"

"You don't get it, Mr. Jones," the Chief said somberly. "We're in it. But so far only a few of us at SpaCom know it. Not even the president is aware of the situation yet, although he'll have to be briefed and give his approval soon. He doesn't put much stock in the Engels stuff. When he hears this, I expect that'll change. Welcome to Soviet Relations 101, Mr. Jones."

CHAPTER 27

THE EXIT

W e are at 35,000 feet and descending," the Aeroflot pilot announced in heavily-accented American English, the standard international airline language. "Weather is clear in Tehran and we should be landing in an hour or two."

"Isn't that rather vague?" Madeis asked Hans, seated next to him.

"Not at all. These are Soviet pilots."

"I can't believe it was so easy," Madeis said.

"Why not? I always take assistants with me to these conferences. And who better to accompany me than an experienced clerk and a translator, right dear?" he asked, reaching across Madeis and patting Tanya Yublenka on the knee.

Tanya looked pale, but managed a slight smile. She thought that it should have exhilarated her, but she felt exhausted from the effects of learning that she'd become employed again. Another backwards reaction. Her assistance to Hans would not end with this trip, of course. She would be his personal secretary upon return to the USSR for as long as he needed her.

The trip itself saddened her. At least a little. She felt like a prisoner let out for a walk in the sun. One was watched constantly when working abroad for the new Soviet Union. Defections were bad for the state's image. The other thing was that she'd always shared such trips with Gregor and—

Never mind! she thought. There was no good to be had pursuing that tendril of memory. She told herself to save it. To save it, cherish it—for when he was found. Or for the future, when things were sorted out, somehow.

"A graceful flight. A state of grace is always better than being in the state of Russia, eh?" Hans joked to his son.

Madeis gave him a warning look, indicating with his eyes the man reading the newspaper across the aisle. The man was one of Hans's two "shadows." The other sat near the rear door; they always watched the doors. "It was so unexpected, her being assigned to work again," he said to his father.

"I asked for her. I'd no intention of watching her slowly starve while you fiddled around trying to help her out in your overworked personnel department on your duck-food salary."

Good, Father, Madeis thought, cover for my part in the matter, in case the shadow has cat's ears.

"As to you, Madeis, well, I requested you, too. Oh, don't look so surprised. I explained to them that I'd never been on vacation with my son and it was time he saw more of the scientific world. I might have hinted that you had hidden scientific inclinations."

"That'll be the day Romanoff takes a torch to Lenin's waxed likeness in the Kremlin."

"Who knows what this trip might inspire, eh?" Hans winked at his son.

Madeis caught a reddening around his father's eyes and suddenly thought, he *knows*. Damn it, he knows I don't intend to return!

Hans turned his face toward the window.

They'd passed over the Aral Sea and would soon cross west of Ashkhabad, then angle along and over the Elburz Range and down to the Plateau of Iran into Tehran, the capital.

Let his father believe he'd set up things for his son and Tanya. Madeis knew the real story. He'd argued to Karpov that getting Tanya this job and taking her to Iran was another way of "softening" her, a romantic vacation. Boris, who had been preoccupied with other work, had approved with barely a comment.

His escape plan had the virtue of simplicity. The two of them could play the role of tourists when there was nothing to do at his father's conferences. The shadows only cared about Hans. He was resolved to seize the opportunities as they arose and create them if they didn't. He knew it would be his only chance.

CHAPTER 28

THE EMBASSY

The new British Embassy in Tehran was, to Trevis's way of looking at things, a magnificent improvement over the old one. After Iran began to reopen to the West in the late '90s, the Brits had taken extensive precautions to protect their reclaimed abode from the types of truck bombs which had taken out American and French embassies in the Mideast and in Bosnia. However, they'd not seriously considered the threat of an ultralight plane loaded with plastique crashing into their roof. That unfortunate oversight eventually forced them to rebuild from scratch.

The new building was beautiful, Trevis decided. It was a fountain-studded series of rectangular concrete and glass fractals descending from twin central structures.

The old 1951 Dodge taxi screeched to a halt next to the building.

Kevin was marveling at the mint condition of the cab. "I can't believe how asphalt-hoppin' *cherry* this babe is!" he said. "Look at the radio! It's gotta be the original, real wood speaker grill and—"

"Polish and shine, every day," the cabbie said, grinning back at Kevin. Kevin had been surprised to learn how many people in the city of ten million spoke decent English. They spoke several other Western languages in addition to native tongues—the dominant Persian language, Farsi, but also Kurdish and Azerbaijani.

"My grandfather bought it after the Big Two, you know," the cabbie said. "When Americans were the good guys."

"Great car," Kevin said, ignoring the politics.

"Then my grandfather gave it to my father. Now it's mine. I make money with it," he said, patting what, to Kevin's amazement, appeared to be genuine leather upholstery, though it didn't look like cowhide.

Following his eyes, the cabbie said, "Hey! This is the right stuff, huh? Used to be the family camel. But he got sick one day. Big family tragedy."

"I'll bet."

"But what the hell's bells, huh?" The young Iranian's teeth were even brighter than Moe's.

"Don't ever sell this vehicle, son. It's fantastic," Kevin said, handing over a fifty dollar bill.

"Thanks, Yanks! No Satan in America anymore!"

"We're late," Trevis said curtly. He never had understood the U.S. male's fascination with cars; especially ones so old and heavy that they could probably do double-duty as tanks.

"Hey, buddy, *you're* the one that's supposed to know this town. How come you didn't speak up his third time 'round?" Kevin asked.

"It's changed," Moshe said. "I expected to come in on Makhsus Road, not south skirting the Imperial Palace along Mehrabad. Anyway, that was after I figured out we'd arrived the other side of town at Tappeh Field. I don't know what they're doing; remodeling, I imagine. Foreign investment again, you know. They obviously had to divert our plane. At least you got to see the Shah Mosque, the University of Tehran, and the famous Jalaliyeh race track. What more do you want on your first day?"

Kevin didn't buy it. Moe always knew *exactly* where he was. He'd probably had some reason of his own for wanting to be late. That meant he was telling the truth about landing at Tappeh Field instead of Mehrabad Airport—or, the Gate of God, as it was now officially called.

Kevin grumbled. "Blocks for balls it's cold!" he said, zipping his parka as they approached the entrance. "I thought Iran was hot all the time."

"No, not always. Most of it sits on a high plateau. In many ways, not that different than your Denver. Almost the same latitude, believe it or not."

The British guards efficiently triple-checked their ID at two entrances—an outer and an inner—before they were ushered through a maze of hallways. They eventually arrived in a spacious room with a tinted, heat-reflecting window facing a large interior garden.

"Who are these people we're meeting?" Kevin inquired after ten minutes alone.

"What?" the Mossad man asked, looking back from the window where he'd been studying the garden's pool, which was filled with golden Koi and blooming purple water hyacinth.

As mission point man, Trevis had become more and more preoccupied in recent weeks. Kevin so far had felt about as useful as a bruised thumb on Moe's left hand; and Moe was right-handed. When he'd expressed his frustration, Trevis had simply said, "Walkingfar is never wrong. He knows you'll be valuable when the moment arrives." The answer hadn't satisfied Kevin. What moment? How would he know? And in order to do *what*?

"I don't know exactly who the Brits have for us," Trevis answered. "They didn't have much to do with it. Streeters."

"Huh?"

"They walked in off the street. Luck."

"Oh."

"They may be a break for Engels. That's why we're here."

"Defectors from Russia?" Kevin asked, fishing again. Moe was the head that carried their secrets. "Seems like guys are strollin' right up to us these days. First Valdez, now these."

"Does it, indeed?" a robust voice asked from the doorway.

A short, stubby man with a huge red moustache, beady blue eyes, and shiny bald head marched in, hand extended. "Brian Monmouth, Gentlemen. Bee-Eye."

"British Intell—" Moshe started to tell Kevin.

"Right. Figured," Kevin said, shaking hands first. "Glad to meet you, sir. Kevin Jones with State."

"And of course you're the famous Moshe Trevis," Monmouth said, immediately turning to the Israeli. "Coffee? Tea? No? Fine. Shall we, then?"

He gestured to two brass-and-vinyl chairs in front of his desk. Kevin hadn't sat in them because he'd thought they might, just possibly, be modern art sculptures.

Trevis whispered in Kevin's ear, "He's just a low-level message-carrier. We both outrank him, so don't call him 'sir.' We have total authority over this case. He doesn't like it."

"What's that? What's that?" Monmouth asked, cocking an ear.

"You have charges for us, I believe," Moshe said, ignoring the inquiry.

"Yes, well. Er, now, see here. Your Mr. Walkingfar—impressive, that Blackfoot fellow, eh? Yes, he has briefed me a bit. By scrambled vid line, that is. Nasty business, this Soviet thing, right? Precisely so, gentlemen. In this together and all that, aren't we?"

Getting no response to his fishing questions, he depressed an intercom switch and said grumpily, "Sally, be a good girl and snatch the three of them up here straight away."

Smiling and steepling his hands on his desk blotter, he lowered his voice to a confidential level, "Seems to be a bit of genuine buggery we've got here, eh? How does it look?"

"Don't worry, we'll *cork* this bottle," Kevin said.

"In the *Soviet Union?*" Monmouth asked, laughing skeptically. "Now that, I daresay, would nearly require an act of war, wouldn't it, my macho Mr. Jones?"

"Damn it, they started it!" Kevin retorted, then caught Moshe's slight shake of the head.

"Well, really, it's a chicken and egg type of thing, isn't it?" the Brit retorted. "But what can one do? Wipe out mankind to prove you Americans right? No profit in that!" He chuckled, shaking his head patronizingly.

"Mr. Monmouth," Moshe said quietly, "we're not here to discuss the merits or misconceptions of British foreign policy as seen through the eyes of a minor civil servant. You may've seen the sun long ago set on *your* empire. That doesn't mean we're going to let it set for everyone else."

"Well, that's quite uncivilized!"

At that moment the door opened and two people walked in. One was a young, tall blond man; the other, a slender dark-haired woman. The woman instantly reminded Kevin of Carmen Sevens, the Spaceman's secretary, whom Kevin had been dating almost since his first days at SpaCom.

"Gentlemen," Monmouth said stiffly, "these people are asking for asylum in the United States. But as we're the nearest thing to a Yank embassy here in Tehran, naturally we are the logical choice. I hope you appreciate it. May I introduce Madeis Plechl and Tanya Yublenka?"

CHAPTER 29

THE DEBRIEF

"Why are there no windows?" Tanya asked Kevin, who sat beside her in the 10-passenger SpaCom TAV-7. Trevis was busy several rows back, already beginning the debriefing of Madeis.

Kevin said, "There are." He reached across her and touched a button labeled, "Vid." What looked like bare wall in the place where a window would have been on a normal airliner, snapped to life as a 31-inch, high-resolution, flat monitor. It revealed a purple-black sky, pinpricked with white stars, and the round, silvery-blue sweep of the planet nearly a hundred miles below. Tanya gasped.

"See? *'Lectric* windows! Hell, got a couple in my house, back in the states," he lied. "They're the thing lately."

"But such expense. Glass is surely cheaper."

"Yeah, and at hypersonic speeds, it melts like a slug in salt. Which breaks planes. Which are damned near as 'xpensive as Rooster eggs."

"Roosters do not lay—Oh." She smiled.

Kevin winked. "Gotcha."

Tanya had instantly liked the big American. She sighed. Too much was happening. First the unexpected job. Then a flight out of Russia to Iran. Then Madeis's forcefully steering her without explanation into the British Embassy. Yet he hadn't trusted the British, insisting on seeing the Americans. When they finally came, actually one American and an Israeli, they had flown her and Madeis directly off the Embassy roof via the present plane—to where, she didn't know.

How had they even been able to do so? Weren't the Americans and the Iranians enemies?

When would they return to Russia? What about Hans and her duties to him? She was most puzzled about Madeis. Why would the Americans be so intensely interested in a mere *clerk*?

She looked at Kevin Jones and asked, "And what is he to you?" She gestured with her thumb toward Madeis.

"To me? How would I know? I'm the hired help."

"Please," she asked, placing her hand on his arm, her eyes pleading.

"Okay, here's the deal. Your boyfriend says he knows somethin' real high on the ol' intelligence totem pole. Can't tell you more 'til my buddy there gets—"

Trevis tapped Kevin lightly on the shoulder. Passing him, he wagged a finger to follow.

"Sorry, gotta go," Kevin said, giving Tanya a thumbs-up sign. He patted her cheek. "You keep that pretty chin up, hear?"

As he drew Kevin to the front of the plane out of Tanya's earshot, Trevis said, "This is a disaster. Or a gift."

"Don't get poetic, Moe. I'm too stupid."

Trevis unfolded a paper. "This is a part of it. He had several hidden inside his boots. Photocopies stolen from KGB files in Krevesk."

"Hey, this is an industrial map of one of the cities that we were sup—"

"Exactly. I'll save you further trouble with your rusty Russian. It says not one, but *six* towns produce the virus simultaneously!"

"Okay, but why a disaster?"

"Don't you see? It raises the stakes. It's much harder to deal with six sites. Many times more complicated. What if we can't get them all?"

"Take the optimistic view, Moe. If we don't try, they win for sure. Besides, the Chief says the war's already started. It just ain't on TV yet."

CHAPTER 30

THE SPAT

Well, what do you think?" the president asked his wife as she brought them a tray of snacks. On evenings when he did not work late—and there were fewer of them in recent months—it was their habit to watch the late news together. They were early. The TV was on, muted.

"Sweetheart, I've known you intimately for decades, but I'm still not a mind-reader," Annette Washington answered.

"The whole thing, I guess. The economy, the arms control deal. How they work in tandem, as seen by my one-woman simulation of the great American public."

"So that's it," she said, snapping her fingers, "I knew there was a reason why you brought me with you all these years. It never was my beautiful body or wanton ways. Well, I think most people are behind you."

"With hatchets and pitchforks?" he asked, picking up a sandwich.

"Not exactly. I admit I didn't think the tax cuts would have such a powerful effect. Who needs Christmas?"

Washington glanced at the TV. A Pixar animated apple was doing a dance dressed as Santa. 'Twas the season.

"Who's it helped more, though; me, or Buck?"

"Buck may've been first to push the idea of cutting arms in order to pump money into the economy. But it's not a new idea. It's the ones who *do* the thing who get remembered."

"Well, I—oops. What's this?"

Annette turned her eyes to the TV and punched on the sound. The picture was filled with roaring flames. The camera panned back to pick up a correspondent in the foreground.

"I'm standing over a half-mile away from what's being called the greatest refinery disaster in American history. Approximately two hours ago, this huge gas storage yard erupted in a series of explosions which some residents feared was a nuclear attack. That's how ferocious the blasts were.

"Officials estimate that over a hundred tanks of various flammable liquids have gone up in this field of about five times that. Despite repeated media inquiries, neither fire officers nor the owners of the facility will hazard a guess as to what touched off the explosions. Police estimate that over three-quarters of them occurred within a minute of each other, maybe faster."

The president glanced at his wife and shook his head, putting down his sandwich. The news was a great appetite suppressant.

"An interesting side-note," the announcer said. "This particular refinery is one of only two U.S. sources for the large quantities of hydrogen slurry fuels used to power the U.S. military's hypersonic fighter fleet, as well as the growing inventory of hypersonic business planes. Space Command officials in Colorado tell us that while the country has enough in local storage to last for a few weeks, supply problems will almost certainly develop from this unexplained disaster . . ."

"Well, thank God," Washington said, muting the sound.

"For what?"

"That things have cooled off between ourselves and the Sovs. I'd hate to have to jump into a war with the Ruskies short of a crucial supply like that. Those hydrogen-powered TAVs are what would let us get the high ground. In peacetime this is no disaster strategically."

"I don't know—"

"Take it easy," he said, patting her hand. "In a week, hell, this blowup will have blown over, a dead issue. I guarantee. Besides, with nigh on eighty percent of our and the Russians' long-range missile forces topping off the trash cans by this weekend, I'm sure that's where our good pals in the press will be directing their attention."

Washington grabbed another two sandwich halves, stacked one on the other, and took a huge bite.

"Sam, that's cheating!"

Her husband had gained twenty pounds in the months since he'd kept his promise to quit smoking.

He nodded and she began to say something, but his attention was inward.

Everything was working out fine, he thought. With the final few score of the ICBMs to be sawed apart in weeks, the U.S. and Soviets appeared to be *en route* toward true disarmament. The president's initial perplexity over their sudden offer had long ago vanished. If he'd had any doubts about either the missiles or the military cutback in the U.S., they'd been drowned in the favorable reports on the economy. America was truly "back on track," doing what it did best—producing and creating work and opportunity for its people. Even the Soviet economy was doing a little better. They'd started another push to encourage trade with the West. True, it wasn't much yet, and many previous such efforts had gone bust, but if the momentum kept rising—

"That, at least, is something Buck can't claim, right?" Annette was asking.

"What's that? Sorry, I was daydreaming."

She glared at him.

"Lately, it seems to happen a lot when I'm around."

What's eating her? he thought.

"I was talking about your tying the missile agreement to freer emigration from the USSR," she said.

Washington shook his head and answered, "Buck battled that one tooth-and-nail. I think he was surprised that the Sovs put up so little resistance when I asked Romanoff for it."

"How well are they doing?"

"The Sovs?"

"Jeez, isn't that who we're *talking* about?"

Washington ignored the retort. "Uh, not bad. They've let twenty thousand people out so far, mostly Jews and dissidents. They were the ones we were most concerned about. But their foreign minister says it'll go up, if the demand is there."

"Oh, for Pete's sake, Sam! If the demand is there?" Annette sneered. "Typically Soviet. That's exactly the kind of two-faced attitude that makes me leery!"

Washington groaned, flipping off the TV. In recent weeks he'd become steadily more annoyed at Annette's wariness.

"Net," he said, "I know you don't trust the Sovs. God knows, I've heard it enough recently. But isn't there a positive angle on this for you? Nothing at all?"

"Nothing I can't look at in black light," she snapped.

She crossed her arms and leaned away from him.

"Meaning?" he asked.

"Meaning, Sam Washington, that I really don't think you *want* to hear it. Not from me, anyway."

She hated it when he sighed in exasperation, but he did it anyway, before he could stop himself. She studied his face a moment, took a deep breath, and said, "Okay. I'll give it another shot. I think it's great that the economy's picking up, okay? But what's the price? If the Sovs are so all-fired eager for peace and a better life, how come they haven't relinquished state ownership to the private sector industries they re-nationalized back in the late nineties? I cruised the Internet news archives for awhile last night, and guess what, Sam? The Sovs have broken almost every single privatization promise they made to you and two previous presidents. How's that for trust but verify?"

"But they have loosened *some*. For instance, they've—"

"Piddly stuff. Damn it, Sam! A year ago, you would have agreed with me that it's a smear on their windshield. Nothing to equal even a tenth of what Lenin did under his New Economy Policy back in the twenties. And I remind you that was reversed, too."

"By Stalin, not by Lenin."

"Certainly. And maybe not by Romanoff, but what about his successors? Lately you're always talking economics, so let me ask it in those terms. Where's the gain to him? I don't see it. It smells wrong. If he's not shifting his military's money into the civilian economy, Sam, *where is it going*? What does this get Romanoff strategically?"

"Well," Washington said, forcing a hollow chuckle as his wife shot him mental daggers, "maybe he figures that if we build our economy up enough, we'll bail out his, too."

"I give up!" she said, slumping down in her chair.

"Hey, you asked for a motive, didn't you?"

Annette wearily rubbed her eyes. "Sam," she said, "it bothers me that all you have in answer to my serious question is a flip theory like that. It bothers me even more that the *U. S. President*, responsible for the lives and freedom of three-hundred million people in this nation alone, is so worried about the next election that he's forgetting his military history. And another thing," she said, suddenly standing and wagging her finger at him, "I don't like the way you've been giving Glenn Young the run-around!"

"Huh? Where'd that come from?"

"He called me. He wouldn't say what he wanted, but he's been trying to get an audience with His Highness of Oval for weeks and can't get past the frackin' secretary!"

"That's enough!" Washington boomed, standing and clenching his fists, towering over her.

But she stood her ground and shouted back, "Sam, you'd better be right about all this! And, and," she began to cry, "and whatever happened to my respected insight into the American public? What happened to your really listening to me and seriously—oh, screw you!"

"Net," Washington started to plead, reaching for her. She slapped his hand away and bolted. In a few seconds, Washington heard the door slam to her seldom used private bedroom.

He paced the living room for a few minutes, then decided that this was one of those times when Annette was simply way off base. The reason he'd blocked out Young was because he kept needling him on that moldy Engels thing. He kept wasting everyone's time by dragging around a penguin corpse, demanding more autopsies. Washington had finally told Ella Paxson to politely inform Young to take it through channels. In practice, that meant through Buck, feud or no feud. But imagine the gall of Young to call and complain to the president's *wife*!

Anyway, Buck had assured Washington that he'd seen the latest reports of SpaCom's High Eye about Engels and there was nothing to them but thin speculation and fat ruminating. Washington remembered that Ella had said that Brighton, too, had rather stridently demanded still another meeting on Engels. Washington had refused, telling Ella to hang up on Bill when he'd tried several times, against orders, to push it. Well, if the CIA chief would learn to get to the point and keep his priorities in order, this lesson wouldn't have been necessary.

No, waiting awhile wouldn't hurt either Bill or Glenn. Let the puppies back in too soon after they'd diddled on the floor and they won't get the point. It bothered him a bit, in the far back of his mind, that he'd used such a disrespectful analogy of the men, but not as much as the way Annette had become so critical in recent weeks. What had gotten into all these good people, anyway? Why were they so worried about nonessentials?

Aw, the hell with it, he thought. He was angry and tired.

He went to bed, tossing and turning for an hour. But thoughts of the rapidly recovering economy and his rising standing in the polls eventually soothed him to sleep.

CHAPTER 31

THE COYOTE

T hat's what I am," Ben Liddell muttered to himself, "a scruffy old coyote. Bone and gristle for meals."

A man at the bar glanced at him and edged away a seat. Liddell didn't notice.

Liddell was reporter, writer, editor, and publisher of a small but reputable national letter on U.S. defense and strategy. Most of his stories and analyses came from the open press. Others originated from a network of defense and aerospace contacts established over many years. This, however, was different.

For a week, he'd been hoofing among bars in a dozen tiny towns in Texas. They were all within a stone's throw of a "ghost" division of the U.S. government. It wasn't to be found on any payroll list or in any directory. No one knew its real name. At least no one was supposed to.

However, Liddell had learned what the insiders called it: Mech Morgue. In its depths, scores of technicians purportedly worked night and day. Their chief function was autopsy.

In answer to his phone calls to Colorado Springs, Space Command denied it had any facilities in the Apache Mountains between New Mexico and the Rio Grande.

Yet Liddell had struck up conversations with a half-dozen locals who had seen guards in black and blue uniforms preventing the unauthorized from wandering within close view of some kind of facility. From shards of overheard conversation, he suspected a few locals worked there, but none offered the tiniest bit of information. They had reminded Liddell of the folks he'd met years earlier in Tonopah, Nevada, where the F-117A Stealth fighter had been secretly deployed. Lips as tight as walnut shells.

He fingered the turquoise string tie with its garish red ends. The tipster had mailed it to him. It was a sign to a man he didn't know by name or sight. Sooner or later, if he cruised the drinking houses of the area, he had been told, someone would spot the odd tie and make contact.

Liddell hoped so. The drinks were expensive and you could only nurse so many without being thrown out or looking foolish. Each day by mid-afternoon, the alcohol gave him a headache—and a deeper hole in his always-shallow pocket.

He sighed, drained the last few drops from his glass, left a medium-sized tip, grimaced and got off the bar stool to leave.

"Excuse me," a small, pudgy, balding man in front of him said, "I couldn't help but notice your wonderful tie."

"Yeah," Liddell said slowly, "it's a killer."

"Could we, uh, go somewhere else?"

"Sure. It's up to you. Long as it's someplace with aspirin."

The man led Liddell about ten miles up a winding, dusty, back-hills road to a run-down house trailer. He nudged his new Chrysler between a row of mangled mesquite bushes and the back of the trailer. Liddell parked his rented Chevy behind the Chrysler and got out. The unseasonable heat, blowing in from Mexico, was stifling, despite the elevation. Liddell's shirt was sticking to his back and his socks felt like sponges.

"Okay to park here?" he asked.

"Yes, sorry about this. It's my brother's place," the man said. "He's, uh, working now."

"Sure," Liddell said, shrugging.

An old air-conditioner hummed efficiently inside a dim living room. The contrast of temperatures made Liddell shiver.

"Drinks?" his host asked.

"Water. And that aspirin, if you don't mind."

"Of course. I forgot."

Each man sat on low, brown fabric couches. The cushions were shredded on the edges and arms. The likely cause, a scrawny gray tabby cat, lay on a chair, flickering open a scarred eye now and then to watch Liddell.

"That's Sage. As in brush, not wisdom," the man said.

"Never underestimate the ugly," Liddell said. "Look at me."

Liddell was a big, rough-featured man, more of what you'd expect a bouncer in a raucous saloon to look like.

"Eh, heh-heh," the man chuckled, adjusting bifocals on a reddened nose bridge. "Our mutual contact said you publish a defense magazine?"

"Newsletter. Similar, but smaller, like a digest. Few thousand readers. It's a living."

The man gulped, as though trying to swallow a ball of cotton. "Gosh, this is hard to get out for some reason."

"You think something's going on that the public ought to know about," Liddell prompted. It was one of his standard lines.

"Er, no, not the public. Absolutely not!"

Oops, Liddell thought.

"Oh, dear, no!" the man emphasized. "I think *someone* ought to know, though, if you get my drift."

"Look," Liddell interrupted, kneading his aching forehead, "I've spent a lot of my own money to get here and find you. If you're not going to give anything, I might as well cut my losses now. I can't afford chicken-out games." He made a disgusted face and stood to go.

"No! Wait! Please."

Liddell sat down. That method usually worked.

"Okay, then," the man said. "Let's say I'll leave it to your discretion."

"You've probably got nothing to worry about. Life is risky. But I think the risks are minimal here." Another standard line.

The little man fidgeted.

Liddell pulled out a pad and pen. He also flipped on a tiny digital recorder hidden in his shirt pocket, remotely activated by the click of his pen. It could store over five gigabytes of voice data. Liddell had a good memory, but he believed in backup systems. Redundancy was a lifeblood of defense; any defense.

"I have to tell you," the man said, "that my opinion at the Mech Morgue is a dissenting one. The two others at my level are unwilling to believe what's going on. They are refusing to include my conclusions in the reports being forwarded to High Eye, directly to Walkingfar. You know who he is?"

Liddell nodded.

The little man reminded Liddell of a squirrel caught in the rain far from home. "I sound like a balloon-head, don't I? Somebody who's got a grudge, maybe. A whiner."

"You're nervous. Anybody probably would be, given the circumstances," Liddell said in a deep, reassuring voice.

"I wish the others felt as you." The man glanced at his watch, half rose, sat. "I can't stay here long. My brother will be back in two hours. I've developed a theory which covers the angles. That's part of my job, you see; like the fellows who analyze airline crashes, except on a broader scale."

"Okay," Liddell said, jotting notes.

"Well, I suppose I should back up and give you the broader picture. You see, for quite awhile now, I've been tri-chair of a team here investigating some superficially unrelated events. They include a bomber and tanker which were lost nearly two years ago. Also a weird incident in which a man lost a leg while driving down an Oregon freeway in the middle of the night. Then, there was a burst dam which took hundreds of lives."

"Out in Oregon?"

"Yes. And there was the case of a TAV forced into orbit and then blown up, almost killing General Young himself. More recently, there was a huge, unexplained refinery disaster. Additionally, we're looking at—"

"Hold on. Let me get this straight. Mech Morgue thinks all those events tie together? How in the world could that be?"

"Er, that's the wrong question. If I'm right, what ties them together is not 'in the world' at all."

CHAPTER 32

THE EVIDENCE

O h, Miss Allison, hello," Ella Paxson said. "The president is expecting you."
"Great," Jeanne Allison said. She motioned over her shoulder and Gen
eral Glenn Young strode around the corner.

Ella spoke sharply, "Sir, I'm afraid *you* can't—"

Young put one hand on her desk and leaned toward the small, graying secretary/confidante of the president. "Ella," he said," I sure as hell wouldn't be here without an urgent reason."

Ella had years of experience judging people and estimating when exceptions were warranted. She regarded Young for a few seconds, then let both visitors enter the Oval Office.

"I take it you've got steak for my barbecue, Glenn," Washington said, suppressing his surprise and throwing Jeanne Allison a you-better-know-what-you're-up-to scowl.

"I do, sir," Young said.

"Well, sit down, both. He's what you had to talk about?" Washington asked Allison, thumbing toward Young.

"No, I have my own meat, Sam."

Washington raised his eyebrows and turned back to Young.

"Mr. President, the Soviets found a biological warfare virus at Engels."

"Pardon me? How do you *find* something like—"

"In the ice, in a core sample. Very old. It got loose. Modern man is as vulnerable as a drunk co-ed in a frat house. The point is, the Sovs have gained control of the bug. They're planning to use this one on us, sir."

A chill touched Washington between his shoulder blades, like a spider running up his back.

"Glenn, I hope you've got a mighty strong nail to hold your picture to the wall. Spell out the essentials."

"We intercepted the virus. It came up through Mexico via a drug courier."

"You've *got* a sample of the bug?"

"Damned lucky it was, too. We analyzed it, kept a little, neutralized the rest, sent it on its way. The courier's contact split the supply. There were fifty small vials. He delivered them to an equivalent number of subsidiary contacts, all deepcover Sovs, we assume. Over half were unknown to the FBI's foreign-agent database. We've established that five of these people will release their portion of the virus—now harmless, of course—within weeks, on the first of February. We've an outline of what appears to be an authentic Soviet plan to aerosol the stuff in two stages. The live virus is easily spread by respiration—like a common cold. Sir, they're under the impression that they are going to carry off a first-strike epidemic."

The president's face went white. His heart sounded like a machine gun in his ears.

"Initial targets are relatively small and isolated," Young continued. "They are two West Coast towns: Coos Bay, Oregon, and Eureka, California. And three inland western cities, Spokane, Washington; Lubbock, Texas; Boulder, Colorado. A disgruntled Soviet KGB man defected to us with photocopied documents sealed in the lining of a boot. Cleverly done. We flew the guy and the documents directly back to the Springs."

The president had slid down in his seat, leaning back, seeming to retreat from the implications. Young glanced worriedly at Allison.

"Mr. President," she said urgently. "We have to deal with this. The Sovs have developed a vaccine against the bug. They've been inoculating for over a year. They've got all their important dacha-dwellers as well as two-thirds of the general population protected. Most everyone else in the USSR will be secure before VR-Day."

"VR?" Washington asked weakly.

"Virus-Release," Young said. "According to my genetics guys, it appears there's no way *we* can easily prepare a vaccine for this if the Sovs try to smuggle in another batch. They may well do that once they discover nothing's happening with the old one. Even if they suspect that we intercepted it, there are so many corridors for smuggling into this nation, that they would be assured of getting it in again. New Sov doctrine, like the old, forbids action unless their estimates of the correlation of forces is favorable. But they can be confident on this one. Look at how futile we proved ourselves in trying to plug the drug trafficking routes. Rest assured that the Sovs duly noted that failure."

"You're sure they've got time?" Allison asked Young.

"Affirmative. We *may* make a prototype vaccine before VR-Day, perhaps enough for our strategically valuable people, like you, Mr. President. But to test and mass produce a vaccine is another question. The bug is quirky. We've never seen anything like it. Even if we had a vaccine now, then going full speed, it'd still take us three months, more likely six or eight, to inoculate everybody. There are 300 million people in this country. Hell of a logistics problem."

Adrenaline pulling him out of his shock, Washington seethed, "Reed assured me this couldn't happen! Bastard! I'm getting him over here right now!" He reached toward his intercom.

"Uh, sir, I wouldn't," Jeanne Allison said. "Not until you've heard everything."

Washington reluctantly pulled his hand back.

"According to some of those photocopied documents," Allison said, "the Soviet plan is to first *demonstrate* the power of the virus against those five small towns Glenn mentioned. As soon as the media get hold of the horror stories, we expect President Romanoff to begin demanding concessions, probably to you, privately at first. He won't want to admit to the world that he was responsible. It would spoil his nice-guy image. And he'll probably let you save face. He's one smart Cossack."

"Concessions, hell!" Washington roared. "You're talking international blackmail. I don't get it. What's his point? We're already giving him everything he could want."

"Apparently not, sir," Young said. "We still have our freedom."

Washington's face twisted through several expressions. "You're not saying they still want the whole ball of wax?" he asked. "Not the old world-domination crap? Surely they know we wouldn't let them."

Allison and Young were quiet a moment, then Young pointed out, "Unless they believe they hold an untrumpable card, Mr. President. Look at it the way they might. By VR-Day, we'll have scrapped all but a few of our long-range missiles. It'd be hard to reliably know which of those remaining would make it through their version of an SDI. Despite what the arms control advocates say, it would be damned near impossible to know about any long-range nukes they've kept in secret, especially the road and rail mobile ones like upgraded SS-24s and -25s."

"But Buck said our eyes could verify—"

"Sir, we've never had eyes that can see deep underground. Additionally, our human intelligence is far from perfect. So if the Sovs really want to hide something, believe me, they can. The Chinese have probably been doing it for decades, too. No one has any idea how many ICBMs they've got. Saddam did it. Syria did it. Even Israel did it. There are deception precedents everywhere. The Sovs *could* do it, sir. Thank God we've got some SDI left, even if it needs updating."

"What you said earlier," Washington asked, "do they have an untrumpable card in this virus?"

"Maybe not, sir," Young answered carefully, "but it will take a massive effort by us to show them otherwise. First, you'd better listen to what Director Allison here has to say. I'm afraid it won't be easy for you to hear."

Washington gave a curt nod. You *will* see this through, he told himself. He turned clearer eyes to his National Secretary Council chief.

General Reed was jaunty when he walked toward the Oval Office an hour later. Things were going so *well*, he mused. It must be more good news.

"Come in, General," the president said, his face set with determination, and not much friendliness. "Sit down."

"Sam, what gives?" Reed asked, still standing.

"I said *sit*," Washington ordered. "Read this."

He roughly shoved a paper across his desk toward his old friend. Reed sat down slowly on the chair's edge, leaning to pull the paper forward. He read it, then jumped to his feet and yelled, "Resign! What is this horseshit, Sam?"

Washington shook his head sadly. "It's no use, Buck," he said. "I know about the pills."

Reed froze, started to protest, then sank back into the chair. He stared at a spot on the ceiling, his face unreadable.

"Why, Buck? Why didn't you come to me for help?"

Reed momentarily looked three sizes smaller inside his uniform, but he then became defiant. "Wouldn't've done any good, Sam! We don't have the stuff in this country. Only the Sovs have the pills. Nonaddictive; at worst, only mildly so. Erased Sal's desire for the wire after the first one. Gave her back to me, damn it! So I had a lot to be grateful to the Sovs about."

"Just how grateful were you, General?"

Reed tried good-buddy persuasion. "Nothing to worry about, Sam. Not to speak of. They didn't want much. None of our really important secrets. Just enough to get us to the bargaining table, really, and break the disarmament deadlock. For Christ's sake, man," he exclaimed, rising again and waving his hands, "what the hell do you think they've been burning, cutting up, and decommissioning—fire-crackers?"

"You are under orders to sit, General."

"I—you—well, yes, *sir*!" Reed finally answered, sprawling insolently back into his chair and giving a sloppy salute.

The president flipped on the intercom. "Send 'em in, Ella."

Reed looked alarmed. "Send who?"

Allison and Young entered, followed by four husky Marines who immediately positioned themselves on either side of Reed.

"What's this bulls—?" Reed began.

"General, I'm hereby relieving you of your command. Under charges to be duly named and detailed, I'm also ordering you arrested and held incommunicado in a military prison, the location of which you'll not be told."

"That's *illegal*!" Reed yelled, lunging forward out of the chair. Two Marines pushed him back down.

"Not under a presidential emergency order, it's not."

"Emer—" Reed started to ask, bolting to his feet.

The Marines instantly grabbed him, two to an arm this time, shoving him down.

"You think you can railroad *me*, Sam? You can't! I'm a presidential candidate!"

"This is under a national declaration which I've just signed," Washington continued, driving his voice implacably through Reed's protest. "As you know, under such terms, you can be held for the duration."

"Duration of what, damn it?" Reed demanded, shouting in his best debate bluffer's voice.

"Get him out of here," Washington said to the Marines.

As he was forced, kicking and struggling, Reed bellowed, "I have a right to know what's going on! I have rights!"

"You sold them to the Soviets," Washington said, as the Marines dragged Reed out the door.

Washington turned to Young and said briskly, "General Young, you are hereby elevated to the position of head of Joint Chiefs. As I see it, with Grieve McDouglas still out, in my administration's scheme of things that also makes you defacto defense secretary."

"Thank you, sir," Young said.

Washington smiled grimly. "You and your organization have earned it. You didn't nod off when I almost did. Now then, Ella is already informing the other chiefs about your promotion. Within the hour, we'll have a national security meeting. Jeanne, get together what you need."

Allison nodded and left.

"Now, General, it sounds like we're at war. You said you had a plan to deal with it. Let's hear it."

As Young pulled material out of his briefcase, the president thought to himself. Net, I'm so *damned* sorry. Your warning bells were right, sweetheart, and I wouldn't hear them. For all our sakes, I hope Paul Bunyan didn't wait too long to sharpen his axe.

CHAPTER 33

THE LIFT

P eter Donahue was an editor for the *Washington Times*. Evenings, after his stint of military rumor-chasing, he stopped in for supper at Washington National restaurant south of the Pentagon. He was biting into a cheeseburger when the public address system announced that all outgoing flights had been cancelled.

Fog, Donahue thought. Again.

He glanced out the window. Puzzlingly, the night was clear. As he watched, a plane took off. He shrugged. Must be squeezing a last liner out, he thought, before the fog rolls in. But as he ate over a period of twenty minutes, he watched a dozen planes land and ten more take off.

He frowned, paid his bill, and sauntered purposefully into the terminal turmoil. The place was aroar with angry passengers demanding to know why their flights were leaving without them. Donahue pulled out his press credentials and talked his way into the terminal supervisor's office. He and the supervisor, Joe Franklin, were old friends.

"What's going down, Joe?" Donahue asked.

"Wish I knew. Thought you might. Well, you won't believe it, Pete. We just got orders ferried in from the President of the U.S. himself to cancel all outgoing passenger flights for the next *two days*. Refueling everything that comes in and sending it straight east."

"East? East is ocean. What? *Overseas*?"

"Yep. London, Hamburg, Brussels, Madrid, Istanbul, you name it. Every damned airliner, every company. Never saw anything like it. You oughta call some of your people in the military."

But Donahue was already out the door heading for the Pentagon building.

It was two in the morning in Wiesbaden, Germany. At one of many U.S. Army barracks, a sergeant roughly flipped on the lights.

He yelled at the top of his lungs to dozens of sleeping troops, "Alright, you angel crotches, peel off those chastity sheets and gear up! Move, move, move, move, *move*, MOVE!"

Dozens of men came groggily awake, grumbling and complaining, tumbling out of their bunks and into their fatigues.

"No drill, babycheeks!" he growled. "Get your pimply little puke-butts in motion!"

Sergeant Jefferson had never before used such emphasis with his men. His nickname was "Teddy Bear."

"You've got three minutes to be good-to-go for march condition!" he bellowed.

"What's up, Sarge?" one man asked, pulling on boots.

"You're all headin' home at the boss's orders."

"What boss is that?" someone else asked.

"*The* boss!" Jackson yelled. "By declaration of national emergency. Orders of the commander-in-chief. Otherwise known to you memory-holes as *The President*. Get your asses in overdrive! I'm countin' a minute gone and you're lookin' late to me!"

Within a half hour at the many airports across Europe, people were amazed to see runways packed toe-to-heel with American civilian airliners. Every couple of minutes, troops by the dozens, the scores, the hundreds, were boarding and lifting into the night sky, heading west.

CHAPTER 34

THE WITHDRAWAL

T om Rosco was whistling lightly as he stepped into the Oval Office. The Oval was not the place all presidents had found conducive to work. But Sam Washington took care of most business there. Rosco understood; he, too, liked lots of "pacing room."

It was six in the morning and Washington was hard at work. He'd had a scant three hours sleep. A coffee decanter sat next to him and a freshly-poured cup steamed near his elbow. Rosco had no idea what the big man's mood might be, but didn't think he looked particularly haggard. Whatever had prompted the momentous decision announced the previous evening, Rosco respected its scope. While the real "press-sec," Donald Ray, recuperated from a car accident complicated by pneumonia, Rosco was taking his place. He hadn't been in on the full-bore discussions which had gone on all night in the Situation Room two evenings ago. Apparently, few people had. Rosco didn't resent it, but curiosity burned. The summary Ella had given him was unsatisfying, though he'd faithfully forwarded it to the world's media.

Washington's White House had no official chief of staff, but Ella Paxson served the role. Only the President and Ella knew that every important discussion in the Oval Office was piped directly into an earpiece she wore. People assumed it was a hearing aid; a misconception she encouraged. For important group discussions, where her eyes as well as her ears were required, Ella sat in as a minutes-taker— inconspicuous, listening, providing an objective "second-mind" for the president. It was an oddball system, but it worked.

Of course, Ella *had* been in on the all-night session. She'd briefed Rosco. While he had no proof, Rosco felt there were bucketfuls that he and the American public hadn't been told.

All this flew through his quick mind as he placed a stack of front-page photo-reductions on his boss's desk.

"Thanks, Tom." Washington said, glancing up. "Stick around a minute. Let me finish John Hancocking these bills and we'll see what America's finest analytical minds think of me today."

"Well, the Europeans are squawking their heads off," Rosco said.

Washington signed his name again and snorted.

"Hell, Tom, they squawk anytime we change any major policy. They complained when we hadn't yet put medium-range Pershing missiles over there. Then they didn't like it when we did. They wanted us to do 'our fair share' by keeping U.S. troops on the front lines against the East Bloc. Then they bitched because the troops had to do maneuvers somewhere and chewed up their farmers' fields. Then they said our deployments were 'provocative' to the Soviets and designed to make their countries the battleground of the next war in Europe—until the Soviets surprised everyone and took back most of Eastern Europe. Then the West Europeans demanded that we send *more* troops over. So let me guess. Now that we're pulling out, they feel like we're shirking our NATO commitment."

Rosco chuckled, "Darned near perfect. Take a look at *The New York Times* blast. It's on top. Typical."

The headline groused: "U.S. JERKS TROOPS FROM CONTINENT! NATO ALLIES YELL 'FOUL'!"

"I'll *bet* they yelled," Washington said, quickly paging through the other clippings, then disgustedly shoving them aside.

"Sir, mind if I say I don't exactly grasp your motivation?"

"It's pretty simple," Washington lied. "As I said to the country on TV last night, I'm fed up with the drug traffic. We're going to stop it. Once and for all. The only way to do it is by lining our borders with troops. We've sent so many boys back to private life in recent years, that we don't have enough at home to handle it. So we'll bring 'em back from overseas. The Europeans are going to have to defend themselves. My first worry is this country and I think the drug problem is a better use for our troops."

But Rosco had done some arithmetic. "Sir, we've got about eight thousand miles of border along the 48 states alone. If we station a hundred thousand men, that's only 12.5 men to the mile. And that doesn't cover Alaska at all."

"You didn't take your arithmetic far enough, Tom. It amounts to one man for every 420.2 feet of contiguous border. Think it's a good enough hollerin' distance in case of trouble?"

"Well, when you put it that way . . ."

Washington smiled, "Tom, the Joint Chiefs assure me it'll be enough. Don't worry. Things'll work out. Oh, almost forgot to ask. How're the broadcast boys taking it?"

"Mixed. The more conservative old-timers don't like it. They say we're givin' up forward-deployment advantages, although they like the idea of finally closing the drug lines. The more liberal, older and younger, think it's okay to leave Europe—a disarmament step, you know—but don't like your jumping on the drug traffickers. Same with most of the libertarians. Civil rights concerns. So nobody's completely happy. As usual."

The two men exchanged small talk for a couple minutes, and then Rosco departed.

The drug-battle cover had been General Young's idea. There was no hope of stopping a new virus shipment forever. The U.S. was a free-trade nation. There were thousands of bulk-cargo shipments daily. Sooner or later something would slip through with one of them. However, for now, Washington hoped, the Sovs would have had to stop and reconsider their tactics. That would take time, and time was all he wanted to buy.

In a move which some Europeans and not a few members of the press were calling "panicky"—but which polls showed delighted the average American with its audacity and determination— Washington had commandeered the entire U.S. thousand-plane domestic air fleet the day before. By using all available U.S. cargo planes, most overseas troops and their dependents were already almost all home. Except for skeleton base crews, the last would depart from West Germany and Britain by nightfall, U.S. Eastern time. Most of their equipment would follow within a few weeks. Some of it was "being considered" for donations to the Europeans in order to soothe their troubled brows.

The airlift was the largest and fastest ever witnessed in peacetime. But, he mused, as he poured another coffee, the airlift may be the easy part. Even after the troops arrived home, it would take a month to fully redeploy them on the U.S. border. Because of the danger of that drawn-out uncertainty; because of his deepseated fear of biological warfare; because of the churning, righteous anger and almost unendurable embarrassment which he felt at being betrayed by Romanoff; because of all that, he wanted action against the Soviet bug-bases as soon as feasible.

All he needed to get the action underway was a phone call from Young, who was setting up the mission details.

Even as he thought about it, the phone rang.

Over the intercom, Ella said, "I think this is it."

Washington took a deep breath, ran his hand over his face, picked up the receiver.

"Sir, we're set," Young said. "On your say-so."

Washington paused only a moment, considering the enormous consequences which he might bring upon the nation by his next few words—and the even greater consequences if he failed to say them.

"Good," he said. "Melt those mothers."

CHAPTER 35

THE HOSTAGE

Boris Karpov sat at his office desk looking at the two people he'd called in. They were a man and a woman; an inventor and a hostage. The two held hands. Their faces were drawn. The woman was slender and shapely with only slightly-graying blond hair. She looked ten or fifteen years younger than the man, although both were nearly the same age. The man was white-haired and ruddy-faced with a moustache and a paunch.

Karpov carefully poured three glasses of vodka. He stood and offered a glass to each of his guests.

Both refused.

"No?" he said. "Then let me."

He raised one of the glasses. "Mir!" he said.

"To *peace*, Boris?" the woman asked.

"Yes, Soviet-style!" Boris grinned. "The peace of control. You know something of that, no?"

The woman shivered; the man turned red.

"Imagine it," Karpov went on. "No more dog-eat-dog competition among, or from, the capitalists. No more fear of war hanging over us all. And, by my fat dead sister's ugly body, we three had a part. A major part in the launching of this grand, new Soviet future!"

"And no more liberty," said the woman. "No more innovation. No more new ideas. No more breezes across the Iron Curtain to stimulate our—"

"Nyet!" Boris countered, slamming his palm onto the desk top. "Not so!" Then, smiling: "They'll still come; just at a more reasonable pace. Even ancient China progressed; slowly, but it did. We will, too."

The man said, "If you consider a hundred years between inventions to be progress."

Boris chuckled. "Such a catastrophist. But I think the USSR has a running start, don't you? After all, the West has many times handed us the technological baton. Our engineering libraries alone can keep us going for a millennium. Besides, we'll have the whole world to help us—at our command!"

"Creative minds don't work well on command, Boris," the woman said. "Technical libraries are useless without the liberty to exchange and review the—"

Boris waved her to silence and sneered. "You're living refutations of that Western cow-dung. You two worked well on command. Gritting your steel-capped teeth all the way, but you did. You developed the vaccine," he said, holding the second glass up to the man, then draining it.

"And *you*," he said, holding the third glass toward the woman, "his wife, the mother of a usefully misguided little KGB agent, you helped keep him happy while he did. As you have all these years! To your great comfort. Mir."

He drained the last vodka, stretched his short, puffy body and stood.

"Now, then, old grudges aside," he said. "I'm again offering you the opportunity to leave Krevesk. You'll have your own dachas. You can live out your years in peace."

He motioned to the man, "You'll even have an institute named after you. Students of the future will revere the name of Hans Plechl."

Hans looked at his wife, Anna, the woman Boris Karpov had secretly brought back from Iran so many years ago, the woman whom Karpov had threatened to torture to death in front of Hans had he not done as he was told. She was also the woman whom Hans had once thought he lost, whom he hoped had escaped to the West. But she had instead shown up soon after he had been moved to Krevesk. Through all the years in Krevesk, he had been permitted to visit her only three times a week at designated hours at her luxurious apartment. She was the woman whom he had never stopped loving and for whose love he had deceived his own son, and probably civilization itself. She was the woman whom Boris Karpov had kept, until now, as his reluctant, but still-beautiful mistress. It had been a bargain, Soviet style.

She looked at her husband and nodded. "It will do us no good to stay here and die. This way, we'll have a few, uninterrupted years."

"If you believe this stub-headed bastard."

"Stop it," Anna cautioned, looking fearfully at Boris, knowing his extreme vindictiveness.

But Karpov just smiled. He knew the pain he had caused over the years. It was more than enough to savor for a lifetime.

~ *PART III* ~

DELUGE

CHAPTER 36

THE MOTHERMELT

Operation Mothermelt was the first deep combat mission of the B-2 bomber. A prototype "flying wing" vehicle, the original B-2 was unveiled in November 1988, right after the presidential election. When planned, hundreds of B-2s were postulated for construction. But in the build-down frenzy following the Cold War's "end," a miserly forty planes were actually built. Only twenty were still functional, although progressively upgraded.

Using SpaCom's satellite-relay laser communications system, USAF squadron commander Colonel J.D. Szalecki briefly checked the status of the other five B-2s in his mission. All were fine. All were bearing down on their targets, skimming the uneven ground at 100 feet. Each was cruising at just below the speed of sound. Despite their huge size, the planes' giant new Phase Echo noise suppressors made them eerily silent in their passage.

The aircraft had entered the Soviet Union hours earlier from separate points, unchallenged, timing their approaches so that all six jets would arrive simultaneously. Their targets: six Ural towns that manufactured and stored the deadly Engels virus.

Each bomber carried four of the U.S.'s most powerful weapon, the nine-megaton BP-53 nuclear bomb. The "P" stood for "penetrator." The warhead was contained in a wedge-shaped casing designed to burrow the bomb far into the earth before exploding. Actually, the correct term for the penetration was "splash." It could best be understood as a problem of fluid dynamics because at certain speeds, in resistance to specific projectiles, even the hardest surface behaved as a liquid.

A modification of the ordinary B-53 nuclear bomb, which, until Reagan, had not been deployed since the Vietnam War, each warhead was capable of completely collapsing ultra-hardened underground shelters. The BP-53 could even take out bunkers covered by hundreds of feet of reinforced concrete and steel.

Col. Szalecki wondered what had prompted this drastic mission. He'd been taught at war college that a well-conceived strategy avoided being forced into extreme solutions. Who had dropped the ball?

He didn't dwell further on the subject. Immediate events were accelerating.

He glanced at the data displays of several ultra fine liquid crystal HDTV terminals. He saw nothing out of place and gave his co-pilot a thumbs-up. It would be mere minutes now. Virtually flying itself with its GPS(Global Positioning Satellites)-enhanced, terrain-matching guidance system, the plane was gliding down a valley in the foothills of the Urals, heading for a place called Krevesk. Forests, rocky patches, small flashing streams, an occasional glimpse of animals and isolated structures, all highlighted by brilliantly moonlit snow, sped beneath the craft. To Szalecki's eyes, the snow glowed golden, an effect of the coating on the B-2's windshield.

"Coming up on minus two," the bombardier said into Szalecki's headset.

"Arm warheads," Szalecki ordered, exactly as they'd drilled in the simulators a dozen times the day before.

"Warheads armed."

Szalecki glanced at the red flasher which lit a corner of the fire control visual.

"Pilot confirms."

Although he was ready to die if necessary to complete his mission, Szalecki wanted to live. He wanted to get back to the States and turn on the news and see whether he'd started World War Three. In fact, he doubted he had.

In the briefings, he'd been assured that Soviet war doctrine did not regard a limited nuclear attack as reason enough to respond with total retaliation. He'd known about that doctrine for years, of course, and believed it. After all, it had come straight from material stolen from the Soviet high command itself.

The current mission was a specialized one, against unique targets. It was a pre-emptive strike much like the Israelis had used against the Iraqui nuclear reactor or the Libyan bio/chem weapons plants years ago. The only difference was the type of weapon. There were conventional types of penetrator warheads. But only BP-53s could *guarantee* that everything was "C3": compressed, crushed, and cooked.

Szalecki, like most servicemen, had felt a clammy horror at biological warfare. It employed a weapon that one couldn't see, couldn't hear, couldn't smell, couldn't easily stop once it got loose. Viruses didn't play *fair*, damn it! Szalecki welcomed the chance to melt this one before it could be deployed against his country, his buddies, his friends, his relatives.

"Thirty seconds," his co-pilot said. "Target will be in sight on top."

Szalecki confirmed the information, then said, "Gentlemen, let's step on some bugs." His voice was flat and calm, but he felt sweat trickling along his cheeks beneath the complicated, sensor-packed flight helmet.

"This can of Raid's for you, Romanoff!" he said aloud as he sent the plane soaring several thousand feet.

At the apex of the climb, he spotted the small city far ahead in the moonlight. He could even see the distinctive square target area, enhanced by his helmet's computer display. Deep beneath the town square—a small park called Inspiration, he'd been told—was the area's manufacturing and storage center for the virus.

"Starting the big stomp," he said.

He nosed the B-2 into its dive. The maneuver not only presented a knife-edge target to any would-be anti-aircraft missiles or radar-controlled guns that might, by a fluke, spot them. It also gave the BP-53s more kinetic energy for penetration.

"Warheads on auto-go."

"Five-thousand feet; four . . ."

Two lights flashed on the weapons load screen. The bombs were away.

"Infect *that*, you bastards!" his co-pilot said.

Szalecki grinned, kicking in the "Big Mach" hydrogen burners. The burners boosted the B-2 to roughly quintuple the speed of sound, something the plane had not orginally been designed for. But the jet had been modified, making low hypersonic bursts possible. Its copper/titanium/aluminide edges glowed despite their hydrogen slush refrigeration. The bomber flashed over and away, unconcernedly outrunning the minimal shock from the underground detonation.

Ten miles and ten seconds from what had been Krevesk, Szalecki brought his plane back below the speed of sound and began hugging terrain again along an erratic, pre-planned out flight path which would, for a few minutes, keep them close enough to their target for another run if the two bombs had failed to detonate. The plane was too low, too far away and at the wrong angle to solidly confirm the damage.

One by one, the other planes checked in. Within twenty seconds, Szalecki verified that each had delivered, was past its target, and on widely varying courses. None had encountered ground-fire or interference of any type.

In a moment, the official word came down by encrypted satellite signal.

"Mothermelt squadron, this is SpaCom. All mamas are slag. Repeat. Recon confirms perfect hits. *All* mamas are slag."

A chorus of cowboy whoops, rebel yells, and football cheers echoed through the squadron's headsets.

"Not bad for a bunch of *air*-breathers," the anonymous SpaCom operator said sarcastically.

"Thank *you*!" Szalecki said. "Your daddy sucks vacuum!"

"Compliment accepted, Tweety Pies. SpaCom out."

CHAPTER 37

THE CALL

In a huge new War Room, begun in the Reagan era and finished only five years earlier in the depths of a Colorado mountain, the president and the people who'd approved operation Mothermelt were not cheering. Everyone was staring at the center screen, the one which showed a polar view of the Soviet Union and North America. Despite knowing that it was unlikely, they were waiting to see if Soviet missiles would rise in retaliation.

Glenn Young spoke up, "Folks, you might as well get busy with something else. If it happens—and it's far-fetched that it will—you're not going to see it for hours. As I explained before, the Sovs'll take quite a bit of time to evaluate. They can't even be sure at this point who caused it. I remind you that over twenty nations now have nuclear weapons and almost twice that many have ICBMs and several have stealthy bombers."

Before ordering it, the president had told only a select few about the nuclear strike. Later, once it was explained to a wider crowd in the War Room, no one had objected. They were all too stunned by the thought that the U.S. might finally, after decades of fretting, be entering the "Big One."

However, among the president's "core" group, there had been strong disagreement over the form the strike would take.

"In poker," Ella Paxson had said, "it's fold, call—or raise."

Young and Allison had urged him to raise. Vice President Leininger and Sunderleaf had opted for a strike with conventional precision-weapons, coupled with a warning that more strikes could be expected if the U.S. found further evidence of hostile intent.

The discussions had gone around and around, technically, politically, strategically.

Washington had finally decided to raise. He had three reasons.

First, a conventional strike—a "call"—would not guarantee complete cooking of the virus and facilities.

Second, if it did not, the virus could be moved elsewhere and they'd never know *where* to strike again.

Third, and perhaps most important, he reasoned that Mothermelt was the only way to show the strength which the Soviet's audacity demanded in return. In Washington's view, a virus attack was even worse than a nuclear strike.

But the hand wasn't over.

"General Young, sir!" a female technician yelled from the floor beneath the giant screens. She was pointing at the far right display, the one indicating the nation's various strategic satellites. The "Star Wars" weapons platforms were outlined in bright blue. But of the one-hundred, a dozen were glowing red. As everyone watched, another eight joined them, then ten more.

"What the hell's going on?" Washington demanded, noting that a state of near-panic was sweeping through the military personnel, like a bad earthquake through a busy office.

"Finding out now, Sir," Young said, picking up a phone. He calmly began asking questions. "Did you check for display or diagnostics malfunctions? Okay. What do the alternate tracking stations say? Yes, all right. Get a world-wide check on that. You did? They do? What's the cause? Well, it makes no sense. Looks like a system display burn-out from this end. Our big board doesn't show *any* enemy anti-satellite or beam tracks. The other boards don't either, eh? Well, find out. Could be a common software glitch or bug, God forbid. If it's not, then it means it's for real and they've got to be using *something*. Whatever it is, it uses matter and energy and they both leave traces. Yes, so you said. I can't accept that, Major. Nail it down, damn it!"

He hung up more abruptly than he'd intended just as five more platforms turned red. Someone let out a low whistle. Someone else, apparently overcome by tension, stuck his face in a wastebasket and let it taste his breakfast. Several in-tense, low-voiced arguments among the technicians had broken out.

Young made another call to the new, deepened strategic radar headquarters at Cheyenne Mountain.

"Spaceman here, General Warren. General, do you have—? 'No idea how' isn't good enough! Listen, are you *sure* they're going out? An absolute confirm? Well, sorry about the expletive, General. It's pretty hot here. There, too, huh? Call me if you get better news."

Washington and Sunderleaf exchanged alarmed glances. Young looked like he'd just heard about a death in the family. After two more phone calls to other divisions of SpaCom, the General turned to the president and said, "Sir, there's no doubt. Someone's systematically cooking our entire space defense shield."

Seven more platforms glowed red.

"Like a gator pullin' ducks underwater," Sunderleaf muttered.

The president's hands were shaking. He lit a cigarette to cover. After taking a moment to absorb the situation, he asked in a surprisingly steady voice, "Why didn't they fight back? Our satellites, I mean. I thought they could defend them-selves."

"They can't identify the source of the attack, Mr. President. They don't know who to shoot back *at*. None of our sensor systems, anywhere in the world or above, is tracking the attackers, whoever or whatever they are. Every radar, laser, or vi-sual we train skyward shows those platforms cracking up, disintegrating. For no apparent reason."

"Correct me if I'm sniffin' the wrong panther-print, General," Sunderleaf said, "but I've always heard there'd be only one likely reason to snuff the other fella's shield. That's to clear th'way for a nuclear missile attack. Am I wrong?"

Washington felt his temples go cold at Sunderleaf's words. He looked at General Young, who shook his head.

"We don't know its the Soviets," Washington cautioned.

"Whomever, then. Same story."

But as the hour ground on, there was no sign of ICBMs rising from the Soviet Union or from any other nation or from the oceans. All the U.S. SDI satellites had disappeared, swept from orbit by an unseen broom. However, Soviet satellites *were* still in orbit. And so were all other nations' satellites. In fact, so were the U.S.'s military J-STARS, Milstar, the Big Bird spy rigs, LANDSATs, commercial communications, mining/geological satellites, and so on. It made no sense to Washington. Only America's anti-missile laser battle satellites had gone down.

Young excused himself to talk to his staff.

"Well," Washington said to Sunderleaf, "I've got a feeling we're going to find out soon enough. Whoever did this has got to *want* something. The more I think about it, the less it sounds like a prelude to war."

"Oh? Then what?" Jeanne Allison asked, joining them.

"Blackmail."

"Right. In the meantime," Allison informed him, "this thing's gotten into the wind. Seismological labs everywhere picked up our nukes in Russia and word's hit the Internet. Amateur astronomers have noticed our missile-defense satellites are gone. Took the media awhile because it seemed too outlandish. But now their various sources are putting things together and it's the most fun they've had since I-don't-know-when."

"Guess I'd better get a whopper of a story together, or panic's going to start."

Allison shook her head. "Sir, look at how well people handle themselves after tornados, floods, hurricanes, or last year's Ebola epidemic in Atlanta. This nation is made of builders, creators, doers. People like that don't stampede, Mr. President. In whatever you're planning, I think you should count on that."

Washington felt an unaccustomed lump in his throat. "Jeanne," he said, "you should've been a coach."

"I am, sir. Girls soccer."

"Who're those two on either side of Walkingfar?" the president asked, pointing to the big 'Chief.' "Don't recall spotting them around before."

"Couple of Spaceman's guys. Their names are Jones and Trevis. They're the ones who got the KGB defector."

"Remind me to shake their hands."

"Yes, sir."

"Jeanne, Walkingfar has an idea worth chewing. He suggests a Goliath-sized bluff: I announce that the satellites are still up there. A secretly added stealth device has been turned on and is now going through extensive tests. Part of planned improvements to our SDI system."

"It's ballsy enough that it just might hold the lid down. But, you know, some of those amateur star gazers are going to make the case that they saw satellite fragments hitting the atmosphere and burning up."

"He suggests we say we're test-firing some of the platforms' kinetic energy 'cloud-gun' missiles. As allowed in the last space-missile treaty. Perfectly legit."

Allison smiled. "Hmmm. Cloud-gun pellets make lots of nice flashes when they hit air. But eventually—"

"Yeah, I know. Eventually the aerospace community itself is going to point out that there's nothing in the literature indicating that such a cloaking device is possible. But if we're lucky, that'll take a considerable amount of time. All I want to do is buy a bit, 'til we figure out what's going on and how to counter it."

Allison frowned, then asked. "Has it occurred to anyone that we can use the 'nothing-in-the-literature' argument *two* ways?"

"How's that?" Washington asked, lighting and dragging on a fresh cigarette, exhaling the smoke off to one side.

"Well, if the aerospace community comes up with the theory that someone had to have knocked off our satellites—based on the debris—we just say there's nothing in the literature that justifies their theory! As far as I know, there isn't. We demand that they show *us* the evidence of how it was done. Put the onus of proof on them. That way we retain the high ground."

Washington's eyes slowly crinkled. "Jeanne, you're a gem."

"Yes, sir. Meanwhile, another suggestion. Announce that you're touring the new war room and other military bases here in the west. Legit excuse. But I'd suggest that some of the rest of us fly back to Washington for a day or two at a time, just to show our faces. Otherwise somebody's going to wonder why the entire presidential line-of-succession happens to be huddled away together in a bomb shelter."

Three days later, a call came from the Kremlin.

"Well, Mr. President," Romanoff said, "as one of your Western proverbs puts it, have you had time to grab the bull by the tail and face the situation?"

"Situation, what situation?" Washington asked, as though Romanoff had inquired about something no more important than a bowling handicap.

"The loss of your defense satellites, of course," Romanoff said archly. "Makes one feel a little naked, nyet?"

"What are you blathering about? We've merely activated a cloaking—"

Romanoff spat a Russian expletive. "Come, now, Washington. You and I are grown men. We both know the new USSR is the only nation advanced enough to have brought off something of this magnitude."

"I know no such thing," Washington shot back. "We know what we have, and our cloaking systems are working. Too bad you can't see through them."

Romanoff hissed, "We can do this not just to satellites, but to anything. Do you understand? Anything?"

"So you say."

"Yes, I do, Mr. President. Now you have forced my hand! Watch your aircraft carrier *Nimitz* in the Mediterranean. See where your intransigence has brought you."

The connection went dead.

Fifteen minutes later, the Secretary of the Navy was death-voiced. "Sir, the *Nimitz* is gone. Sunk. Straight down. Her Aegis shotgun cruiser observed it a few minutes ago. Sir, there were over 5,000 good men aboard. Damn it, no one saw anything coming, sir! What the hell's going *on*?"

"How many were saved?" Washington demanded.

"At best, a few hundred. We're still fishing some out."

"I'm sorry," Washington said woodenly. "Do what you can."

"And now?" Romanoff asked, five minutes later.

"Mr. Romanoff," Washington replied icily, "do you realize that you now *have* declared yourself party to sabotage? The biggest incident since World War Two?"

"No!" Romanoff yelled. "Knocking off your SDI was the biggest!"

"Stop the silly claims and games," Washington said.

Romanoff took a moment to control his fury. "You lost many fine men on the *Nimitz*. How many more of your innocent people do you want on your conscience?"

"Mr. Romanoff," Washington said, feeling a rage rise from the depths of his spirit, "the moral blame lies not with the victims, but with the aggressor. By your own admission, that's you. And I'm going to make sure you live with it."

"You are the one harboring grand delusions! Moral debates are irrelevant now. Don't you see? You've *lost*, Mr. President!"

"I don't see it that way."

Romanoff hung up. After discussing the conversation with Young and others, Washington turned his ear to Ella Paxon.

"Sam," she said, "this sort of thing isn't usually my field, but there just might be a way to regain the initiative."

"I'm open to anything right now, Ella," he said.

His advisor of decades leaned closer and began to talk in detail.

CHAPTER 38

THE DEMONSTRATION

I t was ten o'clock in the morning. Dressed in a dark brown suit, the President of the United States was back in Washington, D.C. Although several of his advisors had asked him to perform from the safety of a Colorado war room, he'd conditionally refused. For at least this act, he wished to appear as vulnerable as the American people. Ninety percent of them would have to weather whatever would arise without the benefit of a good shelter—although, in fact, only a petulant minority would begrudge the president one.

"Ladies and gentlemen of the United States," he said to the TV cameras, "for the past several days, we have been at war with the Soviet Union."

Across America, the blunt statement caused human action to lurch to a stop.

In Rapid City, South Dakota, a trucker listening to a restaurant radio stopped a cup of coffee halfway to his mouth.

In Los Angeles, a young woman listening on a radio headset in a health club halted her exercise bike in mid-stride.

In Atlanta, five go-getter car salesmen scrambled toward the television in the employee lounge.

In New York, a black man, a white man, and a Latino who'd broken into a home to steal a new, fold-screen TV, silently watched it instead. They would leave without taking the set.

In Honolulu, Hawaii, two elderly Japanese businessmen watched the president from their hotel room, vaguely remembering stories their fathers had once told them about war.

In Salt Lake City, a young man sitting near his wife put his hand around her shoulder as she continued nursing their young son.

In Fort Lewis, Washington, several off-duty soldiers put down their beers and began to freshly contemplate their futures.

"That we've been at war," said the president, "has been true in fact, if not in official pronouncement. As of this moment"—he stopped his address, pulled out his fountain pen and signed a document—"it *is* official."

A president had great discretion in the use of the military. Over five-hundred instances of "executive action" had taken place since 1798 when President Adams ordered the capture of 90 French ships. But to actually *declare* war, Congress had to act. For the strategic effect he hoped it would have on the Soviets, Washington wanted it in ink—on television. He laid the pen aside, placed his big, ruddy hands flat on the document and continued.

"I won't insult you by urging you to remain calm. The American people have always been level-headed in crises. I'm confident you'll hold that courage. But there are things I *will* request. First, in the dangerous days ahead, I ask you to pull together with me in spirit and back me as your Congress has. I conferred with leaders of both houses yesterday evening and asked them to prepare this declaration."

He patted the document.

"After reviewing the facts in closed session, they agreed that the magnitude of the threat warranted it. After you hear the facts, I hope you will feel as they did."

Employing digital visuals, complete with maps and animation to illustrate his words, he sketched the story of the Engels virus; Mothermelt; what he termed Soviet sabotage of the *Nimitz*; and part of Romanoff's subsequent threats to him. There was barely a soul in the nation who disagreed with the president's reasoning that the Soviet actions required a firm response.

"One thing I emphasize," Washington said, "is that the U.S. remains confident. We have all our major armed forces intact, *including* our space defenses, which are now under the protection of a new electronic cloaking device."

He smiled wryly, radiating complete confidence.

"We have, hopefully, opened the eyes of the monsters in Moscow who contemplated the biological assault on our innocent population. That would be an action which I, personally, regard as more wicked than nuclear aggression. Thus, our limited nuclear preemptive strike was, in my estimation, mild. Operation Mothermelt showed that we have the means to carry out retaliation deep into the Soviet Union, regardless of Moscow's own sorry strategic defenses."

In his office back in Oregon, Ben Liddell paced in front of his TV screen as he puffed a cigar and glanced at the scattered notes from his meeting with the little man in Texas. Liddell was trying desperately to figure out how the editor of a tiny defense newsletter might quickly gain the ear of the President of the United States.

"John Kennedy once promised that this nation would pay any price to preserve liberty," Washington said, beginning the conclusion of his talk. Tom Rosco appeared briefly at the president's side, handing him a sheet of paper. Washington scanned it, then went on, "I've received word that in the last few minutes, in retaliation for the destruction of the *Nimitz*, an American submarine has sunk two Soviet aircraft carriers, the *Yeltsin* and the *Andropov*."

Washington leaned his husky shoulders forward.

"Mr. Romanoff," he said quietly, "I'm not kidding around. I know you're watching this address. I urge you to reconsider. Take this insanity no further."

He redirected his final remarks to the American populace.

"Most of you are probably wondering what you can do to help. For the moment, just keep doing what you normally do. But do it a little better. If this war should drag on, we'll need the full power of the U.S. economy to pursue it successfully. I refuse to burden us with unneeded regulations, restrictions, or rationing. I will not endanger the vitality of our economy from within while we fight a dangerous enemy from without."

He paused and put as much feeling into his voice as he could muster.

"Ladies and gentlemen, this is the largest threat that our Lady of Light, our Lady Liberty, has ever faced. In the coming days, I ask you to stand by her. For if she dies, civilization will enter its longest night."

After the "off-air" signal from the cameraman, the president let out a huge breath. Under his suit, his body dripped with sweat. Then he looked alarmed. For a second, he didn't understand the meaning of the noise. Every person in the room— Ella, Tom, the vice president, cabinet members, two of the joint chiefs, senators, representatives, technicians, even the few permitted media correspondents, including the normally surly Ernest Pomp—had burst into applause. All Washington could do was nod; he didn't think his voice would work.

Annette Washington had been standing out of camera range. She moved to him, gave him a kiss on the cheek, and whispered, tears in her eyes, "We're with you, Sam!"

The president looked at the First Lady. In a low voice he said, "Net, I wish I had listened to you sooner."

"No, that's behind us," she said, putting a finger across his lips. She kissed him quickly and left him to his work.

"Fine job!" Tom Rosco said as soon as the private moment was over. "Uh, the media are demanding a news conference."

"Not for a day or two, fellas," Washington said, raising his voice and directly addressing the news crews still in the room.

There were a few grumbles, but one by one, everyone shook his hand and congratulated him. In ten minutes, most people had cleared out, but Washington asked Rosco to stay.

"Tom, from now on, I want you in on the Situation Room get-togethers. I think you deserve the full picture through the duration."

Rosco grinned. Washington clapped him on the shoulder. "Let's get to it, before Romanoff can wind up again."

Romanoff, however, was an astute student of strategic surprise. He had already done his winding.

Within five minutes of Washington's speech, Allison was on a secure phone.

"Sam," she said, her voice tensely controlled, "something big's going on in Europe. The reports are sketchy, but they're coming in fast and it looks—well, creepy."

"Creepy, huh?" Ella was standing in the doorway. "Hold the thought, Jeanne. Yes, Ella?"

"General Young's on the phone, too. Says it can't wait."

"Jeanne, can you hold?"

"No! *Listen* to me, Sam. Somebody's knocking out NATO! Flattening facilities as easy as popping balloons at a carnival sideshow," Allison said. "Virtually every important command center's gone and—"

"Jeanne, stay on the line. I'm putting Glenn on with us."

"It's NATO, sir—" Young began.

"I know," the president said. "I've got Jeanne on the line, too." He punched a couple keys. "There, see each other? Okay, Jeanne, continue."

Allison ran a hand through disheveled hair. "NSC data show most command posts of the alliance have been seriously damaged or destroyed. Ground wave emergency network towers across Europe have been disabled as have various fiber-link back-ups. We still have communication satellites; lucky or planned, I don't know. Also, there were some posts they possibly didn't know about which are still functioning. Air and other bases are losing fuel dumps and munitions bunkers like a string of firecrackers. I'd say it looks like a coordinated, massive Spetsnaz operation. I can't think of what else it'd be, but perhaps General Young has ideas."

Young stepped in. "Got to be sabotage this time. SpaCom infrared showed explosions all over the Continent. Most of them were small, but some had certain characteristics of tiny tactical nukes. Maybe back-pack versions buried by Sov commandos long ago. No one's tracked a single incoming missile or artillery shell. PAVE-PAWS phased-array radars and other big systems throughout the Continent and Britain are scrap. JSTARS and mini-RPV airborne radars are filling in the gaps, now, but some of them are being smacked down, too. How those were sabotaged, I don't know."

"Shit," Washington said.

"The deep kind, to be technical. Sat-pics show that as many as a thousand British and German frontline main battle tanks, including the newest ceramic-armor Leopards have gone up in smoke. Luckily, though, not many men with them; most were off-duty at the time. But here's the toad on the stool, sir. We estimate that no more than a fifth of the combined NATO air power is left. It was fried right on the ground—interceptors, tankers, bombers, recons, you pick it. The few planes that got up are buzzing around like bug-bombed bees. They want to fight, but there's nothing to shoot at. Remaining AWACS report no hostile missiles, fighter-bombers, artillery, rockets, beams—nothing has come over from Russia. Not even our Big Bird sats saw anything, and they *should* have given the best look-see."

"What about Soviet ground advances?" Washington asked, dreading the answer. "Are they moving West?"

"Negative, sir. And that *is* almighty strange. Everything we know of their doctrine says that Sov first- and second-echelon forces should already be moving on Germany. But they're bunkered up like it's any old peace day. Gives me the willies. If I didn't know better, I'd say it's like the Sovs aren't even aware of all this."

"That makes no sense," Washington said, forcing his voice to stay even and unalarmed.

"Here's another blast up your leg, sir. The entire operation appears to have started no earlier than *during* your talk on TV. The one you just finished. Although, of course, we've no idea how long the mayhem will continue."

"Surely such coordination is impossible—" Washington started to say.

Ella stuck her head in the room and whispered that the CIA chief was on hold. The president triple-windowed the screen and Brighton came on.

"It's Europe, sir. It appears—"

"Getting it from Allison and Young now, Bill. You're late, but on the screen with the three of us now." He updated Brighton on what had been said. "Anything to add?"

"Yes, sir! It's stopped. Like a rocket burned out."

The president, Young and Allison all looked at Brighton's image as though he'd just turned into Daffy Duck.

"I'm serious," Brighton said. "And Radio Moscow is taking 'credit.' The Sovs are calling it their 'Five Minute Demonstration'—in retaliation for our nuking six of their towns and—"

Young interrupted, reading directly from a fax sheet handed him. "High Eye's confirmed that, sir. And—" He frowned, rereading the fax. "Romanoff is demanding that Europe relinquish control of its armed forces—directly to the Soviet High Command, to the Stavka."

"Coming in now worldwide from all the Soviet news monitors," Brighton said. "Already hit the Internet. The Russians are demanding total, instant control of NATO forces."

The red phone rang. Grimly, Washington picked it up.

"So, you see," said Romanoff, without greeting, in the manner of addressing a naughty first-grader, "we can, indeed, do as I said. Oh, but I agree with your speech. Please, let us bring this foolishness to a close. Tell your allies to cooperate."

"You mean, obey," Washington said, wondering wildly how badly he'd underestimated the enemy. Buck up, man, he thought. Don't let Romanoff knock you out of the boat.

"No snappy retorts?" Romanoff asked. He laughed, then his voice took on an oily tone, "Mr. President, we do not wish to destroy the world, merely to be a legitimate part of it."

"Romanoff, who are you kidding? You've got to change your underwear or the stink persists."

"You'll pay for that, Washington!" Romanoff snarled.

"You want me to pay anyway. What's the difference?"

"Enough! You have *one* day to think about it. And don't even consider hitting back again, Mr. President. Not on any scale. Has it failed to occur to you that we let your stealth bombers through? How else, in the world's eyes, could we justify the magnitude of our current retaliation against NATO, eh?"

Washington heard a caustic cackle as the Soviet leader disconnected.

CHAPTER 39

THE U.N.

After atomic desecration of the innocent Soviet heartland, what *did* the NATO alliance expect?" the Zunduwanian Ambassador, Machel Gufawna, demanded of the U.N. General Assembly. He gestured in all directions at once, jangling and clacking dozens of gold chains, ivory beads, and talismans hung haphazardly from his neck, wrists, and ears.

"Did NATO think the Soviets would say, 'Oh, ho! Yes, yes! Please, Mr. NATO, come *bake* more of our people! And, yes—*eat* them, too! They are so tasty!' No? Then perhaps by offering a *plate* and *napkin*—"

The British Guyana delegate, Jeffrey Hempstead, serving under new rotation rules as floor president of the assembly, banged his gavel.

"The ambassador from Zunduwa has sixty seconds left in which to speak, or whatever it is he's doing. He will please refrain from imputing cannibalism."

The Cuban and Nicaraguan People's Democracy ambassadors began to clap loudly in unison. Soon a hundred other "Third-" and "mid-world" delegates joined them.

Gufawna bowed to the crowd, grinning, making some sort of obscure hand-motion which involved repeatedly touching one ear and his crotch.

Hempstead said, "We stand in recess for one hour."

He knew that this was a sure way to halt Prince Gufawna for the day. He would head to the nearest bar, guzzle beer and God knew what other substances, and then, laughing and ogling, stumble off to an expensive hotel suite with a half-dozen of his giggling, overweight wives.

As the hall cleared, U.S. Secretary of State Craig Goldstein left his seat where he'd been filling in the week for the regular U.S. ambassador, reportedly flu-ridden. Goldstein found a phone and called the president.

"How's it going?" Washington asked.

"I'm afraid it's swung way over toward the Soviets. Almost no one seems to be able to forgive us the use of the nukes."

"The virus *would* have been okay?"

Goldstein chuckled harshly. "I know. But I'd say that out of 180 countries, it's running about 160 against us. A few have stood by us. Britain, Israel, several others. But the Germans were particularly disgusting. I thought they were with us. Instead, they offered the Soviets a hundred-billion dollars bribe, a no-repayment economic 'loan.' Everyone who wanted to has spoken today. Nobody had much to say, except for a few die-hard allies and the Prince of Zunduwa."

"*That* showboat? Well, I've had enough of this ship-jumping. Let's go with what we planned. I've been incognito for three hours and it's only a few more before Romanoff's going to want his answer. We'll see if your deal throws him a curve."

"Oops. Incognito for three hours? Then you don't know that your old friend is loose. The British Ambassador heard it on the news during the morning coffee break here about an hour-and-a-half ago. The ACLU has gotten Buck Reed out of jail."

"What? How the hell—"

"Somebody tipped them on where he was being housed. Then they found a sympathetic Supreme Court justice—that old rascal Carlan Whitman—to order Reed's release on $100,000 bond."

"A judge can't override a wartime executive order to the military! Not even a Supreme Court Justice!"

"One of the networks mentioned in passing that Reed had gotten the pen warden's kid into West Point years ago. So, when the ACLU lawyers showed up with a release order for Reed, the warden was sympathetic. He was probably the ACLU's tipster, too."

"Goldy, Buck is like a cruise missile with a random number generator controlling his course. He could blow anywhere, anytime."

"He's gotten the media's ear already. Has plans to make the rounds of Congress. There are more than a few people taking him seriously. They don't know the inside story on him like we do, and Buck can be extremely persuasive one-on-one."

"Tell me about it," Washington said, remembering how he'd fallen for most of Buck's line on the peace-loving "new" Soviet Union.

"The chair recognizes the honorable delegate from the United States."

A reaction of boos and hisses drowned out the small amount of polite applause on the United Nations assembly floor.

Goldstein pulled his microphone closer and cleared his throat. When the noise stopped, he directed his attention to his detractors, which meant the majority.

"I hope the delegates with their indelicate manners and delicate backbones have enjoyed themselves. It was their last chance."

As though feeling a small temblor, the assembly shifted and murmured in apprehension. Even the cocky Soviet delegate looked mildly startled.

Goldstein held up a sheaf of papers.

"I'll be leaving the details of what I'm about to say with Mr. Hempstead on my way out of here. There's one for each of you. Now then. By the order of the President of the United States, I'm informing you that by decree of emergency presidential powers, my government is revoking its U.N. membership and support, and ordering these buildings closed. As of the end of the next sentence, the U.N. in New York is out of business. This circus is *history*, folks."

For a full ten seconds, no one said anything. Then almost two hundred men and women shot to their feet at once, trying to speak—only to discover that the power to the entire public address system had been cut.

Goldstein casually got up, walked over, handed Hempstead the details, then strode out, whistling.

As each delegate obtained his copy of the order and left the hall, he found the place filled with U.S. Marines, federal marshals, and badged FBI agents. Marines were already searching and escorting the U.N.'s vast staff out of the building. They were told to return to their embassies. No floor delegate was allowed back in his U.N. offices unless his name was on a "friendly" list. Few were. The president's reasoning was that no hostile delegate was going to be given a chance to confiscate, shred, or otherwise dispose of the decades worth of documents in the building which might prove seriously antagonistic to U.S. interests.

After he'd informed the president and left the building, heading for the airport back to Washington, Goldstein thought: So, it's finally done!

Even less than the president, he had never approved of the fact that the U.N. was essentially a taxpayer-funded forum for America's worst enemies and detractors. And the FBI had long told both branches of the U.S. government that the place was little more than a glorified spies' nest.

It took a war, the Secretary of State thought, to lead us to act on that information. We'll see if it gets us what we hope.

It did.

They started as a trickle, but within four hours, calls poured into the White House from over 100 countries, assuring the U.S. that *they* were not among its enemies. Each caller was politely thanked and told again—as detailed in the sheet which Goldstein had left at the U.N.—that U.S. foreign policy was being strictly revised. Those nations whose actions supported both a philosophy of maximum freedom for their own citizens and the U.S. in its present struggle with the Soviet Union, would be given the fullest trade privileges. Those whose actions did not, would find their "most favored nation" trade status and all other aid revoked for at least five years.

There were to be no exceptions. More than a few "Western" nations found themselves in uncomfortable positions.

All of a sudden, all countries had a decision to make about which example of nationhood was more valuable. On the one hand, there was the planet's largest, freest and richest trading republic—the nation which was the source of over a quarter of the planet's production. On the other hand, there was the planet's largest tyranny, which even now was trying to vastly expand the number and size of the nations attached to those horrific strings of red. It was a choice between two Titans, one good and one evil; between an era of light or an era of darkness.

CHAPTER 40

THE RESCUE

In the North Atlantic some 200 miles southeast of Angmagssalik, Greenland, and due east of the King Frederick VI coast, U.S. Naval forces were still pulling a few Soviet survivors out of the water. So far, several hundred had been rescued from the aircraft carriers, the *Yeltsin* and *Andropov*. Hours before, they had been downed by American Waterweasel "micronuke" torpedoes. The Soviet seamen were astonished at the resources which the Americans were expending to find only a few missing men—*enemy* missing.

Several things about the incident were unusual. Both carriers had been way out of their normal ranges. The *Yeltsin* was usually in the Black Sea and the *Andropov* in the Mediterranean. In recent weeks, the two ships and their support groups had met off Athens and pushed out of the Med. They'd made their way up the European coast all the way to the Lofoten Islands off Norway.

The support vessels continued north into the Barents Sea, but the carriers inexplicably headed directly west, then south along Greenland. The U.S. Navy's assumption had been that they were going in for repairs at the Soviets' sheltered shipyards at Godthab on Greenland's west coast. Each vessel had, separately, been there before. The Sovs had built the shipyards ten years earlier during a Danish flirtation with "improved relations." The North Sea oil reserves were not what they once were, so the Soviets were able to get their space on Greenland in exchange for supplying the Danes with crude. The oil came from the USSR's recently-tapped major offshore find in the Kara Sea between the Yamal Peninsula and Novaya Island. The Soviets claimed that the field held more oil than lay under Kuwait, over 120 billion barrels.

As unprotected as they had been on their way to Godthab, the two carriers were logical targets for U.S. retribution for the *Nimitz* sinking. On presidential orders, that's where the U.S. Navy had struck. The ease of the success had elated most of those involved. But there were a few who worried, including a young naval intelligence officer aboard the new, treble-hulled Ohio III class submarine, *USS Reagan*, the ship which had actually sunk the carriers.

It was almost as though the Soviets had offered the two vessels for sacrifice, he thought. In a sense, the Sovs were giving up little. The carriers were noisy, slow, older models. Modern Soviet open ocean carriers were massive HC hovercraft that could travel at over 200 knots, each loaded with twice the number of VTOL fighter jets as the *Yeltsin* and *Andropov* combined. The U.S. had nothing comparable, preferring by budget necessity to rely on its dozen aging carriers, C-17s, B-2s, and TAVs to reach global trouble points.

The officer checked the latest satellite shots of the Med and Black Sea to see if any HC carriers had been assigned to replace the two rust-buckets. None had. He made another note.

He chewed his lip. There were other odd things about the situation.

The Soviets had done no reconnaissance fly-overs of the American rescue and had not demanded that the survivors be returned. Further, many rescued told crazy stories about being recent gulag prisoners.

The "eye" man mulled over his notes for awhile and then suddenly paled. He rushed to the cabin of his superior.

The *Reagan*'s captain agreed with the young man's startling assessment. The sub was still on the surface, aiding as it could. The captain relayed his concerns to the main rescue ships, advising them to cease the search and leave the area immediately.

"Sorry, Cap," the rescue commander drawled in a plainsman's twang. He'd never liked boat bosses. In his view, the deep-ocean big boys were a snotty, cowardly bunch. "You wanna turn tail and run from th' mess you made, Cap'n, 's up to you."

"You were advised."

He ordered the *Reagan* to dive. Three days later, it showed up at Norfolk, Virginia and the captain was unsurprised to hear that none of the five rescue ships or the dozens of helicopters were seen again, at any port in the world.

Several minutes after the *Reagan* had left the rescue scene, a recon specialist in SpaCom's High Eye was using a photonic computer to scan the area of the rescue. The new machine permitted incredibly fast and detailed surveillance by military satellites, twenty times what had been possible in the late '90s. The whole system was called "Dop"—for digital-optics photonics.

It didn't stop there. The reconnaissance images were also *read* by Dop. Incorporating enormously sophisticated neural network variations of software used to guide cruise missiles, Dop had the ability to recognize things that humans would—except humans could not read as rapidly, by a factor of billions.

Dop beeped.

"Watcha got, Honey?" the specialist asked the machine, using his pet name for it. The machine was "brilliant." It could intelligently understand over 140,000 words of human speech once it got used to an operator's voice. "Honey" could also speak, but the officer usually preferred to read the answers on the lower part of the screen before him. Speaking seemed too public for the fondness he felt for the machine.

"Look," Dop printed in red letters, zooming in on a small square of North Atlantic Ocean. In the center of the picture was a life raft. As the specialist watched, a human figure shivered, curled in a fetal position.

"Honey, get precise coordinates on that!"

Instantly, Dop responded, drawing on data from the Global Positioning Satellite network, printing out the latitude and longitude, down to the precise inch. The specialist called Walkingfar and passed on the information. Within two hours, an aquatic lift-and-land "LAL" SpaCom TAV had flown to the area, rescued the survivor, and transported him to High Eye headquarters in Colorado.

Walkingfar, Kevin Jones, and Moshe Trevis, as well as Madeis Plechl and Tanya Yublenka, who'd been flown down from their safe house in Denver after crash-training courses, walked into a small room. Through a one-way glass, they saw a shrunken, haggard man, sitting in a chair in an adjacent room. He smoked a Marlboro cigarette and fidgeted.

Madeis was learning to act as a "XOI" —pronounced "zoy" — for "extra observer/integrator." It was an exotic title which meant simply that in a debriefing or interrogation, he noted reactions, connections, and mannerisms that the main questioner might miss. He liked the work and was a natural at it, or so his trainer, Moshe Trevis, had assured him. Trevis, meanwhile, was watching Madeis. Madeis would have been appalled, but there was still some small question in General Young's mind as to whether Plechl was for real or a Soviet plant.

Tanya Yublenka looked at Walkingfar. He nodded. She squared her shoulders, eased down a side hall and entered the room with the haggard man. She moved slowly, as she'd learned to do. Walkingfar was teaching her to be a "doc," an "MD," Main Debriefer. For reasons he would not explain, he thought that she had a knack for it. Still stunned to be in America at all, Tanya was grateful for any productive work. And this would keep her close to Madeis. Increasingly, it was his face, not Gregor's whom she saw in her dreams.

The emaciated man flinched when Tanya entered.

"You're safe here," she said in Russian, then introduced herself.

"Georg Shkuropat Yaroslavl."

"Can you tell me why you were put aboard the *Yeltsin*?"

He shrugged. One cheek began to twitch. He dragged on his cigarette. "We were told—several from my gulag camp—that it was our only chance to get out. They laughed. We were afraid they would dump us at sea."

"What did you see after the *Yeltsin* went down?"

He curled a lip. "I was swimming for my life!" He stubbed out the cigarette in a ceramic blue and black SpaCom ashtray on the table between them. His fingers were shaking.

"You found a life raft," Tanya prompted.

"Yes. I huddled in the bottom, recovering. When I finally looked up I saw fog. Before the *Yeltsin* exploded, it was clear. They had let us walk on deck, you see, for exercise. I was near the front of the ship, looking ahead, when something behind me blew up."

"Those were U.S. torpedoes."

The man's eyes went wide for a moment, then he shook his head. "We are at war, then?"

"We are."

He thought about it for several seconds, mildly shocked that anything *could* shock him after his years in the gulags.

"The blast threw me overboard. When I looked back, the ship was listing. Somewhere I'd heard that one could be sucked under by a sinking ship, so I swam."

She lit two cigarettes and handed him one.

He was so gaunt that his smile looked skeletal.

"So you got in a raft. Then?"

"I drifted deeper into the fog. It glowed, but just now and then, in flashes. Blue. Violet. Far away, here and there, I saw other men in life boats. If they were only partly in the fog, I would see a flash, there would be smoke, the rafts would jerk, dip behind swells, and then I wouldn't see them again."

"You mean like they were hit by bombs?"

Yaroslavl shook his head and shivered. "No. I've seen explosions. There weren't even gunshots. This was like nothing else. A glow, a hissing, maybe, then the rafts would be gone. It was like an evil sea magician made them disappear."

CHAPTER 41

THE CONTACT

B en Liddell, like many seasoned journalists, tried to keep a rotating "call" file on his important contacts. The idea was to regularly keep in touch. If he didn't, sources tended to drift away or feel miffed, which could be worse. He knew he needed to be world's better about his updating process; if it could be called one.

"No more regular than this system is," he mumbled. "It needs a laxative."

The computer began bringing up the subscribers employed by SpaCom. As they came into view, he "print-screened" the names and addresses, one by one. After a few minutes, he had a list of fifteen. Two were at SpaCom's Colorado offices.

Their rank insignia were a silver spaceship-over-arc and a silver nova—a colonel and a brigadier general. Yes, he remembered the general now. He'd subscribed three years ago when he was but a single silver spaceship, a lieutenant colonel. His name was William V. Brand. Brand had moved up rapidly. That could happen in SpaCom, if you were good enough.

Liddell picked up the phone receiver and punched "memory" and the number "37," his auto-dial number for SpaCom's info desk. He identified himself and asked for the general by his little-known nickname, "Goat," a play on "Billy." Liddell asked that his call be transferred in order to save a second long-distance charge.

A familiar, strong voice came on, "Well, Ben, how the *hell* are ya?"

"I'm doing okay, sir," Liddell answered. "Congratulations on your promotion. 'Fraid I never had a chance to send you a card."

"Well, thanks, Ben. It's good work. Hey, I enjoy your little rag. Top of the list. Now, what's gnawing at your skull?"

"Don't want to bother you long, General. My reporter hat's off on this one. All between us. I've busted onto some research dope that you might want to pass on up the ladder. It bears directly on this war."

"How's that?" Brand asked, somewhat skeptical, despite his respect for the writer. Too many media people—even with the best intentions—felt they knew more than the brass. Sometimes they did, too. But not as often as they thought.

"Well," Liddell said, "something big's being stonewalled by a couple of guys over in your Mech Morgue in Texas."

The word "Morgue" was enough to convince Brand that Liddell might, indeed, have "busted onto" something. The brigadier general was silent for a few seconds. Then said, "Ben, that place isn't officially there."

"I know, sir."

Liddell and Brand talked for fifteen minutes. Brand was cautious at first, but asked questions and gradually turned toward Liddell's view.

"General," Liddell finally asked, "if we get out of all of this, and if you or anyone else on SpaCom can ever talk about it on the record, I'd like to be the first to get the inside dope."

"Between us, they're both big 'ifs,' Ben."

"Both, huh?" Liddell said. He felt acid in the back of his throat.

"*Should* it all work out," Brand offered, "how about an exclusive interview with the Spaceman himself?"

"That'd be a plate hard to push away," he answered. "But I think it'd be hard to serve, too."

Brand chuckled. "I'm not blowin' smoke, Ben. His niece and my son recently married. I'm family."

"Congratulations, sir. Uh, actually, it's the first big 'if' I'm most worried about."

"I know," Brand said, his voice becoming huskier. "I've got a grandkid on the way. Like to see the little guy make it into orbit. Well, I've gotta get on this stuff."

"*Bruise* the bastards with it, Goat," Liddell said.

The general laughed, if a bit grimly, and said, "I sure as hell hope to. Take care, you old bulldog."

The nice thing about SpaCom was that it hadn't had time to calcify. Anything important enough could be quickly pushed up the chain of command. It was only an hour later that Walkingfar was on the phone to the Mech Morgue, talking with Liddell's "little man," Dr. Jeff Garreth, about his underappreciated ideas about various, odd events.

An hour later, Spaceman, the Chief, Moshe Trevis, Garreth, Jeanne Allison, and the president had assembled via a scrambled video conference line. Walkingfar and Trevis were at High Eye, Young was in the Colorado War Room, Allison and the president were in D.C., and Garreth was at the Morgue in Texas.

There was one other person, an oriental, whom General Young had ordered brought in on the conversation. He looked vaguely familiar to the president.

"Let me stop you," the president said after listening a few minutes to Garreth. "Do I understand you to say that *all* of these events have an identical cause? That guy losing his leg, the refinery disaster, the dam break, the TAV nose-job, and so on? If so, pin it down, Doc. This war's put us in kind of a hurry."

"I don't know how it works, but I think there's one aboard every Soviet power satellite they've orbited in the last several years. They're supposed to just produce microwave power from the sun's rays and beam it to customers. But somehow the solar source can also be converted into something else, into some kind of devastating, precision disintegrator beam. According to the scientific literature, it shouldn't be possible."

Young looked from the oriental man to the others. "Gentlemen, Jeanne, this is probably a good time to introduce an old friend of mine. He's the only quadruple doctorate at the age of sixteen from MIT. Like you all to meet Tomasito MacGregor. A little older now, Tommy's an expert on quite a few far-out things in physics, isn't that right?"

MacGregor flinched, but nodded.

"Wait a minute," Washington said, snapping his fingers. "I've seen you before, Doctor MacGregor. You were on PBS's Nova, talking about—what was it? Superloo—luminar—"

"Yes, Mr. President. Your memory serves you. Superluminal travel. Travel beyond the speed of light," MacGregor said quietly in a mellow bass voice. "You see, sir, under Einsteinian theory, stretching of the universe becomes an unnecessary rat-warren where a simple hallway might do. For instance, take the parameters for Planck's constant, which is 6.625 times ten to the twenty-seventh. It might be shown under varying quantum contexts that if one were to—"

"All right, Tommy," Young said, stifling a grin. "Some other time on that one. What about this disintegrator ray?"

"As I said, theoretically possible."

"How about an example?" Walkingfar asked. The Chief himself held several doctorates, including one in quantum physics.

"Tunneled antimatter might do it," MacGregor said.

"Refresh me on antimatter," Washington asked.

"Think of it as the mirror-image of regular matter. An electron in 'real' matter, for instance, has a negative charge. The equivalent in antimatter would be the positron. When an electron and positron meet—as when a positron beam is shot into ordinary matter — they destroy each other. A small amount of antimatter emission occurs in beta radiation disintegration and in a number of nuclear reactions. Man has been able to produce various forms of antimatter for decades, but only on a frustratingly small scale."

"What's the tunneling part?" Young asked.

"Oh. Well, it does *not* refer to electron tunneling, as in microcircuitry. It's rather a misnomer. In this context, it's similar to a guiding process. For instance, like that used for an ordinary particle beam weapon. When particle beams were first tested as weapons, they wandered around too much, like lightning bolts. You could send them out, but couldn't predict whether they'd hit anything. Then somebody came up with the idea of tunneling with a laser beam. You send out the laser beam to ionize the atmosphere. This action creates a channel for the particle beam to follow a fraction of a second later. It's kind of like digging an irrigation ditch and then sending the water where you want it."

"I see," Washington said.

"Once refined, the concept worked. As a matter of fact, that's what our SDI mid-course decoy-discriminators do—except at quite low power. They act as sensors. Particle beams work well as sensors, too."

"Fine, but as to—"

"Yes, well, it's possible that a similar idea would work with antimatter. If controllable, it would be an enormously powerful weapon. The control capabilities would depend on the tunneling beam and I don't know what that would be, although it would probably be the least of the difficulties. I imagine that with work, such a beam could be tightly tuned, maybe even made invisible to our normal sensors. It could therefore range from a bunker-buster, as we just saw in Europe, to an individual assassination weapon, as with that fellow who had his limbs severed. It would be astonishingly versatile. But the real problem, as I see it, is to be able to make and store antimatter in useful quantities to begin with. That has been slow, expensive, and cumbersome."

"Both we and the Soviets have been working on antimatter manufacturing problems for years," Walkingfar clarified. "It was a priority with the Air Force way back in their old 'Forecast Two' program. But nobody over here's been able to figure out how to make the stuff in economical quantities. Both the Sovs and we have been making a little for decades, but only in minuscule amounts. At least so we thought."

Washington asked, "Doctor, is there a way to tell for sure that this *is* what the Sovs've got? Antimatter, I mean. And if so, do you have any ideas on how to stop such a weapon?"

MacGregor answered carefully. "Yes, to the first question. If I could study the raw data—"

"Excuse me," Young interrupted smoothly. "Dr. Garreth, we thank you for your services. Time is essential here. Please prepare what is necessary for forwarding your test results for Dr. MacGregor's review."

"But I—Yes, of course," Garreth said, realizing the discussion was about to tread into territory which he was not cleared to discuss. He was clicked off the conference line.

"Now, then," Young said. "This is not so much an issue of the weapons' exact nature, as it is coordinating a surprise attack on them."

Walkingfar added, "Well, true, but it's worse than a numbers problem, sir, because anything we might try to bring against it can be instantly destroyed."

"Well, damn it, you guys are the experts!" Washington said in frustration. "I don't want 'why-nots,' I want a way. What about attacking these things with ground-based lasers as they come over the horizon? Couldn't we knock them out one-by-one?"

"No, sir," Young said. "We don't have enough such weapons, only six, as a matter of fact, and all up in the Montana mountains in secret silos. But as soon as you shoot down even one of their Buck Rogers birds, the Sovs'll trace our laser beam and zap back. Our lasers wouldn't last a minute or two."

"They've got 839 so-called power satellites up as of our latest sweep," the

Chief said. "Two more went up this morning. We've got to presume that every one of these alleged power birds is, in fact, a quantum popgun."

The scope of the implications began to sink in.

"What else could we do?" the president asked, almost instantly knowing the answer. "If we try to get at them with shuttles, TAVs, or any anti-satellite rockets, we're still sitting ducks."

"Is there nothing else?" Allison whispered. "Are we saying that we're at their complete mercy?"

"I won't accept that," Young snapped. "And if we let them think that, we might as well pull down Old Glory and run up the bed sheets now."

"Agreed," the president said. "Any ideas?"

Each person, in turn, shook his head. All except Tomasito MacGregor. He frowned thoughtfully, then said, "What if we could get behind them?"

"Huh?" Allison and Washington asked simultaneously.

"From outer space. It's their blind side."

"Now that our own SDI's been eighty-sixed, we don't have any weapons in space," Young said.

"Not yet," MacGregor said.

"Eh?"

"We don't have weapons above the Sovs yet. But I have an idea, highly unconventional. I've found no flaws in my theoretical base."

The president looked at the others. All except Young shrugged. Young's eyes had narrowed as he contemplated his old friend, MacGregor. He'd seen that look before.

"Okay, Doctor. What do you need?" Washington asked.

"First, I need time. If you could buy me a few weeks—three or four should do it. And give me a single TAV and a good mechanics crew."

CHAPTER 42

THE ACT

President Washington looked at his core group members, one by one. They sat around the dining room table in a makeshift Situation Room in Aspen Lodge, the presidential residence at Camp David, nestled in Maryland's Catoctin range.

The mood was morose. If someone had told them they'd all soon be living on heating grates, it could hardly have been more pessimistic. An unseasonal, thundering cold rain from Canada contributed a claustrophobic touch.

Young told the group, "If we're guessing right, the AM gun—AM standing for antimatter—draws its wattage primarily from the sun. They've got mammoth solar collectors surrounding each of those satellites and each one probably has a weapon aboard. The weapon might be supplemented by mini-nuclear reactors or magneto-hydrodynamic generators, both of which the Soviets have employed in various forms since the 1970s. For instance, they used them for their massive ground-based lasers at Sary Shagen and elsewhere.

"But there's more to it. They must also have devised a miniature converter, a way of economically deriving high quantities of antiparticles. They'd have to store the antiparticles. This would be accomplished with what are called magnetic bottles.

"Then they'd have to have a system for firing the particles earthward at large fractions of the speed of light—*and* focused in a tight beam. A potential tactical wedge: there is some question as to how efficiently the AM beam can penetrate fog or cloud cover."

A few people sat a little straighter. Any sense of hope eased the tension.

"For those of you whose physics history is rusty," Young said, "antimatter was a concept largely formulated by P.A.M. Dirac way back in 1928. He showed that when antimatter collides with matter, they disintegrate. But you can't violate laws of energy and matter conservation. The particles' form is radically changed. That's what's meant by 'annihilated.' More specifically—and this is about as technical as I'll get—their intrinsic angular momentum or 'spin' and their energy are converted directly into photons. Photons are simply the basic particles which make up ordinary light and other frequencies of the electromagnetic spectrum, such as radio signals."

"Let there be light," Craig Goldstein intoned. "I'll bet the Big Guy in the Sky never meant it *this* way."

A few people laughed.

"Maybe, maybe not," Young said. "Depends on how actively you believe He wanted us to use our brains."

Although shocked at the magnitude and nature of the arsenal, the news was somehow a relief. At least they knew roughly what their country was fighting. Before, it had been like thrashing at a ghost.

"In three weeks you'll be needin' to develop a countermeasure? Three weeks?" the house speaker asked. "That seems t' be one damned sunshiny timetable, sir. Personally, an' no insult intended, I doubt there's a 'coon's mask worth of deception left in this bluff you're runnin' on Romanoff. I'd say a tactical retreat's in order. Now hold on! I ain't talkin' *surrender*. I don't aim t' give that cocky Red S.O.B. control over Western Europe or anythin' else. But we're damned short of options an' talkin' buys time. Hell, the Ruskies've been doin' it to us for years at the disarmament table. They get us a'flappin' our jaws an' b'fore we know it, they've fielded a whole 'nother generation of missiles. Or, in this case, some damned science-fiction thing."

"How would you present it to Romanoff?" Goldstein asked. "It's going to look suspicious to him if we cave in early. He might think it's a trick. It could push him into a nuclear attack on the U.S. mainland. Could make him try to smash everything to crush our will to resist."

"Damn it, son, not if you *structure* the bargainin' right! Don't forget, the Sovs are gradualists."

"I don't know, Bake," Allison said. "They seem to be moving like a Nascar driver lately."

"It's just a burst o'speed to impress us, Jeanne, honey! They'll ease back on the throttle if we give the impression of even grudgin' cooperation. We gotta learn to drag it out."

"A bluff's certainly macho," Bill Brighton said, "but how much destruction will we tolerate in the meantime? Especially if Romanoff starts taking pot shots at the U.S.? Not up there, but down here, on home ground!"

"We take what it takes, Bill," Jeanne Allison snapped. "I'd think a CIA chief would know that it's what one always does in war. Unless he's proposing crawling under a rock."

"Now, wait a minute, " Brighton protested, "I didn't mean to say that."

"Of course not," the president interceded with controlled calm. "We *have* to think about how much we'll absorb. People, I've got an hour before Romanoff's going to insist on accommodation. If his past actions are any indication, he's going to bullwhip somebody if he doesn't get his way."

"Maybe a change of subject would jar a few ideas loose," Vice President Leininger said, speaking up for the first time, his measured Midwestern voice helping to turn down the emotional thermostat. "I don't understand why Romanoff let us take out his two carriers. And why is he letting our spy eyes remain up? It seems inconsistent with any intention of blind-siding the U.S. proper."

"It's no fun for a bully without an audience," Sunderleaf said. "And no lev'rage. Wants us to watch, and shake in our socks."

"Don't forget," Young said, "he's playing this on at least two levels and therefore—"

"Let me guess," Leininger interrupted. "First, there's the behind-the-scenes blackmail. But there's also got to be a cover story for the public. The Sovs use public relations as an integral part of war strategy. Romanoff's got to have at least a semblance of an excuse for whatever he plans to zap next."

"But for God's sake," Brighton exclaimed, "he can hit whatever he wants whenever he wants!"

"I believe Romanoff when he says he doesn't want to destroy the world, or even the U.S.," Young stated. "Remember, with our SDI out he could've baked us to briquettes already."

"*Could* he?" Washington asked, a contemplative smile crossing his lips. "I wonder. I sense that Romanoff's somehow still afraid of us. Except for his initial strike against our SDI, and taking out the *Nimitz*, sure. But not us. Does he just want to keep us fat for cooking? Or is it something else? What if he suspects we've got some tusks he can't pull; maybe tusks we're not even aware we have?"

"Well, we do still have our terminal defenses," Brighton said.

"That's no surprise," Young replied. "He can pop-gun our terminal defenses into dust, *then* nuke us. I don't know what Romanoff might fear. But I doubt the Sovs figure they'll have to use nukes, or at least not many. Once word gets around about those ray guns—and I certainly anticipate that our Soviet friend will leak it soon—then the planet's public will be more intimidated than it was by nukes."

"Up 'til now," Leininger observed, blowing out a small cloud of blue pipe smoke, "we haven't been able to conceive of anything less than a nuclear strike as a serious threat to America. That's how we let our guard down. We got smug. We thought we had the ultimate threat covered. Anybody try anything, we nuke 'em to atoms. Not anymore."

"Decision time," Washington said, checking his watch, then smacking his hands on the table top and standing. He felt stiff from the tension. He glanced down at the many notes he'd taken. He picked up his yellow pad and paged through for a few moments.

"Okay, here's the plan for now. We stick to our bluff. It's not played out. There's time left in this hand. I have the sense that our ploy is making Romanoff nervous. And that's exactly how I want him to feel. I want him to wonder if he's misjudged the cards. If he gets nastier, we deflect what we're able, take the blows if we must. I agree that it's wise to be aware of the gravity of our predicament, folks. But don't forget the early symbol of this republic, the rattlesnake. That—not a cowering rabbit—is the image we've gotta hold high."

Romanoff's call came, demanding the NATO surrender.

Washington said no.

Romanoff's response was merciless.

The Soviet orbital guns tore into NATO barracks and field deployment in

Europe. 50,000 troops in thirteen countries died. Another 100,000 were injured, all in a span lasting less than an hour, most from fires or explosions of fuel or weapons emplacements. The hospitals of Europe were jammed.

"Tsk, tsk, tsk!" Romanoff chided when Washington picked up the red phone afterwards. "Another day, another disaster! Well, I give you a week this time. Sift through the rubble and think it over."

A week this time. Not a couple days or a few hours. A full week. Interesting, Washington thought. Was Romanoff perhaps hoping to wear him down, allowing time for international political pressure to build against the U.S.?

Or had Romanoff become the first man to blink in this stare-down?

Washington ordered dozens of military relief and triage teams put together and flown to Europe. He made no secret about it. He didn't think Romanoff would risk attacks on medics. It was true that they'd bombed Red Cross units in Afghanistan. But there had been no universal Internet instant news then; no dozens of competing "total" news networks like CNN International, ABC WorldWide, Microsoft Planetary, BBC-24, or AT&T-AllNews, which were now everywhere in Europe. In this case, the publicity would be much worse for the Soviets than their wiping out 50,000 troops.

Washington also sent ten thousand armed U.S. men, former regular units only recently pulled from Germany, to "guard" the medical teams and other U.S. installations. It was a big gamble with American troops. But it was war, and Washington wanted to learn two things.

Number one, he wanted to see if Romanoff would dare fire upon U.S. ground troops in Europe. If not, it might be evidence that Romanoff had lost the fine edge of confidence. Second, Washington wanted to find out if sending in the help would contribute to solidifying European doubts about America's resolve. And although not yet dominant, there were deep doubts.

It had become clear to European members of NATO intelligence that its principal partner, the U.S., knew more about what was going on than it was admitting. Washington decided that the NATO partners had a right to know the source of the invisible terror killing their sons and daughters. They had a right to know that it was accomplished not by clever sabotage, but by a radical new form of force. Informing the allies had the virtue of upstaging possible propaganda by the Soviets. Washington ordered Goldstein to personally link the allies by secure video and give it to them straight. The "secure" briefing soon leaked out.

"WORLD COWERS BEFORE SOVIET DEATH RAY!" bellowed *Der Spiegel* of Germany. "U.S. PARALYZED!"

"WHERE'S THE EAGLE WHEN WE NEED IT?" demanded a sassy Brussels daily. "SLEEPING IN A SAFE NEST, PERHAPS?"

"HAS BIG UNCLE LOST HIS WILL?" the *South China Morning Post* asked. DOESN'T SAM SEE RED?" the *Rome Daily* prodded.

But such sniping was a minor fraction of media reaction. Most others were more considerate. Stunned, yes. But paralyzed? That was unthinkable. And America was, as it had been for many decades, the only Western heavyweight on the mat. "U.S. REFUSES USSR DEMANDS FOR CONTROL OF NATO," the *European Wall Street Journal* said. "AMERICA URGES ALLIES TO 'BUCKLE UP' FOR 'ROUGH RIDE AHEAD'."

"BUNKER MENTALITY BELTS BRITAIN," the *Economist* of London alliterated. "DOWNING STREET CONFERS WITH CRISIS COUNCIL; RESERVES READIED."

"GERMAN PARLIAMENT OFFERS NEW $200 BILLION GRANT TO SOVIETS," Bonn's *Money Daily* reported. "'INNOCENT GERMAN BOYS MEAN SOVIETS NO HARM,' REPUBLIC'S LEADER SAYS. OPPOSITION PARTIES CALL GERMAN ATTITUDE 'GROVELING.'"

"VISA APPLICATIONS TO U.S. SOAR," said the *New York Times*. "IMMIGRATION OFFICIALS PREDICT MASSIVE INFLUX FROM EUROPE. U.S. RELATIVES PROMISE TO TAKE IN CONTINENTAL COUSINS."

"EUROPEAN, FAR-EASTERN STOCKS NOSE-DIVE," reported *Japan Internet Economic*. "U.S. MARKETS SOAR AS 'SAFEST-HAVEN' OF WEALTH."

"AMERICANS CONSIDER RESPONSE," the *Australian Times* announced conservatively, "COMMONWEALTH LEADERS RECALL AMERICA 'ALWAYS SLOW' TO GET INVOLVED IN OVERSEAS WARS."

At least that's one legacy working for us, Washington thought, reading the news summaries.

At a press conference, he confirmed much of what had "leaked." He did his best to appear confident. While the American people didn't panic, they wanted to know what the U.S. was going to do. In their hearts, they assumed that America could and would do something. As an ex-Georgian President had learned too late, futility and malaise were not in the American outlook. Washington assured his countrymen that the U.S. would "respond forcefully, in time."

"The Third World War will not be won in a day," he told the microphones and cameras. "If we are to win, we must not merely respond, but respond intelligently."

"But you have, after all, declared war, Mr. President, so are you going to nuke 'em or blast 'em with our Romulan SDI?" ABC's Don Samuelson demanded sarcastically.

"Aw, c'mon, Don," Washington said with his best campaign smirk, "you know a sensible strategist never divulges his intragalactic plans."

The NATO allies grudgingly supported the U.S. caution. With their major defense systems wiped out, there was little else they could do. All but Germany called up reserves and tried their best to organize remaining regular forces. The Germans seemed politically paralyzed. Their chancellor was facing a no-confidence vote in the Bundestag, the lower house of parliament. The French, who were, once again, not part of NATO's military wing, and whose forces had for unknown reasons been spared by the Soviets, clammed up on public statements after the last Soviet attack on the Continent. Washington suspected that the French were also biding their time, though in precisely what way, only the French knew. A radically different attitude prevailed in "the boot" of Europe. Death rays notwithstanding, the Italians were boiling.

When the Soviets had wiped out the 50,000 NATO soldiers, a large Italian convoy had been passing through the historic city of Florence. The Soviet attack ignited tons of weapons and fuel in the convoy. The explosions left sections of the venerated town and hundreds of its revered historic treasures in a smoking, shattered shambles. Even more than the deaths of its soldiers, this sacrilege on art and tradition sent Italy into a fury.

The Italians had a new chief of state, one whom old-timers called, "The New Mussolini." He had the nickname not necessarily because of dictatorial inclinations, but because of his overpowering charisma. Antonio Mauro was a handsome, but less-than-well-educated young firebrand. He felt that what NATO needed was someone to expose these Soviets as the charlatans and bluffers that they were.

He directed Italian generals to launch fifty secretly built nuclear supercruise missiles against strategic cities in the Soviet Union. They did. An hour after the launch, the young Italian President and two of his top generals, flush with confidence, stepped out of a limousine. They and six body guards were swept by a twitch of a Soviet antimatter beam and fried on the sidewalk.

After hours passed and U.S. intelligence bruskly informed Italy that no nuclear explosions had been detected in the Soviet Union, the Italian general staff decided to reconsider the defense of national manhood.

CHAPTER 43

THE LINK

I t is quite clear," UPI's chief political analyst, Ernest Pomp, typed into his terminal in the belly of the company's Washington building. He stopped. For a moment he wondered: *is* it clear? Then, only half joking, he thought: if it occurred to *me*, it must be. As a compromise to the remote possibility that it wasn't, he struck the word "quite" and wrote, "It is increasingly clear that by forcing out General Wharton 'Buck' Reed, the administration sought to silence a salient observer—not to mention an articulate rival to the president himself. In our wholesale, if not already somewhat weary, war-time worship of Washington, let us not forget that the elections are only two short years away."

He frowned and deleted the words, "wholesale, if not already." A little alliteration was catchy; too much sounded fruity.

He leaned back, stuck a hand under his sweater, loosened two lower shirt buttons and with dirty fingernails scratched a pimple on the hairy skin of his paunch.

He took a huge drag off his cigarette and blew smoke at a tiny picture of President Sam Washington taped to the edge of his monitor.

An early riser, Pomp wrote, "Pomp and Circumstances" every morning between three and four, Eastern. By 4:30, it was clearing the teleprinters and computer screens across America, assuring that it would be one of the first, and therefore influential, opinion pieces that editors saw when they arrived at work.

President? Pomp thought. Who needs to be president when he can be the Media Pope? He smirked, scratched, and smoked.

"Almost daily," he pontificated into his keyboard, ash falling between the keys, "the consensus around the nation's capitol carries questions. 'Why did our president incarcerate his own, former best friend?' That is perhaps the smallest of the questions. Bigger ones are lighting up everywhere, like lamps blinking on in an early fog."

He paused and grinned crookedly. That one would be quoted.

"Given Reed's background, one might have thought the roles would be reversed. That they were not—that Reed was both a general and a peace advocate— was perhaps an all too accurate barometer of both men's basic consciences."

Pomp ground out his stub and lit a fresh Camel, sat back, and read his column. After running it through the computer's spell checker, he sent it out to the news services.

Buck Reed didn't like Ernest Pomp. The man needed to polish his shoes, straighten his tie, and use a good mouthwash.

Unbeknown to his readers, Pomp had become a behind-the-scenes force at the powerful anti-defense think tank, Strategic Thought, Inc., or STI. He had free use of a computer and frequently ghost-wrote articles for the organization's newsletter and the dozens of position papers which STI distributed to college and high school campuses. STI offices were closed between midnight and six, but by arrangement, Pomp was allowed to work then. The secrecy was at Pomp's request. He saw no point in risking another level of attack on him by the conservative media. They were still a minority among the "majors," but they were such loudmouths.

Pomp met Reed and a man whom he assumed was a bodyguard at a side entrance to STI and led them to his cubicle.

Reed had read several of Pomp's sympathetic columns—much like the one which Pomp had just finished—and had called to request a meeting. Pomp had set it up and Reed had been unsurprised at the columnist's choice of locations. Reed had long ago read FBI domestic surveillance reports documenting Pomp's close association with STI.

Pomp plopped down in a chair and motioned to another. Reed sat down, but his bodyguard remained standing, never more than ten feet away. Pomp blew smoke at the guard once, then ignored him. He hated musclemen.

Reed frowned and said, "Pomp, I can't say I'm crazy about you."

Pomp puffed his cigarette and shrugged. "It's an alliance, General. That's all. So what more can I do for you?"

"As you know, I set my sights high. It's the way I am. I'm not only going to shake this trumped-up treason charge, I'm heading for the top. I'll be frank. I want you to help me smell like a rose so I can reach the Rose *Garden*. I want the White House and I'm going to get it two years from now—if we all make it out without being crisped by my opponent's stupidity. What you're doing in your column is superb. Just the kind of media-pumping a campaign needs. But I need STI, too. If you can get the STI grass-roots stompers to goose my campaign—"

Pomp shook his head and more ashes fell onto his sweater. "STI's registered non-profit. Can't get involved in political campaigns. Illegal."

"Don't bullshit me, Pomp!" Reed snapped. "All you've got to do is make sure a good bundle of those pamphlets and brochures STI hands out all over the country have my basic defense line in it. The public'll take it from there. Now, will you do it? And if so, what'll I be on the hook for?"

"Hook, General?" Pomp shook his head. "Why, there's no hook. None at all. I receive full payment by the sheer goodness of your position."

He gazed at Reed through a cloud of smoke and smiled.

Reed looked at him uneasily for a moment, then nodded, and said, "One of those Kantian types, eh? Virtue-is-its-own-reward, and all that? Fine. I can live with it."

"You'll have to."

Reed blinked, "What's that supposed to mean?"

"Not a thing."

Reed abruptly stood, automatically shook Pomp's outstretched hand, nodded to his bodyguard, and left.

But in the elevator, he experienced an urgent desire to shower. He shoved his hands deep into his pants pockets, like plunging them in antiseptic.

CHAPTER 44

THE RING

I t's a gap," Ella Paxon told her boss in the middle of a bite of steak. Washing ton, Ella, the First Lady, and the vice president were sharing an early dinner at the lodge. The cold rain of the last few days had temporarily stopped, but dark clouds continued to roil. "I mean, it makes no sense," Ella said. "If they're so confident in their anti-matter rays, why resort to nuclear weapons?"

Two days earlier, the Italian generals had worked themselves up into another frenzy and sent a fresh flock of cruise missiles at the Soviets. Using mainly their AM guns, the Sovs had knocked out the cruises, but had then responded further, nuking historic Florence.

"Did you see those TV and video reports? Horrible!" the First Lady said.

Washington grimaced. "Yeah, I saw." More than you know, he said to himself, remembering close-up intelligence photos.

"*New Pravda* is claiming that it's justifiable retaliation," he said. "They're telling the world press that the Soviet High Command saved tens, maybe hundreds of millions of innocent peasants at the price of tens of thousands of Italian *aggressors*."

"And thanks to Buck and his crowd, our citizens are starting to believe them— even though the Sovs initiated the mess," Ella said. "It's absurd."

The emerging turn in public sentiment was incredible; a bafflingly swift switch toward isolationism. Rarely were Americans isolationist after being attacked. To top it off, a nut case was leading the cheers to run for the presidency.

"Sam, its a gap in their strategy, an inconsistency," Ella persisted, gesturing with her fork. "Sure, they felt they had to teach the Italians a lesson. Strategically, I can see that. But what would the best way have been?"

"Using their beams," Leininger spoke up. "A surgical strike, perhaps at all the Italian generals or naval facilities."

"It almost seemed desperate," Annette said.

"Now there's an intriguing thought," Leininger observed.

The other three looked at him.

"Suppose," he said, "that their AM satellites aren't solar powered? Or nuclear powered? Or what was it? Magneto hydrodynamically powered?"

"Don't follow you," Washington said, sampling his own wine and then taking a mouthful of mushrooms-and-onion stir. Most of his food had gone untouched and was growing cold. He put down his fork; hell with it; it'd be good for his waistline.

"What if they don't have the one thing we've assumed—the one, crucial item that MacGregor and Young and everyone else has been taking for granted. A converter."

"Now *I'm* lost," Ella said.

"Me too," the First Lady admitted.

"The converter is the thing that SpaCom assumed has been the Soviets' breakthrough, right? It's what makes the guns economical, portable, rechargeable."

"Yeah, that and the gizmo that clears a path for the beam through the atmosphere." Washington said.

"Our scientists are saying that it's only by miniaturizing their anti-matter-maker that they were able to achieve what they have. But what if it wasn't that way at all? As everybody keeps saying, there's no literature on it, anywhere. Well, what if what we think exists, doesn't?"

"Nice thought, but it won't wash," Washington said. "High Eye's labs and the independents we brought in—including a few guys from Europe and Japan—have confirmed that it's definitely an anti-matter gun. The spectroscopy and a bevy of other tests, most of which I don't fathom, are positive."

"No, no! You miss my point! I'm not denying that they've got the AM guns up there. I'm talking about the fuel. Was it *really* made in orbit—by what proof? What if it's made in the ordinary way, in big facilities on the ground? What if it's got to be shuttled up? More significantly, what if they lifted it up there only once for each satellite?"

Ella dropped her fork.

"Good Lord," Annette said, starting to grasp the implications.

"If so," Washington speculated slowly, "then you're suggesting the fuel they've put up is *it*? All they've got?"

"Could be."

"That may be why they resorted to nukes against Florence," Ella said. "They absolutely had to teach the Italians, and by implication us, a big lesson, but didn't want to waste their antimatter reserves."

"Which implies," said Leininger, "that if we're clever, we might be able to exhaust them." He popped a piece of steak into his mouth and grinned, proud of himself. "Why not put our hats on some sticks and fool them into using up their bullets?"

"There's only one way to test it, you know," Young said on the video phone later.

"I know. I've got a couple ideas . . ."

They discussed them, then Washington asked, "Anything developing from the crews you've got working?"

"Well, I don't understand all the springs and gears, but one of MacGregor's guys has figured out how to track the Sovs' rays by using portable ionization detectors. I guess they track the thin path of the AM beams, atmospheric interaction, or rather, that of whatever clears their path—we still don't have it nailed down. It's tricky, but Tom says he can train operators to get pretty good with it; he's already got guys running through simulators. We're finding that sub-warfare guys are best at it. Whatever the technical details, it's a passive principle and compact. That means our use of 'em is unlikely to be detected," the Spaceman said.

"You mean from now on we can tell exactly which AM guns are firing when?"

Young nodded, "You got it, sir."

"Damn, that's great! It'll tie in with my own idea, if we can forge it into a plan."

"If your hunch is right."

"How's MacGregor's main project?" Washington asked, somewhat unenthusiastically.

Young's face clouded. "Well, Tom says it's proving tough as thistle. Not three, but more like six weeks, earliest."

"Too long."

"Much. Problem is finding or fabricating parts. Nobody seems to understand what he's trying to do and he won't get super specific. I could order him to, but try that with him and you don't get anything but a Southern California impression of Mr. Oriental Inscrutable. He's been bashed and battered a lot for his so-called far-out ideas. Hypersensitive. Guess I don't blame him."

"Well, I'm not going to count on his stuff being ready. Glenn, I want you and your guys, and anyone else you trust, to come up with a tactical scenario for my suggestions. I think they're the basis for a good retaliation strategy, or at least as good as a ground-hog can muster against a hawk. My outlook is that the hawk may have a few sore talons. I won't be an armchair general, Glenn. But I stress that we must act soon. It's got to begin well before Romanoff's week is up and that's a paltry four days from now. It's the only way we can steal the initiative. In other words, I want a grand surprise."

"You got it, sir," Young said, feeling charged.

"Oh, one more thing," Washington asked, "you keeping this inter-service rivalry damped? I don't want it flaring up at a crucial moment."

"Okay, so far. They have their peacetime differences, but they're patriotic, sensible men. This is war and they're all pulling together. They're not all like Reed, sir."

"Thank God. Give your crews my best."

"I will, sir."

Washington noted that General Young's voice and demeanor were those of a much older man these days. War is an agent of age, the president thought, remembering his own haggard face in the mirror that morning.

In early 1988, partly in response to reporters' inquiries, the U.S. Army Missile Command at Redstone Arsenal in Huntsville, Alabama admitted that it had successfully tested an antiaircraft missile called a "Patriot," in a new mode. One of the tests, it said, had occurred nearly two years earlier against an older Lance missile.

On November 4, 1987, a second test took place, this one against another patriot. Both targets had been simulating re-entering Soviet short-range ballistic missiles; both targets were destroyed.

That was the beginning.

By 1990, the Patriot was tested in the Gulf War. Then the United States fielded 6,200 upgraded Patriots in 75 batteries of 103 firing units in Europe. An unknown number of test missiles were also based in Texas. By the late nineties, these missiles had been further upgraded to anti-tactical and anti-medium-range ballistic missiles and their numbers quietly tripled as preparation of one part of the U.S. SDI. Shortly after, to the loud, but brief howls of the Kremlin, the U.S. withdrew from the anti-ballistic missile treaty of 1972 and more powerful fuels were introduced and new computer software was added to the missiles. The upgrades enabled the Patriots to function as anti-ICBM missiles and to double as faster variable-range anti-satellite strikers. By the early 2000s, the numbers were vast. Nearly 60,000 of the Raytheon product, now termed "P-6s," were spread among locations around the world, including ten thousand in mobile hardened canisters in Europe. Nearly 20,000 P-6s, in addition to thousands of shorter-range missiles, super Gatling guns, and other devices, surrounded critical U.S. bases and command, control, communications and intelligence centers.

Soviet human intelligence and overhead reconnaissance had helped destroy five-thousand of the P-6 missiles in Europe in the initial Soviet attack on Europe. But thousands more remained, their locations uncertain to the Stavka of the Soviet Supreme High Command.

Two days before Romanoff's latest deadline for NATO's surrender, half of the worldwide inventory of Patriots was, within minutes of each other, reprogrammed to anti-satellite mode; the other half was left programmed to anti-ICBM status. This required a mere flick of a switch; the software was digitally stored inside an EMP-proof optical memory.

Simultaneously, every phased-array ship-based radar of the U.S., as well as its main stationary PAVE-PAWS and rail-mobile phased-array systems, were fed full battle-management software. This enabled them to track the nearly 900 Soviet antimatter satellites and prepare the radars to direct P-6 missiles against the Soviet weaponry.

The battle picture was this. At any instant, there were 150 orbiting Soviet AM guns over a slice of the globe roughly the size of the United States or Europe—150 AM guns for each sixth of the planet. Some of these guns were in transpolar orbits, so as to rotate complete coverage over all parts of both hemispheres. Others were in interlacing orbits, primarily covering the middle third "waistline" of the planet.

Fifty-four thousand deployed P-6s remained in the U.S. worldwide inventory. Out of the 27,000 Patriots activated to anti-satellite status, 29 would be assigned to each Soviet antimatter battle-station. Another 18 would be assigned to each of the Soviets' 50 kinetic energy weapon (KEW) battle platforms, to the

USSR's "outdated" SDI, which consisted primarily of "smart rocks," small missiles housed in radiation-hardened space "garages."

The idea was that as each battle station was taken out, battle-management computers would switch remaining missiles toward untouched targets.

"Understand that, despite the raw numbers, we don't have much to field against each Soviet target and that these are only averages," Young said, briefing his general staff on the plan cleared by the president. "I expect it will be extremely difficult to bust the Soviet orbital ring—hence the name, Operation Hard Ring. Frankly, our backs are already against the wall—or rather, down against the dirt. If we don't pull this off, gentlemen; if their rate and duration of fire is greater than we expect; we may be cooked as a country. We're fighting our way out of the bottom of a pit."

He pointed an infrared remote "mouse nose" at the huge war room HDTV monitor which carried a multi-colored schematic of the earth and locations of Soviet AM satellites. As he pointed, the schematic began to move in time with his explanation, illustrating the projected course of battle.

"We'll begin our attack with concentrated firepower against only about 100 of the stations after they top the horizon in range over Europe. We'll use the Patriots remaining there and others aboard U.S. and NATO vessels. We have about 100 THAAD high-altitude rocket-killer missiles we might be able to bring on line, but that's iffy. They've been mothballed since Clinton killed that program."

"Why start there?" an Air Force general asked. "And why against 100 targets? Why not fewer and concentrate our shots?"

"Good question. First, we're back-timing the strike in order to hit those battle stations which we believe are *already* low on antimatter—in other words, those AM sats which were responsible for the last big attack on Europe. Now, it turns out that some of them were also involved in the first hit against NATO. An oversight on the part of the Soviets, but we thank them for their smugness. It means some of their AM birds ought to be doubly low on energy. They'll be among our primary targets.

"The reason we don't want to concentrate too much is that it allows rising battle stations a less challenged field. Remember that at over seventeen grand an hour, those AM babies take only about ninety minutes to orbit. With about 900 of them, they're dawning at an average rate of ten per minute. In our case, we're given a few minutes window across the section of the surface that our Patriots can efficiently handle.

"Now, these numbers aren't written in stone and we'll be constantly updating, but the bottom line is that we'll be facing a minimum of around eighty Sov battle stations at a time. I stress, a minimum."

"Whew!" the Marine Corps Chief exclaimed.

"Amen," Young said. "Actually even that's optimistic. About a tenth of the AM guns are in transpolar orbits and consequently take longer to get anywhere sideways. But at those velocities, you can see why we have to start shooting pronto at the primaries and why we also have to keep their heads pinned down, meaning that we can't concentrate too tightly. It's like keeping up cover fire on the ground while your assault troops rush in. If you *only* shoot at the main enemy nest, the other nests'll cut your assault team to ribbons."

The Marine nodded.

"Now, once the ring is breached, if it can be, we want to have a hotdog double-banquet. We want to eat the meat from both broken ends. We'll fire primarily from safer positions beneath the breach, but we'll also set up crossfire from below unbreached areas in order to diffuse the Soviets firepower further. As it is, by shooting mainly from under the hole, once we make one, we should be able to prevent their concentrating as much damage at us. The curve of the earth will keep the bulk of their guns off-angle."

"Because of the atmospheric distortion problem, we strongly suspect that their AM beams work best shooting straight down, or at least damned close to perpendicular. To take advantage of that presumed limitation, we'll transfer attacks right around the globe, timing them to follow the breach ends. This'll put them at a disadvantage on the first sweep because their unaffected sats won't know what to shoot at on the ground and won't be able to reach the rockets that reveal themselves by their launch signatures.

"Now, it's not quite as simple as that," he paused.

"This has been *simple?*" someone piped up.

Young smiled, but plowed on, for there wasn't much time.

"Our P-6s don't have the straight-angle hindrance low down, but of course as they rise, the horizon scoots back and they become subject to more of the Sov stuff. I stress that we don't know the AM's true angle of fire. Maybe it's narrow; maybe they can rotate those guns to counterattack anti-satellite weapons, ASATs. However, the Chief's guess is that only a few are significantly rotatable as ASAT weapons. This is because the primary aim of the system seems to be ground and mid-atmosphere control—in other words, tactical or theater support."

"I take it," a Navy admiral said, "that we need only exhaust their guns, not necessarily kill 'em?"

"Correct. No bullets is as good as no gun."

"How sure are we that these mothers *can* be depleted?" an Army general asked.

"It's a calculated risk based on a fairly lengthy chain of reasoning. Personally, I think it's correct. So does the president."

"Will there be other diversions to draw their fire?" someone else asked. "A few noisy firecrackers behind their ears wouldn't hurt."

"Absolutely. The Italians, the French, the British and the Israelis will be launching what remains of European cruise missile fleets—some 8,000 of them, I understand—prior to our initiating Operation Hard Ring. That should drain a lot of juice from those Buck Rogerski pistols. The Brits and French also have some hardened ICBMs they might be able to launch when things get confusing enough. There's no point trying them too soon, though. They'd be as vulnerable as sleepy ground squirrels. However, when the smoke and haze hit, a lot of 'em'll probably sneak through, at least far enough to force a diversion of antimatter beams. Same goes for our ICBMs and SLBMS, our sub-launched missiles—and our sea-based cruises.

"One thing in our favor is that it appears the Soviets have never developed an efficient plane-based cruise-missile interdiction system. We don't know why. Maybe it was in anticipation of their AM system taking the load. They plan their military acquisitions in twenty-year hunks. Nevertheless, the Italian experience confirms other intelligence. The Sovs only seem able to stop about ten percent of a cruise attack with lookdown/shoot-down interceptor jets or surface-to-air rockets. The Rooskies used mostly AM guns against the Italian attacks. That means we can be fairly sure our cruise launches will, indeed, divert a hell of a hunk of their AM fire."

"What about using our sub SLBMs as ASAT weapons?" another Army general asked.

"We've reconfigured about half of them to do just that. But the Peacemakers and D-5s are big, expensive candles. We'd rather see what the cheaper Patriots can do first. Remember, even if we break the ring, the Sovs'll still have their entire land-and-sea-based arsenal intact. We'd be advised to keep some stuff in retaliation reserve. We don't have enough bombers to hold all their main targets at serious risk, and we're not even sure the B-2s can penetrate unless we first zero-out their orbital guns. We don't know if their AM eyes saw the B-2s that went after their six cities or not. Russia says yes, but that may be a convenient lie."

"What about the B-3, the Plate?" an Air Force man asked.

Young hesitated, not entirely liking the answer he was forced to give. "The president says we don't bring out the Plate until there's no other alternative. It's cover isn't to be broken unless total defeat is imminent. When they start hitting bunches of our cities like they hit Florence, then I imagine we'll be discussing that. Other questions? No? You have your orders, gentlemen. Let's pull the ring out of the bad bear's nose."

CHAPTER 45

THE DENT

Y oung had named the area of the AM ring which had been partially self-depleted *The Dent*. At 8:00 p.m., Greenwich Mean Time, as *The Dent* neared Europe, the passive beam detectors were activated. They would spot, trace, pattern analyze and record the source of Soviet antimatter strikes. The data would be used to project how much firepower might be needed in order to wear down individual battle stations.

As battle stations went dead from apparent depletion, the number of strikes each had made would be used to build a profile of Soviet fire reserves. That would be used to forecast which enemy satellites were weakest and thereby most vulnerable. The collated information was crucial in order to husband the West's relatively meager anti-satellite resources.

As the detectors lit up, thousands of cruise missiles jetted out of hidden NATO locations in Europe and from dozens of ships at sea. All the missiles headed toward the Soviet Union. Most carried conventional loads, but the Sovs had no way of knowing which were which. They would have to go after them all.

As the scenario began, thousands of U.S. military personnel around the planet held their breaths, wiped sweat from their brows, shifted their feet, gnawed styrofoam cups, sipped coffee, smoked, fidgeted, joked, scratched, stared, bit lips, tapped fingers, as soldiers throughout history had done to handle stress at the beginning of crucial battles.

It took several minutes, but Soviet AM satellites in and slightly ahead of *The Dent* finally began firing at the attacking cruise missiles.

"Interesting," Young observed to Walkingfar in the war room as they watched the high resolution depiction of the battle. "It took them quite a spell to integrate."

"You mean that the cruises were away?"

"And to decide to act. Their sensors and initial targeting reactions aren't that fast, even if their guns are."

"Don't forget the guys who push the 'start' buttons. It may simply mean that they were caught off guard."

"Let's hope so. They were supposed to be."

A few minutes later, in the deep blast shelter off the Black House basement suite, the president picked up the red phone and heard Romanoff's grating, angry voice.

"Washington, are you merely retarded or are you also insane? Don't make me wipe your country off the face of this planet. We are quite capable of doing so!"

"Oh, I wouldn't count on it," Washington said. "We've got a few cards up our sleeves. Besides, I'm not 'making' you initiate anything, mister. You started this ugly circus, so you can damned well pull down the tent and pack it up."

Romanoff gave a harsh chuckle. "I give you credit for being a bull, Washington. But in a fight, the bear always wins, because the bull doesn't know when to run. Surely you don't wish to prod me into a full-scale nuclear conflict? Into rash action?"

Washington snorted. "What you've done so far is not rash?"

"We are chess masters, not football Neanderthals. We'll simply burn your missiles out of the air. We are invulnerable to such puny attacks. Your SDI queen is already gone. You, Washington, King of the Ruling Circles, will soon face checkmate."

"Our queen *is* up there, Romanoff. You simply can't see her."

The Soviet ruler snorted contemptuously and hung up.

Mere moments after his call, the NATO Patriot anti-satellite rockets began roaring skywards, their new ultra fast-burn, high thrust fuels shoving them up from locations throughout Western Europe and surrounding waters, even from points as far south as the coast of Nigeria and Namibia. Patriots went up from the Atlantic and the Mediterranean, from the North, Baltic, Barents and the Black Seas. Others streaked out from Israel and Turkey and Kuwait. As *The Dent*, the weak spot in the Soviet AM "hard ring," moved steadily east, its satellites were forced to take on the bulk of the defense against the cruises and P-6s. The NATO missiles had been launched from points as widely scattered as possible. This compelled the Soviet AM guns to spend more time retargeting and refocusing their beams than if the enemy had been more closely drawn.

The first thing that was learned by U.S. monitors was that Walkingfar's judgement had been accurate. Except for a few specially designated ones, the battle stations had limited fire-angle flexibility. The Soviets did, indeed, prefer to fire their guns as close to straight down as possible.

Despite the stricture, they kept ahead of the NATO antagonists for several minutes. If the allies couldn't break the ring over Europe, Young thought that they wouldn't have another chance until before *The Dent* rose over the Japanese longitudes. That, unfortunately, would give the Soviets nearly a half-hour for regrouping. The U.S. plan would work best if the ring could be broken in the initial encounter. That way, the Far East follow-on attack would be able to "eat the meat," to begin chomping at the weak, broken ring ends. Using island and ship and boat based P-6s, the process could continue right across the Pacific, the U.S., the Atlantic and Europe again. As the gap grew, Young and his tacticians had other infections ready to throw into the wound.

"There!" one of the war room technicians shouted. "There it is! And another!"

Sure enough, two red monitor lights blinked, indicating that a pair of enemy satellites had been put out of action.

"Field monitor teams confirm two Sov AM birds have ceased firing. AM ionization trails no longer detectable."

"Got another one! Busted it!" Walkingfar shouted, his eyes glittering as he glanced at Young.

"Three more gone!" a different, high-voiced technician piped up. "All direct P-6 hits!"

"Six more!" a woman officer cheerfully cried out.

Someone whistled as another person shook a fist in the air and said, "They beam, but we cream!"

Watching quietly off in one corner, wishing he had something to do, Kevin Jones whispered to himself, "Snort *that* pepper up your noses, you bastards!"

Within four minutes, a total of thirty-seven AM guns had been neutralized and Young assessed the situation on the big screen. There was a clear, although narrow gap in the ring. It was a ragged and slanted line, running roughly from Oslo to Marseilles to Lagos to Walvis Bay. But it was there.

"We've broken the sucker!" Young said loudly. "Now let's chew up the ring ends as much as we can before they disappear down Mamma Russia's dress!"

His comment was more of a pep-talk than an order, for battle-management teams had standing instructions to do precisely that. The Patriot batteries methodically banged at the edges of the breach, widening it quickly. By the time it passed into Soviet territory, ninety-eight of the death-ray machines — over a tenth of the total — had been blown away or depleted.

Meanwhile, the fresh AM guns crossing Europe were occupied going after the many NATO cruise missiles still heading toward the Soviet Union, as they would for hours, most being slower-moving, low-flying subsonics.

Young punched up battle data on a terminal. While heartening, it still didn't look that good strategically. Considering that these had been the weaker of the Soviet satellites, the cost had been high for the P-6 ASAT inventory — about a dozen Patriots per AM gun. It had taken half of the activated anti-satellite Patriot arsenal in and around Europe to do the job. Young had hoped for a better score. He looked at Walkingfar and pointed to the big screen. The big Indian nodded stoically. He'd seen the data, too, reaching similar reservations.

But then, as always happens in war, human nature got the better of the aggressor for a few moments. The next wave of nearly undamaged, undepleted Soviet AM guns began a wild attempt to roast the land-based Patriot batteries which had been involved in the breach-making attack.

"Looks like they calculated and kept track of our boost locations," an Air Force general remarked.

"They don't want to give our Pats a second chance next orbit," Walkingfar observed. "But they're sure wasting a lot of firepower. This is an emotion-driven response. They can't be targeting carefully. Hell, they're letting fly so much anti-matter, they're practically spraying it! Tsk, tsk, tsk!"

He winked at Young.

After the breach moved over Soviet territory, unexhausted Patriot batteries had swiftly headed for shelters different than the ones from which they'd emerged while the breach was above Western Europe. Exhausted batteries had been abandoned. To assist the survivors in their run for cover, the Army had poured out an infrared and ultraviolet reflecting, anti-sensor smoke "ASScover" camouflage.

As the Army chief eventually reported to Young, the Soviet retaliation had done significant damage to allied hardware. The angry beam assault had hit over a quarter of the exposed NATO missiles before they could hide. However, only 400 men had died in the overall skirmish, and two-thirds of them had bought it when two Navy cruisers were beamed and sunk, one in the Baltic, the other near Cyprus.

Young reflected that the toll could have been worse had the Soviets had more time to bring their own precision surface-to-surface missiles to bear. But the targeting for those weapons required accurate reconnaissance and assessment against an enemy that had proven fluid. At least this time. The allies had momentarily caught a cocky Ivan off guard.

It looked like the president's hunch about Romanoff's strategy was close. There was no hint yet that the Soviets wished to launch a massive nuclear or conventional assault. They still believed that they had a vastly superior hand and could force U.S. and European capitulation at relatively low cost.

Despite the limited allied success, Young wasn't sure the Soviets were wrong. It was early in the game, and he reminded his top people that the U.S. gains had come dearly. Yet for another fifteen minutes, the Soviets wasted antimatter stores in a fit of retribution. Their beams pointlessly swept NATO personnel quarters, slicing and dicing them, setting many ablaze. This was fine with Young. Most of the men in those quarters had evacuated before the attack, so it was primarily the structures themselves which were hit. Romanoff was cooking snail shells.

Abruptly, as though a giant switch had been thrown, the Soviets seemed to realize their folly and stopped the tantrum. In the Colorado war room, for ten seconds there was quiet. It reminded Young of the sudden, unearthly silence following the end of a heavy artillery barrage.

"Somebody slapped *somebody* in the face," a SpaCom colonel and ex-TAV fighter pilot remarked. Cheers, congratulations, relief rolled through the room.

In the Black House, Sam Washington wiped sweat from his brow with a handkerchief and winked at Ella Paxson. "Round one to us," he said.

"Round two," Ella said twenty minutes later as she, the president, and the remainder of the core group not in Colorado gazed up at the Black House situation screen.

It was Young who made first direct contact. "Expensive, but looks good so far," he told his Commander-in-Chief. "It'll get hotter now. We're a long steal from home plate."

"Keep at it," Washington replied. "We're rooting for you here beneath the Potomac."

"Thank you, sir."

The breach was no longer a dent. It would soon rise over Inchon, Kwangju, Taejon, and Seoul, South Korea and encounter the Patriot batteries there. But before that, the Soviets faced another cruise missile threat. Thousands more of the hard to detect missiles skimmed out of shelters and ships, heading for Soviet military facilities on Sakhalin Island and points north and northwest in the USSR. The antimatter guns were forced to commence firing, discharging their precious energy stores in order to protect the Motherland and some of her more important ground facilities from attack.

But another variety of malt was flavoring Young's tactical brew. Unrealized by the Russians, their lead AM guns were about to face a new challenge off the coast of Tientsin, China. Some forty miles to sea, a U.S. submarine had deployed a self-inflating giant rubber raft. Aboard it floated a unique weapon: a mobile *flex-lens*, double-beamed laser — a MFL/DBL, or *muffle-double*, as the mechanics called it. This weapon could effectively fire into space by nearly instantaneously correcting for atmospheric turbulence. The first beam was a "pathfinder." It bounced off a target and returned to the platform where sub-based computers analyzed the dispersion of the beam. They then directed the main laser to split its ray into many separate ones which would find paths through the turbulence and converge in a pinpoint of destruction. The system was driven by the boat's own nuclear reactor in combination with a bank of giant capacitors. The capacitors were explained in news releases as "rapidly discharging power-storage devices, sort of ultra-quick-release batteries." The power was ferried upward to the laser on its floating platform through a superconducting cable. The sub stayed several hundred feet down and almost a mile away, out of range of all but a lucky Soviet nuclear blast.

A certain amount of fresh data about the antimatter guns' vulnerability to lasers had been gleaned during the height of the battle over Europe. An experimental SpaCom ground laser, placed by secret treaty with the French government in a remote nook of the Jura Mountains not far from Morez had fired scores of quick bursts at Soviet AM guns, using various amounts of power. The casings of the AM guns were found to be heavily shielded against laser penetration. But SpaCom analysts discovered that the beam weapons' targeting sensors could be "flash blinded" when held in battle mode, which they would be as they entered the Japanese theater.

The blinding eliminated them from use for several minutes. During that time, they were open to attack by other means.

Targeting information for the floating laser off China was provided by a second floating platform of phased-array radars cued to the sub's fix-and-follow (FAF) system. The systems's operator, a young specialist of only twenty-two, waited until there were over fifty targets in view on the trailing side of the breach. That was about all he figured the equipment could handle. He hit an "enter" key and the laser began a rapid-fire discharge skyward as its gyroscopically stabilized bed on the platform kept it steady against the swell of the ocean.

The laser blinded forty-two of its Soviet targets before the forty-third antimatter gun beat it to the punch and sunk the floating platform. The sub's commander ordered the firing of planted charges, destroying the phased-array platform so its miniaturization technology would not fall into unfriendly hands. Then, using a quantum-wired, blue-green laser communications beam — which could deeply penetrate ocean water — he notified an airborne Voyager drone relay station of the successful blindings. The drone, a robot which cruised at over 90,000 feet, forwarded the information to Patriot battle management banks in Korea.

The first thirty Patriots to reach up from there managed to kill twenty-two of the blinded AM guns. Another thirty P-6s out of Okinawa got the other twenty.

Someone thoughtfully radioed news of the kills to the submarine. A highly controlled and brief celebration ensued below the waters of the Gulf of China as the submarine dived deeper and left the area. Five minutes later, the boat shook mildly from the shock of three Soviet nuclear blasts over the area where the launch platform had been.

The blasts were duly noted by the Chinese. Indeed, the Chinese "Dragon Flame" high commanders had monitored the battle closely. They had neither condemned nor praised either side. But now, with nuclear bombs detonating off the Chinese coast, certain key Party and military leaders in Beijing made what would prove to be the most monumental decision ever for the future of their empire.

As soon as the blinded AM guns were blasted away, thousands of ASAT Pats in Korea, Japan, the Philippines, and Northern Australia began hammering away at the western edge of the breach. Young had decided to let the eastern edge drift by. The purpose of this tactic was both to maximize what little surprise his forces might retain and to test the theory that the breach was wide enough so that one end of the broken ring could no longer easily defend the other. Part of this depended on how many of the more versatile, wider-angle Sov guns had been eliminated from action near the breach.

Walkingfar's guesstimates held. As the breach grew, the ends found it impossible to assist each other. At that point, Patriots slammed against both ends of the ring and the breach broadened faster. The breach was becoming a gulf. By the time the trailing eastern edge passed Hawaii, the leading western bank stretched all the way to the Sargasso Sea in the Atlantic. After not quite an hour-and-a-half of battle, the break in the ring of orbiting beam lasers was nearly eight-thousand miles long. An irregular string of two-hundred-eighty-four antimatter battle stations had been destroyed, including most — perhaps all — of those which had been in transpolar orbit.

Again, the cost had been terribly high. Eighty-nine percent of the ASAT-activated P-6s had been expended.

As everyone from corporals to generals slapped each other on the back and gave high fives, General Young stood with his hands clasped behind him and looked grimly at the war room's big monitor. If this continued, he figured, he'd have to activate all the remaining Patriots on the planet in order to wipe out only 300 or so AM guns. But that would leave an equal number untouched in orbit.

Because Patriots were the core of the U.S.'s anti-ICBM ground based arsenal — although there were other "terminal" defense weapons — its depletion would leave the U.S. and its allies far more open to a Soviet nuclear strike. There were still the Gatling guns, swarm jets, a few THAADS, Arrows and other rockets, and a scant number of lasers, but they wouldn't be enough to stop the Soviets' remaining ICBM arsenal — depleted as it was.

He didn't dare fire anymore P-6s. On the other hand, if he didn't, any lingering doubts Romanoff had about Washington's audacious bluff that the U.S. SDI was intact, but "cloaked," could go up in smoke. Young privately believed that the Soviets had complete confidence that they had knocked out the American orbiting anti-missile rocket weapons. But, if he could convince them otherwise, or just create significant fresh doubt, the vaunted Soviet strategic masters might head back to chess school. If so, it would buy the U.S. a lot of time — perhaps victory.

Despite the fact that the Patriots' locations were masked, it was open knowledge that the U.S. had a large domestic reserve of Patriots protecting its military facilities and Capitol. Stupid, Young thought. The U.S. had years ago disclosed the precise numbers under legally questionable Clinton executive order modifications to the '72 ABM Treaty. But that's the way it was; generals were expected to fight despite the foolish finagling of politicians. The longer the U.S. refused to fire its remaining P-6 banks, the less Romanoff might wonder if he'd really wiped out the American space shield. As it stood, there was a slim chance Romanoff might think the U.S. was holding a truly cloaked shield in reserve.

Now came the big test, the second part of Washington's gargantuan bluff, to see whether the U.S. could change a frail but lingering Soviet doubt into a certainty — into a certainty that the American SDI was still there, even though it was not.

The plan implementing Washington's "impossible" bluff was the Spaceman's own.

CHAPTER 46

THE STONES

Walkingfar's brain felt like his tongue: like it had done a month's duty on the bottom of somebody's shoe. From a quiet cubicle off the Colorado war room, he picked up a black and blue phone. A businesslike voice immediately answered, "Goliath."

"Slingshot," Walkingfar replied. He replaced the receiver and strode into the war room's beverage bar and got coffee.

Two minutes later, ten of SpaCom's "Missionary" (for "multi mission") transatomospheric planes rolled out of hardened hangers. They screamed off runways at Beale Air Force Base, California, the same base that had launched most of the old U.S. SR-71s, the Mach-3-plus spyplanes mothballed in the late '80s and then partially demothed in the mid '90s until TAVs came along.

The Missionary TAVs carried only half their normal loads of fuel. Their forays would be short. These particular TAVs were unmanned, but remotely piloted via "telepresence" links with humans on the ground. Each plane carried a special five-ton payload of 100 yard-long cannisters.

The Missionaries headed heavenward, moving east at a steep angle, fanning out into the maw of the breach. Within a few minutes they were moving at 11.4 kilometers per second. The planes were at escape velocity, on the verge of achieving orbit. But at that point, they rotated upside down and exposed their bellies to space. As their conformal bomb bay doors slid open, the planes released special payloads and screamed back toward earth. The cannisters continued on into orbit, spreading out into pre-designated paths that would eventually place them above and parallel to the orbits of the live Soviet AM guns.

While the cannisters were coated with a combination of "stealthy" paints and composites and were not spotted by Soviet radar, a new Soviet enhanced infrared detector did sight five of the robot TAV mother ships. A few of the more versatile antimatter weapons on the trailing Hawaiian breach edge began firing at the TAVs. Four were destroyed before the rest of the team dipped below the AM guns' sight-horizon and back into the atmosphere, ultimately landing at six different East Coast Air Force or SpaCom bases.

The blue and black phone rang. Walkingfar snatched up the receiver. He noted that his palm was slippery with sweat.

"Stones afloat," said a voice, young and as strung up as a kitten on coke, though trying hard not to show it.

"Good job, son," Walkingfar said. "Take the day off."

"Thank you, sir. Better stay on duty, though."

Walkingfar re-entered the main war room, caught the Spaceman's eye, and made a "perfect" sign with his thumb and forefinger.

Young called the president.

"Got our rocks off," the SpaCom general said.

"Got my fingers crossed," Washington said, expelling a tense breath. "Your guys really think the things'll work after *all* this time?"

"Not much left to bet on, sir. They were cosmoline-preserved and most tested out okay in diagnostics. We didn't lift any that didn't. Wish we had more."

The "stones" were tiny anti-missile missiles, the remnants of the aborted Brilliant Pebbles program begun in the eighties. Proposed in the waning days of the Reagan administration by former Lawrence Livermore Lab's head Lowell Wood, the Pebbles program had envisioned anywhere from 3,000 to 10,000 of the cheap, tiny, virtually undetectable missiles orbiting the globe. Employing a breakthrough in infrared sensor technology, the pebbles were to have been able to automatically destroy any rockets rising from uncoded locations, meaning from any enemy location. Friendly launches were to give off bursts of infrared code, letting the miniature missiles know to leave them alone. But unfriendly missiles, minus the code, would automatically be attacked. There were other, classified ways in which the missiles could know when to fire, such as by keying on updates of the latest intelligence estimates of Soviet mobile missile locations. Also, friendly rockets were to contain a secret mixture of elements in their fuel which could be detected by orbiting spectroscopy sensors.

But after a prototype production run of 1,200, the plan had foundered on the political reefs — on two long-standing fears held by two powerful groups.

The first group was a majority of Congressman who were frightened of any space-based system which could fire on the enemy without the constant presence of "men in the loop," without humans actually pressing all the fire buttons. The Congress had demanded a man in the loop despite the fact that the high velocities of space interceptions made it physically impossible for a human to react optimally during the heat of battle.

The Congressional fear of automation, a kind of military Ludditism, was exaggerated and exploited by a second opposition group, the Joint Chiefs of Staff. The JCS of the time was battling the impending creation of what could one day become SpaCom. JCS didn't want Pebbles because it worked too well. The JCS staff was, at least for a time, dominated by men who were afraid that space operations would take away their traditional ground-, sea- and air-based methods of deterring the enemy. The dissenters on JCS were politically overwhelmed.

In the end, a majority in the House, citing JCS arguments, as well as similar ones advanced by technically ignorant media, killed the Pebbles project. Any attempt at deployment was declared illegal. Only the exigencies of the war had now allowed the dregs of the Pebbles program to be legally pressed into service. Fortunately, the old SDI office, with the help of a few farther-sighted Senators, including a young firebrand named Baker Sunderleaf, had had the brains to mothball, rather than destroy, the few Pebbles produced. As bigger, more cumbersome, and far fewer SDI platforms had gone up, the "stones" had stayed undisturbed. They'd been almost forgotten, preserved inside a special, anti-oxidant-saturated gelatin.

"Well," Washington said to Young, "if this doesn't cause Romanoff to become a born-again believer in our bluff, I don't know what will."

"And if he doesn't believe, he'll have no reason to think he'll fail to win by attrition by waiting us out. Our battle progression estimates show that without slinging the stones, even if we were to take out another third of his AM guns with our Pats, Romanoff would win. He wouldn't have to fire more than a few nukes to do it. Maybe none. The numbers would all be on his side. That is true no matter if we tried to use our entire remaining ICBM and SLBM force in addition to the P-6s. He'd come out with at least a good number of AM battle stations and most of his offensive nuclear force, including missiles he's probably hidden from us. At that point, when he talked, we'd have to listen damned politely."

Washington grunted an indecipherable curse, then asked, "All right. How much time do we have?"

"An hour and a half. Three hours at the most. If we haven't changed his mind within two more orbits, I don't see how we can. If you want my best guess, we'd better be able to do it during the next loop. If we've got an SDI, he'll expect us to use it then or not at all. In other words, once and for all he'll call your bluff."

Washington narrowed his eyes and muttered, "He'll *expect* it then."

"Pardon, sir?"

"Hmmm. I know I said I'd leave you to fight this your own way, Glenn, but let me hit you with a thought."

"Not much time for modifications, sir," Young cautioned.

"Yes. But here it is, quick and dirty. If Romanoff expects our SDI counterattack sooner, maybe we should save it. It'll be more of a shocker."

Young considered for only a few seconds. "But I doubt he expects it at all."

"He's got his doubts, General. I'm sure of it. There's not much else I can imagine that would cause that undercurrent of uneasiness I pick up from the man. He wants to believe his own experts, but he isn't really sure — because he knows the U.S. has surprised him before with secret weapons."

"But, damn it, sir! If we save the stones, that means we're going to have to blow almost all of our Pats! It's bound to make him a lot cockier than he's been. Remember, even if they don't know where they're hidden, the Ruskies've got a pretty fair idea of how many P-6s we've deployed over the years."

"I know, Glenn, I know. But if we use our Pats first, it means he'll be more shocked when we blind-side him with the stones — claiming they're our cloaked SDI, of course, and suggesting there're plenty more where they came from. If we're going to deflate him, I suggest we make it count. I want to squash his scrotum at the moment he's prancing around naked and proud."

"Surprise is always a great theory, sir. But I still say it's an awful chance in this instance. Those Pebbles are old. Diagnostics on the ground are one thing. Whether they'll work reliably upstairs after all these years is another question."

"How many AM guns has Romanoff got left, Glenn?"

"Latest count says the underside of 600."

"Well, you're the general. You do what's best."

After Young hung up, he frowned, then called his general staff together. He put Washington's idea to them. To his amazement, most of the staff agreed with it. The staff was starting to get the hang of space tactics. Somebody had even dragged out an old copy of *The Shape of Wars to Come* by David Baker and quoted from it.

If Romanoff got cocky after the Patriot exhaustion, most of the generals felt his primary objective would still be conquest with minimal damage. Besides, as an Army staffer pointed out, an hour and a half was not exactly sufficient time to invade Europe. It was, though, as a Navy admiral noted, plenty of time to gloat and let your guard down.

Young decided to save the stones for the later orbit, as the president had suggested, providing nothing new turned up.

As the leading end of the chewed-up ring passed Hawaii and moved toward the mainland, a few more P-6s began soaring up from ships in the Eastern Pacific. By the time the lead ring-end crossed the West Coast, and the land-based Pats began ascending, the AM gun-count was down to 550. Progress, but far from enough.

Now came the part which Young, the president and nearly everyone else feared most: the launching of the U.S.-based Patriots. Retribution against the American mainland — another tantrum — was possible. So far, U.S. homeland had been spared, but no one thought it would be spared forever.

Then, the first of two unexpected events occurred.

It was never discovered who did it, but someone leaked a brief and fairly accurate account of what was going on — including an account of the "high" danger of Russian nuclear attack — to one of the Internet news outfits. Within minutes, what had been a trickle became a torrent. Civilians tried to leave American cities and the vicinity of any military base, power station, defense industrial plant or other possible target for the fire from above. In the major urban areas, human action gridlocked.

While most Americans didn't panic, it only took a tiny minority to spark a lot of chaos.

On the Golden Gate Bridge, over 50 people killed each other in fights using tire irons, fists and guns as they tried to force their way out of the city.

In Chicago, 300 people were trampled to death as they tried to get out of a stadium where word had hit at halftime in a hockey game.

In Los Angeles, the Watts district erupted in fires and looting as the panic invited criminal opportunity.

In New York, a power overload blacked out a section of Manhattan, sparking a rumor that it had been caused by a nuclear attack. Twelve-thousand people died in their frenzy to squeeze down the stairs of office skyscrapers.

In Florida, a Puerto Rican revolutionary group, armed with stolen Stinger hand-held missiles, used the opportunity to shoot off the wing of an airliner. The airliner crashed into the center of Miami sending up a huge fireball and killing 1,500. Assuming that it was a Soviet attack, panic riots erupted in the city, fires broke out, and hundreds more died.

In Atlanta, airport authorities grounded all outgoing flights, but one captain rebelled and sent his 747 into the air without authorization. A thousand feet up, it clipped an incoming European Airbus and the ensuing crash killed 800.

In Reno, Las Vegas and Atlantic City, the power stayed on and in the casinos people simply spent faster, pulled harder on the one-armed bandits, and hoped the whole thing would blow over soon. By keeping them off the streets, their gambling for once kept them healthier than many of their fellow citizens.

While the Soviets fired at the U.S.-based Patriots in the short, fierce battle over the American mainland, they did not throw another wasteful tantrum with their precious anti-matter guns. The U.S. was spared the outburst that had taken place after the European Patriot attack. While the AM guns could doubtless have damaged an important percentage of U.S. military facilities, the Soviet Stavka strategists were now grimly content to limit themselves to anti-missile missiles actually fired or known.

"Romanoff's afraid of American public opinion afterwards," Brighton observed to the president. "Doesn't want it said that they had anything against the U.S. populace, even if they are fighting a war with its 'ruling circles.' Looks like you're right about his playing it tight, trying to avoid a general conflagration. I wonder if we would've gotten one if you hadn't declared war."

"The mistake," the president said, "would have been to *under* react. In fact, although I might not have believed it a few months ago, I'm convinced that that's what's been wrong with U.S. policy toward the Soviet Union since that corrupt country's founding. Not to mention a few other countries."

"Hear, hear," Sunderleaf said. "It's never been enough to say 'bad dog' to the bear. You've got to whack him with a fencepost now and then or he'll start raidin' pantries."

"When we get out of this, I'm going to suggest a general strategic review with exactly that premise in mind," Washington said.

"So maybe gunboat diplomacy was underestimated?" Jeanne Allison asked.

"No maybe about it," Washington said. "Oops, here we go again."

Everyone focused on the big monitor as another phase of the lightning-fast war got underway.

The video schematic showed a new series of dots. These dots were in yellow and represented the projected locations of the "stones" orbiting above the Soviet antimatter weapons. The stones had gradually spread to cover a surface area some ten thousand miles long and five thousand wide — fifty million square miles. Below, the majority of the active Soviet weapons, in a lower and faster orbit, had caught up to the stones and were passing under them, unaware of the danger above.

The Soviet guns were firing at Patriots and a few British sublaunched ballistic missiles rising out of the central Atlantic and off the far western edge of Europe.

About a minute into the renewed European firefight, the U.S. laser in the Jura Mountains of France began shooting blinding bursts — much as the sub-driven laser off China had done. Using a new tactic of shorter, more random shots — which gave Soviet detectors less time to home in on the ground gun — the Jura laser blinded not just forty-two, but sixty-seven Soviet battle stations before being destroyed. Sixty-three of the blinded Soviet weapons were then taken out by Patriots and four MIRVed (multiple-warhead) French ICBMS reprogrammed for the purpose.

By the time the breach approached the Iron Curtain, it had been widened to 13,000 miles. Half the Soviet ring of weapons was now gone. It was an improvement, but far less than what Young had wanted by that time. He'd hoped to have destroyed two-thirds.

Walkingfar assessed the damage: "Over 90% of our Pats are gone and we only smacked about a quarter of what we thought we'd do. It's not looking good, guys."

"Better make those rocks count, then, and soon," Young said.

He looked at the situation screen. For the moment, the Soviet antimatter guns were silent. And all the U.S. Pebbles were directly over the Red battle stations.

Young said to the face of the president on his computer screen, "We're falling way behind, sir. I'd say it's now or never with the rocks. The surprise should be as good now as waiting for another orbit or two. In fact, we'll never be in a better position. They've got around 450 of their beasties still alive up there. I suggest that we give 'em a shot from half our rocks to see how many AM pistols we shoot out of their fists. Hold the rest of our rocks in reserve."

"Go for it, Glenn," Washington said.

But as Young was about to issue the order, the second major unanticipated event began to happen.

There had been no hint, nothing in the recent news, no intelligence tips to suggest it would occur.

Someone yelled, "Jesus H. Crucifix! Look at that!"

Everyone in the war room jerked his head toward the giant screen. Brilliant purple lines showed a flowering of thousands and thousands of anti-satellite missiles rising from the Chinese mainland.

"I'll be frackin' damned!" Young shouted. "They're helping? They appear to be attempting to create another breach!"

As the rest in the war room grasped the significance, cheers, applause and whistles broke out — and instantly stopped. Because now newer, red-violet lines were also showing on the monitor.

"Oh, shit," Young said, "God in Heaven blessed shit."

Several hundred Chinese ICBMs were thundering upwards under the cover of their smaller anti-satellite missiles. While the smaller missiles engaged the Soviet AM guns, the ICBMs were clearly heading for the Soviet Union itself.

"The bear is about to be roasted," a female technician blurted into the momentary silence.

The Soviets suddenly realized their predicament. AM guns frantically tried to fire back at the new source of attack, focusing on the ICBMs.

"Whatever the Chinese intentions are," Walkingfar shouted into the confusion, "let's take advantage of it. Now!"

Young issued the order to activate half the stones.

On the screen, yellow lines streaked down from out of "nowhere" in higher orbit, intercepting Soviet antimatter guns. The tiny U.S. missiles caught the Soviet tacticians by such a total surprise that hardly any of their guns were able to rotate to defend themselves. Nearly a hundred of the Pebbles missed, but over four hundred hit their marks. Within three minutes, all but a few dozen of the Soviet guns had been destroyed. Within five minutes, more Chinese ASAT missiles took those out, too.

The world's first death ray battle force had been defeated.

"Uh-oh. Fryin' gophers," Kevin Jones said aloud, pointing at the giant screen.

"Ten-kay detonation over Leningrad," Jeanne Allison said, reading the duplicate indicators in the situation room beneath the Capitol. "Looks like some of our own cruises are getting through, the stealths with nukes."

As she finished the sentence, five more lights flared over Leningrad, Plesetsk, Bobruysk, Volgorad, Smolensk.

The remaining undamaged U.S. cruises, most of them subsonic, had been weaving their way toward Russian targets all through the beam battle. The Soviets had taken out most, but some were penetrating. The Soviets had no AM guns to help them out anymore.

"They've got to be scrambling every jet they've got," Young said. "For all the good it'll do 'em if their planes are only 10% effective against cruises."

Lights popped on over Korsakov and Orlavo on Sakhalin Island.

"Those weren't cruises," Walkingfar said. "Not the last two. Chinese ICBMS."

"Oh, Lord," an Air Force general said, staring at the big screen open-mouthed. Someone else whispered, "God have mercy."

New lines were rising from China. Another larger wave of ICBMS.

"What the Hell! Don't they know it's over?" Washington yelled as Young thought the exact same words 2,000 miles away in Colorado.

"Get me Premier Zhao on the phone now!" Washington ordered to the room at large. For a moment, no one did anything, then Bill Brighton, the CIA chief, leapt forward to comply. In a minute, Zhao was on the line.

"Ah, yes, Mr. President," he said, as though he'd just served the Russians nothing more extraordinary than tea.

Washington brought his vocal cords under control. "Premier Zhao, are you aware that all the Soviet antimatter guns are down? There's no further point in diversions!"

"Quite," Zhao said drily.

Vice President Leininger hissed, "Sam, they're sending up a third wave of nukes."

"Premier Zhao!" Washington said urgently. "There is *no need* to keep diverting the Soviets. They can't fire back. Mr. Zhao, this is insane!'

"Is it, Mr. President? By whose standards?"

"But the Soviets are *down*, finished! They won't dare do anything more —"

"Perhaps not this year, Mr. President. Ten or twenty years from now? We prefer the longer view." He let the words hang and then said, "There is a rabid dog running too close to our back yard. There is only one thing to do about a rabid dog. When you get the chance, you kill it."

"Wait! Just call Romanoff and talk —"

"No!" Zhao interrupted, his voice as cold as wind off a Manchurian glacier, "We are not subject to Western drivel about fair play."

"But your own people, they'll suffer the fallout from the prevailing Westerlies! You're right in the path of the fallout from the worst of your own attacks!" Washington pleaded.

"Mr. President, why do you think we've spent the last four decades building shelters under our cities? Your intelligence services knew about it. Why do you think we did it? For precisely this opportunity, of course. The fallout problem will not last long for us. And only a tiny portion of our people will die, a few millions, perhaps. Your people, on the other hand, will not have the benefit of civil defense foresight. We are infinitely sorry for that. You Americans, with your open trade, have been generous to us in recent years. It will mean needless suffering for many of our friends. Even so, we will take the brunt. You should be grateful for that. Besides, you shouldn't let silly anti-nuclear fears blind you. The fallout will be much less by the time it crosses the Pacific. You can weather most of it merely by staying indoors for a few days. Good day, Mr. President. Say good-bye to the Russian dog. He shall bother the world no more."

Zhao hung up.

Washington looked at the situation screen while asking for Young on the phone.

"Now what?" Washington demanded, after briefing Young on his talk with Zhao.

"Sir, we're already at Defcon One."

Defcon One stood for the highest condition of U.S. defense readiness.

"The Chinese are not firing at us, so there's not much we can do except to sit tight."

"Ah, nuts!" Walkingfar growled.

On the big screen, tracers showed ICBMs rising out of the Soviet Union.

Washington saw it, too, and asked, "Which way, Glenn? Are they coming down our throats?"

In a moment, Young answered, "Not yet, sir. Looks like they're all stabbing at the Chinese. But there're a lot of them. At least 2,000, including intermediate rangers not far from the Chinese border. That's a heck of a lot more than we thought they had left. But not as many as the Chinese had hidden from us. God, I'm glad they aren't shooting at us!"

"Can we do anything about it with our remaining stones?" Washington asked.

"They've passed too far east. It'll take nearly another hour to come around. By then, I'm afraid it'll be over. Now it's a race to see whose anti-missile defense systems hold up the best, the Sovs', or the Chinese's. This is one time when I'm hoping both sides of Reds have the best damned rocket-shooters you ever saw!"

"Amen," Washington said. "But let's keep our powder dry in case someone starts poking burning sticks our way."

He and the others watched while the human race's first, massive nuclear exchange began spot-blackening the planet's largest continent.

The big brothers of "eternal fraternal" socialism used thirty minutes and over five hundred megatons of nuclear destruction to decide who would rule Asia.

Disproving the old saw that "no one could win a nuclear war," the Chinese did.

Of 1,638 nuclear missiles which actually detonated on both sides, 720 hit the Soviet Union and 318 hit China. The rest were taken out by various remaining "conventional" Soviet space and terminal defenses and by unexpectedly numerous and effective Chinese defenses. Worse for the Soviets, a large percentage of the Chinese missile re-entry vehicles penetrated deep underground before detonating. This had the effect of creating a massive compression shock wave which crushed even the deepest, most heavily reinforced Soviet shelters. The Soviet Politburo, Stavka, and much of the Nomenklatura leadership were crushed and buried alive.

The Chinese had not only used tens of thousands of Patriot-like missiles to intercept the Soviet ICBMs, but over a dozen forms of other weapons. One of them was a vast, rapid-firing, computer-controlled complex of Gatling guns "orbiting" over China aboard high flying planes. Another surprise was "pop-up" space interceptors. These were not radically different from the U.S.'s "stones" — the main difference being that the Chinese stones never hit orbit. They were shot up above the atmosphere, released by their "elevator" boosters and within seconds intercepted incoming Soviet warheads with deadly accuracy. The Chinese never admitted whatever sensing system they used. U.S. analysts guessed it was some sort of wide-angle, optical radar. Young recalled reading of a plan of "pop-up" lasers that had been circulated but abandoned in the early days of SDI. The Chinese had apparently salvaged and expanded on an unexpected virtue from an old American idea.

In China, thirty million people died in the exchange; a tiny two percent of the population, including almost none of the leadership. In the Soviet Union, 150 million died; half the population, including virtually all the leadership.

CHAPTER 47

THE HEGEMONY

T he nuclear exchange wasn't the end of it.

Within a week, the pundits and observers, the analysts and geopolitical strategists, the commentators and speculators of the world began to ask each other interesting questions. The main question they asked, and argued, was whether the decimated Soviet Union might have yet another chance at becoming a free, constitutional republic. The Bolsheviks in 1917 had ruined the first chance. Stalin's destruction of Lenin's 1920s New Economic Policy had spoiled the second. Yeltsin's successors had wrecked the third.

The Chinese smiled and ignored the entire discussion. They were not interested in speculation. They were acting.

Announcing a new Asian "hegemony," twenty million Chinese troops, tanks, planes and millions of tons of hidden equipment swept into their bloodied, irradiated Soviet neighbor.

The Chinese conquest of the USSR took exactly a month. The dispirited Soviet Red Army scattered like a flock of bedraggled pigeons. There was little the U.S. could do, even if it had wanted to. The Chinese invasion was too big and fast, and the U.S. was suddenly, urgently busy re-fortifying NATO — against China.

In the summer of Washington's third year in office, the Chinese declared that the new Soviet Union no longer existed. Its scores of "republics," from parts of Eastern Europe to the Bering Strait, were declared "autonomous regions" of the People's Republic of China. China was now the largest nation which had ever existed. The USSR's remaining military facilities still flew a red flag, but not one with the Soviet hammer-and-sickle.

To the astonishment of Western observers, the Chinese executed few of their new subjects, perhaps twenty thousand; the surviving local managers of the Soviet "holy trinity," the Party, the KGB and the military. Most Soviets were peacefully absorbed into the new system. The conquered Soviets complained, but adapted, as their ancestors had done for centuries. When one has learned that taking orders is almost a metaphysical condition of man, a switch to a new master is not such a large step.

The adaptation was lubricated by the fact that the Chinese were not nearly as rigid as the Soviets in their economics. The Beijing leadership had been introducing capitalist incentives since the late days of Jimmy Carter. The Chinese had discovered that the Communist Party could, with proper supervision by secret police, fatten itself and its military arsenals enormously faster by tolerating a large dose of capitalism. The Chinese were not free by Western "civil liberties" standards, but were awash in liberty by their own.

While the Chinese agreed that they had much to gain by trading with the West, it did not mean that they accepted the West's "inevitable" military superiority over them.

"And that," President Sam Washington said, "is why the Cold War is not over. It's just against a new enemy. I wish it were otherwise. And I'm terribly afraid that this new Cold War will be harder to win. No matter how free we are, a nation that is only half as free, but five times as populated, is going to be a severe strategic challenge. The new Soviets were only perhaps a fifth as free as the Chinese are now, and *they* came within a pin's width of beating us. Extreme vigilance is required."

He paused to sip water and survey the gathering. The people seated in the large dining room consisted mostly of the core group and senior military — those who had been deeply involved in overseeing the actual war. A few other guests were there.

Jeanne Allison, Baker Sunderleaf, Craig Goldstein, Bill Brighton, Ella Paxson, Kurt Leininger, and Tom Rosco sat at a table directly in front of the podium. At another table were the Joint Chiefs and their wives. Behind them were Walkingfar, Moshe Trevis, Kevin Jones and Lieutenant Carmen Sevens. Also at the table were Madeis Plechl and Tanya Yublenka. Filling out the room were selected military, state and intelligence officials who had been instrumental in the Soviet defeat. Congressional leaders and their wives sat at three of the tables. No members of the press had been invited, although they'd be briefed and given video tapes or digi-chips of the president's talk later.

Washington noted Buck Reed sitting at a center table not more than thirty feet away. Washington felt like making a sour face, but controlled himself. He'd not wanted Reed there. But the man's lawyers and a sympathetic judge had given Reed his freedom and he was a legitimate presidential candidate, although no longer Washington's most popular challenger. Reed was running a slow 22% in the polls. Not only had the exposure of the trial hurt Reed's image, but Washington himself, hero of the war, was suddenly undefeatable. He led in the polls by three-to-one over his nearest rival from the other party. Out of courtesy, Washington had invited the other declared candidates before Reed had been cleared by the courts. Once he was, there was no way Washington could politely refuse to let Reed attend.

Washington glanced at his wife seated at the speaker's table to his right. She noticed for the first time that her husband had a streak of gray in his beard. She smiled; she thought it looked good. He held her eyes for a moment, then looked down at his notes and continued.

"It is my profound fear that the Chinese will be a tougher foe than the Soviets ever were. I know some will take this to be alarmist, or even cultural prejudice. But I believe it. I believe it because of several factors. I hope you, and those who replace you and me in the years ahead, never forget these things.

"First, because they are economically more open than the Soviets were, convincing the West to refuse to trade with the Chinese will be next to impossible. Thus they will constantly benefit from our technology and our financial investment.

"Second, because their military is controlled by a small ruling oligarchy, unlike us, they will face no populist political pressure to skimp on military spending. What we view as a growing relaxation of relations and broadening friendship with the Chinese may well be viewed by them as nothing more than a strategic wedge. We must be wary of that.

"Third, we don't know for sure if we totally destroyed the Engels virus. If there was another lab producing it, the Chinese may discover it. We need to guard against this possibility. In fact, we need to take the whole bio-warfare issue a lot more seriously.

"Fourth, they have undoubtedly discovered the Soviet antimatter technology. It is a devastated system and may take them years to rebuild and effectively use. But they have the lead on us and may maintain it. I hope this is not the case, but I beg you to never shunt aside the possibility that the Chinese may have strategic goals almost incomprehensible —"

Washington never got the chance to finish his sentence.

Buck Reed was rushing toward the podium with a service pistol that he should never have been allowed to bring into the room. He was screaming something incoherent and his face was red with a sick, twisted rage.

Two tables away, the room went into slow motion for Kevin Jones. He saw the pistol in Reed's hand. As Jones rose from his seat, the pistol was already halfway to firing position. As Jones reached Reed and grabbed his wrist, the pistol had barely moved an inch and nothing else in the room had seemed to move at all. Reed was still looking at the president as Jones ripped the pistol away. The force caused three of Reed's fingers to bleed and it dislocated his thumb. Jones hit Reed across the temple, laid the gun on the floor in front of the podium and scooted back to his seat as the slowdown effect stopped.

Kevin watched Reed slump sideways and collapse ten feet from the president. Four secret service men rushed in and then stood for a second, perplexed. A moment earlier Reed had had a gun. Then there had been a blur of — something— and now Reed was out cold and the gun was at the president's feet. The secret service people confiscated the weapon, hauled Reed away and hustled the president out, looking uneasily over their shoulders at the crowd, wondering if Reed had cohorts, wondering what they had seen.

Walkingfar and Moshe Trevis were not confused. The Chief looked at Jones straight-faced and said, "You good-for-nothing rust-bucket reject! I *told* you that you'd come in handy someday!"

Lt. Carmen Sevens, now Mrs. Kevin Jones, simply looked bewildered. Someday, thought Kevin, I'm gonna have to explain it to the little lady.

Tanya Yublenka brushed a strand of hair from her face in the crisp, spring wind. She looked up at Madeis Plechl, her husband, like herself a U.S. citizen for the last year. Gregor is gone, she thought, realizing that she had finally accepted it. This man is different. But, forgive me Gregor, he is as good. She squeezed Madeis's arm and followed his gaze to watch the small plane land on a bright green grass runway.

They were in a section of Montana near Bozeman, where she and Madeis worked at a nearby SpaCom linguistics research facility. The day before, the Chief had called to tell them that there would be a surprise arriving by plane. Walkingfar had grown close to both Plechl and Yublenka and had been Plechl's best man at their wedding. He had flown up from Colorado and now stood beside them, hatless. The wind whipped his longish black hair and lent his raw-boned face a wild, exhilarated look. It's a look that his ancestors would have fully understood, Madeis thought.

The plane bumped twice and taxied toward them. A rear door of the Cessna opened and a white-headed, portly man climbed out and then turned to help an elderly woman. Madeis Plechl walked to his father, incredulous. He took Hans Plechl by his shoulders and hugged him as they both shed silent tears.

In a few seconds, Hans broke away, looked at his son, patted is cheek, and said, "The Chinese didn't have any use for lucky old Germans. We survived in a shelter that the bombs missed. Karpov chose to hide with the big boys. His bones will make some future anthropologist happy, I'm sure."

He turned toward the woman. "Madeis, I'd like to introduce you to your mother."

Anna Plechl looked at the face of the son to whom she hadn't spoken in over three decades, who had been nearly an infant when she'd last stood beside him.

Off to one side, unnoticed, Walkingfar's face cracked into a huge grin as he watched them embrace.

Maria stretched luxuriously. She turned her head to look at Hernando, who wore a slightly smug smile.

"I presume," she said, "that this was the proof you required that becoming an American would not be the equivalent of emasculation."

"Go to sleep, psychiatrist," he said with mock gruffness.

She chuckled and snuggled against him.

Ben Liddell sat fidgeting in the waiting room of the Spaceman's office.

"So," he said, after a few moments, addressing the attractive young woman behind the lone desk, "you're his secretary. What'd you say your name was?"

"Lieutenant Carmen Jones," she said, smiling. "Nervous?"

Liddell answered gruffly, "Not in the least. Been interviewing the big brass for twenty years."

He tried to light a cigar and burned his fingers. Carmen stifled a grin.

Then Young was at his door, walking toward Liddell with his hand outstretched.

"Ben, about time I stopped bumming freebies, don't you think?"

Liddell half tripped as he rose to shake hands, with "the general who beat the Russians."

"C'mon in," Young said, clapping the reporter's shoulder, "and tell me how it'll feel to be awarded a SpaCom Silver Nova hero's medal."

"Huh?" Liddell stammered.

Young led him into his office, laughing.

Annette Washington opened her eyes dreamily and looked at her husband as they gently separated their bodies.

"I love you, Mr. President," she said, pulling the sheet up to keep off the chill of drying sweat.

"Me, too," he replied, rolling onto his back and stroking her cheek with one hand.

"Sam?"

"Hmmm....?"

"It's not over, is it? I mean, not ever."

"What?"

"Being wary. Watching out. Defending against more surprises, like the virus or the beam guns — or who knows what. It's a new world, but it's still primitive."

"Oh, that. Yeah, but our little corner's pretty nice for now, isn't it?"

"If we can keep it. Can we?"

Sam Washington found himself thinking of a certain Oval Office painting of an historic river crossing. In his mind, he saw a proud face looking out over a winter waterscape.

Washington's eye crinkled and he said, "Yes."

Moshe Trevis and Kevin Jones strapped themselves into the seat of the experimental TAV. In the past year, under the best SpaCom pilots, they'd learned to fly the vehicle. Either man could handle it, but just in case his faster reactions were needed for an emergency, Jones was piloting this premier flight to test a radically new capacity.

He looked down at its designer, Tomasito MacGregor, and switched on his headset radio. MacGregor backed away from the foot of the cockpit and crossed his fingers. Moshe waved from the rear position.

"Well, Tommy," Trevis said to MacGregor, "it took not three weeks, but a year. Now the real test, huh?"

"Just do it," MacGregor said, nodding and backing away to safety. Jones gave a thumbs-up, revved the TAV's J-SCRAM engines, and taxied to takeoff position.

He got clearance from the tower, acknowledged it, and sent the plane thundering down the runway. As the g-forces pinned Trevis to his seat, in a flash he finally understood why Kevin Jones was so fond of old American "muscle" cars. He smiled at the back of Jones's head.

At somewhere over 200 mph, the ordinary jet portion of the engine kicked over to the SCRAMs and the hypersonic plane rapidly rode twin hydrogen flames past the sound barrier and up through the Mach multiples. As it achieved escape velocity in the mid-Mach-20s on the edge of space, Kevin radioed back, "Okay, Tommy, here goes."

MacGregor replied, "Don't talk about it, do it!"

With his thumb, Jones felt the special button on the flystick. He took a deep breath and pushed.

To observers on the ground, the plane disappeared. To Jones and Trevis, there was a slight feeling of vertigo. Other than that, nothing seemed to change. Then Kevin used maneuvering thrusters to rotate the plane. Below was the earth, the size of a marble; a pea-sized moon revolved around it.

Moshe expelled a low whistle. A chill ran over the backs of Kevin's arms and legs. He said into his headset, "Tom, we're still here."

Seconds later, the signal reached Earth and Tomasito MacGregor heard the rest of what Jones said: "You brainy bucket of bolts, you were right! The light-speed barrier can be cracked! We just damn did it! We're way the frack out here, at least twice again past the moon's orbit. Now what?"

Moments later, they heard MacGregor's reply. "You mean you overpaid goof-offs don't know? It's time to claim the galaxy for Uncle Sam!"

Kevin grinned and said to Moshe, "Better dig Old Glory out of the trunk, Moshe. I aim to find a place to plant her."

"How about Mars?"

"Good as any — for a start."

ABOUT THE AUTHOR

B orn in Austria, E. G. Ross was raised and educated in the small logging community of Lebanon, Oregon. He entered a career in journalism and economics while attending the University of Oregon.

Since 1986, Ross has edited and published *Understanding Defense*, a highly respected international newsletter. Each month, he also conducts World Intelligence Briefing, a live update on world events and defense technology. For many years, he was a radio news director and reporter, airing over 3,000 commentaries and 23,000 news stories, including 1,200 science reports. He sold stories to NBC, ABC, CBS, the Associated Press, United Press International, and Mutual Broadcasting.

His articles and letters have been published in *The Freeman, International Money and Politics, Foreign Policy Perspectives (*Libertarian Alliance of Great Britain*), Science News, Reason, Air Force Magazine, TV Guide, Gold Standard News, Full Context, The Register-Guard, Journal of Civil Defense,* and others. In addition to his defense letter, he currently edits and writes two other publications: *The Objective American* and *The Positive Economist Bulletin.*

Ross has been an instructor at the university level and lectures frequently on defense, economics, and self-improvement. He also narrates science films, is a cartoonist, and oil paints. He lives in an Oregon rain forest with his wife, Suzy Peterson, who is a telecommunications engineer, artist, and business manager.

For a sample of Ross's newsletter, *Understanding Defense*, write to 1574 Coburg Road #242, Eugene OR 97401 or email to 74434.3474@compuserve.com.